GOOD GONE BAD

A FALLEN MEN NOVEL
BOOK THREE

giana darling

To the Love of My Life.
You are the man who taught me that still waters run deep, that Prince Charmings can be bad boys and that love is all the more beautiful for the obstacles you have to overcome within yourself and outside of each other in order to be together.

"There is nothing either good or bad but thinking makes it so."
William Shakespeare, Hamlet, Act 2, Scene 2.

PLAYLIST

"God's Gonna Cut You Down"—Johnny Cash
"Every Rose Has Its Thorns"—Poison
"Short Change Hero"—The Heavy
"Born to be Wild"—Steppenwolf
"Give My Love to Rose"—Johnny Cash
"I Hate Myself for Loving You"—Joan Jett & The Blackhearts
"Snake Song"—Isobel Campbell & Mark Lanegan
"Not Afraid Anymore"—Halsey
"Dirty Deeds Done Dirt Cheap"—AC/DC
"Like Real People Do"—Hozier
"Gun in My Hand"—Dorothy
"No Good"—Kaleo
"Real Wild Child"—Iggy Pop
"Once Upon A Dream"—Lana del Ray
"Game of Survival"—Ruelle
"It Will Come Back"—Hozier
"If I Were a Boy"—Beyonce
"Hazey"—Glass Animals
"Make Up Sex"—SoMo
"Die for You"—The Weeknd

"Can't Help Falling in Love"—Elvis Presley
"Hot Blooded"—Foreigner
"Die A Happy Man"—Thomas Rhett

CHAPTER ONE

Harleigh Rose

IT WASN'T THE FIRST TIME I'D SEEN A DEAD BODY, AND I KNEW it wouldn't be the last. Not living the kind of life I did as both a student nurse and the daughter of an outlaw motorcycle club Prez.

Blood didn't freak me out.

Violence didn't deter me.

One was simply biology and the other was basic MC theology.

I'd seen enough cadavers to fill a classroom, too many bodies to fit out in the pigpen at Angelwood Farm where The Fallen took their dead bodies and so many injuries it was no wonder a bleeding wound seemed as insignificant as spilled beer.

Still, I'd never seen a dead body like this.

Probably because I'd seen my boyfriend, Cricket Marsden, a lot of ways—angry, manic, happy, high, and humored—but I'd never seen him dead.

The blade was wet in my hand, slipping against the blood coating my palm like grotesque red satin gloves. I couldn't stop staring at Cricket's handsome face paralyzed in horror and wrath long enough to drop the cleaver to the ground.

Honestly, I didn't even know why I owned a cleaver. But it had been there when I'd reached blindly behind me into one of the kitchen drawers and grasped the first cool handle my hand made contact with.

I'd expected—at worst—a wooden spoon to jam into his eye. At best, a butter knife to stab him painfully but not mortally in the shoulder.

Instead, fate or something like it had pressed the awful square weight of a cleaver into my hand and in my mounting panic, I hadn't realized the significance of my improvised weapon until it was lodged in the junction between Cricket's long neck and his tattooed shoulder.

Blood was everywhere in an instant, all over me like I'd jumped into a rain shower. I choked on the blood as it sprayed between my lips but I didn't take a step back because my eyes were hooked on Cricket's brown ones, which were obliterated by his blown pupils from the mammoth amount of drugs in his system. They widened in shock at the impact of the sharp metal as it tore with blunt force and no finesse through his connective tissues and his mouth opened like a second wound as it embedded irreversibly in his clavicle.

We watched each other as I killed him, caught up in a tangle just like we always had been. Our union was destructive, something I'd first sought out just to taste the tang of danger and feel the thrill of rebellion. I was an MC princess, so I knew outlaws, but Cricket wasn't smart enough to be called even that. He was reckless and always had been, searching for the next thrill because he always grew bored with the last. The only thing he'd never grown bored with was me.

At first, I'd been flattered. He was a hot guy with an addictive personality and I was the drug that lit him up and burned him from the inside out. In different ways with the same heady result, Cricket gave that to me. I was a girl surrounded by men too busy to pay attention to her with a mother who'd rather hit up smack or snort coke than brush my hair.

It was a cliché, but clichés existed for a reason.

I just wanted to be loved and Cricket did that.

He did it so hard it left bruises; metaphorically at first, just around my heart like strangle marks, and then later, physically too.

The drugs whipped his love up like a storm, epic and powerful in a way that had me paralyzed in awe even as it swept me up in its fury.

I'd been telling myself for a long time not to let him hurt me anymore.

I wasn't the kind of girl to have an abusive boyfriend.

I had things going for me that included more than my abundance of hair and bluer than fresh denim eyes. I knew I was good looking, full of personality and pretty damn smart if I put my mind to it.

I had good friends and more, the best family any girl could ever have known.

Resources to get me out of the thick, stinking mud of Cricket's hold.

I didn't use any of them.

At least, not until now, not until it was too late and the only resource I had left at my disposal was an inconveniently placed cleaver.

The blood was cooling on my skin, drying in abstract patterns that pulled my skin tight the way old sweat does after a workout.

Still, I remained there, kneeling over my boyfriend's dead body.

I was almost a fully qualified nurse, so my training should have kicked in while I watched the blood arch like calligraphy drawn in red ink through the air and over the walls of my small kitchen, over the pristine white of my thin dress. But they don't train you in university what to do if you accidently sever the carotid artery with a meat cleaver when your high, abusive boyfriend tries to rape you with the butt of his gun.

So, when he'd fallen to the linoleum with the knife lodged deep in the junction of his shoulder and neck, I forgot everything, dropped to the floor beside him and started to pull the thick steel blade from his neck.

Blood gushed over my hands, warm and slippery so that the wooden grip glided through my fingers and thudded to the floor.

Cricket gargled in protest, blood pooling at the sides of his mouth.

It reminded me that you should never pull out a foreign object until you have a way to staunch the blood flow and you know exactly what the damage is to the surrounding area.

It reminded me that there is approximately 5.5 liters of blood in the human body.

It didn't take a nursing degree to know that most of that measure was pooling hot and smooth like wet silk under my knees.

A man was dying on the floor of my apartment.

Not a man, *my man*.

And he wasn't just dying. There was no heart attack, no car accident.

Only me.

His murderer.

My man was dying on the floor at my feet because I had killed him.

I searched wildly for something to save him with even

though I knew—*I knew*—he was going to die and do it soon. My eyes landed on the phone Cricket had knocked to the floor when he'd caged me against the counter. I slipped in the blood as I lunged for it, ignored the bloody smears my fingers deposited on the screen as I dialed the number.

I was on autopilot, but that didn't explain why I called *him*.

My dad was the best person to call. The President of The Fallen MC and a ruthless protector of his loved ones, Zeus Garro would know exactly what to do with a dead body, how to clean up the mess and make it seem like nothing had ever happened. He'd make it so I could return to my life as I'd known it, princess of fallen men but removed from the taint of their sins. I could wake up tomorrow morning and do as I always did, grab my Double-Double coffee at Tim Horton's and make my way to the last of my exams as a normal student, your average girl. The blood would still coat my hands like phantom gloves as I filled in the little bubbles in the answer booklet but no one else would know because my dad would have disappeared the body and the trauma of it all like some kind of outlaw magician.

I could have called my brother by blood or any of the brothers by the club, Nova would have charmed me out of my panic while Priest, silent and competent as a predator, took care of the body. Curtains would make it seem like Cricket had never even been to my apartment, deleting snapshots of footage from random street cameras that had captured my dead boyfriend on his way to my house. They'd think about calling in Cressida, my brother's girlfriend and one of my best friends, but they wouldn't because they'd know better than I would that it was my dad's wife I needed, the husky, strong tones of Loulou Garro in my ear telling me I was a warrior just like her and I'd fought a battle there had been no choice but to win.

I could have called them all, but I didn't.

Instead, I called a ghost, a man I hadn't seen or heard

from in three years. A man I'd had a crush on since I was a girl because he was everything good and straight and *true*. Even as a child I'd known, he was too good for me. We existed in the same world but in the way of the hero and the villain. We crossed paths but only in times of disaster, when I found my mother blue with near-death on the floor of our kitchen, when my father went to jail for manslaughter or when I stabbed a pencil into Tucker Guttery's thigh because he stole a kiss from me in seventh grade. I was a storm of calamity, cast adrift on a sea of black doings and loosely drawn rebel rules. He was an old growth oak with roots sunk deep into rich earth, limbs stretching wide across the sky, standing sentry across centuries as the world toiled away beneath its leaves. I could whip around that kind of man, cause hurricanes with my spirit, quake the earth with my tempers, but none of it mattered. He would remain untouched no matter what I did, no matter what anyone did.

He was just so simply and profoundly *good*. I think that's why I always liked him.

And it might have even been why I called him.

To punish myself by facing a man who wouldn't disappear my sins but rectify them. It was his duty as a cop to arrest me for what I'd done to Cricket and part of me yearned for that kind of justice, and to be properly defined as an outlaw in a way that my outlaw family refused to do. To be punished for the first time in my life for all of my many misdeeds, big and small.

I didn't expect him to answer, not really. Not after three years and no contact, not on his old number.

But he did.

"Harleigh Rose?"

I breathed short puffs of panicked air into the phone.

There was a pause and I knew that wherever he was, he would be shifting to the left, curling his shoulder into his ear to create a protective barrier, us against the world. Only then did his deep, smooth voice deepen further as he said, "Rosie? Tell me what's happening."

A sob bloomed in my throat, the petals clogging my airway and the thorns tearing up my throat as I choked on the wet rose of his name for me.

Rosie.

Like I was some sweet, young, innocent thing with pigtails in her hair instead of human blood and plasma.

"Lion," I gasped through the wreckage of my throat. "I did something bad."

These were the words I always said when I called him to get me out of trouble.

Countless misdemeanors throughout my youth: underage drinking and public intoxication, bodily assault (that pencil stabbing and some other—warranted—attacks), trespassing and some minor theft.

They were the same words but a different tone.

Usually, I was a brat, taunting him with my rebellion, trying to get a rise out of a man who was interminably calm.

Not now, and he knew it.

"You at your apartment?" he asked.

I nodded my head then realized he couldn't see me. "Yes."

"Twenty minutes," he said in a way that made it a promise. "Hang tight, Rosie."

He hung up before I could ask him how he knew where my apartment was or that I even had one.

The phone fell from my numb fingers as I looked down at Cricket again.

He was dead.

I stared into glassy brown eyes and gave into my shock.

It seemed to me that I blinked and he was there, looming in front of me like some righteous angel come to condemn me to hell. The waning sun filtering in through the windows cast a halo around his broad fame but obscured his face in a veil of shadows. I didn't need to see it to know he was handsome. I'd memorized his features a long time ago, the broad crest of his forehead over the strong brows, the pure jade green of his eyes and the way they creased at the corners in a constant brooding squint or in a rare grin that broke open the planes of his face so that his blazing spirit poured through like light through cracks in the darkness. He was handsome enough to be famous but worn in a way that made him sexy, like a weathered cowboy or a sheriff from the Wild West. He even smelled like that, warm and comforting like sun-kissed man and freshly tilled earth.

Even submerged in a deep haze of shock, I knew him.

I'd know Lionel Danner anywhere, anytime even if I was blind, deaf, and struck dumb.

"Jesus Christ," he cursed as I blinked up at him.

He was in front of me in two long strides, his rough tipped fingers delicately pinching my chin. I stared up at him as he took stock of me with implacable eyes, noting the blood drying on my skin and clothes, the dead carcass that was Cricket lying on the floor at our feet.

He seemed more concerned with me than the very dead body.

"What the fuck did that piece of shit do to you?" he grumbled low in his chest.

I blinked and wished that I could find my voice because I wanted to laugh at him.

I wanted to tease him and ask why he wasn't assuming it was *me*, as it always had been, who had done something wrong.

I wanted to cry and ask him what *hadn't* Cricket done to me?

But for the first time in my life, I had no voice.

I was just as much a body without soul as Cricket was dead on the ground.

"Rosie," he said, more of a breath than sound.

I watched him from deep within myself as he shifted into a

crouch before me and his fingers on my chin slipped in the blood splatter then tightened almost painfully.

The hurt grounded me, but it was the vivid clarity of his green eyes that pulled me like a hand from the depths of my wretchedness.

"For once in your goddamn life, you are going to listen to me and obey. I'm going to get you up out of that bloody swamp you're sittin' in and put you in a chair. Then I'm going to call this in. While we wait for the police to show, you're going to look me in the eye and tell me what happened here. You hear me, Harleigh Rose?"

I was nodding before I could even process his words.

His glare hardened. "Wanna hear that voice."

"Why do I need to look you in the eye?" I asked, surprisingly steady.

My soul felt weak and failing in my chest and I wondered if murderers killed their goodness right along with their victim.

"'Cause you don't distract me with those pretty blues, I'm going to murder that piece of shit all over again for whatever he did that made you feel the need to stick a blade in his neck."

Emotion rumbled under the ruins of my spirit and threatened to bubble up my throat.

Danner read the question in my eyes and his stern face softened from severe creases into smooth, rumpled silk.

"You didn't murder him in cold blood, Rosie. I don't need you to give me those words for me to know the truth of this."

"You haven't even seen me in years," I whispered through the tears that were sudden and insistent at the backs of my eyes. "How could you know that?"

He moved his other hand around the back of my neck and wove it into the sweat damped hair there then tugged it back firmly, just enough to make me hiss in surprise. The action was oddly calming and without conscious thought, I found myself tilting my head to expose my neck to him. Taking my cue, the hand on my chin slid down my jaw and wrapped around my throat, his fingers and thumb pressing gently at my pulse points on either side of my neck.

"You think I don't know that under all that thorny sass you got a heart as tender as a budded rose, you can think again," he said in that flat, sure tone.

Like he was reading someone his or her Miranda rights or reciting a code from the police academy. Like what he was saying was an irrefutable, absolute fact.

In a way he was, if there had ever been a chance of me *not* loving Officer Lionel Danner, it was obliterated by that moment and those words. My heart was imprisoned by his, regardless of his lack of interest.

"I still gotta call it in," he told me, stern but gentle, a contradiction he'd mastered. "If you thought I was gonna let this slide because you're you to me, you were wrong. You didn't call your daddy, you called me, and I'll get it sorted just like he'd get it sorted for you but my way will be a fuckuva lot different and more *legal* than his, yeah?"

When I nodded, shadows passed over the grass green of his eyes like clouds overhead. His jaw ticked as he stared at me like that for a long minute before standing up and sticking out a hand to me. It was a deeply tanned hand attached to a strong wrist threaded with thick veins that ran up and over his corded forearms. A strong hand at the end of a strong arm on the body of the strongest man outside of the club that I'd ever known.

Reeling from everything, including the powerful resurgence of my childhood adoration, I mutely took his offered hand and let him peel me off the tacky blood spill. My core throbbed dully, painfully and my skin felt tender all over like the flesh of an overripe peach dropped to the floor. Still, I sat in one of my slightly wonky wooden chairs and watched him as he pulled out his phone and called in the accident.

I didn't listen to the words he said as he talked to the operator at the station. Instead, I watched the way his firm, beautifully formed mouth worked over the words, watched his pink tongue click against his square, white teeth. It was a disturbing situation to find myself so physically drawn to another man when my old one was barely even cold on the ground, but I'd always been irrevocably drawn to Danner and observing him in his element, Good Cop In Action, centered me.

Again, it felt that I blinked and there were people there, flooding through the doors of my apartment with equipment and cameras, in blue uniforms with squawking walkie-talkies. I jumped when three of them tried to corner me while Danner was busy talking to two people studying the body. I couldn't seem to hear their voices properly. The volume was there, but the words were fuzzy like the adults in Charlie Brown cartoons.

Wah wah wah, wah-wah.

"Back off, Sterling," Danner ordered, suddenly pulling me half behind him so he could face my interrogators.

The huge black man named Sterling rolled his eyes. "Just doing my damn job, Danner. You clearly got personal ties to this one. I think it's me who should be telling ya to back off, eh?"

Danner crossed his arms over his chest and stared down the man in response.

Sterling lasted all of thirty seconds before he awkwardly scratched the back of his head and muttered, "Damn, Danner, I'm just trying to do my job."

"And you can do it but you'll do it at the station and I'll be in the interview room with the both of you. I arrived on the scene after she called me in distress. It's obvious that even if the victim didn't succeed, he attempted to rape her. This case will be opened and shut within forty-eight hours, and you and I both know it. So, cut the posturing, do *your job* and I'm sure that promotion you've been chompin' at will come 'round sooner rather than later, now you're gettin' down to doin' some actual work."

I blinked at Danner and I wasn't the only one. He'd always been quiet, even reserved to the point of fading into the background. It was what had made him such a good cop, everyone was always overlooking him, underestimating him. That man was gone and in his place was a leader, the cold, ruthless kind of man that set my pulse to racing.

I watched his three colleagues physically stand down and lower their heads the way betas might do in deference to the Alpha of a wolf pack. I felt the animal impulse to tilt my head and bare my neck to him as well.

"You've been in deep with the RCMP for three years, Danner. You think Van PD is gonna be hot on you interfering in a murder case?" Another cop said, this one short and slight with a wispy mustache.

"As a matter of fact, you better sweep this up good and fast so it doesn't compromise my play with the RCMP. You wouldn't want to be to blame for fuckin' up a year's long investigation, would you? And you think I've been in deep three years and I don't have connections to pull in if I gotta? Harleigh Rose Garro is my responsibility, Sterling, so listen hard and hear me clearly when I say, she isn't goin' through this shit without me."

A sob ripped through my chest, unzipping the tight lock on the emotions overstuffing my chest so that they spilled through me. I shook with the impact as my shock ruptured and pure horror and agony overtook me.

"Oh my god," I choked out through the tears as I buried my face in my hands. "I don't deserve this."

And I didn't mean Cricket and the attempted rape and the murder. I probably deserved all of that. Karma or some bitch like that for all the ways big and little that I'd been careless and disrespectful and just straight up *wrong* over the years.

But no, that wasn't it.

There was no way in any world, in heaven or hell that I deserved to have a hero like Lionel Danner in my corner.

As if hearing my thoughts but probably responding to the horrific sound of my ugly sobs, he turned slightly to swing me under his arm in a tight hold even as he continued to issue orders. "Now, get someone to take her goddamn pictures and do an examination so we can get her out of these bloody clothes and into something clean. I'm takin' her to the station myself and Sterling, you wanna show what a big boy cop you are, you stay here and get this mess sorted."

CHAPTER TWO

Danner

I WAS SPEAKING WITH THE TRAUMA COUNSELOR WHEN THE door to the North Van Police Station crashed against the wall as it opened and a hoarse voice called out, "What the motherfuckin' fuck do you think you're doin' talkin' to my fuckin' girl without her fuckin' lawyer and goddamn father present?"

I closed my eyes even as the station went wired around me. I thought about counting to ten but giving the President of The Fallen MC ten seconds of vulnerability was ten seconds too many. The six foot five behemoth currently stalking towards me like an enraged, feral jungle cat was not the kind of man you wanted to fuck around with.

I knew that.

It was a lesson one might argue that I'd learned the hard way, when I'd let his teenage wife get abducted by a rival MC.

15

Regardless, I knew not to fuck with him now.

Unfortunately, Zeus Garro didn't know that he'd earned my reluctant respect, so I was braced and unsurprised when he stormed right up to me in a room full of wary cops, lifted me with a huge ass hand by my throat and slammed me against the wall two feet behind me.

Fuckin' *fuck*. That hurt.

I let him do it though. The only way to stop a man like Zeus Garro was to shoot him in the head or lie down in the face of his fury and hope it passed you over. As I'd been in the fuckin' outrageous position of giving a shit about his kid daughter for the last fifteen years, I chose not to shoot the fucker in his thick skull.

Still.

"Stand down, Garro," I said calmly.

His eyes flashed like knifepoints and his grip on my neck tightened.

There was no doubt in my mind that this man had killed men with that very hand or that he had killed them for a lot less than wrapping their daughter up in a murder case.

Fear germinated in my belly then bloomed into something better, something bold and beautiful like a poppy cropped up over dead bodies. I was the rare kind of man that fed off fear, that relished the challenge of conquering the beast and making it submit to me in the end.

I smiled languidly in the face of the beast before me and leaned into his grip, a silent dare that had Zeus Garro snarling. "I said, stand down, Garro. You're going to kill a cop in a room full of cops? You won't live a breath past the second my spine snaps."

"I'll throttle you myself, if you don't tell us where Harleigh Rose is," a sweet voice, sweeter than spun sugar and melted chocolate, called to me over his shoulder.

I ground my teeth when I realized Loulou Garro, formerly Lafayette, had followed her husband into the station.

I was a feminist.

But fuck if I hated when women got involved in men's business because I'd never found a way to say no to them.

"Louise," I acknowledged her easily as if her monster of a husband wasn't strangling me toward a slow death. "Call him off and I'll get you to Harleigh Rose."

A golden hand appeared on the top of Zeus's shoulder and like magic, the tension dissolved in his muscles a second before he dropped me from his painful clutch and stepped back with a low growl.

Loulou stepped forward just as he reached back for her. It was a small thing, but that little symphony of synchronicity hit me in the gut. Sure, Louise had been seventeen years old when they got together and Zeus nineteen years her senior but that move right there, that was the reason I didn't find it disgusting in the least. If anything, my gut clenched with something startlingly close to jealousy. Not for her, never for her. Louise was almost too gorgeous to be made of flesh and blood, yet she was one of the most human people I'd ever met. In another life, one where she'd stayed good and I'd finally conquered my constant battle to be the same, we could have ended up thrust together.

But as I looked at her now, heavily swollen with Garro's babies under her virgin white dress with shit kickers on her feet, I was glad for her that life hadn't turned out that way. She leaned into Garro instinctively and her huge blue eyes sparked like a lightning streaked sky as she glared me down.

"The fuck you get my sister into?" King Kyle Garro yelled across the station as he stepped through the doors, holding them open for the slight woman trailing in behind him.

At least Cressida Irons, his better half, had the grace to look mildly embarrassed by the spectacle.

"We don't know it was his fault," she whispered, tugging on King's hand to keep him from storming at me exactly like his father had done. "He's gotten H.R. out of more situations than anyone else. Hear the man out."

King redirected his glare from me to his woman, but his face softened into an affectionate grin as he looked down at her.

Man, those Garro men were whipped.

Again, there was a pang in my chest that had nothing to do with my high blood pressure.

"Haven't seen this motherfucker in three years, H.R. hasn't been in trouble with the fuckin' pigs in three years and suddenly here he is and my girl is in trouble again?" Garro ground out. "Start explainin'."

"She called me," I said.

I could have said more but I was a man of few words and I knew they'd get me. Harleigh Rose had called *me*, a man she hadn't seen in years, to help her out of a woman's worst nightmare. She'd called me. Not her father, her brother or a member of the club she'd been born princess of.

She'd called me.

I rubbed at that sore spot in my chest as it warmed and pulsed.

"She called *you?*" both Garro men growled.

Loulou and Cress shared a knowing but troubled look.

I shrugged and crossed my arms over my chest, signaling with a slight head nod to the four or five lingering cops warily watching the family that it was cool to go back to their work.

"She did. Cricket showed up at her place high on a cocktail of illegal substances, which, apparently, wasn't unusual," I paused preemptively, knowing Garro enough to know he'd curse like a sailor at that. "This time, he was angry for a number of reasons. One, being that he was high on a potent combination of crack, marijuana and cocaine and that shit would turn a toddler into the Hulk. Two, that he'd recently been passed up for a promotion with the Berserkers MC, somethin' he's been working on for the last two years. And third, Harleigh Rose had just issued the last in a line of attempts to get rid of him, this one done by dragging an old trashcan in front of his apartment door, filled to the brim with stuff he'd left at her house, and this she set on fuckin' fire."

Despite themselves, Garro and his son smirked proudly at that.

Yeah, Harleigh Rose was trouble, born and fuckin' raised.

"She'd just filed a police report," I continued, and then watched their smiles get crushed under heavy frowns. "He'd started to stalk and threaten her. Filed a restraining order last week and got a friend from school to testify to the fact."

"The fuck?" King asked. "Why wouldn't she come to us with that?"

Cress leaned into him and spoke softly, "You think on that for a second, honey, and I think you'll find your answer."

"I'm not thinking on fuck all," Zeus growled. "Why the fuck would she go to the pigs about that little shit?"

I thought about the sight that had greeted me when I entered H.R.'s small downtown apartment. It wasn't just the blood lacquering her torn clothes and bared skin. The abuse and terror went deeper than that. There were hollows under her sharp cheekbones and deep, dark shadows under her flat blue eyes, signs of sleep deprivation and malnutrition. She was too skinny and too flat, even her honey hair had lost its luster and her eyes, eyes that normally flashed with sass and wonder, were dead.

Whatever that now-dead piece of shit had done to Harleigh Rose over the last three years had taken its toll and had been for a good long while. I knew H.R. well enough to know that by the time she realized she was in an abusive relationship with a scumbag, she would be too proud to ask for help. She'd stick it out thinking that she was the one who had gotten herself into the mess in the first place and so, she was the one who had to get herself out of it.

It was a good philosophy sometimes.

Completely disastrous in this case.

Not because the loss of Cricket (nee Taylor Marsden) was a travesty.

But because underneath Harleigh Rose's crown of thorns and venom laced tongue, she was as tender as a fresh bloom and I hated that she would now carry the weight of taking a life.

I should have been there.

Though, it was pointless to chastise myself.

It was in the past, for one.

For another, I hadn't whiled away the time. The last three years working for the RCMP in their Organized Crime Undercover Investigations unit was the highlight of my career and not only because I was out from under my corrupt father's thumb in Entrance, BC.

But all of that was really bullshit next to the real reason I hadn't been there.

I'd had to leave for exactly the reason that I was now wishing I had stayed.

No self-respecting cop should fall in love with an MC Princess.

No moral gentleman should act upon his most deviant desires *at all*, let alone with a girl so much his junior.

No man could fall in love with a woman who would be his downfall but more, he hers without at least attempting to escape that fate.

And I had.

Only now, both H.R. and I were paying for that choice.

"Danner, clue in here please." Loulou's voice pulled me out of my thoughts.

"She didn't call because she's been abused, at least mentally and verbally, for years and by the time she noticed it, she didn't want to shame herself by telling you all." I lifted up a palm to them when they all started speaking over each other and then waited for them to fall into reluctant silence. "When was the last time you saw her?"

"Last fuckin' week," Garro snapped.

"She visit you or you come down here?" I shot back.

I read the answer in the tick of Garro's furred jaw, in the way King ran agitated hands through his long hair and both women slid just that inch closer to their men in a silent act of comfort. She had visited them up in Entrance, in her haven, a place she could escape Cricket and the harmful, shameful way he claimed to love her.

Rage seared low in my gut like an unchecked burner. I knew if it wasn't turned off soon, it would light my whole body on fire in a way I wouldn't be able to control.

"Not like you to let a thing like this go unchecked," I said quiet-like.

My lack of volume didn't blunt the blow of the words the way I'd hoped.

"Watch your fuckin' self. You don't know shit all about my family," Garro snapped and I could see in the way his body vibrated that he was a breath away from pounding my face in.

I leaned back against the wall and crossed my booted foot over the other. "How do you figure that, Garro? Those three years you went away, your kids were more at my place than yours with your strung out excuse of a wife. I was the one who first taught your son how to fire a gun. *I* was the one who bought your daughter her first ride, who made sure it had pink skull and crossbones on it just like she wanted, and then *I* was the one who taught her how to ride. So, tell me again how you figure I know fuck all about the Garro kids?"

It was a brutal speech, and one of the longer ones I'd ever made, but the lingering wrath that curdled my blood made it impossible to care about the flinch of pain that rocked Garro like the strike of a bullwhip. Loulou looked about ready to whip me herself, but it was King who seemed the most impacted. He stared at me with wide eyes that betrayed the fact that he was still fresh, a recruit of The Fallen instead of an initiated brother at arms. Only a man without blood on his hands could look at a cop like that; like a little boy who hero worshiped the cop next door.

I watched as he shook himself out of it and his jaw set to ticking, a bomb about to detonate. I wondered idly who he was angrier at. Me, for being right, or himself, for agreeing with me.

"You throw that in his face one more time, I don't care if it's tomorrow or in twenty years, I will personally cut off your balls, Danner."

I looked down from Garro's eyes to see Loulou leaning forward, little teeth bared, a biker built like a Barbie throwing threats at the feet of a cop. It should have been funny, that image, but it wasn't. It wasn't because I could see the ferocity in her eyes, read the restrained fury in her body and the pain at her lips that made them twist funny in the corners. I'd hit a nerve not only for her man but for her as well. After all, he'd gone to prison after killing the man who'd shot Loulou as a little girl right through her chest in a gang war that erupted outside a fucking church.

I hooked my thumbs in my pockets and raised an eyebrow at her. I couldn't let her know, any of them know, how much I reluctantly admired them, their courage and conviction, the way they fused themselves together into one fucking beautiful family unit.

I tried not to spend too much time near the Garros because each time I did, my moral compass went haywire in the face of their magnetism.

"They aren't done with her yet," I told her blandly.

She blinked then put her little claws away and tipped her chin up like the snotty Princess she'd been raised to be. "Fine. We'll just wait right over here until you're done interrogating a victim."

She tugged Garro away by the hand and with one last

vicious glare directed my way he stalked after her, already tugging his phone out to update the brothers or call them to arms. It was lucky Cricket was already a dead man 'cause the damage Garro would've done to him once he found out the extent of his crimes... let's just say that death by cleaver was a hell of a lot less painful.

King lingered a second, peering at me in that brooding way he'd mastered even as a kid. "What're you still doin' out here? Go make sure those fucks aren't fuckin' with her."

I locked eyes with him as warmth loosened the dozen knots tied in my chest. Even after all the years and all the bad blood, it felt good to know the kid still believed in me, at least a little.

I gave him a curt nod then turned on my heel, shooting a quelling glance at the nervous rookie officer on duty behind the front desk as I stalked from the front bullpen, up the stairs and into the back where the interrogation rooms were.

They hadn't been fucking with H.R. when I'd left. I'd spoken with the two interrogating officers, laid it out for them that this wasn't about takin' down an associate of The Fallen, but helping a long-time victim work through her shock and horror after taking a life.

They'd gotten me, mostly because I hadn't given the option not to.

But as soon as I saw Timothy Guzman, I knew things had gone to shit in my absence.

He proved me right by immediately stating, "You gotta bring her in, son."

Heat raced from the base of my spine up my neck and I had to physically bite back the fury to keep from throttling the man next to me.

I took three deep breaths before I faced the middle-aged piece of shit I had to call my superior.

"First off, not your son, Sergeant Guzman. Not going to tell you again," I paused, waiting for him to acknowledge it with a terse nod. "Second, I told you once I told you fucking twenty times, no."

"You can't just say *no*," he said through his teeth, slamming a fleshy hand down on the counter in front of the one-way mirror that looked into the interrogation room Harleigh Rose was currently sitting in. "This is official business and I'm your boss, Danner. This isn't some suggestion box at a fucking coffee shop."

I glared at the five-foot-three sack of shit that technically ran the Combined Forces Special Enforcement Unit for the province. He was a paper pusher, a schmuck that wouldn't understand fieldwork if a bullet bit him in the ass.

"And I wasn't suggesting shit. I was *telling* you that under no fucking conditions will I be involving a victim of abuse and gang violence in my investigation."

"You don't run this show, Danner. Your daddy may be Staff Sergeant up in bum fuck Entrance, but down here, in this city, I say what goes. And I say that Harleigh Rose, a far from innocent, born affiliate of The Fallen MC, is the perfect confidential informant to get us inside information from The Berserkers."

I ground my teeth together and tried that counting to ten thing.

It didn't work.

"No," I stated, then turned away from him to see Sterling and Farrow staring at me with dual expressions of awe and irritation.

No one stood up to Guzman. He was completely incompetent, but he was a bully, and he had no problem with making a cop's life absolutely miserable if he felt they needed to be 'reminded who was in charge.'

Only, no one bullied me. I'd been effectively bullied by my father for too many years to count and when I took down the Nightstalkers MC, I finally had enough notoriety to get out of Entrance and away from his corruption. Now that I was free, there was no way I was taking orders I didn't believe in.

Not anymore.

Not ever-a-fucking-gain.

And especially not when following orders meant I'd have to use Harleigh Rose as an inside asset in the most dangerous gang British Columbia had ever seen.

"I'm fine with that, Danner." Another voice, deeper than any voice I'd ever heard otherwise, sounded over my shoulder and I turned to find Sgt. Renner, the head of Project Fenrir and my immediate superior, at my back. "But if she gives us any indication she still has serious ties to that MC, I want you on her, you hear?"

Immediately my bestial brain concocted an image of me *on* H.R. the way I'd wanted to be on her since she turned sixteen and went from gangly kid to fucking gorgeous woman; her endless legs wrapped near to twice around my hips, her streaky gold and blond hair laid out across my pillow and her long neck under my teeth as I bit into her, fucked into her, branded her as mine.

Only I hadn't given in to the urges when I'd had the chance. In fact, I'd run away from them as fast as I fucking could because the thought of her was nearly too much, but the reality of her was impossible.

Guilt slithered through my veins like a toxin, infiltrating my system before I could rationalize the feeling. I'd been too chicken shit to get involved with her then, and she'd lashed out by turning to the worst possible option.

Cricket.

So indirectly or not, I was to blame for her abuse, for his death.

I rubbed a hand roughly over my face, trying to scrub away the weariness there. I'd become a cop because I was born the kind of man that couldn't sit idly by while injustice was done. I'd known the first time I stood up to a bully, six years old and scrawnier than most of the girls in my grade, and then promptly been beaten on my ass by said bully and three of his friends, that I would keep standing up and fighting wrong for the rest of my life, even if it meant getting beaten down each time.

I'd known there would be setbacks, that a badge and a code of honour didn't mean I'd be able to rectify every misdeed. What I never could have prepared for was the knowledge that my own father would force me to act out those misdeeds or at the very least, cover them up. That system was in place for a reason yet so many innocent people were condemned and so many guilty slipped through the cracks, their way greased by money slicked palms and handshake deals.

And now this.

Now, Harleigh Rose, a woman who radiated confidence and pure fucking joy, was sitting in an interrogation room coated in her abusive boyfriend's blood, physically torn by his hands and degraded by his actions.

And fuck if I didn't feel that worse than all the other trans-gressions rolled into one.

"I'll watch her," I muttered, to the man I actually admired enough to give a response to. "But she's a victim here, Serge. I'm not feelin' keen to take advantage."

Serge's big hand clapped over my shoulder and gave me a squeeze. "Don't like to see a woman, any woman, assaulted sexually or otherwise. But you've got to face reality here, Danner. The girl didn't just make her own bed, she was born in it."

I shrugged off his hand but gave him a terse nod. I wondered for the thousandth time if children were inherently accountable for their parents' offences, if there was receipt of sinful debt written into our DNA, if we were karmically wired to live bad and do bad because it was in our blood. And not for the first time, I couldn't answer definitively even though I'd spent my entire life trying to prove otherwise.

My distracted gaze focused on the room in front of me and I immediately frowned when I noticed who had replaced Sterling and Farrow in the interrogation.

CHAPTER THREE

Harleigh Rose

"You murder anyone before, Miz Garro?"

The asshole interrogating me even looked like an asshole. Slicked back hair thick with styling cream, an even tan that spoke of artifice—either careful rotations sun tanning in his yard or even worse, at a salon. It was obvious he was no stranger to a salon either way because his nails were better manicured than my ratty-assed chipped black fingertips. I couldn't stop staring at them as he moved his hands over a stack of papers meant to intimidate me. They were slim-fingered with perfect oval nails buffed to a high shine and palms so smooth I just bet he moisturized every night before bed.

"Not a stranger to being on the wrong side of the law, are

you? Daughter of Zeus Garro. I just bet you were born with the thrill of rebellion on your tongue. Let's see, we got some petty theft, physical assault charges, and destruction of public property," the other officer, this one a smug looking, masculine brunette grinned thinly at me as she listed my crimes.

I shrugged one shoulder. "Honestly? I shoulda been given a medal for decapitating that statue of mayor Benjamin Lafayette. He was steaming piece of shit so really, I did a public service."

The asshole awkwardly swallowed his startled chuckle, which made me like him more, but the lady cop sneered at me.

"Flagrantly disobeying the *law* isn't a laughing matter, Miss Garro. And I find it interesting that you could retain your sense of humor after you claim that Taylor "Cricket" Marsden assaulted you and tried to rape you with his gun."

I swallowed past the sudden swell of bile at the back of my tongue. I could still feel the press of metal against the inside of my thigh, how cold it was against the hot blood that seeped from my torn opening.

It would have hurt anyway, a comment like that, no matter that I'd grown up livin' the kind of life that meant I'd been born with a thick skin that only grew more calloused with time. It hurt more that a woman was givin' that shit to me. I may have been raised in a club of biker men, but it was their women who'd raised me and taught me that there was nothing so sacred as the bond between women.

"Not one for the sisterhood, are ya? Judging a woman on how she's gotta move past something like that," I said softly with a click of my tongue.

"Difficult not to judge a biker's daughter with a rap sheet started when she was thirteen and now she sits there laughing about vandalism after she's killed a man. For all we know, you like it rough and the one who got out of hand wasn't him, but you with that knife and an opportunity to take a shot at a rival gang to your daddy's."

There was a loud bang from outside the door and asshole cop even shifted uncomfortably at her insult but I ignored it to casually lean forward over the metal table between me and Bitch Cop to say, "No one ever taught you a woman doesn't have to act like a man to be powerful, did they? Us women, we got more power in our pinky finger than most men hope to wield in their entire lives. And a part of that power is supporting your sisters, believing them when they confess and supporting them when they fall. Shame," I clucked again.

I watched with satisfaction as the lady cop progressed like a paint sampler from rose to vermillion red.

Then, I continued.

"And just to add, you aren't half as smart as you think you are if you believe I'd date a man for four years, let him beat me and treat me like shit for the last two of those, just to wait until he finally tried to rape me in order to kill him for the betterment of my 'daddy's gang'? Which, correction again, bitch, is a fuckin' *club of motorcycle enthusiasts.*"

I leaned back in my chair, trying not to let a wince of pain ruin my smug grin. Bitch Cop's face was screwed up so tight she looked like an ad for constipation medicine.

"You're done."

I startled slightly even though I'd vaguely been aware of a commotion outside the room. Just as quickly, I settled back into my smug grin because I knew that voice and I knew what it stood for—justice, peace, faith—and what it stood behind—*me.*

Danner rounded the table, all grace and coiled power, a great cat stalking its prey and doing it boldly because stealth was nothing next to the other tools in his arsenal.

"Stand down, Jacklin. The Captain's watchin' and you don't want to make any more of an ass of yourself than you already have," he said as soon as he reached Bitch Cop's side, leaning down heavy into the table so that his face was looming over hers.

A hissing noise of irritation built in the back of her throat. "You're not even supposed to be in here, Danner. You're not even supposed to be in the goddamn station, the position you're in. The fact that you *are* says a hell of a lot, none of it fucking *ethical* about your relationship with Miz Garro."

"You wanna talk ethics when you're sitting there blatantly insulting a victim of fucking sexual assault after she had to take a life to save her own?" Danner roared, so mired in his rage that I worried he was going to go all The Hulk on everyone.

I reached over to hook my finger in one of his belt loops and tugged so his fury twisted face turned to me.

"I'm okay," I told him, my voice pitched low, just for us.

Ever since I could remember, Danner and I occupied our own space together, a separate frequency of sound bubbled up around us so that it was us and only us who understood the other. It ballooned around us now, close and intimate, eradicating our three-year separation into dust.

"You're not," he protested gruffly.

His strong hands were flat and stiff on the table before me, lined with veins and muscles that extended up each thick finger and around each wide palm. They were such capable hands, calloused from shooting and guitar, strong from sports and yet tender as a feather touched against my cheek.

I placed one of my hands over his on the table and stared into his furious eyes. "I will be. Just get me out of here. You know cops give me the creeps."

Humor cracked through the anger in his face like a broken pane of glass. "I'm still a cop, you know, H.R.?"

"Oh, I know, but at this point, it's the devil you know versus the devil you don't," I said with a blasé shrug because I knew it would make him smile.

It did, just a slight twist of his lips but it was enough for me.

"Sorry to interrupt this intimate moment,' Bitch Cop said scathingly. "But we weren't finished with her and *you* shouldn't risk your ass by being here, Danner."

Danner practically snarled at her and I wondered if it had been the last three years that turned him feral or the fact that I'd almost been raped.

It didn't matter. The Lionel Danner I'd known was now only a gilded frame around whatever kind of man he'd become, one I got the sense was much, much darker than the one before.

"You're done, you need a follow up then you contact Miss Garro tomorrow. She's still covered in her abuser's blood, Jacklin, have some empathy."

Bitch Cop opened her mouth to spew more poison, but the pretty cop beside her laid a restraining hand over her arm and shook his head. "Danner has a point. Let the girl get cleaned up and rested. We can make a house call tomorrow."

Her eyes flashed but then she looked over her shoulder at the one-way mirror and I knew she was remembering that Danner had said the Captain was back there watching.

"Let's go before I get hives," I muttered to Danner, clutching his stiff hand in mine as I moved towards the door.

I was trying desperately to be light-hearted, to hide behind that titanium coating of barbed humor and faux confidence but I'd been born an outlaw and the walls of the police station were closing in on me.

And I couldn't afford that claustrophobia, not when my family was no doubt gathered in the police station front room, braving their severe hatred for all things law to see me as soon as humanly possible. I needed to batten the fuckin' hatches, cage the break down that thrashed like a wild thing inside my chest. I could feel it eating at my heart, gnashing into it with hard, sharp teeth and ripping away big, bloody chunks, but I didn't flinch, promised myself I wouldn't tremble.

At least, not until I was alone, sequestered in my daddy's house like an MC Rapunzel safe in a chain link protected metal tower.

"Rosie," Danner interrupted my thoughts just before I could descend the stairs.

I closed my eyes tight against the pain of that pet name and took a deep breath before I said, "Yeah?"

He tugged at my hand gently so I swirled to face him. His face was heartbreakingly beautiful, stern features softened by pain and concern, his eyes so green they glowed against his golden tan, his thick brown lashes. I blinked hard then looked away, angry with myself for being so easily bedazzled by him. Firm fingers took my chin in their grip, tipping my head back slightly so I was forced to look up into his face. His gaze swept over every corner of my expression, detailing every scar, every angle, plane, and curve of my features. I wondered if he was matching reality to memory, if I looked different than I had three years ago. There was a scar on my left cheekbone, just under my eye where one of Cricket's rings had broken the skin, and another on the lower right corner of my bottom lip where my tooth had cut through the flesh when I'd fallen to the ground during one of his rages. One hand moved to cradle my left cheek, his thumb swiping over the slight scar, while the other thumb dragged over my mouth, pulling it open into a pout.

Tears pricked my eyes even though I tried to steady myself with short, shallow breaths. "Stop," I breathed.

He ignored me, his features metal hard and melded into shape with the heat of his rage and the cold of his pain. He leaned down into my face and spoke softly into my open mouth, hoping to feed me the words in a way I could easily digest.

"I want to apologize, but how can I when there are no

words to erase what was done to you? You know, I'm a man of action, not words, Rosie, and fuck me, if I could, I would bring that bastard back to life and write a poem for you on his body with my fists and his blood. And you know, I'm not religious, because fuck that, but for you, I'd pay penance every day with a flogging, write lines until my fingers were numb and broken, self-flagellate until I was mutilated, if it meant taking this pain, this memory and especially, my part in it, away from you."

I shuddered under his hands, sucked in a breath so big it ached in my lungs, and then let it out low and slow. I needed the air to prop me up, to inflate my shape for just a while longer so I didn't dissolve into a puddle of tears right there on the floor.

"You're such a fuckin' martyr," I told him, aiming for sassy but falling uncharacteristically short. "This isn't your fault."

His hand tightened briefly on my face, but I didn't flinch because if I knew only one thing in my life, it was that I was safe with Danner.

"I left," he muttered.

"You did," I agreed, then because I wasn't the kind of girl to hold back, I added, "It hurt like a motherfucker."

His eyes flared. "Same for me."

"Your choice, so I got no sympathy for you there. That said, don't be a fuckin' idiot and assume that your desertion led me to staying with a madman for longer than I should've. You didn't use to be so full of yourself."

"Rosie—" he started, but I'd found a flicker of fire in my belly and I latched on to it.

I shoved him away and backed up a few paces. "Stop calling me that, Danner. I'm not your Rosie anymore. My life doesn't have anything to do with you. *I* fucked up, *I* killed Cricket, *I* was the fuckin' cliché that let her man beat her because my head wasn't right. Not you. Not my dad like that Bitch Cop implied. *Me*. Thanks for coming for me, thanks for gettin' me out of that fuckin' box. If you need to pay penance, there, you did it. Now, we can be done. Again."

"Fuck that," Danner snarled, the tendons in his forearms clenching in a way that I noticed was delicious even through my increasing delirium. "You think that's the end, you haven't grown up as much as I would've thought in the last three years."

"Fuck you," I shouted out at him with bared teeth. "You don't know shit!"

Infuriatingly, he just raised an eyebrow and crossed his corded arms across his chest. "I'm the one just got you out of this shit, Harleigh Rose, you think I don't know shit?"

"This bullshit doesn't define my life," I yelled at him, furious at the idea.

Too furious to notice the way his lips twitched with satisfaction, to wonder why he was antagonizing me after what I'd just been through.

Too furious to realize that he was giving me strength in the only way I knew how to take it—furiously—so that I could go out into that main room and face my family with strength the way I wanted to but was just seconds ago, incapable of doing.

"It doesn't," he agreed. "But I knew you at seven, eleven and seventeen. I drove you and King to school, shot the shit with you at Mega Music for hours every Sunday for years. You think three years means I don't know you, Rosie, you're fucking *wrong*."

"I don't want to see you a-fucking-gain, *Officer* Danner," I sneered at him, my anger like a flaming sword in my hand, weaponized and ready to take on any adversary.

I frowned as Danner pressed his lips together, to keep from smiling it seemed, and slid his gaze lazily over my body. I was covered in blood and bruised, my fingertips black with police ink, but he looked at me like I was something magnificent, something worthy of awe.

"I know you still amaze me," he muttered, even as we

heard commotion at the bottom of the stairs and then King was taking them two at a time to get to me while my dad shouted at a cop who was trying to restrain him from going up after me. "Know it in a way that I know you'll never stop doin' it."

I blinked at him, my anger momentarily forgotten. Never, but *never*, had Lionel Danner confessed his attraction to me, not even after the kiss that changed everything so many years ago.

"H.R. Christ, fuck me," King growled in my ear a second before he was wrapped around me, his long arms gentle as they wound me up against his chest.

I closed my eyes, breathed in a lungful of his clean laundry scent and forgot about Danner, about Cricket and blood and the weight of a cleaver in my hands. My brother was there and, two seconds later when even thicker arms clenched around the both of us, I knew so was my dad.

"My baby girl," he croaked, and I knew there was a sadness in his gut so deep it made my big, bad biker dad close to tears. "I got you."

"Yeah, we got you," King muttered into my hair.

The fear I hadn't realized was looming over me began to dissipate, because there was nowhere safer for me on this planet than between my two Garro men. My eyes snapped open to search for Danner, because I knew in a way I couldn't describe that I felt the same way about him, but he was gone.

CHAPTER FOUR

Harleigh Rose

I WENT TO THE FUNERAL.

It was a stupid idea.

Yeah, the police had swept the real details of Cricket's murder under the rug, but there was no longer any reason for me to associate with the Berserkers MC and if you were given an out from a world like that, if you were anything but certifiably insane, you took it.

I'd always been a little off my rocker.

I wanted to go to that funeral.

Mostly, I wanted to spit in Cricket's face before they incinerated him into ash, but another part of me, one that was born into the MC culture, had too much respect for the traditions of club life to ignore my duty as Cricket's 'old lady' and not attend.

There was also the fact that my safety depended pretty fucking heavily on the Berserker brothers believing in the cover story the police had concocted for Cricket's murder. I didn't know the details, but I knew enough about cops to know it might be flimsy at best, so it was up to me to watch my own back.

So, I guilted Lila into giving me a ride out to North Vancouver's secluded Cate's Park for the funeral, decked out in my biker babe finest, skin-tight black skinny jeans tucked into chunky heeled black leather boots, a black lace-up V-neck and my requisite black leather jacket. My thick head of hair was a tousled, wavy mass down my back and my blue eyes were rimmed in kohl. Inappropriate for most funerals but this was a biker gathering, it was my duty as Cricket's old lady to show up looking strong and beautiful, to show his brothers the kind of woman he'd been capable of keeping.

I felt no obligation to him, *obviously*, but I was still my father's daughter and even though I'd been Cricket's, I was a Garro first. I represented The Fallen MC and no woman born to them would be weak enough to look sullen or angry or unkempt.

I kept that shit inside my blackened heart and when I strutted through the caramel sand toward the black mass of bikers surrounding the hand-hewn canoe containing Cricket's shrouded corpse, I did it with a smile pasted on my blood red lips.

"Afternoon, guys," I practically purred as I stepped up to the front line of mourners.

My heart was beating strangely, too furious and too slow, brutal gong strikes against my ribs every few seconds that made my breath hitch. I tried to control my pulse because if anyone would notice something like that, it would be Wrath

Marsden, Vice President of Berserkers MC and Cricket's much older, much cooler cousin.

I could feel his eyes on me instantly, the hot, hard weight of them like one of his big, scarred hands pressing into my chest. He was bracketed by Berserkers Sergeant at Arms, Grease Montgomery, and the Prez of the entire MC, Reaper Holt. They were two of the scariest men I'd ever laid eyes on and definitely two of the most terrifying men I'd ever met, which was saying something given my upbringing. Despite the attention they demanded, I only had eyes for the man at their center.

Wrath was the kind of biker who'd been adopted into it. Raised by two alcoholic parents, mum a stripper and dad the bouncer at a nightclub, he came from rough and learned early that the easiest way out of poverty was to channel his sheer size—six foot six at the age of sixteen and fully grown—as a tool to lend to the gangs that ruled the streets. He started as a lowly enforcer for the Triad, the Chinese crime syndicate, and then quickly discovered the appeal of a Harley between his thighs, prospecting for Berserkers at the age of eighteen and now, twelve years later, he was VP. This was no little thing given his youth and it was directly correlated to the amount of blood he'd shed with those hammer-like fists and the amount of blood he'd saved from being let within their own ranks thanks to his above-the-average-biker IQ.

As if this wasn't terrifying enough, Wrath was good looking. You think there isn't something threatening about beauty, you haven't seen it, not really. There is so much power in a pretty thing, in its capacity to rule your thoughts and puppeteer your actions. It's a shiny thing and we're all just crows, helpless against its appeal.

Wrath was one of the shiniest things I'd ever seen, so beautiful it was terrifying and so terrifying it was, to someone who appreciated such things, beautiful. I'd never seen a bigger man, not even my goliath dad was as tall and carved from granite muscle, but all that hardness was softened by a thick, lustrous fall of golden-brown hair and large eyes so clear and pale a blue they looked like the placid surface of a lake. His mouth was lush, a thick curve above and below that cut up the darkness of his beard and amplified its ridiculous prettiness.

Over the years, I'd made a study of Wrath Marsden but not because he was pretty.

No, I'd made a study of the Berserkers VP and ruthless killer because he had made a study of me.

I had the feeling that if his cousin hadn't met me first, he would have had me in his bed in a heartbeat.

He watched me then, his jaw tight but his face otherwise impassive. There was a threat there somewhere, I could read it in the absence of his expression.

He didn't buy the story of his cousin's death.

More than that, he didn't believe I hadn't had a hand in it.

Fuck.

"Harleigh, baby," Reaper said, his voice as smoldering as the plume of smoke billowing out from his cigarette plugged mouth. He opened his short, stocky arms to me. "Come to Reaper."

I went without hesitation even though the thought of being touched still sent violent chills through my body.

Reaper Holt wasn't someone you disobeyed.

He wrapped me in a tight hug, his nose burrowed into the crook of my neck because we were the same height with me in my tall boots. I tried not to shudder as he took a deep whiff of my scent, and his fleshy hand fell down my back to curl over my ass, giving it a pat before he released me.

"Lookin' good, baby," he told me, his bloodshot brown eyes twinkling.

He was somewhere in his fifties, but he had the libido of a teenager. He'd never been married but as far as it was known, he had twelve kids, all by different women, and those were only the ones who'd had the balls to come forward to get money for child support. I didn't understand the appeal but then, you didn't have to find Reaper appealing to bang him. I'd spent my entire life watching women drawn into the biker gang fold, entranced by the thrill of rebellion, of taming a bad boy, of reveling in sin.

Sleeping with an outlaw was like sleeping with a wild animal. Only the very stupid or very courageous braved the risk that that animal would turn, tear out your eyes and eat out your throat before you could blink. I knew women who'd chosen well, the brave ones, like my step-mum/best friend Loulou Garro and my brother's woman, Cressida Irons. They hadn't tamed the mustangs they'd found, they'd just learned to ride 'em well, over the uneven terrain of their biker lives and through the wilds of their often-violent realities.

I knew the stupid ones too. Tons of them.

I was also one of them.

Cricket was an animal and not even one worth trying to tame or trying to ride. He was something small, shifty and feral, a raccoon out in the daytime that's starvin' and crazed.

For the millionth time in the last four years, I wondered how I ever could've been taken in by him?

And for the millionth time, the same answer came to me.

There a small part of my self-esteem that was corrupted, sunk through with a rot so deep that all the confidence on top of it was startlingly precarious. And that rot stemmed directly from my bitch of a mother.

I'd been loved by men all my life, I trusted them to take care of me, even more than that, to *treasure* me.

It was a woman who had taught me to hate myself, that I had nothing to offer and nothing to gain from life because I was nothing myself. Not even worthy of my mother's love.

So, I'd made a mistake. I'd chosen to trust the male gender implicitly and I'd shunned that putrid corner of my soul where self-doubt and loathing hung out like high school slackers. And in ignoring them, I'd allowed them to vandalize my entire soul with their anarchy until I'd become exactly what my mother wanted me to be.

Nothing.

Cressida had done her research, frantically trying to find answers in her precious literature that could explain where they, the family, went wrong in raising me. I could have told her it wasn't her or them, least of all my father. Sometimes all it takes is one bad egg, and all that.

She hit on the statistic on the Canadian Women's Foundation and Child Help website though.

Children of abuse are twice as likely to be abusers or victims of abuse in their adulthood. They are almost nine times as likely to engage in criminal behaviour as well, which made me laugh. King was a prospect for my father's outlaw motorcycle club, and I'd had a rap sheet since I was thirteen.

It didn't make me feel better to know that there was science behind my pathetic actions, but it helped my family so I stayed quiet while they hunted down information to feed the gaping maw of despair in their guts.

The monster in the pit of my belly stayed starved.

"Sorry 'bout Cricket," Reaper interrupted my ill-timed daze to say. "Good kid."

I could feel Wrath's sharp eyes digging into my chest like the point of a blade so I was careful not to make a disgusted face at those words. Cricket was not a kid, he'd died at twenty-four, and he was in no way, shape or form good.

Instead, I let tears fill my eyes to the brim but not over. It wouldn't do to overact, and they would expect me to be tough twice over, as an old lady and, more, as a Garro.

"Can't believe it," I whispered, looking from Reaper to Grease to Wrath and back again so they could all catch a look at my drowning blue eyes. "Tell me you know who did that to him. Tell me you'll get 'em."

Grease stepped forward, his pockmarked face further

textured by a nasty grin. "Oh, we'll get 'em. Got solid intel that it was them fuckin' Red Dragons."

I whistled gently and rocked back on my heels, genuinely surprised that the cops had thought to pin it on the Asian organized crime syndicate based primarily in downtown Vancouver. It was a ballsy move, way beyond moving a pawn on the board, they had placed their Queen in jeopardy on the off chance of taking down two gangs for the price of one.

"Does this mean war?" I asked.

Reaper stroked his long goatee and shot a sideways glance at Grease. "Not convinced it was them chinks. Was thinking maybe it might be a rival MC."

I frowned. "Anonymous MC sticks to Langley, I didn't know you had beef with them."

"We don't."

I blinked at Reaper, my mind whirring until *click*.

"You think it was The fuckin' Fallen?" I demanded, taking a step forward so I was in Reaper's ugly face.

He shrugged. "Was a while back now but I'm sure you remember your Uncle Crux there murdered three'a my brothers in cold blood."

I remembered. I was a girl so I could never be a true member of The Fallen but I was their Princess, and though I was sheltered from the outside world's atrocities growing up, I knew all too well the mayhem of MC life. My great uncle Crux had been, to put it fuckin' mildly, a psychopath. He killed indiscriminately just because he had a thirst for blood and violence the way an alcoholic does for booze.

He'd even killed members of his own fuckin' chapter.

So, my dad killed him and took his chrome and iron throne.

To some, that might make their father into a murderer. For me, it made him into a hero.

I didn't say any of that to Reaper. I was careful with him. He was too happy to have a member of the Garro family within the Berserker fold, and he often pressed or tried to manipulate me for inside information.

He was a thug with a loyal following. It was easy to deceive him.

It was Wrath, standing quietly just behind him that posed a challenge.

"The club's business is their business, what do I know about it?" I suggested with a shrug. "You know how it is even better than I do."

"Yeah," he said, squinting hard at me. "Just wonderin' if maybe your daddy picked up his old uncle's torch against us. Think it's likely?"

Digging.

I wanted to roll my eyes but to a biker like Reaper that meant blatant disrespect that he would rectify with his fists.

"Let's think of it this way, The Fallen's got a good thing goin' with their product and you got a good thing goin' with your gun trade, you think they want to start a war over somethin' they don't give two fucks about takin' on themselves?"

Reaper stared at me with his beady eyes for a long minute, but I didn't flinch.

"Bitch has got a point, Prez," Wrath said quietly.

"Yeah, maybe," he muttered, but I could tell by the way his eyes shifted to Grease, who was bouncing lightly on the balls of his feet, that they were itchin' for something, and I had a powerful inkling that that something was Fallen men blood.

"Let's get this done," Wrath suggested, clapping a huge hand over Reaper's shoulder. "The brothers are ready to celebrate Cricket's death back at the clubhouse."

"They'll wait for my fuckin' say so," Reaper barked, his hackles raised by any semblance of someone taking control other than him.

He hated Wrath for his smarts just as much as he was

grateful for them. It was a fine balance and one that Wrath miraculously kept in check.

"Whatever you say, brother. Just got my eye on the weather. Looks like rain and it'll be one dud of a sendoff if we can't even light this fuckin' thing."

All four of us looked up at the June sky curling at the edges into clouds the colour of charred paper. Reaper grunted, his concession to Wrath, and then stomped off towards the waterline.

"Let's do this," he yelled out, and everyone that had been chatting immediately fell into a massive semi-circle around him.

Most clubs have their own funeral rituals, usually something authentic to their origin or culture. The Fallen tosses coins into the coffin to pay the deceased's way with the ferryman just as they did in ancient Greek times.

Berserkers were a little more intense, almost to the point of being heathens.

I watched as ten of the strongest brothers grunted and hefted the canoe heavy with Cricket's corpse into the air on their shoulders. As one, the crowd around me began to hum and stomp their boots into the damp sand. I added my voice to the keening swell of sound and if mine was tinged with pain and edged with anger, no one noticed.

The canoe-bearers walked into the cold Pacific without a shiver, the men at the front up to their cuts in the freezing brine before they let the canoe go with a sloshing shove.

The crowd stopped their humming as the brothers returned to shore and Wrath handed Reaper a massive, modern crossbow. The Prez twisted to Grease who dumped the tip of a cloth wrapped arrow into a jug of gasoline and then lit it on fire with his lighter. The sound it made was loud in the dead silence, the hiss of a snake about to attack.

I watched without breathing as Reaper adjusted his stance and let the arrow fly high into the sky. Less than a second later, it thwacked straight into Cricket's gasoline coated chest and roared into flame.

I stared into the inferno and silently damned Cricket to the furthest reaches of Hell, condemned to a fruitless, endless task like Sisyphus rolling his boulder up the hill again and again. It was only fitting given that's what I'd done for the last four years, struggling to push the weight of his crimes against me, against our love, off of my heart.

"He loved you," said a deep voice, rough in a way that spoke of a pack of cigs a day. "Used to say, 'got me the prettiest girl in the whole wide world.'"

I couldn't fight the shiver that yanked on my spine. "Sorry for your loss, Wrath."

His breath was hot on the skin of my neck and I could feel his body curved over me, shielding me from the others while simultaneously intimidating me with his size. He was an idiot if he thought his sheer mass would scare me. Clearly, he hadn't met my father.

"Never understood why he went on about your looks," he continued as if I hadn't spoken. "Sure, I've no doubt you'd look fuckin' fine takin' my cock, or any man's, but I also thought Cricket was missin' the point of ya."

I swallowed thickly but infused my voice with my signature sarcasm. "You sure know how to compliment a woman."

"That point being, the brain in that pretty head. See, I've got these questions that've been needin' answers since you took up with my cousin. Like why the fuck would an MC princess hook up with a man from a rival MC? Why would she stay loyal to him when he started takin' that beauty and desecratin' it with bruises? Why would she love him when he didn't even get the point of her beyond the pretty set of her face?"

"Seems like you've spent a fuckuva lotta time thinking about me, Wrath," I murmured, tucking my chin into my left shoulder so he could see the curve of my cheek, the red of my lips curled up and the way my eyelashes fluttered like fans. My ass pressed back slightly into the seat of his groin and I was triumphant to find his cock lay hard against his thigh. "Maybe these are questions you're asking as a man and not a cousin."

He breathed hard in my ear as I ground down on his erection then stepped away. His hand lashed out quick as a flash to wrap hard around my wrist and jerk me back into him. "Maybe, I am. But remember this, Harleigh Rose, man or cousin, I'm *always* the VP of this club. You'd do best to remember that you're playin' games with a brother who's not afraid of violence and murder."

The anger that had lain dormant in my belly since the moment Cricket attacked me in my apartment, beat me and tried to rape me, flared to life as bright as the flames surrounding his now charred corpse. I ripped my hand out of Wrath's grip, spun to face him and pressed my knee *hard* into his groin, up under his tender, swinging balls.

"Yeah, well you remember this big man. I'm the princess of The Fallen MC, not some sniffling Disney nitwit without the means to save herself. I'm a warrior princess, the kind that'll cut off your balls and serve them for fuckin' tea, you feel me? So next time you threaten me, why don't you remember *that?*"

I pushed off his chest and stalked farther up the beach away from him. I didn't start breathing again until I'd got twenty paces without Wrath following me. There was no doubt in my mind that Wrath had his eye on me, in more uncomfortable ways than one.

"H.R.," a throaty voice called, and I turned around to see Laken Bard, my one and only true friend in the Berserker bitches.

I tipped my chin at her but kept moving. "I gotta head."

She frowned and shouted, even though it drew eyes I didn't want to both of us, "You're comin' to the clubhouse for the wake."

It wasn't a question, but up until that point I hadn't been sure I would go. Laken was reminding me in the only way she could that I didn't have a choice. If I wasn't at my old man's wake, it would be noted and even though I was technically done with the Bersekers, for them no one was done unless they'd cut the cord themselves. I had to give them the opportunity to do so.

"Yeah, see you then," I called out, about to turn around and catch a ride with one of the bikers who was already leaving when I caught sight of a tall, blond man wrapping his arms around Laken.

Even before I turned to fully face them, I knew in the depths of my chest who would be holding her, because my body knew intrinsically whenever he was in my vicinity.

I shouldn't have recognized him in that brief glimpse, not with the leather cut snug tight across his broad chest, a snarling wolf patched across the back under the "Berserkers MC" top rocker, and a bright red, green and black tangle of a tattoo peeking out from under it.

The man I knew him to be wore Timberland boots, not motorcycle shit kickers, plaid shirts not dirty tees, and he always had his clean, shining gold hair smoothed away from his forehead instead of the mess it currently fell in over his eyes.

I dragged a deep, steadying breath into my lungs before looking back at him and it still hit me harder than seeing Cricket burn, to see Officer Lionel Danner tangled in a passionate kiss with my best girl, Laken Bard.

CHAPTER FIVE

Harleigh Rose

THE BERSERKER CLUBHOUSE WAS NOT LIKE THE FALLEN'S. IT was a huge four-story Victorian house on a big lot in West Van. The club owned both lots on either side of it, one that was converted into a massive garage for their bikes and equipment and the other they rented to nomad bikers and Berserker affiliates to cut down on nosy neighbors and noise complaints. The cops basically lived on the opposite side of the street, constantly looking for a reason to take down the club but after twenty years of existence, the club remained largely unscathed.

They were there then, watching from an unmarked car

that we all knew was cop issued. No one cared. The night would get rowdy, no doubt, as only a biker's wake could be, but it was nothing worth arresting us over. Besides, I had it on good authority from Cricket, who was not the kind of biker that kept things from his woman, that the club had a number of higher-ups in the force on payroll.

So, the party was bumpin' and no one gave a fuck the police were outside the door. Bikers were packed to the gills, chapters from all over the province and as far as Saskatchewan were in the city for the funeral even though Cricket had only recently become a fully patched member. Still, his cousin was the VP of the mother chapter so everyone wanted to pay their respects. Cricket had done his best to keep me away from Berserker MC gatherings, which was probably his one redeeming quality in the end, so I didn't know most of the people offering me their condolences and it was easy enough to lie with my smile when I gave them my thanks.

"Honestly, honey, you were way too good for Cricket anyways," Sheila told me as she sipped casually from her half-empty mickey of spiced rum.

"Sheila," Sarah reprimanded her with a quick, apologetic look at me as if she was responsible for her friend's insensitive remark.

"What? It's true. Even Cricket knew it."

"Doesn't much matter," I told them both with a thin smile that I hoped would read as sad and not disgusted. "He's gone now."

"Exactly, that's what I'm tryin' to say," Sheila cried out, three sheets to the wind and then some.

Most of the mourners were at least as drunk, if not more fucked up on harder stuff than booze. I'd never liked going to Berserker parties because the brothers were known for the prolific use of drugs. It had always seemed ironic to me that the Berserkers, who ran guns, were hardcore users while The Fallen, who sold grade A weed, stuck only to the soft stuff.

"Tryin' to say what?" Sara said with an eye roll.

"It's H.R.'s time to move on up! We all know she's hot enough to take on one of the big boys," Sheila said with a hiccough riddled giggle.

"Most of them are taken," Jade said. She was Grease's old lady though the moniker was a misnomer because the chick was a solid two decades younger than him.

"Not Wrath," Sheila sing-songed. "And I seen him look at her."

"You saw shit," Jade hissed. "Always thinkin' somethin' is what it ain't. What're ya doin' lookin' at Wrath anyways, slut? He's way above your paygrade."

"Don't be a bitch, Jade," I said mildly. I'd grown up around biker babes, I knew how to navigate their jungle better than anyone ever could. "The girl is trying to pay me a compliment, which is appreciated. Though, Sheila babe, it's got to be said, this is my old man's wake. I'm not ready to talk about moving on *or* up, at the moment."

The three women had the good grace to look mildly chastised even though Jade did it looking like she'd swallowed a dozen lemons.

"I'm gonna get another beer, need anything?" I asked, walking backwards away from them so I could see them shake their heads.

I turned on my heel and ducked easily through the mess of bodies littered throughout the rooms. The swell of sound and human smells made me nauseated, and a small part of me reasoned that I'd been recently traumatized, so feeling anxiety in enclosed spaces, especially those filled with men, and those men holding very little respect for women's autonomy, was probably *not* a good idea.

Even as I thought it, I shrugged it off. I'd never been a "good idea" kind of girl, and I didn't see any reason to start then.

Of course, that was a stupid decision to make and I

learned that about thirty seconds after I made my resolution to stay.

"There she is," Twiz said in the same second as he shot out of a small guest bedroom and tugged me inside it. "We were lookin' for ya."

"Feels like fuckin' Christmas," Pink Eye said over the sound of his clapping hands. "Ding Dong the Cricket's dead, and we can get his girl!"

"Not a Christmas song, Pink," Mutt pointed out like he was the smart one when he definitely was not.

I struggled against Twiz's big body as he pushed me against the wall then gave up and glared at him. "What the fuck do you think you boys are doin'?"

Twiz ducked his furry face down to trace his tongue up my neck in one long, slimy trail. "You're up for grabs now, babe."

"And we grabbed you first!" Pink Eye practically shrieked, so tweaked on a cocktail of drugs that for one terrifying moment my mind's eye morphed his young, pimply face into Cricket's handsomer, deader one.

I tried to keep my wits about me, but my body's nervous system was flooding with adrenaline, making my skin sweat and my brain melt into a useless puddle. It didn't help that Mutt was reaching between my body and Twiz's to grab at my tit.

"You said you grabbed me first," I panted slightly through my words. "But there's three of you."

"Yeah, we know you can be a feisty little bitch," Twiz muttered into my neck. "So, we figured we better grab you team-like."

"You gonna fuck me team-like too?" I asked.

Twiz and Mutt both froze against me, but Pink Eye started to jump up and down squealing *yes, yes, yes!*

But I knew Twiz and I knew Mutt. The former was an ex-pro football player for the B.C. Lion's that tore his ACL, got hooked on his painkillers and got in with the club after having to pay back his dealers with enforcement work. He thought he was all that, but his gut, his lack of hygiene and his concussed-one-too-many-times brain did not speak to a good kinda man.

Mutt had a chip on his shoulder the size of Texas. He was a mix of minorities, Mexican, First Nations and Pilipino that made him astonishingly handsome. Unfortunately, he was also born a straight up psycho; a multiple offense sex-offender, incarcerated for manslaughter for the last decade, he'd just gotten back out on parole and he was eager to reclaim his place in the club.

They both wanted me, but they didn't want to share. They wanted the thousand-dollar Garro chip in their back pocket so they could cash it in with Reaper, break me down and crack me open until all The Fallen secrets were exposed and they could be the ones to reap the rewards.

They thought Cricket was dumb, or not hard enough on me, that they could be the ones to ruin me.

Happily, they were too fuckin' stupid to succeed.

"Really, boys, I'm surprised you didn't think about this. Who's gonna get to claim me in front'a the Prez?" I asked, aware that Twiz's grip had slipped on my hands he had pressed to the wall. I just needed him to take a little, itty bitty step the fuck back...

"I caught 'er," Twiz grunted.

"The fuck you did," Mutt growled, and changed position so that he was no longer looming over me, but Twiz. "Was my idea in the fuckin' first place to take her!"

Twiz twisted to face his accuser and there it was, that slight movement that gave me enough room to raise my knee and jam it ruthlessly into his gonads.

Happily, Mutt took the same opportunity to attack him with a crunching punch to the jaw. I ducked out from the wall just before he slammed a reeling Twiz into the space I'd just occupied. A lamp crashed off the side of the bedside table in the commotion and I hoped Pink Eye was too preoccupied with the skirmish to notice me slip out the door.

Hope is such a stupid sentiment.

I cried out as a strong hand caught me by my flying hair and jerked me backwards so hard that tears immediately sprung to my eyes and raced down my hot cheeks.

"I GOT HER!" Pink Eye screeched like a demonic child as he drew me tight to his chest and wrapped his thin, but stupidly strong arms around me.

I kicked my legs out into the air, trying to launch forward with enough momentum to throw him over my shoulder. I was tall, over six feet in my heels, and I'd done the maneuver before but Pink Eye was strengthened by a medley of super-sonic drugs and he kept hold of me well enough to take us both tumbling to the ground. We landed hard, me on the same bruised hip that I'd fall on when Cricket knocked me to the ground. Pain exploded white hot in my side and rico-cheted shrapnel edges of agony through my entire body.

"Fuck!" I screamed, momentarily blinded by the pain.

Pink Eye took the opportunity to straddle me, wrapping me so tightly in his wiry limbs that I couldn't breathe, couldn't move. Panic overloaded my system in a flash as I was thrown back to my assault. It was only the horrifying, blood-curdling scream echoing throughout the room that brought me slightly back to my senses. At least enough to realize that it was *me* making that noise.

"What the actual *fuck?*" A deep voice boomed through the room, my siren's wail a warning before his explosion.

Wrath followed up his words by peeling Twiz and Mutt apart, because they were between Pink Eye, me and the door. Mutt went flying across the room into the opposite bedside table, the pink lamp there splintering under his weight.

Twiz just flattened himself against the wall, which seemed

to enrage Wrath, who stopped moving passed him and turned on him with one heavy, brutal punch that knocked the big biker to the ground like tumbling Jenga blocks.

My head swirled as Pink Eye continued to mutter victoriously in my ear and hump my leg. I made eye contact with Wrath for a split second as he turned away from Twiz to face me and there was something in his eyes I hadn't ever expected to see.

Sympathy and, even more, encouragement.

It was the visual equivalent of "get up, fuck him up, make him sorry he ever took you down."

He'd save me if I needed it but that one look was a reminder that I *did not*.

With my eyes still on his, I wedged my chin into Pink Eye's neck, angled my mouth and savagely bit down on his ear.

His howl of pain ripped through my eardrums but I held on even as he thrashed, and when he jerked hard away from me I still held on even as a chunk of flesh ripped loose from his lobe. He rolled over onto his back away from me, but I followed him, hovering over him so I could spit that bloody morsel into his warped face.

"Don't fucking touch me," I whispered hoarsely. "Next time you do, it won't be your ear I rip the fuck off."

Pink Eye glared at me, gearing up to cobble together the last of his biker badness so he wouldn't be a complete embarrassment.

I saved him the trouble and punched him in the throat so hard, I felt something crunch.

"What the fuck happened in here?" Reaper asked from the doorway, Grease, Jade, and Shrek all behind him.

I stood up even though my legs were trembling and fisted my hands on my hips, ready to defend myself to a jury that would always side with the man.

Only, I didn't have to.

"Tried to claim 'er," Wrath said, stepping up beside me with his colossal arms crossed.

"And you got a fuckin' problem with that? She's Berserker property, her old man died it's only fittin' she get herself another brother."

I tensed all my muscles so I wouldn't shudder. This wasn't how things were done in my father's MC. A woman was owned by no one unless it was with *her* consent, and then she was considered untouchable by others, an old lady fit only for her man. The biker sluts that hung around the club-house were not even good enough to be considered Fallen property.

"The fuck? Her man just fuckin' bit it, she doesn't get time to, I donno, mourn?"

I closed my eyes at the sound of his voice. I'd convinced myself seeing him wrapped up with Laken was just a mirage my trauma-riddled mind had conjured to fuck with me.

But no, Danner was there just behind Reaper, his arm slung around Laken, his hair in disarray over his bright eyes.

It killed me that I loved the disheveled biker look on him.

I shoved that thought aside though because there was only one reason Danner would be buddy-buddy with an MC.

And that was to take it down.

My blood pressure spiked as pure joy raced through my veins.

Reaper shot Danner a look, but it wasn't as pissed off as it could have been. "You think we're gonna give up Garro pussy? Think again, Lion."

Lion.

I swallowed thickly and clenched my hands into hard fists.

His club nickname was *my nickname.*

Lion for Lionel, obviously.

But also, because I'd never met such a lion-hearted man before. Growing up, he'd been the king of all the manly beasts in my jungle so it seemed fitting to give him such a nickname.

I both hated that these deplorable men used it, and loved that Danner thought to offer it to them.

"Doesn't seem that special from where I'm standin'," Danner drawled with his face tucked into Laken's absurdly thick black hair. She giggled at him even though she was my friend, and went on her tiptoes to offer him a wet kiss.

Bitch.

"It is," Reaper said firmly. "Now, Wrath was gonna tell us why he kept a brother from takin' her for his."

What he meant was, why Wrath stopped a brother from raping me to claim me, like we were in some 17th-century feudal clan system.

"He was—" Twiz started to protest from where he sat slumped against the wall, a club slut between his thighs as she tended to him.

Wrath quelled him with one violent look.

"Was more than one of 'em," Wrath stated, then with such a small beat of hesitation, I was sure no one else noticed it, his long arm unwrapped from his chest and rewrapped around my hip. "Doesn't matter much now, she's mine."

"What?" I demanded, at the same time that Grease guffawed.

Wrath's hand squeezed my hip almost painfully.

"Since when've you wanted an old lady?" Reaper asked, his eyes narrowed to slits. "What's that you say, fresh pussy is the best pussy?"

"Like you said, you think I've gonna give up my shot at Garro pussy?" he retorted easily.

Reaper stared at the both of us for a long moment, but it was Danner's gaze I could feel burning holes in my armor, burrowing so deep I worried it would scar. Wrath must have sensed his president's reticence because before I could blink, his lush mouth was on mine, his beard scraping deliciously against my skin.

Wrath was kissing me.

And it was a good kiss.

No, amazing.

He didn't kiss like a giant of a man with hands so calloused they abraded my neck where he held it just like his beard did my chin.

He kissed like a man with all the time in the world to worship a woman and make her body sing.

I almost could have enjoyed it if I'd actually *wanted* him to kiss me, or if I didn't still feel the ache of Cricket in my bones.

If I didn't want and hadn't always wanted the undercover cop whose burning gaze was on us now.

Wrath pulled away after a long moment, his unreadable eyes as blank as ever as he stared down at me for a beat before looking at the crowd.

"Fine, you want 'er, brother, can't think of a better man to have at 'er," Reaper sanctioned with a jerk of his head.

"Keepin' it in the family, eh, Harleigh?" Grease said with a lecherous waggle of his eyebrows before dissolving into laughter. "Hey, Wrath man, you get tired'a her, you send her my way for a night, yeah?"

"Yeah, brother," Wrath said quickly before I could bare my teeth at the scumbag Sergeant at Arms. "Though got a feelin' in my dick, I won't get tired of her real quick."

"Good," Reaper said loudly, his voice ringing with authority. "Glad to have that shit done with. Now let's fuckin' party, got somethin' to celebrate now."

There was an answering roar as everyone filed out of the room, conflict forgotten even between the feuding brothers Mutt and Twiz who laughed at something as they shoved each other out the door. Only Danner remained in the frame, Laken gone, his arms free to cross over his chest.

"You got a problem, brother?" Wrath asked pointedly as he tugged me closer into his side.

Danner waited a beat too long to be respectful then

smiled, "Nah, man, we're good. Just takin' a look at the prize you won."

"Yeah?" Wrath asked, anger creeping in at the edges of his voice.

I tried to catch Danner's eye to tell him to back off, but he was preoccupied, cheekily shrugging his shoulder. "Looks like her name, beautiful as a rose. Mind those thorns though, yeah? I have a feelin' they might getcha in the end."

CHAPTER SIX

Harleigh Rose

IT WAS THE EARLIEST HOURS OF THE MORNING WHEN I FINALLY made my way home from the wake, and the emptiness of the streets in downtown Vancouver didn't help to settle my unease. It was a safe city, and even though my apartment could have been nicer, I lived in a good part of town far away from the drug-riddled, crime invested horrors of East Hastings Street. Besides, I carried the Sig Sauer handgun my dad got me one Christmas in my purse as well as a flat, slim blade Bat had given me tucked into my boot. I was a biker babe, I could handle myself.

But fear still ate at me like the encroaching night. It was the first time I'd be back in the apartment Cricket had tried to rape me in. I'd spent the last week holed up with my family back in Entrance, sleeping in my childhood room, curling up with my dad and brother on the couch, going shopping with Cress and Lou, out for drinks with my girl Lila and the other biker babes. But it was time to face reality. Even though my dad wanted to sell the apartment immediately and put me up in a hotel in the meantime, I knew the Berserkers would notice that shifty behaviour. I was a spider caught in a web of her own making. I'd made it, and now I had to lie in it.

My hand was on the door handle when I heard the whisper soft rasp of footfalls on carpet. In the next two seconds, I had my gun in my hand trained dead center at the chest of the man who'd dared to creep up on me.

"Good reflexes," Danner noted tersely even as he continued to come at.

I knew I should lower the gun, that Danner didn't pose *that* kind of threat, but I held statue still as he walked into the barrel, its small, lethal opening pressed up against his chest over his heart.

We locked eyes over the gun. I could feel his strong heart beat against the weapon and for one crazy moment, I knew he'd let me shoot him.

"You shouldn't surprise a woman alone in a dark hallway," I told him finally.

"And a woman shouldn't arrive alone and unprepared at the funeral of her abusive dead boyfriend," he ground out, leaning closer to me in a way that ground the gun even deeper into his hard pectoral.

I bared my teeth at him. "You think they wouldn't'a found that suspicious, me staying away when my man's been murdered."

"Suspicious maybe, but at least you'd be out of sight, out of fucking mind, Harleigh Rose. You think that club isn't thrilled to have you in their fold? They got a Garro on their side of things and I think they proved today that they'll do anything to keep you there."

"It's a good thing I want to stay there then, isn't it?" I threw back at him, digging my gun into his chest so hard he winced.

"Why the fuck would you want to stay with those bastards?"

"Same reason you're undercover with 'em," I hissed, rising up on my tip toes so I was right in his face. "To take them down."

I took satisfaction from his startled blink and resulting frown. "Are you fucking with me?"

"Nope."

"Let me rephrase," he growled, easily disarming me, popping the safety back on and dropping the gun in my purse. "You *want* to be fucking with me. Even you aren't crazy enough to volunteer as a snitch for the cops."

I tossed my hair over my shoulder, watched his eyes dance over the glorious length of it, and smirked. "Never underestimate a woman, Danner."

"Like you're the average woman," he muttered.

"No, which is exactly why I want to do this. They're not like The Fallen, you think I don't got a line in the sand between good and evil just because I was born with a different code of honor? Berserkers are *not* good men and they definitely don't do good things, one of those things being allowing, no, encouraging Cricket to beat me into submission. So, yeah, I'm crazy enough to want to snitch on the most dangerous and disgusting MC in the nation, and I'm also crazy enough to pull it off."

Danner ran a hand roughly over the almost lethal edge of his stubbled jaw in frustration. "Can't believe you're saying this shit when I nearly came to blows with my senior officer to keep you out of this shit."

My heart pulsed. We weren't romantic people, Danner

and I. We didn't exchange poems, or letters or any of that crap.

We exchanged barbs and coded taunts that seemed cruel but were really pieces of our heart offered up on a bloody platter, an offering of vulnerability that no one else would understand the significance of. Coming to blows with someone over me was basically the equivalent of handing me a bouquet of flowers and a box of chocolates.

So, my heart warmed and bloomed even as I threw up thorns to hide it.

"Don't need you speaking for me, I'm not sixteen anymore," I reminded him then deliberately ran my fingers down the exposed expanse of my chest, right between my pushed-up tits.

His eyes followed the movement even though a muscle ticked in his jaw. I loved frustrating him, proving his basic goodness wrong with temptation. I hadn't seen Lionel Danner in three years, but it was as if no time had passed at all. We were still playing the same games we had before, and somehow, they hadn't gone stale with time.

"You needed me speaking for you when you were sixteen because you'd get yourself in impossible situations and the only way out of them for you was through *me* standing up for you. Surprise surprise, haven't seen you in three years, first time I do, you're needing me to speak up for you a-fucking-gain."

I tried to grit my teeth against the urge to flinch but the pain those words sent radiating through me was too great. Never, not once since I'd met him at six years old, not once in the hundred times I called on him to be my champion, had he made me feel weak or exploitative.

He read the look in my eyes before I could hide it, cursing under his breath as he stepped closer so his big belt buckle was pressed to my belly. "Rosie, you're too easy."

"Too easy?" I seethed.

His eyes were soft even as his lips curled cruelly. "Too easy to rile up. How is it possible, when all it takes is insinuation to set you on fire, that you've got so much dead in your eyes?"

I swallowed painfully as his big, coarse hand pressed flat to my chest then slid up to wrap, finger by finger, around my throat, up against my pulse. Slowly, deliberately, he squeezed.

"Tell me, rebel, how I should react when my beautiful, dilapidated rose wants to put herself in another dangerous situation when she stills wears the mark on her skin of the last one?"

"I can take care of myself," I told him thickly, irritatingly moved by his words, by the sound of his voice calling me 'rebel' again when I hadn't heard it for so long.

He leaned closer, his minty breath fanning over my parted lips. "Know it. Also know, you're not alone, not ever with the kinda family you got. Don't know when you stopped countin' me as one of them, but I'm gonna take care of you too, Rosie."

I opened my mouth to blindly protest for the sake of protestation when his lips moved even closer, the silky plush edges moving over my own as he said, "Brought Hero. I'm gonna go down to the car, bring 'im up and then do a walk-through of your place. I would insist on staying the night, but I know you got your fucked-up independence issues, so I'll let that slide so long as you take the dog."

God, he brought Hero.

I hadn't seen him in three years and the ache of his loss was almost as poignant as Danner's.

He read the delight in my eyes even from a nose length away and those lips against mine smiled before his hand at my neck gave me a firm squeeze then released me.

"Stay," he ordered as he turned on his booted heel and headed back down the hall.

"Not your dog, Danner," I called after him, a second too

late because he was already out the emergency exit and descending the stairs.

Still, I heard his laughter through the walls.

"Fuck me," I muttered, leaning back against my front door with a soft thud.

My pulse was set to fluttering, my blood helium light in my veins as it bounced through my body. I hated that Danner made me so light, so weak and fragile in a way that even I had to admit felt beautiful. But as beautiful as it was, it was also dangerous, especially in my world. I couldn't afford to be anything less than titanium, especially if I wanted to convince Danner to let me help with his investigation.

If he really didn't want me involved, I wondered what I would do. More than that, I wondered *why* I really wanted to help in the first place. A snitch, in my world, was the lowest of low, a gnat to be ground ruthlessly under your heel once discovered.

I searched myself for that rotten core in the heart of me that had allowed me to endure Cricket's abuse, just in case I was turning into some kind of self-flagellating freak, but it wasn't there. Thank Christ.

Instead, I found a sliver of something like a piece of wood stuck beneath my fingernail. The idea that if I didn't find a way to stay in Danner's world, he'd leave me again.

This time forever.

I pressed the heel of my hand to my aching, palpitating heart.

A second later the clatter of nails on concrete and the jingle of tags drew my gaze to the stairway door a moment before it shot open and the second love of my childhood life burst through.

"Hero," I whisper-yelled through my suddenly swollen throat as I dropped to my knees and opened my arms.

The golden retriever sprinted the length of the hall in seconds, pink tongue out in a doggy smile even as he whined a hello. I caught his considerable weight against my chest and held him tight to me as he attacked my face and neck with kisses. Christ, he still smelled the same, sweet and fresh like crushed autumn leaves in a crisp wind. My fingers instantly went to his downy soft, slightly crimped ears to give them a good rub and he groaned with delight into my neck as he licked at it.

I closed my eyes, buried them in the fur at his ruff and let myself shed one tear that felt like a million. God, but I loved this dog. More than most people could ever love a human, I felt the chain linking Hero's heart to mine tangibly as I held him.

"You missed our girl, didn'tcha, champ?" Danner said, prompting me to look up at where he leaned with one booted foot crossed over the other against the wall beside my door.

He had a hard face, one suited to brooding and stern reprimands, but it was his eyes and a uniquely expressive mouth that told me how deeply my reunion with his dog affected him too.

I continued to rub through Hero's glossy, perfectly golden coat. "Not your girl."

He raised one dark blond brow and inclined his chin at Hero who was sitting on his rump staring at me with happy brown eyes. "Right, well he's almost more yours than mine. I knew he'd be happy to see you, stand guard for you."

I felt an itch in my lower lip that meant it wanted to tremble, but I ignored it. "I got a gun, a knife and, if memory serves, a cleaver somewhere in my apartment, I think I'm good."

He shook his head as he muttered, "Only you would make a joke about the fucking murder weapon days after using it to kill a man."

"If you can't laugh," I said with a shrug even though I could still feel the awful weight of it in my hand.

"I'm going to check out the apartment, stay here with

Hero 'til I give the all clear," he told me as he bent down to root through my bag for the keys.

"Yes, sir," I said flippantly even though I knew it wasn't casual, I knew I'd see the muscle tense in his square jaw and feel the flare of heat emanate from his body.

He ignored me as he opened the door, flipped on the switch and disappeared farther into the apartment.

"Bossy," I told Hero, who responded by lifting a paw and putting it on my bent thigh.

I laughed into his warm, clean fur and wrapped my arms around him for one of the best embraces of my life.

"Clear," Danner said from the doorway, something working behind those jade green eyes as he stared at his dog and me. "I'll get you two settled, you're tired."

I rolled my eyes as he turned back into the apartment, calling Hero to him with a click of his tongue. I dusted the dog hair off my black pants and followed after them.

Danner was in the kitchen, unloading a dog dish, food and a thick, rolled up blanket I recognized as Hero's doggy bed because I'd bought it for him five years ago.

"Make yourself at home," I muttered drily as I moved passed him to the fridge, grabbed a Corona and hit the cap off on the side of my chipped countertop.

He stared at me as I took a long, cool pull from the bottle. "Gonna offer me one?"

"Wasn't planning on it."

His lips twitched, but he returned to pouring feed into the bowl then placing it on the ground, then doing the same with a water dish.

"I want you to take him with you everywhere, H.R.," he ordered again like I was some lackey.

"I've got class," I reminded him. "I'm not done for another three weeks, and I can't very well drag a dog with me into my labs."

He stuck his hand into the pocket of his deliciously soft,

faded jeans and emerged with a folded piece of paper. He waved it in the air then thumped it down on the counter. "Got you a note and everything."

"What am I, blind now?" I asked angrily.

"PTSD," he said without missing a beat as he finished setting up Hero's stuff and turned to settle his lean hips against the counter across from me. "You need him in case you have a panic attack."

"That's bullshit," I cried, slamming my beer bottle so hard against the counter that beer sloshed over the edge and onto my hand. "I'm not fucking traumatized. Look at me," I dared him with a licentious sneer, gesturing to my tight, cleavage-bearing biker babe outfit. "Do I look fucking traumatized to you?"

"It's a wound you wear behind the eyes, Rosie," he said, folding his arms across his chest and tipping his chin up at me like he was settling in to ride out my anger, a bull rider seizing up his mount and finding it amusingly lacking.

Anger seared through me hot and heady as my daddy's rye whiskey. "You're not in charge of me, *Officer*," I hissed at him. "I know you haven't noticed but I'm a fuckin' adult now and I can do whatever the fuck I want."

Danner stared at me in that implacable, asshole way he had that gave away nothing but made me feel about two inches tall, childish and truculent.

"Not in charge of you," he repeated slowly, his mouth moving around the words in a way that made them *cursive*, smooth and rounded and emphasized. "Never have been, though can't say, Rosie, that the idea of it hasn't crossed my mind. Takin' all that wild and leashing it, breaking it under a firm, calm hand… *yeah*," he drawled. "Thought about it."

I blinked at him. In all the years I'd know Lionel Danner I'd come to know many things about him. He was an old-school gentleman, the kind that held doors open for women, that said 'please' and 'thank you' without thought. His reserve, dedication to justice, and smooth, low Canadian drawl gave him a cowboy sheriff vibe like John Wayne or Paul Newman, men who had morals and loyalty in such abundance that you felt like a jackass just standing beside them.

He was *not* a flirt. Oh, women threw themselves at him in McClellan's where he was known to throw back a beer with his partner Riley Gibson and his other cop buddies, or in Mac's Grocer, or anywhere they could reach him. Some even ventured out to the piece of land he'd bought on the outskirts of Entrance where he'd kept a few horses and a potbelly pig I'd named Irwin. It wasn't unheard of that a group of them would congregate Sunday mornings at the corral to see him work with one of his wild horses.

But he was discreet. I knew he dated, or the very least, fucked any number of women, but they didn't talk about it, even though the urge to brag must have killed them, and I knew it was because Danner demanded that. As a lovelorn girl, his secretiveness gave room for my fantasies to blossom even though he'd always treated me, at least until the very end, like a kid sister or pal.

This was the second time he'd made a sexual innuendo with me, and honestly, my poor love-sick body could barely handle it.

I blinked again and suddenly, he was in front of me. There was nothing in his features, shallow hollows and steep cliffs of stony bones and golden skin, but his eyes were so alive they burned.

"Not in charge of you, but as I said, I'm gonna look out for you even if you don't like it. So, you're taking Hero with you wherever you fucking go, because you love him, you miss him and you need that affection right now, but also because he's a trained retired police dog and he'll kill a man before he lets you get hurt. You understand me, Harleigh Rose?"

"You can't just come back into my life and run roughshod all the fuck over it, Danner," I said, but the sass wasn't starched like it should have been. The warmth of his body so close to me made it wrinkled at the edges.

He flashed one of his rare, million dollar smiles and it hit me right in the womb. "Hero takes two cups of chow in a little warm water twice a day, needs twice daily walks as well, an hour each if you can hack it."

I scowled at him and humor creased his face into interesting planes I wanted to trace with my fingers.

"And quit it with this Berserker MC business. Stay away from Wrath and the boys, and you see me, you act like you barely know me unless it's inside these walls."

"Whatever."

Danner bit at the corner of his grin then moved away to crouch in front of Hero, who sat contentedly to our side wagging his tail.

"You take care of our Rosie, okay boy?" he said, cupping the pup's face and looking into his eyes the way he would a young boy.

Hero let out a gentle woof of affirmation and trotted to my side the second Danner stood up to leave. I wanted to shout out an insult, something to keep him on his toes and secure me the coveted last words. Instead, my head was filled with romantic delusions, with the lurid image of Danner breaking me under a firm, calm hand...

"Lion," I called before I could stop myself.

He paused with his hand on the door handle and I distractedly noticed that there were more locks on my door than there had been before the accident. I swallowed when he shifted slightly to face me and I could take in the long, muscled length of him. It killed me that I couldn't look at him without wanting to put my hands on his body, through his thick, glossy flaxen hair and down the ridge of muscles in his back to his high, taut ass. It killed me even more that I didn't have the right to do so.

"Thanks for lending me Hero," I said and then in invisible

ink written in the space between us I added, *and thank you for always taking care of me.*

"My job, Rosie," he said softly, and it was, but what he meant was that he felt taking care of me was his duty just as much as being a cop was.

Even though I'd never said the words out loud, he knew.

I'd been his since the day he bought me my first rose.

CHAPTER SEVEN

Harleigh Rose

2008

Harleigh Rose is six. Danner is sixteen.

I REMEMBER THE DAY STARTED WITH A SLAP.

I was six years old so young, but still old enough to know better than to wake up my Mum when she was sleeping off a hangover. It was getting late though, mid-morning, and it was Sunday, which meant it was time to go to Mega Music down on Main Street so I could get a new record. It was tradition. Sure, Dad started it, not Mum, but if he wasn't around, then he made her *promise* to take me instead. Mum and King didn't care much for music. Mum was too busy with her boozin' and partyin', and King was all about his books so after the record store, even though we didn't have a whack of money, our next stop was the bookstore.

But Dad and me? We loved music. Not the stupid, tinny new stuff they played on the radio that Dad said sounded like a bunch of 'snot nosed cry wankers' or 'straight up douchebags,' but the old stuff, like Black Sabbath and Guns n Roses. Dad loved AC/DC best, so I did too. I'd been a daddy's girl since I could cogitate and so even though I was upset Dad wasn't around to take me himself, I was still excited to go to Mega Music and pick out a rockin' record to show him when he finally got back from where work at The Fallen MC took him.

So, I decided to brave the beast and wake up Mum.

It was the first calamity of the day, but it wouldn't be the last.

I could smell the vodka as soon as I pushed open the door to her room. There was an overturned bottle on the ground that she'd knocked over, probably in her sleep, and it wet the floor all along the side of the bed. It smelled gross and chemical, like nail polish remover, and I held my breath as I tiptoed through the sludge.

"Mum," I whispered, and put my hand on her cheek, admiring the black nail polish I'd stolen from one of the biker whores at the clubhouse. "Mum, it's time to go."

"H.R.?" my brother's voice hissed from the doorway. "What the fuck you doin' in Mum's room? She'll kill you, you wake her up."

I frowned at him. "It's Sunday. We have to go to Mega Music, Old Sam's going to be waitin' for me."

Old Sam was called that because he was really old and he seemed to have been that way for at least half a century. He owned Mega Music, which wasn't mega at all but actually a really small record store that refused to sell anything else like iPods or MP3 players because he was hardcore like that. I loved him. I loved him almost as much as I loved my dad and that was saying something. I didn't want to keep Old Sam waiting because I knew he'd have a piece of Hubba Bubba gum ready for me and a record all picked out to listen to.

"You wake her up, swear H.R., there is *no way* Mum'll take us out," King whisper-yelled at me.

He was only eight, but he thought he knew everything. Honestly, I kinda thought he might've because he was always reading those thick books and quoting dead people. I didn't care about dead people, I only cared about living ones like Dad and King and Old Sam and the brothers of The Fallen, but quoting them sure made King sound smart.

"She'll take us 'cause she doesn't, Daddy is gonna be so angry," I reminded him of something he knew.

Only problem was, Dad could get angrier than a bear coming out of hibernation, but Mum was like a rattlesnake, only one twitch away from coming at you with a venomous mouth.

I slapped my hand lightly against her face a few times then when that didn't work, I pushed hard at her shoulder.

She woke at the same time she lunged for me. One second, she was dead to the world and the next she was coming at me like that rattlesnake, a curse hissing across her tongue and through her teeth to poison me. Her hand was against my cheek so briefly, it was almost like it didn't even connect, only the pain that exploded after that flash contact made me reel back from the bed.

My hand flew to the burning pain in my cheek, but I didn't let the tears in my eyes fall out of them because Mum hated when I cried, especially when she was hungover.

'Sides, it wasn't the first time Mum laid hands on me and it probably wouldn't be the last.

King cursed from his place in the doorway, but he didn't make a move. Makin' a move only made Mum angrier.

"Fuck! What're you doin' wakin' me up? You so selfish you can't let your Mum sleep in once in a fuckin' while? You such a little girl still you need me to wipe your ass for you or something?"

I bit at the corner of my lower lip because it threatened to capsize into a trembling pout. "No, Mum. But it's near on noon and it's Sunday so it's Mega Music day."

Mum was pretty. I knew she was pretty even as a little girl because Dad said she fished for compliments from everyone and always came back with a fat catch on the line so I heard more people than I could count say so. Only then, her pretty face was sour with irritation and it was a look she gave me a lot so I didn't think she was the prettiest.

I didn't look like her and I think it bothered her because even though I had gold in my hair it was dark, more caramel coloured than true blond like hers and King's. Otherwise, I looked like a female version of Zeus Garro. I also acted like a female version of Dad and this, for whatever reason, often pissed her off.

Like now.

She rolled her eyes so hard I thought it must've hurt and pushed my hand off her shoulder so she could roll away from me in bed. "Mega Music is shit, Harleigh, and I'm tired. Go watch TV or somethin' and if your fuckin' father has the decency to remember he's supposed to take you Sundays, he'll be 'round to get ya."

"Mum," I tried again. "*Please.*"

"Close the door behind you and keep the TV on low, yeah?" she grumbled, already half asleep.

I stared at the back of her head. Her hair was twisted up and spun thin like an old rat's nest. I stared at it, happy for the spot of ugly on her. I stared at it and hated her so much that my little body shook with it.

"I hate you," I whispered, but Mum was already back asleep.

"Hatin' never did no one any good, H.R.," King muttered as he took my arm and pulled me out of the stinky room, closing the door softly behind us. When he faced me, his face was serious like an adult's. "You gotta be smarter than hate, yeah? You don't like Mum? Can't blame ya, but you don't let that rule ya."

"Why not?" I pouted.

King grinned and tugged on the end of my messy ponytail. "'Cause I don't wanna take a grumpy girl to Mega Music with me."

"We're gonna go anyways?" I nearly shrieked.

"If you keep it down, we will," King ordered on a harsh whisper. "Now get your shoes on and let's go."

I started to turn on my heel and sprint to my mini biker chick combat boots, but I stopped mid-step, lost my balance, righted myself and then turned around to face my brother again.

"You love me, don'tcha?" I asked him soberly.

He grinned his grin that girls already loved. King was only eight, but, man, did he have game. "Yeah, H.R., I fuckin' love ya."

"How much?" I demanded, because I knew I could.

I might have had a shit mum, but my men loved me, my brother, maybe, most of all.

He shoved at my shoulder and rolled his eyes, but his voice was so warm as it poured over me it felt like soft, tropical rain. "Enough to take ya to Mega Music instead of meeting Shelley Newborn at Stella's diner for a milkshake and a kiss."

"She has braces anyways," I told him something he already knew as I tugged him down the hall toward the front door. "I'm saving you from bloody gums. You can do better."

"Such a chick thing to say," King argued as he swung out of the house behind me and slammed the door shut as a tiny 'fuck you' to our mum. "Sure, she has braces, but have you seen her tits? First girl in the grade to get 'em, and H.R., you're not a dude so you don't get just how much a bloody mouth is worth some one-on-two time with those beauties."

"Horndog."

"Brat."

We grinned at each other so wide, we looked dumb and then before I could sass him right back King hiked up his loose-fitting jeans and took off in a dead sprint.

"Last one to Mega Music has to buy the winner a pop," he called out.

I wasn't angry with his head start or even when he won, mostly because I didn't have the money to buy him a pop and he'd find that out soon enough, but also because Old Sam would give me some Hubba Bubba so King was the one that was going to lose out in the end.

He was already inside when I pushed open the poster plastered front door to Mega Music, but I didn't go looking for him among the stacks and bookcases filled with records. Instead, I went straight to Old Sam.

"There she is, *oh ye*, there's the love of my life," Old Sam sang out to me, doing a little shimmy as he did it.

I laughed at him and fell just a little more in love with him. I didn't have a grandpa, because my dad's parents were dead and my mum's wished she was dead, so it kind of felt like Old Sam was my grandpa. He suited the part too. Even though he wasn't a biker, he'd lived a hard life of rock concerts and partying as a roadie before settling in Entrance at Mega Music and I liked the tales age and experience had written in his creased face. He wore his hair funny, a retro-style I was too young to realize was reminiscent of Elvis and James Dean.

When I reached him, I threw my little arms around his legs and squeezed. He laughed in a way that was somehow *jazzy* and patted the top of my head.

"There she is," he repeated softer, then pushed me away gently so he could bend down and look me in the eye. "You been a good girl this week?"

He asked me this every week and every week I shot him a

little grin and batted my eyelashes at him. "Not this week, Old Sam."

I was only six, but I knew men, I'd been reared by the manliest of them, and I already knew how to wrap them just so around my little finger.

Old Sam laughed then winced as his knees creaked when he straightened. "You make an old man feel young, shinin' such beauty in my store each week."

"It's my favourite day, Sundays," I told him.

"Right on, girl, mine too. Now, where's your dad at, huh?"

I shrugged even though it was weird that Dad would miss a Sunday with us, at least without calling to tell us why first.

He pursed his lips and darted his eyes over at his cell phone lying on top of a stack of records, but when he looked back at me, he was smiling. "Right, pick a paw then, princess."

I watched him stick his hands in his pockets then offer them to me with fists tight before slapping my little hand over one of his big ones. "Left!"

He tipped his hand over and opened his palm, revealing a package of strawberry watermelon Hubba Bubba gum.

"Yes!" I shrieked with a fist pump. "My fav!"

Old Sam winked at me. "Don't I know it? Now, I pulled some Johnny Cash fer ya, today. Why don'tcha go take a look while I deal with somethin'?"

I wrinkled my nose even as I popped a thick piece of bubble gum in my mouth and started to chew. "That's country music! I hate that shit."

"Girl, you don't know shit about that shit. Don't spew what yer daddy told ya without listen' fer yourself. You got a mind of your own in that pretty head?"

I fisted my hands and plunked them on my hips. "And don't forget it!"

"That's what I thought. So, go the hell over to your spot

and play what I pulled fer ya, think you might like this brand'a country."

I chewed my lip. Country music sucked, my dad had told me that all music outside of rock was for the musically uneducated. But I trusted Old Sam. He pulled records for me every Sunday and he never disappointed. So, even though I could've thrown a mini tantrum and it would've been fun to argue with Old Sam about it, I took his advice and made my way through the disorganized stacks to my little corner with the record player.

There was a man in black on the worn sleeve and "At Folsom Prison."

Reverently, I slipped the record from the cover and placed it on the turntable. I held my breath as the first few strains of his rendition of Blue Suede Shoes rumbled into the room with me.

I wasn't a musician. In the last year, I'd tried the guitar, the piano, and singing (don't even get me started on that failure,) so I couldn't produce beauty with sound, but since I was a baby, so they said, I loved it. I was a woman with a deep well of emotions raised by a bitch mother and a brotherhood of men who mostly didn't know their emotional ass from their elbow. So, I had a lot to feel and not a lot of ways to say it.

Music was that voice for me, and even at six years old sitting cross-legged on the floor of Mega Music, I knew that it would play a vital soundtrack to my life.

Johnny Cash's "Give My Love To Rose" was playing when I noticed him.

First, it was just an extra twang of notes, a thrum of chords added to the scratch and smooth of recorded music that pricked my ears and made me turn to look over my left shoulder.

And there he was.

Sitting on a turned over crate, one Timberland booted foot

up against it, the other pressed to a mess of sheet music on the floor so his thick thighs were spread apart and taught against the worn denim of his jeans. His muted gold hair fell over his face as he bent over a blue guitar, obscuring everything but the fine cut of a strong nose and the edge of a lush mouth that moved silently with the lyrics of the song. The way he cradled that guitar hit my six-year-old gut in a funny way. He had big hands that seemed too strong for his long, gangly limbs but they held the instrument tenderly, coaxing sound from the neck with his firm fingers, teasing it out of the body with a feathering touch.

He held that guitar like it was the love of his life, so it was no wonder that the swell of music he made with it made my nose itch with tears.

Both he and the music were the most beautiful things I'd ever seen in my short life.

I must have let out a quiet gasp because suddenly, he was looking at me.

He had green eyes.

God, they were the greenest living thing I'd ever seen. Greener than freshly watered grass, than the light filtering through a thicket of fir trees onto a patch of pacific northwest moss, and the green of an overripe lime. Looking into that color surrounded by a full fringe of short, spiky brown eyelashes under thick, slanting brows, I stopped breathing.

He didn't miss a beat in the song as he locked eyes with me and added his smooth, low voice to Johnny's growling rasp.

The song wasn't about falling in love, but it was about a man leaving behind a woman named Rose and a son when he went to jail. It shouldn't have been profound, I was a six year old with no context for the song, but it gave me a shiver of premonition up my spine that made my teeth ache.

When the final refrains died away and Johnny's voice came back over the record speaking to the prisoners, the teenage singer finally tipped his head in a gesture much like any of The Fallen men would do and said, "You like Cash?"

I wanted to say yes because I was in love with his prettiness. He was only a boy and he was so good looking, it should have been vaguely feminine, but there was a somberness to his character, a weight and sternness to his face that reminded me of a *man*.

But I didn't, because even though I was young, I was still a Garro.

"He's not shit, I guess, but he's country."

The boy's eyebrows shot up, wrinkling his forehead in a way I liked. "You hatin' on country music? You are Canadian, right?"

I sniffed at him, my crush totally forgotten in the face of his challenge. "Uh, I'm prob'ly more Canadian than *you*. My family's been here since forever. And FYI, not all Canadians like country."

"You live rural, small town like we do, you like country."

I snorted. "Don't know who you hang out with, but country is for losers."

He smiled slightly in a way that told me he didn't smile very much. "So, you don't like Cash."

I chewed my lip because I *did* like Johnny Cash. His voice so deep and growly reminded me of my dad's, and his country music didn't *sound* country.

"It's basically rock," I told him, taking a wild stab at an argument to justify it.

He bit back the corner of a smile. "True. He was a cool guy though, he was arrested a bunch for pretty minor offenses during his life, but he made a point to play at prisons 'cause he understood their trouble."

A bunch of The Fallen brothers had been to prison, so I'd been visiting penitentiaries for years. I liked that about Johnny, but more, I liked that this strange boy liked that about him too.

"Here," he said, carefully placing the guitar back in its open case then unraveling to his full height. "Let's try At San Quinten."

I froze as he moved beside me to slide a new record under the player, only my lungs working hard to steady my suddenly fleeting breath. He smelled good, like fresh tilled earth and hay with the slight musk of man. If I could get close enough, lie down and close my eyes, it would smell exactly like lying on sun-warmed grass beneath a big summer sky.

He squatted beside me to switch out the records and turned to me when he was done, close enough that I could see the beginning of wispy stubble on his jaw. When the smiling creases beside his eyes flattened with anger, I realized that he was close enough to see the faint red handprint against my check.

"Who the fuck did that to you?" he demanded.

His voice was like the lash of whip cracking through the air, but his hand was soft as a butterfly kiss against my chin as he tipped my face to better see the bruise.

"What do you care?" I asked, even though my lip was curling under and the backs of my eyes were hot with tears.

What did this stranger care that I'd been hit? I wasn't used to that kind of empathetic generosity from people outside the club and their families. Usually, outsiders sneered at us or scuttled around us like beetles.

"What do I care?" he repeated, as if he couldn't believe I'd asked. "Someone hits a sweet kid, you think I wouldn't care about that? You think anyone would let that go unchecked?"

"Yeah, I don't know you. Why'd you stick your nose into messy business that isn't even your problem?"

His face tensed with rage then settled with sympathy. "'Cause I'm not the sorta guy who can walk by tragedy without doing something about it, okay? And I sure hope you aren't that kinda girl either."

I thought about it for a second. "I beat up this stupid guy on the playground last week because he called my best friend Lila ugly. She's isn't ugly, my dad says she'll be a real looker when she grows up."

Again, he bit the edge of his mouth like he was trying to stop a smile. "Yeah, well can't say violence is the answer but I'm glad you don't let that pass you by. It's our responsibility as decent humans to look after each other, otherwise, we're all sunk. So, I'm going to ask you again, who did this to you?"

I chewed my gum anxiously then decided to answer him by blowing a big bubble with my Hubba Bubba. He stared at the pink balloon as it stopped an inch from his face then shook his head when I popped it with a loud smack.

"You're not going to tell me. My dad's important, I can get him to help you."

"My daddy's important too," I told him proudly, because Zeus Garro was the youngest officer the club had ever voted in.

He squinted at me, his eyes greener than traffic lights, encouraging me to *go, go, go* and tell him all my secrets. "What's your name?"

"What's yours?" I shot back instantly.

Another bitten-off grin. "Lionel."

I wrinkled my nose. "That's a stupid name."

"Yeah? Yours is better?"

I scoffed into his face, liking that I was close enough to see the deeper ring of green around his outer irises. "Duh. It's Harleigh Rose 'cause I'm a biker babe."

Something flashed behind those eyes that made me lean back from him.

"Now you know my name, you wanna tell me who hit you?" he asked in a low, metallic voice that I recognized from my dad and his brothers when they weren't screwing around anymore.

"What the hell're you doin' with my sister?" King's voice

called out from behind me and an instant later I was snared in his arms.

The boy stood up, so much taller than my kid brother that he had to bend his neck to look down at us. "Making sure she's alright. She's a kid, shouldn't be alone in a store even in a town as small as ours. We got outlaws living here."

"No shit," King laughed meanly. "Think we can handle 'em more than you."

I knew he was taking in the teenager's nice outfit, his button-up shirt under an open blazer and pants so fancy they even had a crease in the front.

"You judging a book by its cover?" Lionel retorted, his arrow hitting home in a way that said he understood rebels.

We weren't about judgment, not ever.

I could hear King's teeth grinding above me. "When you don't got much else to go on, what's a man supposed to do but assume and move to protect?"

"A man?" Lionel laughed. "What're you, eight years old?"

King puffed his chest out, constricting me even more in the tight circle of his arms. "Now you judgin' based on my age? I'm eight, but I've been learnin' to defend myself and my family since I could walk."

Lionel lifted up his hands in a gesture of surrender. "No doubt in my mind that you can. Just checking in on a little girl who has a handprint plastered to her cheek."

King's arms spasmed around me. He hated that for me, for us, but there wasn't much he could do. She was our mum.

"Sometimes, you gotta play the long game," King said cryptically. "Not that it's any of your business."

"Could be," my teenage friend said with a shrug. "You let it be. I've got the means to help you two get away from the biker fold, get you somewhere safer."

"Nowhere safer than with Daddy," I spoke up.

"H.R., King, get over here," Old Sam yelled suddenly from the front of the shop.

Seconds later, shots rang out through Main Street. I'd heard the innocuous *pop* sound before and instantly knew it for what it was, what it meant.

Death.

Before they could stop me, I ducked out of King's arms, swerved around Lionel's outstretched hands and booked it to the poster covered glass front door. I pressed my face to a gap in the posters and peered out.

Nothing.

But I had this feeling, this sensation in the pit of my gut like the gates of Tartarus had opened and these horrible monsters were spilling forth, wreaking destruction on my body and taunting my soul.

Something was wrong. So wrong, I knew whatever was happening outside the doors of Mega Music was big enough to change my life.

Looking back and knowing the woman I'd become, it's not so surprising that I defied reason and safety to yank open the door shielding me from gunshots and run into the street. I vaguely head Old Sam bellowing after me then King fighting with him as he was held back from following me, but I was too focused on finding the source of that sound, on making sure it wasn't what my gut was telling me it was.

Main Street was a long stretch of quaint shops, eateries, the courthouse, town hall, police station, a big park, and First Light Church.

The church was across the street from Mega Music and towards the ocean, but I could see immediately that the chaos stemmed from there.

There were men in leather cuts everywhere, my father, and his brothers.

My heart seized.

I started sprinting down the asphalt.

I only made it half a block, close enough to the action to spot my father standing closest to me at the edge of the parking lot, when hands snared me from behind and pushed me to the ground. The pavement scraped my palms as I went down but the weight of the person caging me to the street didn't descend. I twisted my head to look up at my captor and found Lionel's face, stern and strong over my shoulder.

"Let me go," I demanded.

"Not gonna happen."

"Let me go!" I screamed as another shot, this one somehow louder than the rest tore through the air.

My head jerked toward the action and I saw with startling clarity, my father, his arms around someone smaller, rock back from the impact and fall to the ground.

I screamed.

I wasn't old enough to have a worst nightmare, but if I'd been forced to think about it before then, seeing my father fall would've been it. He was my idol, my favourite human on the earth, the person who'd taught me what loving even was.

Not understanding that, not needing to, I felt my entire world implode as I watched him fall.

I screamed so long and loud without breath for well over a minute that in the end, Lionel's arms around me, pulling me up and against his body so he could carry me away from the scene, I passed out.

And later, when I woke up on the couch at my house, King arguing with my mum in the kitchen about the fact that Dad was in the hospital and would be arrested for manslaughter and I knew that I'd been right, that my whole life had changed in the course of a Sunday morning, there was a rose on the table beside me.

I'd never held a rose before—my family weren't exactly flowery people—so I wondered at the depth of the red petals, tightly furled but just opening in the center, a vortex as complicated as it was beautiful peeking out for me to see.

There was a sticky note stuck to the table beneath the rose.

Sorry for your loss, Rosie.

You need me, you call.

-Lionel

Then his phone number scrawled underneath.

"Almost threw that shit out," King said, stalking into the living room with both his hands stuck in his long hair. "Shouldn't get close to a Danner."

My hands automatically clenched around the rose and the note, a thorn pricking my thumb so blood smeared over the phone number.

King was smart enough to pick up on it, and he sighed as he flopped down beside me and tugged me into his arms. For the first time since I'd heard those shots, I felt like I could breathe again smelling his fresh laundry scent, feeling my brother's arms so much stronger than mine wrapped around me.

"Kills me, but the guy was right. I can't do much to protect you and now Dad's," he cleared his throat when it broke over the word, "now that he's goin' to prison, we gotta fend for ourselves. Want you to keep the number, H.R., and I want you to use it if you gotta, even if it means goin' against mum and what the club stands for."

"But," I whispered through the tears in my throat. "The club comes first."

"Nah," King said, his voice so heavy with wisdom, I wondered how the words didn't pin down his tongue. "We're just kids. Thinkin' we need to put ourselves first for now."

I carefully unfolded my fingers from the crumpled note and touched my bleeding fingers to the small, block script there. My mind memorized the digits immediately and over the course of my adolescence, I would come to call that number dozens of times over, whenever I needed Lionel Danner to shield me just as he had that day from the massacre at First Light Church, but to this day, I kept that bloody Post-it note carefully folded in my wallet as a reminder of the first time he saved me.

CHAPTER EIGHT

Harleigh Rose

WHEN I WOKE UP, IT WAS TO THE SMELL OF BACON AND I KNEW what that meant.

My dad was there.

I hoped like hell Loulou was there too because she always had a calming effect on him and I knew he was pissed as hell at me. He'd been cool with me while I recuperated from the incident at his house in Entrance, taking me for a ride on his bike like I'd loved doing since I was a girl, touching me affectionately whenever we passed each other, and basically, giving me room to recover without getting all up in my shit about my poor choices.

Clearly, that time was over.

Hero was pressed full length to my side, his sweet chops on my thigh facing the door when I opened my eyes, but he'd turn to look at me when I lifted my head.

"Hey, buddy." I rubbed his ears and smiled as he licked my hand. "I'm surprised you didn't freak out at my dad breaking into my apartment."

"He did," Zeus Garro said from the doorway to my bedroom, his great big body taking up the entire width and height of it. "'S a good thing Lou was 'ere and the beast knew 'er or I'd be seriously chewed up by now."

"Can't believe I slept through that," I muttered, looking down at Hero as he lapped at my hand happily, totally at ease with my dad.

I'd been told dogs had good instincts and Hero was the best of them so it was no surprise he knew my dad didn't pose a threat to me, only to anyone who would fuck with me.

"You're beaten down, H.R., your body needs time to recover, but instead'a doin' that, you shot like a bat outta hell to come back down to Vancouver and attend that fuckin' piece of fuckin' shits funeral. Wanna explain' that to me?"

"Not really."

"Yeah, baby girl, wasn't a request."

I blew a messy lock of blond-streaked hair out of my face and huffed petulantly. "How 'bout you give me time to get ready for the day and I might feel more like chatting?"

"How 'bout ya brush your teeth and meet me in the kitchen in less than two minutes and I won't haul your ass outta bed myself and make you answer my questions?" he suggested casually.

"You're such a bully," I muttered as I shoved the covers back and slid to the cold floor then stomped over to my bathroom.

He caught me with a gentle hand on my arm as I tried to move by him. "Nah, sweetheart, I'm no bully and I won't have you sayin' somethin' like that again, jokin' or not. What I am is a father whose worst fuckin' nightmare came true when he found out someone has been layin' a hand on his princess, the apple of his fuckin' eye, for years with 'im none the wiser."

"Daddy," I whispered, suddenly a little girl again. I turned into his body and clutched at his favourite AC/DC tee as he wrapped his tree trunk arms around me and squeezed.

"Not mad at you, Harleigh Rose, mad at myself for becomin' a self-centered bastard."

"Never," I swore. "Never have you been that guy, Dad. You've had a lot goin' on the last four years and honest to Christ, I tried everything I could to make sure you didn't know."

He made a sound low in his chest like a wounded bear. "Didn't trust me with it?"

"Didn't trust myself anymore," I told him honestly. "I didn't know how it started happening and I didn't know why it wasn't stopping. I," I sucked in a deep, stabilizing breath, "I tried to stop it, Daddy."

"Fuck me," he said into the top of my head. "I'd kill him again if I fuckin' could. I'd make it the slowest death in the history of man, skin 'im layer'a skin by layer'a skin, carve 'im up inch by fuckin' inch until he was swine food. I'd have Priest bring 'im back from death time and time again like only he can, just so I could do it all over again."

I hummed against his hard chest and patted his back soothingly. "Yeah, Daddy, I know."

"Hate you had to take a life, even though I'm glad as fuck karma got 'im in the end."

"Yeah," I agreed, because it was the poeticism of ending my own victimization that made the fact I was a murderer a little more palatable.

"Doesn't go away, baby girl," he murmured.

"What?"

"The blood on your hands. But promise you, when it's

done for the right fuckin' reasons, that shit doesn't feel like a stain, it feels like a fuckin' badge."

"Believe you," I said, and it was true, I always did.

"That's my girl. And I want you home, Harleigh Rose, soon as exams are done, you're back in Entrance, safe and loved."

"Okay," I said, because I might rebel against him and the club, but at the end of the day, there was no one I trusted as much as him.

"Good. Now the food's gonna get cold you don't get your ass in gear and come eat with me and your family."

"Be right out," I said when he gave me a squeeze and let me go.

I smiled when he bent down to give Hero a pat on the head. "Lou's been wantin' a dog for a fuckin' age. Don't give 'er any ideas, yeah? Think we'll have enough on our hands with fuckin twins."

I laughed and rolled my eyes. "Like you wouldn't give Loulou the world if she asked for it."

Dad grinned then sobered, swinging an arm out to cup me by the neck and bring me back to his front, his forehead dipped down to meet mine. "You'll find a man feels the same way 'bout you, who'll treat ya like the princess you are."

I swallowed thickly, feeling Hero pressed against my side, feeling the phantom of Danner's hand wrapped securely around my throat, a necklace of possession I wished I could brand into the skin there.

"Yeah, maybe." I gave him, even though I wasn't sure I agreed with him because the only man I'd trust with me wasn't mine to have.

Later, when I was showered and dressed in my over-sized Hephaestus Auto tee from The Fallen's garage, I padded into the main living room of my apartment with Hero by my side to see my entire family packed into the small space.

My brother sat in one of the spindly chairs at the dining

room table, his woman, Cressida straddling his lap and facing him, her hands in his tumble of curly blond hair and his hands at her ass. They were laughing loudly at something, which was something they did a lot of together, but they both turned to look at me the second I hit their space.

Nova, not my family by blood but by right, was thrown across my sofa, a hand over his eyes, his legs spread, one over the back of the couch and one over the coffee table, his dirty boots still on. Even hungover as I knew he probably was, he looked beautiful lounging there, like some Greek God fallen from Olympus. He peeked out from under his arm when my best friend Lila, sitting on the ground at his side painting her nails on the coffee table beside his boot, hit him in the side at the sight of me.

If I rounded the corner, I knew I'd see Dad in the kitchen finishing up the bacon, adding it to whatever his wife had whipped up for breakfast, probably lemon ricotta pancakes knowing my step-mum, but before I could take that step, the woman in question was in front of me beaming so bright a smile at me I blinked.

"Harleigh Rose," she rasped softly in her husky voice, and just the sound of my name in her mouth made me want to cry again.

Man, I was turning into a fuckin' wuss.

Before I could blink again, she was against me, her caramel scent in my nose and soft hair against my cheek. I clutched her to me, loving the warmth of her body and spirit against my aching counterparts.

"You disappear like that on us again, swear to God, H.R., I won't hold your dad back from the rampage he's gonna go on, you get me?" she whispered in my ear.

I smiled into her shoulder before releasing her to give her an eye roll. "Like you can control the monster he becomes when he's on the warpath."

Lou gave me a small, feminine smile as her hand went to

her huge belly, swollen with my half-siblings. "Oh, I have my ways, babe."

"Okay, barf. How many times do we have to have this talk, huh? No more sexual innuendos or information about your sex life with my father," I ordered her.

Of course, she laughed her beautiful laugh and winked at me as we rounded the corner to the kitchen. It was nearly impossible for me to believe that four years ago I tackled her to the ground and beat her up because I'd found out the same girl that got my dad shot when I was six, was the same girl fucking him then. I'd hated her for that and for taking away a massive chunk of his time and attention because I was young and selfish as shit. It was only after she'd been disowned by her family and I realized the horrors cancer had wrecked on her life that I came around.

Now, I couldn't imagine my life without her and I sure as fuck didn't want to imagine my dad's that way either.

I took a seat at the bar as she slid under the arm my dad held up for her while he dished out perfectly crispy rashers of bacon onto plates.

"Grubs up," he called as he twisted down to plant a kiss on Loulou's upturned mouth.

God, the men in my family were sweet enough with their women to give a girl a goddamn toothache.

"How's my pretty girl?" Nova asked, sliding up beside me to grab the plate of food Dad tried to slide to me.

He intercepted it, lifted it to his chest and bit into a piece of buttered toast as he waited for me to answer the question.

"That was mine," I informed him.

"Don't see your name on it and my mouth's been on it now. You still want it?"

"I wouldn't," Lila drawled as she popped up to press a kiss to my cheek and then accept a plate from Lou. "The devil only knows where that mouth has been."

We all laughed as she faked a shudder, but Nova only

shrugged and took another enormous bite of toast. "Who am I to deny the ladies what they want?"

"You're disgusting," Lila said with a sneer as she pushed Nova with a solid hand to the shoulder.

A huge diamond winked in the light as she did so and I gasped. "Fucking hell, Lila babe, please don't tell me that rock is an engagement ring."

My best friend beamed at me and wiggled her hand in the air as she crowed, "You better believe it, baby! Jake proposed."

I launched myself off the stool and into her arms. "You're kidding me!"

"No way, bitch. This five-carat diamond is no fuckin' joke."

We laughed into each other's faces as we hugged and for a moment, the world felt right again.

"Only known him 'bout a fuckin' week," Nova muttered. "But whatever."

"Yeah, whatever, Nova," Cress said, bumping him gently with her hip as she crowded around us. "When you know, you know."

Nova looked to King for help, but he only shrugged one shoulder and smirked, "Sorry, man, my woman speaks truth."

"She does," Lila told just me, her huge hazel eyes bright with joy. "I never thought I'd find someone who loved me back, but I have and he's everything."

I shook her slightly to confirm I got where she was at. My girl had been in love with her best friend, Nova, since she was a freaking girl, but the loveable slut was too busy looking pretty and getting with any woman who threw themselves at him to notice her unrequited love.

So, finally, she'd moved on.

I was happy for her, happier than I could express with my poor lexicon of emotive words so I just gave her that gentle shake.

She was my girl, so she got me and smiled big.

"Right, eat while I talk," Dad ordered as he ushered us to the living room where we all took up seats on available surfaces to eat and listen.

There was a look on his face that I knew well, a troubled kink in his strong brow and glint in his silver eyes that spoke of unease and fury. He waited until Lou was settled half on top of him on the couch to begin but before he even spoke, I knew it was bad.

"This is club business, don't need to tell you women that normally, this shit doesn't extend to you, but for reasons you'll soon fuckin' understand, I gotta loop ya in on this. We're bein' threatened on a coupla sides right now and I need you to be vigilant."

"Javier?" Cress asked immediately, smart enough to understand that just because our one time enemy had been dormant, playing mayor of Entrance docilely for the last three years, it didn't mean he was done being our enemy.

"The cops been sniffin' 'round more than normal, no big deal but they're pullin' over brother's wives and girlfriends, showin' up at our legit businesses trying to hassle employees got nothin' to do with club shit. We're keepin' vigilant but need you to be careful, yeah?"

The guys gave chin tilts, but the women, we looked at each other because we knew by the electric feel in the air that a storm was coming.

"What else?" Cress asked, leaning forward on the arm of the chair she perched on to give my brother's a back rub.

This time, surprisingly, Lila spoke up, her gorgeous tattoos glowing brightly in the early morning light shifting through the windows. "Irina Ventura's started a pornography company outside Entrance."

I frowned. "Okay, why do we give a shit?"

"She's using Javier's drug dealers to get local girls hooked on meth, coke or heroin and then forcing them to perform.

You remember Talia Jenkins? She went to EBA, but she dated Aaron, remember?"

King laughed. "I remember her."

Cressida huffed, which just made King laugh hard and lean back into her so he could tilt his head to grin at her.

"She never had anythin' on you, Cress babe," he said.

"Talia got hooked, she's working for Irina now," Lila continued.

"How is this our problem?" I asked, somewhat callously, but it was true. We weren't the police, we weren't vigilantes so what did this matter?

"They got Honey," King said, his eyes on me even as he absently, gently bit at Cress's fingers.

Honey.

Fuck, they got Honey.

I closed my eyes for a second and let that rock me. Honey was our half-sister through our mother. The most time I'd ever spent with her was the nine months Mum was pregnant with her while Zeus was in jail, her cheating ass having waited not even a few months after he was incarcerated to shack up with another guy. Since then, I'd seen her a sum total of three times and it was clear, Farrah had raised her like a miniature version of herself, and both bitches hated The Fallen and the Garros.

But still, Honey was all of sixteen years old.

"She's making porn?" I asked without opening my eyes, hating the visuals.

"Not yet, Farrah called Dad demanding he deal with it," King replied, an edge to his voice like a serrated knife.

"She's not even his kid," Nova spoke for the first time.

"Still, family's family and she's a fuckin' kid. Can't have that in our town and 'sides, I wouldn't mind takin' those cunt Venturas down," Dad said, and not for the first time I was reminded that heroes come in many different shapes and sizes.

Just because Zeus Garro was an outlaw motorcycle club Prez with a rap sheet didn't mean he wasn't all kinds of good.

"Agreed," King and I said at the same time, then grinned at each other.

"What's the third thing?" Cress asked softly.

Dad looked at Cress then at me and his face went blank. "Berserkers MC approached about partnerin'. I rejected the idea straight out. They didn't take it so well."

"How the fuck else did they think somethin' that stupid would fly with the club?" King asked, leaning forward to sit with his forearms braced on his knees.

"You didn't know about this?" I asked, surprised that King wasn't in the loop, especially now that he'd started prospecting.

He'd finally taken the plunge, but King had been a part of the club since he came out of our mother's rotten womb.

"Haven't been tellin' me shit since I joined the club," he muttered, but his eyes went pale with rage.

"'Cause you aren't a full patched member yet and it's important you fuckin' feel that just like every other prospect does," Dad said, his tone both irritated and bored like they'd had the same conversation a million times.

It made the hair on the back of my neck stand on end because Dad and King were never anything less than thick as thieves.

"That's a pretty bold play," I said carefully. "You don't think I have anything to do with it, do you?"

Dad lifted his steepled hands to his lips and studied me for a second. "Think I don't want you around them even more than I already did 'fore this, that's for fuckin' sure. Reaper an' me go back to 'fore he founded his club. Like to think it was a gesture, back in the day he wanted in The Fallen and Crux turned 'im away. Could be simple as that."

"How do you know they didn't take it well then?"

His jaw clenched then ticked hard, but he didn't say anything.

Loulou did, both her hands on her pregnant abdomen. "We don't know who exactly, but someone's made threats against me and the babies on behalf of that club."

The oxygen in the room evaporated with a snap, and what followed was flat silence, not punctuated even with breath.

"You're fucking kidding!" King shouted, standing up to pace. "You're *fucking kidding me.*"

"That's so fucked up," Cressida said softly, her hand over her mouth.

It was a reaction that reminded me just how far she'd come from being an uptight, prim schoolmarm in the last five years, but how far she still was from being a real old lady or biker babe.

Because me?

Born and raised a biker bitch, formed from biker sperm and in a bitch's womb?

My reaction wasn't external, it bloomed in my heart like a bloody rose wrapped in poisonous thorns. My family was under threat and nothing in the world mattered so much as them, not even me.

So, I knew what I was going to do.

My vague inclination to take the Berserkers down had just solidified into something, long, and strong, and lethal, a flaming sword in my righteous hand.

I was going to end them.

Even if they never actually touched a hair on Loulou and the babies' heads, they deserved to die just for the very thought of it.

Prison was too good for them, but it was a decent substitute for murder as long as every single member of that MC went down with the fucking ship.

"Everyone shut the hell up," Dad ordered firmly over the

clamor of King cursing, Nova and Lila arguing and Cress speaking softly to Lou. "Goes without fuckin' sayin', I should hope, that I'm not going to let one-fucking-thing touch a goddamn hair on Lou's head or get within even a fuckin' acre of her. That understood?" he waited for us to agree with chin tilts and nods before going on. "Good, then put it outta your minds."

"Easier said than done," Cress said softly, tears in her eyes as I stared at Lou.

"Love you, Loulou," I told her but what I meant was, I loved her enough to get involved with the Berserkers MC again and take them down for her.

CHAPTER NINE

Harleigh Rose

I WALKED OUT OF THE NURSING BUILDING AFTER MY LAST CLASS of the day to see a gaggle of students surrounding something in the parking lot. It happened sometimes at UBC, Vancouver was filled with wealthy families and the international students had to be very rich or very lucky to secure a spot at the school so it wasn't unusual to see a Ferrari or Aston Martin in the parking lots on campus.

Personally, I didn't give a fuck. My father owned the premier custom car and motorcycle garage on the west coast, I'd seen 'em all and then some.

So, I was moving passed quickly, already thinking about getting home to Hero and taking him for a walk, having defied

Danner's order to take him to class because it was straight up ridiculous. The MC would never harm me on campus grounds.

"Harleigh Rose," the deepest voice I knew called out over the higher cries of student chatter.

I froze.

Then slowly, already reevaluating my affirmation that the Berserkers wouldn't harm me on campus, I turned to face the group of students in the parking lot.

Wrath sat on his huge Harley Davidson, a soft tail slim with red and chrome accents, but I knew it wasn't the bike that had drawn notice but the big ass, badass biker that went with it. His thick hair was kinked and waving in the wind, his permanent scowl affixed to his gorgeous face, and his big body doing that lean women loved where the whole length and muscled breadth of their body was on display.

I understood the crowd.

I didn't even like the man and I wanted to get closer to catch a better glimpse of that beauty.

But I didn't.

"Gotta get home, Wrath," I called out with a flick of my fingers. "Catch ya later."

"Why do ya think I'm here? Get on," he said.

Fuck.

I didn't want to. I wanted to go home, clean my gun, take Hero for a run, and study for my finals coming up in two weeks. But Wrath was technically my old man now, and we hadn't had the time for us to work out the particulars.

Like the fact that I was *not* going to sleep with him.

I hefted my backpack over the other shoulder so it would be balanced on the bike and trudged over to him.

"Lookin' sweet, H.R.," he complimented me when I came to a stop with my hand on my hip in front of him.

I was hyper aware of our lingering crowd as I tossed my hair over my shoulder and popped a loud bubble with my original flavoured Hubba Bubba. "Wearin' an old tee and jean shorts, Wrath, nothin' to write home to your mummy about."

Given, it was one of my fav tees, one I'd stolen from dad with AC/DC emblazoned in red on the front that I'd tied at the bottom to expose a sliver of my tanned belly and the tops of the fishnets I wore beneath my shorty short jeans. I'd been a biker babe since I could talk, even I had to admit I had the look down pat.

He crossed his arms over his chest, drawing attention to the beautifully detailed tattoos of hellfire blazing across his forearms and up into the demons burning in the flames on his huge biceps. "You think a woman's gotta wear somethin' special to make a man pant, woman? Nah. Attitude is ninety percent of the attraction."

"And the other ten percent?"

He paused as a slow grin split his beard in two. "Don't find that out 'til later, when she's on her knees with your dick in her mouth and you find out how good she is at suckin' ya down."

I snorted, done with our game, and moved to swing myself over the bike behind him. "I wouldn't bet on finding out the decimal power of my suction, dude."

Wrath's laugh was less noise than it was a vibration of movement through his long, wide torso. He settled himself over the bike, waited for me to set the brain bucket on my head and then gunned the throttle just to see the gathering of students gasp and scramble backwards.

"Show off," I muttered under my breath, but if his laugh was any indication, he heard me.

We took off and I hated that I loved being on the back of a bike so much that I enjoyed the ride through UBC's curved roads, glimpses of multi-million-dollar houses through opened security gates, and huge stretches of unobstructed ocean views, the summer sun in full noon bloom over the silver water. The wind was in my hair, the scent of hot asphalt and leather-clad biker in my nose and before long I caved to the impulse to throw my arms in the air and yell indecipherably into the rushing wind.

I was almost sad when we arrived at Bernadette's, Berserker's local watering hole, except they made the best damn chicken wings on the planet so at least there was that.

I swung off the bike, pushed the helmet into Wrath's chest and said, "Meet you inside."

The bar was nothing like Eugene's, my uncle's bar and also my father's club's favourite bar just outside of Entrance. It was grungier, the servers older and haggard, wash-ups from strip clubs and more popular downtown bars, the drinks limited to beer and a few bottom shelf liquors.

I slid into a booth and ordered a Blue Buck and hot wings.

Wrath joined me at the same time the frothy pint was slapped in front of me and ordered the same.

"We gotta talk."

"Yeah, we do. We gotta talk about the fact that I am *so* not your old lady," I told him.

Wrath stared at me implacably with those placid, beautiful grey-blue eyes. "For the purposes'a the club, you are."

I perked up. "Cryptic much?"

He peered at me, his big hands flipping a coaster over and over in his fingers. I didn't know if he did it on purpose, but it was a good reminder that he was not someone to fuck around with.

"Don't want ya like that. Pretty as a fuckin' peach, but like I said 'fore, that don't matter much to me. What does is my own fuckin' business and you don't need to worry 'bout it none, 'cept for the part where you go on pretendin' to be my old lady."

"Think I do need to worry about it," I said slowly, my eyes scanning the biker haunt for any Berserker brother that might've been listening. "If it involves me lyin' to the club."

He snorted. "Let's get this straight, I got my own shit goin' down, but I'm still VP of this fuckin' club and the only reason I'm not diggin' into your shit—shit so rank I can smell it a fuckin' mile 'way—is 'cause I've got need of ya. Reaper might buy that wide-eyed blue stare, but I see your second face, H.R., and I know you got shit to hide, same as me."

I pursed my lips, but I was between a rock and a hard place. He'd saved me from those asshole bikers, sure, but in doing so he'd already inextricably tied us together. If I wanted to take down the MC, I'd have to go along with his plan. And in a way, it was to my advantage to have the VP's protection, especially without having to take his cock.

"So, what's the gig then? We pretend to be together in front of the brothers? I cover for you, they ask where you've been?"

"Sounds 'bout right," he agreed as his beer arrived and the hot wings crashed to the table between us. He watched me lay into the chicken with humor lighting his eyes. "Don't trust you, H.R., but I've got to. You screw me on this, I'll gut you with the same knife they claim killed my cousin. You feel me?"

I spoke through a mouthful of chicken as I ripped a chunk of meat off the bone. "You gut me, you'll have hell to pay with The Fallen. I'd say, give or take a year or two, you touch a hair on my fuckin' head, they'd spend a decade keepin' you right on the edge of the death, torturing you daily for hurting their princess."

"No doubt," he agreed easily, shoving an entire wing into his mouth and then pushing the clean bones out between his teeth.

"So, same goes here. I need cover, you're it."

He blinked at me then his eyes shot to the door as it opened to the sound of a giggling woman. His smile pulled across his face as if tugged by a thread and needles as he looked between the newcomers and me.

"Done."

Two seconds later, I understood why he'd been smiling,

and didn't like that he knew enough to get off on my coming discomfort.

"H.R. girl!" Laken cried as she threw herself into the booth beside me, her arms tightly wrapped around my neck.

I closed my eyes and gritted my teeth against the flash-back, the feel of her wound against me so much like the feel of Cricket locked on top of me, his gun sliding hard and cool down my thigh over the gusset of my panties and under...

"Good to see ya, brother," Danner's voice cut through my turmoil and I watched as he leaned forward to clasp Wrath in a manly handshake/back pat.

"I cannot believe you didn't tell me about Wrath," Laken faux-whispered loudly, her arms still around me but loose. "Were you fucking him while you were with Cricket?"

"Laken," Danner snapped at her before I could answer. "Jesus, woman, you ever dream of thinkin' before ya speak?"

It was weird to hear Danner speak in biker contractions just as much as it sent a tingle of arousal shooting between my legs.

God, he looked like sex on legs in that leather jacket.

I refocused on Laken who looked properly chastised and patted her arm before pulling them off me. "Don't mention it again, babe. But, if you wanna talk surprises, when did you hook up with this guy? What's his name again?"

Wrath poorly concealed his bark of laughter behind a cough, and I shot him a wary look, because it seemed he knew way too much about my history with Danner.

Laken helped herself to one of my wings and said, "Harleigh Rose, this is my man Lion."

"Lion," I mused. "How'd you get that one?"

"When he started prospectin' he was an ink virgin so the boys took 'im down to Gilly's shop and made him get tatted up. He didn't take no pills or shots to dull the pain and he chose a huge chest piece with this lion roaring over his heart caged by a thicket of these roses and thorns," Laken sighed dreamily as she recounted the story, completely unaware of my unnatural stillness beside her. "That combined with the fact that he came off the street with brass balls to straight up ask Reaper to take 'im on as a hang around two years ago, no connection to the club at all, well the guys figured he had the courage of one, ya know?"

I did know. His courage and conviction were half the reason I'd started calling him Lion as a girl. I didn't know anyone so foolishly brave, so convinced of their mission to do good and right wrongs.

I understood the symbolism of the tattoo more than anyone else could know.

Danner was looking at me, his eyes like hot knife points searing into my skin, but I refused to look his way. If I did, all my well-maintained walls would crumble and all that remained would be me in my basest form, weak and tender and *his*.

"You ever heard'a the Cowardly Lion?" Wrath asked.

I burst out laughing, shocked that the big, bad biker knew the Wizard of Oz and delighted that he used it to insult Danner.

Even Danner's eyes sparkled at the cut. "Shut the fuck up, man. You're just fuckin' sore I beat your ass at pool last week and took you for fifty bucks."

Wrath thumped a hand on the table. "Was lurin' you into a false sense'a security. Feelin' a rematch?"

"Bring it."

"Couples game," Laken cried happily, standing up to grab my and Danner's hands so she could drag us over to one of the three pool tables.

They were all occupied but one look at Wrath's bulk and Danner's corded height, both clad in biker cuts, made the people closest to use scurry away.

I hid my smile behind my beer. Intimidation never got old.

"How's my dog?" Danner asked, reaching around me to

grab a cue from the wall, his hard torso pressed against my back. "Takin' good care of our girl?"

"How's Laken?" I asked back quietly. "Takin' care of your cock?"

Danner stared at me for a moment when I turned around and then laughed. I loved the sound of it low and smooth like liquid honey, the way his head dipped slightly as if he was embarrassed, surprised by his own mirth, and the creases it cut in his face, beside those green eyes, around his firm mouth and an especially delicious one cut into his left cheek like a dimple. I could have watched him laugh for hours, but the fact that he did it so sparingly also made it precious, and I coveted that.

"Playin' the game of life here," he told me when he quieted. "My only goal is to make Vancouver a safer place."

"So, why not use Laken to do that?" I ventured, careful to keep my voice down and my lips immobile so Laken and Wrath wouldn't eavesdrop from the other end of the table where they were ordering more drinks.

"She's Reaper's niece and she isn't the brightest," he shrugged.

"Never knew you to be so ruthless," I muttered as I racked up the balls on stained green felt.

"Police think Berserkers are responsible for one-third of all guns illegally seized in this city, and we have the highest rate of gun crime per capita in the country. I've been undercover with this operation for three fuckin' years, H.R., at this point, I'll do anything to bring them down."

I thought about Mute, The Fallen brother who had taken a bullet to the neck while trying to save Loulou, her little sister, Bea, and me from a burning building. I wondered if Berserkers had supplied the gun that loosed that bullet into his neck and my resolve tightened.

"Joining you in this, Danner," I told him. "You don't sort it with the pigs, I will."

"You wanna work for the police when you can't even refer to them with respect?" he asked with a snort.

"Yeah, I do. They've threatened my family, they sell guns to anyone with money and they encouraged Cricket to crack me in half with his fists so I'd spill Fallen secrets. Think I have a better reason than most to get involved here."

Danner's hand went to my hip, out of sight of anyone, caught between our bodies as he stood slightly behind and to the side of me, but I felt the illicit touch like shock paddles to my heart.

"Don't want you involved in this shit, Rosie," he said softly, too close to me, his voice in my ear and breath on my neck.

I shivered violently and his hand flexed on my lower back in response.

"Too late," I said. "Besides, you're so concerned, you'll watch my back."

"Yeah, rebel," he said and his hand dipped lower pressed hot and possessive like a tramp stamp of ownership to my upper ass. "I'll watch your back."

He moved away, and I didn't need to look over my shoulder to know that he stood with his arms crossed, eyes trained on my ass as I bent over the pool table to break the balls.

It was late. There weren't many windows in Bernadette's so it was hard to tell, but the sun had definitely set. I'd slammed back at least five beers and a few shafts, a provincial specialty that was a heady combination of vodka, coffee, Bailey's and Kahlua, but over a long enough period of time that I wasn't as drunk as I could've been, just this side of tipsy.

This was a bad idea, the tipsiness, because alcohol barely affected me anymore except for making me horny as fuck.

And Danner had been too close all night, barely flirting with Laken, instead exchanging glances with me that left me with full body shivers and an ache between my legs no amount of squirming could slack.

I should have been more careful, but I just wasn't that kind of girl.

Some people faced the edge when the occasion called for it. I just straight up lived there, on the edge of reason, on the outskirts of temptation, seducing others to join me there.

And right then, I was trying to seduce Danner.

He was bent over the table lining up a difficult shot to get the green striped ball in the corner pocket without hitting the solid yellow one in front of it.

"Don't mess up," I taunted him, settling a hip on the edge of the table beside him and leaning slightly over his back so he'd feel me in his space.

Laken was in the bathroom, but I couldn't say I wouldn't be doing the same thing even if she was right in front of us.

Danner's white shirt had ridden up with his cut, exposing a taut expanse of lower back to my hungry eyes. I trailed the fingertips of one hand whisper-soft across the breadth of it and watched as Danner flubbed his shot.

His face was hard, marbleized into sexy displeasure. I'd never seen a man wear his discontentment so well, like a badge of authority, a crown of regality. I wanted to get on my knees, kiss his fingers and beg him for forgiveness anyway he would give it to me.

"You'll pay for that play, Rosie," he clipped out quietly, and I could feel his touch against me even though he was inches away. "If you do it again, I won't be responsible for what happens next."

There was a loud commotion at the door that drew my attention briefly to Reaper, Grease, a hoard of other brothers and their women entering the bar. Wrath went instantly to greet them and we should have too, but didn't.

The game Danner and I were playing had just gone from dangerous to deadly.

My heart was beating so hard I could feel it sharp and obvious, tattooing my desire at every pulse point. My nipples beaded into hard points under my shirt, my breath too fast between my parted lips as I turned back to see Danner's eyes still on me. I was lit up with lust like a fuckin beacon and I didn't care.

I just wanted Danner to blanket me with his form of darkness until I exploded into sparks.

"Who says I'll hold you responsible?" I murmured, brushing passed him so my diamond hard nipples scraped against his arm.

"Fuck me, you're trouble. Have been since the day I saw you," he said, but his eyes tracked the newcomers as they intimidated another group into giving up their booths. "You could tempt a saint into sinning."

I bit my lip, unsure if I wanted to admit how hard I'd been trying all these years to do just that. "Wouldn't bet on that. I haven't succeeded yet."

"I'm no saint."

Oh, but he was wrong.

Standing wearing faded, old jeans in the way only he could, the soft fabric molded to his thick thighs, his high, tight ass, his white tee pristine against his tan and that too fit well, hugging every delicious contour of his chest so that it was nearly indecent. He was a North American idol, vital and strong, righteous and just, virile but principled. If all that wasn't saintly, I didn't know what was.

"Seems that way from this side of the table," I taunted, digging at him because I hated him for being so beautiful and so not mine.

He sighed roughly and ran a hand through his dishevelled hair. "Wanting you was never the issue."

I snorted. "Wasn't it?"

"Jesus Christ, Rosie, this isn't the time or place."

Emotions whirred in my gut, the longing and the lust, the frustration and the unjustness of it all, but as usual, I couldn't find the words to parcel such huge feelings into neat little boxes. So, I got angry.

"It never fucking well is," I hissed at him. "You've been spewing that shit for years. You're a man, you want a woman, you fuckin' take her if she wants you back."

Danner gritted his teeth, his eyes darting over to the group which Laken had joined. We needed to go over to join them soon or they'd notice the slight and take insult, middle of a pool game or not.

So, when he started stalking by me, I assumed that's where he was headed. Instead, he powered past me, his hand snatching out to grip my wrist and drag me behind him.

"Lion," I whispered harshly in protest.

But I followed him. I followed him, because I had all my life and I knew I always would.

He dragged us down the hall to the bathrooms then farther around the corner to Bernadette's office at the back.

"Danner, what the—" I started to ask, but then I pushed up against the paneled wall and the long, hard length of his body was pushed up against me.

"You want proof you drive me fucking crazy," he rasped, his forehead pressed to mine, one hand at the back of my head to cushion it from the wall and the other clenched tightly to my ass. "You need me to do something stupid like kiss your sweet mouth in the back of this shit bar while men who'd be happy to kill us are steps away just to prove to you I'd do anything to be near you, on you, fucking *in* you?"

"Yes," I said the word like a curse. "Yes."

The hand on my head fisted in my hair and yanked back so my face was tipped and my lips were parted on a gasp.

"Anythin' for you, Rosie," he said, a savage benediction. And then, he dipped his head and plundered.

I hadn't had his mouth on mine in over three years, and even then, it had only lasted minutes. Still, I'd played that one experience over and over in my head like a reel until the film was warped and spotted with use and time.

Nothing could have prepared me for the feel of his lips on me in that moment.

He shaped my mouth with his, stroked my tongue and bit my lip hard enough to make it ache before soothing it with a long, slow suck. I loved the way he tasted, hot like burning whiskey I wanted to swallow down. I was addicted to the way he felt pressed to me, the iron hard length of him pressed to the aching apex of my thighs, his hand in my hair both causing me pain and preventing me from it.

It was the most beautiful moment of my life, and I was lucky, I'd had a lota really beautiful moments.

There was a crack and a bang as one of the bathroom doors swung open into the wall around the corner. Danner tore his mouth from mine but didn't pull away. Instead, instinctively, he curled over me, the hand at my head pressed me under his chin, his back forming a broad shield between me and whatever threat he thought we faced.

And somehow, that was even more beautiful than the kiss.

"Just the bathroom," I told him quietly.

I felt his sigh, but he remained curved around me for another long beat before he stepped away.

We stared at each other.

His green eyes were dilated with lust, the pulse in his strong throat jumping so high I could see it from where I stood even in the dim light. My eyes dropped lower and stuck on the sight of his cock, so thick and long against his thigh trapped in those soft denim jeans.

It took everything in me not to drop to my knees right there and mouth him through the fabric.

"Harleigh Rose," he said sharply.

I closed my eyes instead of looking up at him. His moment of insanity, I knew, was over. He'd come back into his right mind, a mind that loves order and discipline and hated chaos and rebellion. A right mind that hated everything I stood for.

Was it wrong that one day, I wished he would drop off the deep end of sanity for good and fall right into my arms?

"Rosie," he said again, his voice softer but the word so much more painful.

"Right," I said, opening my eyes to see him reach for me, his beautiful face crippled with indecision. "Think I won that game, eh officer?"

"Don't be hard with me." He narrowed his eyes and took another step closer, but I slid against the wall away from him and started to back away. "You always throw up thorns the second I get close to the heart of you."

God, he was lovely. I wished as I'd only ever wished for him, that I was born a different kind of girl.

But I wasn't the good girl to his good guy and I never would be.

If Lionel Danner wanted me, he'd have to come to me, over to the dark side where outlaws ruled, sinning was routine, and love was blind.

He'd have to be the bad boy to my bad girl.

And I knew, the kind of guy he was, that would never happen.

So, without saying another word, I turned on my heel and fled.

CHAPTER TEN

Harleigh Rose

I HAD NEVER WILLING ENTERED A POLICE STATION IN MY ENTIRE life, but I guessed there was a first time for everything. It was after my classes the day after my bizarre double date with Danner, Laken, and Wrath, and I'd decided to take matters into my own hands, mostly because, after I'd left Danner, I'd joined the Berserkers crowd and learned something of value.

I knew Danner wouldn't involve me in the investigation if his life depended on it, but I figured his colleagues would be only too happy to risk the life of a biker bitch with a rap sheet if it meant bringing down the biggest source of illegal firearm smuggling in the province.

I was proved right the minute I told the receptionist my name and reason for being there. Minutes later, I was set up in a room with a large black man named Sergeant Renner and a very beautiful female officer by the name of Casey.

"So, we're just supposed to believe you're doing this out of the goodness of your heart?" Renner asked, his arms crossed over his chest, a scowl affixed to his face.

Clearly, he was playing Bad Cop.

I shrugged. "The words 'good' and 'my heart' don't have much in common, but we can go with that if you want to be poetic. I'm here because I want to take down the Berserkers. Does it really matter why?"

"It does," Casey explained with a lovely smile that made me instantly dislike her. "We need to know you have the proper motivation."

"A member of their club beat me and tried to rape me, they bring thousands of dollars' worth of illegal firearms into the province every year, which contributes to making Vancouver have the highest rate of gun crime per capita in the country." I unwrapped a piece of Hubba Bubba gum from my pocket and popped it into my mouth. "That good enough for ya?"

"It has nothing to do with the fact that your father is the President of a motorcycle club based in Entrance? To our knowledge they don't have a history of discord, but how are we supposed to believe that you aren't doing this to better your father's club?" Renner asked.

I hadn't thought of that. Of course, they were kind of right. I did want to take down Berserkers MC because of my family, because I wanted to protect them. Not that I was going to tell them that.

"I guess you can't really know, but as you said, there is no history of beef between the two MC's." The two officers shared a look and I felt traction slide out from under me.

"What about this? I promise to limit contact with my family until the investigation is over."

They looked just as shocked as I felt about making that concession.

I spoke to my family every day, even more since the accident. Cress and King had graduated from UBC the year before, but we were used to seeing each other weekly so they called a lot, just to shoot the shit. Loulou and I had been through hell together, so I didn't think it was strange that we texted every day, sometimes just with memes or song suggestions, any excuse to make contact. My dad texted me twice a day, every day since I'd moved to Vancouver for university. Once in the morning before I left for school saying "kick some academic ass today, princess," and the other before I went to bed every night, "dream sweet, little badass."

I loved them. They were a critical part of my day even though I lived an hour away.

But yeah, I'd give that up if it meant keeping them safe.

They wouldn't understand, but maybe I could use the incident as a reason to need space...

"Miss Garro?" Casey asked. "You're that serious about this?"

"I am," I said and I could feel that one word like a signature in blood on contract with the devil.

After all, who better to represent the devil to a biker chick than the cops?

It was basically a breeze after that, which made me mildly uneasy. How many confidential informants did the cops have? I'd have to mention to Dad when this was all over how ridiculously easy it was to convince them to take me on.

They explained the ins and outs of the operation, that I was to look for evidence that would incriminate the club in smuggling and arms dealing. I would report to my 'handler' the wonderfully pretty Casey by text over a newly gifted burner phone only when I had something important to relate, and that from this point on I would be referred to only by my number designation.

I requested the number 69, but cops never had a sense of humor.

Casey was walking me out of the room, confirming that our meeting place would be UBC's Café Ami, when I felt the mood hit the room.

Palpable anger rolled through the station like a nuclear blast, drawing everyone's attention to the front of the station where Danner stood staring at Casey and me.

Oh, boy.

A thrill of delicious fear and anticipation zapped down my back. There was nothing like an angry hot guy to make a girl weak in the knees.

Only... I frowned as the woman beside me laughed and descended the stairs on a glide to come to a standstill before him.

She laughed then rose on her tiptoes to plant a kiss on his unshaven cheek. "You shouldn't be here, mister."

I blinked.

Danner took his eyes off me to look into the face of the pretty cop and he raised an eyebrow. "Renner texted me. Said we had a new asset he had to speak with me about. Please don't tell me it's the Garro girl."

The Garro girl.

Not Rosie.

Not Harleigh Rose.

I shouldn't have been angry, not when I called him Danner for the exact reason he'd just called me by my last name. To remind the both of us that this was a modern-day Capulet vs. Montague situation, and at the end of the day no matter that we avoided it, we stood apart from each other across a great divide.

"Sorry to disappoint," Casey said with another light laugh.

"But I think you'll be happy when you realize how committed she is to this."

"I wouldn't bet on it," he muttered before giving her shoulder a pat and moving up the stairs toward me.

"You are in so much trouble," he murmured to me as he passed by. "And I think you're finally fucking old enough to feel the real pain of my displeasure."

I swayed back from the sheer heat of his words then gritted my teeth so I could focus on what was important. "Another girlfriend, Danner?"

He looked over his shoulder at me, his glare smoldering. "I'll break up with her tonight if you promise to be in my bed, ready to be punished by ten."

My lips parted, releasing emotions I wish I'd kept sewn up tight. Mainly, pure desire and greed.

He flashed me a wicked, lopsided grin that made his green eyes flare and drawled, "Yeah, Rosie, I'll see you tonight."

I stared after him as he strolled away, watching the way his long, strong legs ate up the floor, the way the breadth of his shoulders strained his grey tee and his lean hips made his jeans sit loose enough to shift tantalizingly over his fucking fantastic behind.

When I jerked out of it, I looked around to make sure no one had caught me ogling, then wiped the corners of my mouth for any errant drool. As I walked out of the station and over the three blocks to where I'd parked my car (it paid to be paranoid), I tried to convince myself I wouldn't be at his house that night.

I'd always been a skilled liar, but even I wasn't talented enough to make that true.

I WAS AT THE LIBRARY LATE, MOSTLY BECAUSE MY APARTMENT felt haunted by the greasy essence of Cricket's spirit, but also because I was a good student. In high school, I was lucky enough to get by on sheer intelligence and pure luck, because I didn't try for shit. It was only after I'd witnessed the havoc cancer wrecked on Loulou and thus, my family, that I found a reason to try. I wanted to be a nurse. Not a doctor, though there was nothing wrong with the profession. I wanted to be the unsung hero for the sick and hospital-ridden, the person that developed a relationship with them, gave them what morale and medicine they needed to survive the ordeals life had thrown in their paths. My family was shocked at first when I'd declared my intention, everyone but Loulou. She'd smiled her movie star smile at me and declared it was an awesome idea.

The night was cold for June and inky black. I tugged my leather jacket closer around me, wishing I'd brought Hero with me as I moved to the parking lot. A prickle of unease shot like needles into the delicate skin at the back of my neck when I opened the car door, but there wasn't a soul in sight and I told myself I was being paranoid.

I should have listened to my intuition. I was a woman and it was one of the deadliest tools in our arsenal.

But I didn't.

I slid into the front seat, plunked my backpack on the seat beside me and started up the car. I started to head bang to

"Highway to Hell" as it blasted from the speakers then looked up at my rearview mirror to pull out when I saw him.

A huge figure entirely dressed in black wearing a mask sitting directly behind me.

I screamed, a bloodcurdling sound that ripped painfully up my throat and cut through the sound of AC/DC.

One second later the sound was cut off by a large hand wrapping painfully around the side of my throat, the other yielding a wicked sharp blade that was pressed to my throat.

"Don't scream, bitch. Do as you're told, and you can end the night nice and safe in your bed, yeah?" The voice was clearly a man's, muffled, but deep under the hood.

Other than that, I had no idea who this person was.

"What do you want?" I asked quietly, proud that my voice didn't shake even though my hands did.

My purse was just inches away. If he didn't have his knife to my throat, I could make a grab for it, but his position behind me would make it nearly impossible to shoot blindly on target.

"Drive, princess," he growled. "Make any wrong turns, or indicate in any way that you're distressed, I'll slice open your throat, yeah?"

"Yeah," I whispered.

"Get on the Sea to Sky, I'll tell ya when to turn off."

Even though I was careful to keep still as I navigated the traffic, the blade cut through me like butter, just shallow nicks but the neck bleeds profusely and by the time I took the exit he indicated into Entrance, the entire top of my blue Hephaestus Auto tee was covered in blood.

I knew after only a few turns where he was taking me.

My dad's house.

It was a Friday. Everyone was at the house by the look of the cars parked outside, by the movement of bodies in the golden-lit rooms. Loulou liked to have everyone over as much as she could, especially after getting pregnant. She called it nesting, Dad called it irritatin', but everyone knew he loved his brothers, his family, and he loved, even more, having them in his house.

"You see 'em?" the masked villain asked almost conversationally.

"Yeah," I breathed, fear like a living thing crawling with eight legs up my neck over my face, digging fangs under my skin to poison my bloodstream.

"You wanna keep 'em alive," he noted.

I didn't answer, it was obvious he knew my family was my weak spot.

The door to the house opened as if I'd willed it with my mind and my dad stepped out. With his huge body backlit, he looked big as the Hulk, as capable of defeating villains as any superhero. A whimper slid up my throat and I almost impaled myself on the blade in an effort to swallow it.

I could tell he was smoking. He was trying to quit before the babies came, but it was a hard habit to give up and Lou wasn't a nag, so he was doing it slowly. I wasn't surprised when a minute later, my brother's equally tall form appeared, lankier but growing thick with muscle from spending so much time with the brothers at their gym on the compound.

Dad tossed an arm around him and tugged him close, casually, affectionately in that way he did that made you feel warm to the very bones.

"I'll kill them. Every single one'a them, slow and painfully 'cause, princess, I get off on that shit. I'll start with Louise Garro, pin her down and fuck her then gut her so she loses those devil spawn and knows it before she loses herself too."

"God, stop," I croaked, my eyes burning, so dry, but I couldn't blink, I had to watch my dad with my brother, had to remind myself every second that they were alive and standing there.

"Don't care if it takes me ten years, you fuck with Berserkers MC, I'll kill every last one'a them and save you for last, you get what I'm sayin'?" he asked, wiggling the blade against my throat when I didn't immediately nod my head. "Thought you were smart enough to get me. Gotta say, it would be a shame really if you stick true, that Garro bitch is worth fuckin' even fat like she is."

Fury exploded within my body. I imagined turning on the sick fuck behind me, twisting that knife out of his hand and showing him how I could use it by stabbing him right through his fucking eyes. He didn't deserve to look at my beautiful family. He didn't deserve to occupy the same fucking world as them.

"I'll kill you," I told him, maybe unwisely.

But I was a wild thing, cornered and desperate. You back an animal into a small space, it's only in their nature to fight back, however fruitlessly.

The man laughed and even though it was deeply muffled, I almost recognized the sound. "No, princess, you won't. You don't get this 'cause you can't see the whole picture, but this is a game I'll win."

I gritted my teeth and refrained, barely, from blindly turning and launching myself at him with just my nails to use like claws.

"I'll get out here," he said, again conversational, the fucking psychopath. "But you remember this, remember that I like to sit here at night and watch your daddy and his pretty wife, go over to your brother's place and watch him fuck his woman on their deck. You remember what I'll do to them if you fuck with the MC. And know this, I watch them and someone else, always, is watchin' you."

A second later, the knife was gone from my throat and cold ocean air blasted in from the open door. A moment after that, it slammed shut and he was gone as if into thin air.

Without missing a beat, I peeled away from the curb and hauled ass back onto the Sea to Sky down to Vancouver. I wanted to go into my house, hug my dad, kiss Lou's belly, feel

Cressida's hand in my hair and King's laugh in the air. But I didn't, because somehow, I'd become an unintentional threat to my family.

I desperately didn't want to be alone in my apartment, but I needed to get Hero and ditch the car in case anyone was following me. The dog was waiting at the door and he growled when he saw the state I was in. After I locked the door behind me, I allowed myself to drop to the ground and bury my face in his fur. I clutched big handfuls of his silky tresses and cried into his neck for a long time. He let me, whining occasionally in empathy, licking at my face when I finally pulled away to soothe me.

"I'm never leaving home without you again," I told him soberly, cupping his sweet face in my hands and looking deep into his chocolate brown eyes. "Danner might have to get a new dog."

Hero yipped softly in agreement and wagged his tail.

I laughed wetly then dragged in a few deep breaths to center myself. I'd just been held at knifepoint in my car, I'd had to kill a man in my own apartment, I couldn't go home because my family was under threat and I was a big part of that.

I didn't have many safe places left.

But I had one fortress, one impenetrable safe haven that I hadn't used in years and if there ever was a time to give in, it was then. I packed up Hero's stuff and a bag of mine then called a taxi to take us to Danner's.

He lived in a small house in Kitsilano of all places, a tidy well-to-do neighborhood that didn't exactly suit his persona of a badass biker. Seeing the little shingled home made me miss the ranch-style house he had on a plot of acreage back home in Entrance.

I had to take a few fortifying breaths before I could get out of the cab into the dark night and walk to his door, but Hero kept close, brushing against my thigh with every step and I took comfort from the fact that he would protect me until his dying breath.

I reached the door without incident, which given my life lately, seemed like a minor miracle.

When Danner opened the door, he was smiling, and I loved that. He wasn't a man who smiled often, but he did a lot of it around me and always had. I loved that I gave him lightness to combat his somber spirit, that he weighted my wild impulses just enough to give me cause to think before I acted. We were such opposites, but so beautiful paired.

I hated when the smile dropped from his face and crashed to the floor between us. Before I could lie and tell him I was fine, I was wrapped up tenderly in his arms and he was lifting me and my big bag easily over the threshold into the house. I could hear the sounds of Hero following as Danner locked the door behind us, armed an alarm and then walked with me into a little living room off the kitchen. He sat us down with me straddling his lap, my bag forgotten beside us. Hero jumped up on the couch next to him and let out a contented groan.

I held my breath as Danner gently unwound my arms from around his neck and then tipped my chin down with his thumb so he could look into my eyes.

He had a way of looking at me that seared me to my very soul. It was as if he could read every thought I'd ever had, every feeling I'd never been able to correctly express in the blue of my irises, as if he would happily drown in the blacks of my eyes. He looked at me as if his world began and ended in my gaze.

I swallowed thickly as that look hit the well of emotion at the heart of me and tears sprung forth. "Lion."

"Rosie," he breathed, the thumb at my chin gliding up the angle of my jaw over the shell of my ear and then the hair over my temple with the rest of his fingers. "My Rosie, what happened?"

My body needed to cry. I could feel the lava-like burn of it behind my eyes, the pressure of it in my nose, tightening my throat and clenching my gut.

But I was Harleigh Rose Garro and I'd made a pact with myself a long time ago, the day I saw my mum on the brink of death for the last time, that I was not the kind of woman that cried.

I was strong.

I was thorn-studded roses, smoking gunmetal and the cool heat of weed being sucked down your throat.

I was my own woman before anyone else's and I could hold my own against anyone. The mean girls in high school, Cricket, The Nightstalkers MC, Reaper and Wrath, even my own mother.

God, but I both loved and hated that I couldn't hold my own against Danner. That my body and soul could outvote my mind and give in to the tears, because a huge part of me knew that there was no hiding from Danner. Not when he held my thorny heart in his hands. Not when he'd had it inked onto his chest.

A sob ballooned in my throat and I choked on the effort to keep it down.

Danner's hand moved soothingly over my back then, his eyes on me asking the question silently so that I could answer that way, it moved down to the hem of the tee and slowly, gently pulled it up over my head. He tossed it to the floor, his eyes to my wounded throat instead of my breasts inside a sheer, black and leather bra.

"What happened to my girl?" he asked again, his thumb trailing whisper soft over the cuts then pressing over my thudding pulse point as if to reassure himself I was alive and safe. "Tell me so I can kill them."

He would kill them. I could see it written across his face, his features twisted with heathen savagery and it occurred to me that this wasn't the first time Danner had offered to do bad for me.

In fact, it wasn't even the hundredth.

He'd been going bad for me for a very long time.

It shouldn't have been romantic, his corruption and my culpability, but it was.

There was enough power in that realization for me to give up control and allow myself to be vulnerable with him, so I told him.

About the cold edge of the blade biting then slicing smoothly through the skin at my throat. How hard the hand squeezed the left side of my neck, so hard capillaries had burst and I was already bruising, purple finger marks beneath the blood. About how the chemical response my body initiated in response to the crippling fear, how my breath lacked oxygen so I had to breath hard and fast but carefully so I didn't press my trachea into the blade. My muscles flooded with so much adrenaline they burned with acid and my heart stuttered, failing and starting again and again, each time more painful than the last.

How I kept thinking about dying in that car after everything I'd already been through, without saying goodbye to my family and friends, without ever really being with him.

At that last, he stood up swiftly, caging me carefully in his arms before he stalked down the hallway into a darkened bedroom through to a bathroom. He opened the glass shower door, cranked on the water, and then set me on the sink basin.

Carefully, reverently, he took off my clothes. My jeans were peeled off, his guitar roughened fingers tips trailing the fabric in a way that tickled then burned, next bra, unclasped with a flick of his fingers, and last, my panties torn with a *snap* so quick it was painless.

I gaped at him as he tossed the lacy fabric to the side and lifted me again.

"You know," I told his shoulder. "I can walk."

"Hush," he said as he placed me under the hot spray and closed the door behind us.

I watched in fascination as the water soaked through his black tee and jeans, plastering them to his body in a way that was somehow hotter than him being fully nude.

"Why are you dressed?" I asked as he reached for the shampoo, lathered some between his hands and then turned me into the spray so he could massage my hair into suds.

"Don't want you to feel uncomfortable," he muttered distractedly, obviously focused on giving me the most relaxing head massage in the history of the world.

Those words cut through the thicket of vines and thorns around my heart in one swift motion, leaving me tender and exposed. I stood there naked in the spray, a beautiful, good man washing me because I needed platonic affection and care, not undressing because I'd recently been attacked both sexually and physically a number of times and he was sensitive to that.

I felt honoured, blessed even to have a man so good tend to me as if I deserved it.

"Not possible," I whispered because when I tried to speak, I found that was all I could manage.

My throat was closed, my nose was stinging, and I was crying.

Danner heard me hiccough but gave me the dignity of sobbing into the shower spray until he was done with my hair. He turned me around, pushed me gently farther under the water and commenced rubbing me down with a natural sponge and body wash that smelled like him. I watched through the stream of water as he sympathetically dabbed at the cuts on my neck and worked away the crusted blood peeling on my chest then I closed my eyes to better feel it as he worked the sponge in firm circles over my breasts, slowly swirling from the outer edges to the hardened peaks. I gasped as his hand slid down my stomach and he crouched before me, lifting one of my feet to his shoulder so that he had unrestricted access to me. I could feel his fingertips at the edge of the sudsy cloth, moving up my calves, behind the tender skin of my knee to my inner thigh. I panted into the steam as he carefully swept over the outside of my bare pussy, across my suddenly aching clit and down the other side.

"Lion," I pleaded softly.

He placed one foot down and picked up the other, shifting closer to my sex as he did so his nose was at the tender junction of my thigh and groin, and then started on that leg.

My head hit the backsplash behind me with a thud when he made his way up to my sex again. "Lion, please."

He continued his slow, methodical washing, his face too close to me I should have felt insecure or uncomfortable. Instead, my blood felt molten, singeing through my veins and churning through the raging furnace at my heart.

The sponge pressed hard over my clit on the next path and I hissed.

Done, I twisted my fingers in his short hair and tugged brutally until he looked up at me. The savage desire in my gut blazed when I saw his blown pupils, the flush spread high on his cheekbone. Thank Christ, he wanted me too, even broken and ravaged as I was.

"I need you," I told him, feeling like an exposed nerve beneath a scalpel. Only able to take the plunge because I knew Danner was skilled enough, careful enough to handle me the way I needed. "Please, Lion, you make me feel safe and loved. I need you right now. I've needed you for a long time."

His eyes went black before my eyes as he digested my words and they gave him his high. He turned his head into the inside of my thigh, growled against the skin there and then bit me *hard*.

I gasped at the pain then melted into a full body moan as he tipped his head the other way and took my pussy in his mouth. My fingers spasmed in his hair as he ate at me, ruthless, ceaseless, until an orgasm crashed through me so hard I felt I'd shatter into molecules and floated on the air.

I could hear the wet sounds of him licking up my cum, feel his groan of triumph vibrate through my clit as he added fingers to my clenching cunt and curled them forward.

"Fuck," I cried, jacking my torso forward at the intensity of pleasure, at the shocking feeling of a second orgasm looming so soon over the first. "*Fuck.*"

"Yeah, Rosie," he said huskily, leaning back to watch his two fingers pump in and out of me, to see the way my thighs quaked. "Be a good girl and come all over my fingers. I want your cum dripping down my wrist."

"Fuck!" I cried out as his words splintered the dam holding back that second orgasm and I was swept up in the flood.

"Yeah," he praised, long and slow, still moving his fingers in and out of my grasping pussy but slower now, watching them glisten with me each time he pulled out. "Knew you'd have a gorgeous cunt."

I shivered at the praise and stroked my fingers through his wet hair in silent thanks.

"I think we can do one more," he said, looking up at me with wicked intent.

"I can barely stand as it is," I told him truthfully, most of my weight against the back wall.

He smirked, a curling smile that I felt in my still convulsing core. My hands shot to his head when he lifted me up, walked on his knees closer to the wall so he was directly under the shower and I was pressed to the tile behind it and settled my legs over his shoulders so I was held up only by the strength of his hands at my ass.

"No excuses," he muttered in my sex. "Come for me again, Rosie. Be a good girl."

I shuddered at the thought of being good for him. God,

I'd never wanted to be good for anyone else in my life, or any reason other than him, but fuck me if I didn't want to prove to him just how good a girl I could be.

It took longer this time, his tongue at my clit in flat, broad strokes, his fingers twisted inside me to rub against the walls of my swollen sex in a way that made my skin feel tight and my pulse too strong. He worked me from the inside out, wringing a third orgasm from me brutally, almost painfully, the edge of hurt only making the pleasure that much more phenomenal. I felt utterly used, completely broken apart and strangely clean, as if he had deconstructed me only to reassemble me properly again later.

And he did.

He mended my shattered, terrified soul by washing me once more, quicker this time, before pulling me out of the shower and drying me gently with a big fluffy towel. He did it by carrying me into his bedroom, sitting me on his dresser so he could find a big, old Entrance PD tee to dress me in, knowing I'd be uncomfortable going to bed naked. Then again when he carried me to bed, tucked me, then ordered an eager Hero onto the bed to lay beside while he checked the house and locked it down.

But it was when he returned, wearing black boxer briefs I wanted to peel him out of with my teeth some time when I had the energy, and fidgeted with the sound system beside the bed until the soothing twang of Hozier's "Like Real People Do" filled the room that I knew, if anyone could fix me, if anyone could love the wild, broken spirit that was me, it was Lionel Danner.

He slid into bed and immediately pulled me close so he could curl around me. Suddenly, I was safe. My shield, my Lion at my back and my dog, my Hero at my front. After a night of horrors, after a month of living nightmares, I fell asleep the second I closed my eyes, secure in the knowledge that nothing could harm me.

CHAPTER ELEVEN

Danner

2010

Harleigh Rose is 10. Danner is 19.

I SPOTTED HER RIGHT AWAY. SHE WAS TALL FOR HER AGE, I noted surprised that she'd grown so much in the nine months I'd been away at RCMP training camp, but otherwise, she was unchanged. Same streaky blond hair, so many shades of gold, yellow and honeyed brown that it shimmered even under the artificial lights of Evergreen Gas. She wore her black biker boots, too heavy for her lanky limbs also decked out in her custom uniform of torn denim and a concert tee, this one Pink Floyd. She looked cute despite not wanting to, despite the neglect that was written in her tangled hair, dirty jeans and gaunt cheeks.

It killed me to see those telling signs even after all the talks

I'd had with her mother, Farrah, but it didn't surprise me. The bitch was an addict of the highest order so even having two grown kids and a baby wouldn't stop her from sticking herself with needles and blowing herself high into the sky off of cocaine.

I was about to approach Harleigh Rose and tease her about not spending her Sunday at Mega Music, which is where I'd gone to look for her first because it was where you usually shot the shit when I was home from training. But there was something about her movements, too casual, too slow that made me pause and watch her from my position near the door to the gas station. I knew even before she took a handful of candy bars and stuffed them into the waistband of her jeans that she was going to shoplift.

My whole life I'd been observant, noticed people do things in the half second between the *tick* and *tock* of the clock, in the murky half-shadows of twilight and the dead hours of dawn that they thought they could get away with. Bad things, against-the-law things that I noted and felt no compunction about relating to the police.

I was the son of the Staff Sergeant for one.

For another, I was just that kind of man.

But for the first time in my life, seeing someone act illegally, I was torn.

I didn't want to turn Harleigh Rose in for the inconsequential theft of candy bars, not when I knew she was probably just hungry because Farrah had forgotten yet again to feed her kids.

I wasn't technically on Entrance's police force until I was sworn in next week, but it was still my civic duty to do something about witnessing a crime.

While I vacillated, my morals and emotions at war with themselves, the decision was taken out of my hands.

The cashier had noticed her too.

Who wouldn't notice a pretty kid with all that shining hair loitering around their shop?

"Hey kid," the teenage cashier called out.

Instantly, Harleigh Rose was running.

She was fast and agile so even when the teen lunged for her, she didn't look concerned or afraid.

Only determined.

She was coming right at the door, right next to me as I stood beside it.

It was my time to act, to snap forward and snare her while I could.

But her eyes hit mine as she barreled towards the glass door and they widened almost comically, an aquamarine color so opaque they looked like jewels. Still, she didn't miss a beat. She ran, her eyes on me, and I watched as she raised one brow in silent question.

You going to catch me?

I wanted to laugh at her aplomb. A ten-year-old asking a rookie cop if he was going to stop her from committing a crime, however insignificant?

Then, I wanted to laugh at myself. Rosie asking her Lion if he was going to let her get in trouble, however trivial the consequences of that may be?

I knew without consciously deciding which side would win.

Harleigh Rose breezed past me even as the cashier called out to me to stop her. I made a lame attempt and grabbing for her that I hoped would satisfy him. If her little giggle was anything to go by, it was enough to satisfy Harleigh Rose.

She was gone in the next second.

I dutifully followed the cashier out of the store, searching amid the gas pumps, around the building and at the edge of the trees behind the property for a glimpse of multicolored blond hair, but I knew we wouldn't, and we didn't, find her.

I talked the guy down from filing a formal complaint because everyone on the force new what the Garro kids looked like and they'd ID her in a heartbeat. Then I gave him ten bucks, more than enough to cover the cost of the five candy bars she'd stolen.

Harleigh Rose may have cut a hole through my moral fiber, but I wasn't going to let her rip it wide open.

So, I got in my car and went looking for her.

She was at the first place I stopped. Mega Music.

I heard the song before I even opened the glass door.

Dirty Deeds Done Dirt Cheap by AC/DC.

Again, I had to fight my amusement. No one spoke as eloquently through music as Harleigh Rose and she was only a kid.

"Thought you'd be by," Old Sam said as I entered and tipped my chin up at him.

I hesitated then changed my stride toward the back of the store where H.R. was to go to the counter where Old Sam sat on tall stood.

"What's going on with the Garros?"

The old man peered at me, the folds of skin over his eyes making it impossible to tell if he was even looking directly at me.

"Who's asking?"

"I think it should be obvious," I said slowly, wondering if he'd finally lost the plot. "Me."

"You *you* or you Danner?" he asked cryptically.

Unfortunately, I got him, and I felt rage rip up my back like gasoline lit flames. "I gotta prove myself to you again, Old Sam? You've known me since I was younger than Harleigh Rose. You make me answer that question, I guess we've got a different kinda relationship than I thought we did."

Old Sam chuckled then wheezed and coughed. "It's no wonder you and the princess get along so goddamn well. Both got a temper like *that*," he said with a snap of his fingers. "And both as loyal as all get out."

138

"So?" I asked, unimpressed with his test.

It wasn't the first time someone had forced me to assert myself as independent from my family, specifically my father, but it was only recently that I'd had inklings as to why that was.

Old Sam sobered with a dramatic sigh. "Thought things got better for a while there when Farrah shacked up with Jacob Yves, but then the baby was born with some kinda heart defect 'cause'a her drinkin' while she was pregnant and Jacob went nuts. He left her 'bout three months ago and took the baby. Motherfuckin' prick didn't think to take King an' Harleigh Rose though Lord knows they needed to go too. Since then, H.R. spends more time here than at home, and I hear King's at school 'til they lock it up at seven 'clock every night just to stay away."

I rubbed a hand over my face. "She still hitting them?"

He hesitated.

"Fucking tell me," I snapped. "You think I'll judge you for not doing something about it when for years I've wondered how you stood by and watch this happen? Yeah, it's too late for that, Old Sam. So, *tell me*."

"You don't know what you're talkin' 'bout boy," he said, but he didn't seem angry, only tired. "I call social services on Farrah, you know what happens? They take those kids away from Entrance and away from the possibility of being with their father again. So, they run away like they do, they come to my place and Millie and I take care'a them best we can."

"Okay," I said. "Okay, Old Sam, I get you. But something has got to change here."

"Zeus is up for parole in less than a year."

I nodded, then tilted my head when the music changed and "Hot Blooded" by Foreigner came on.

I rapped my knuckles on the counter as a thank you to Old Sam and then made my way back through the haphazard shelves to the back corner. Harleigh Rose was there sitting cross-legged on a stack of empty record sleeves eating a Snickers candy bar in a way that was hilariously defiant.

I was careful not to grin as I crouched down in front of her. She stared at me insubordinately and ripped off another huge chunk of chocolate covered candy.

"You know the difference between good and evil, Harleigh Rose?"

She tilted her head to one side and squinted at me, but didn't answer because she was smart enough to know she had no fucking clue.

"One has a conscious. See, good people don't abstain from doing bad things. Everyone makes mistakes, gives into temptations, lies, or even steals, but it's the good ones that know when the bad deed is done, there was something wrong in the doing of it. So, maybe the next time they face that crossroads between doing what they want despite the consequences—and Rosie, there are *always* consequence—and doing what they know is right, they make the right choice. At least the majority of the time."

"I'm too young to get a job," she said. "And mum never buys any groceries unless she's havin' a party like she is tonight, then all her friends eat the food 'cause we aren't allowed in the house when they hang out. Lots of times Bat and Trixie take me and King for dinner or give us some money for food, but Trixie just had twins, so they're too busy." She paused then looked up at me with her crazy bright blue eyes and said, "You weren't here, so what was I supposed to do?"

I rubbed at the flare of pain making itself known to the left center of my chest and tried to think of how to answer that question. I was only nineteen, I didn't have much of a wealth of wisdom and what I did have, I figured wouldn't be very applicable to a ten-year-old girl with chaos in her blood.

"First up, you call me. You know my number, you know if you need me, I'll come up from Vancouver and get you what you need, okay?" When she nodded, one of the dozen notes tied tight around my heart loosened. "You also call Bat, okay? Do you or King have a cell phone?"

"No, Daddy gave Mum the money to buy us one, but I think we both know where that went," she said casually, as if the fact that her mother chose to snort that money in the form of coke instead of providing for her children was normal behaviour.

I guessed for Harleigh Rose it was.

My chest constricted again.

"Okay, tomorrow I'll take you and King to the store and we'll get you one."

"King doesn't think we should hang out with you anymore," she told me.

It wasn't like I hung out with the Garro kids, but since their dad had been shot in front of H.R. years ago, I'd felt a certain responsibility towards them. With King, it was easy. Sometimes he'd walk by my parents' house on the way home from school and spot me in the garage, tinkering with my father's old 1968 Mustang Fastback. Even at eight and now twelve, the kid knew more about cars than I did so he'd roll up his sleeves and help out. With H.R., it was a little more complicated, mostly because she was a complicated kid. I'd spend a few hours with her every Sunday at Mega Music, but if Farrah was being a bitch, H.R. often ran away from home.

Straight to my house.

At first, I hadn't known what to do when I opened the door late one Thursday night to see her drowning in the rain, her face red from tears. Happily, my mum had.

My dad was a lot of things, most of them bad, but my mum was an angel.

So, without hesitation, she'd taken Harleigh Rose into our house, fed her, bathed her and put her to bed in the guest room beside their master.

We had a history, the Garros kids and me, but I was still surprised by how much it hurt to hear her say those words.

"'Cause you're a cop now, it's prob'ly bad for your reputation to be seen with bikers," she explained.

I blinked at her earnest expression then laughed. "You and King aren't bikers."

"No, but he's a biker-in-training and I'm a biker chick..." She shrugged. "And King just read this play by an old white guy about two families that hate each other. A kid from each family fell in love and they all ended up *dying* because they shouldn't'a been together in the first place."

I bit back the edge of my grin because I knew she didn't like it when it looked like I was laughing at her. "That's a play by Shakespeare called Romeo & Juliet. It's incredibly stupid."

"No *duh*," she told me with a big eye roll. "But still, you're Lion Danner of the Danners and I'm Harleigh Rose of The Fallen. Your people are cops and mine are bikers. Being friends doesn't make much sense."

God, but she was right.

As evidenced by my moral slip up today when I let her get away with shoplifting.

But I couldn't leave her and King to Farrah's devices, I just didn't have it in me. I liked them too much.

"Sometimes, opposites attract," I told her with a wink as I stood up and pulled her with me. "Now, come on. I've got a date tonight, and I want to talk to your mum when I take you home."

"A date?" she asked me and there was something in her tone that had me turning to face her again. She was looking at the ground, carefully making sure her feet didn't crunch any of the records on the floor. "Who would want to date you?"

"You're too young to understand, but trust me, when you're older you'll get that it's hard to find a nice, handsome guy who's also tall enough you can wear heels around him," I chuckled, because that was exactly what my date that night had told me when I'd asked her out last week.

Harleigh Rose stayed silent behind me.

AFTER WE PICKED UP KING FROM SCHOOL AND I'D TAKEN them to Stella's Diner to grab a quick dinner, I drove them home so I could have a word with Farrah. If that didn't work, as it hadn't before, I'd get my dad to pull her down to the station and have a word with her there.

I was thinking this in the silence of the car, both kids tense as they hadn't been all night knowing that I was taking them back to their mum. Harleigh Rose had tinkered with my iPod until "Sweet Child O' Mine" by Guns N' Roses came on, the lyrics filling the cab of my truck in a way that her voice couldn't.

The song painted a picture of Harleigh Rose with her sky-blue eyes huddled in a corner while her stupid mother shot up, wondering where else in the world was safe for her, if not her home?

I could barely breathe through the weight on my chest as I pulled onto their street and noticed a lineup of cars all around their little bungalow. The second I cut the ignition, I heard the music.

"Stay here," I told the kids as I unbuckled my seatbelt and opened the door.

I could smell the heady fragrance of marijuana in the air.

Fuck.

"You hear me?" I asked Harleigh Rose and King as they both looked at the house then back at me.

"Sure, Danny," King said with a firm nod as he climbed over the middle console to sit in my vacated driver's seat beside Harleigh Rose so he could take her hand in his.

The kid was twelve going on twenty.

I gave them a nod then made my way around the truck and up the gravel drive to the home. I could hear people partying in the back over the noise spilling out from the house and I was surprised the neighbors hadn't called the police.

The door was open when I tried it so I pushed in.

There were people everywhere in varying degrees of nudity. Two women writhed on the floor fully naked as they exchanged tokes of pot and blew the smoke into each other's mouths. Men were lining up to do lines of coke off some *very* young girl's ass and a couple was fucking in full sight of everyone else on the couch.

My fucking Christ, was this what King and Harleigh Rose were subjected to regularly?

I moved through the rooms, bile metallic on my tongue, my fists clenched so tight my short nails cut half-moons into my palms. I wanted to rip Farrah in two and grind her into dust so the Devil could snort her in Hell.

She wasn't anywhere.

I searched the house again, worrying about the kids in the car when there were people like these addicts, felons, and partiers so close by.

Still, I didn't find her.

Instead, when I entered the kitchen for the second time, I found Harleigh Rose standing in the midst of the revelry, her eyes trained on the hall like she'd been waiting for me.

"Rosie, what the hell? I told you to stay in the car," I growled as I pushed between another couple to get to her.

"I found her," she said, her voice dead like the tone of a heartbeat flatlining.

She took my hand and led me through the crowd, back down the hallway and into the master bedroom I'd already checked then behind a cloth partition I'd thought was decorative into a walk-in closet.

King was there too, crouched beside his mum with her head in his lap, but my eyes went to Farrah.

She was utterly still, her lips inked with blue at the edges, crusted vomit at her chin and cheeks.

She wasn't breathing.

Quickly, I shrugged off my jacket and went to my knees beside her body.

"King buddy, need you to take my phone out of my coat and call 911, okay?" I ordered him gently as I found Farrah's thready pulse and silently thanked God.

He didn't respond, but I heard the numbers being punched into the phone and then, "Hi, name's King. My mum had an overdose, need you to send the ambulance."

I grimaced as I used my sleeve to clear her mouth of vomit then tipped back her chin, pinched her nose and started to give her mouth-to-mouth.

At some point, I felt Harleigh Rose come to kneel beside me and place a soothing hand on my back, as if it was me that needed calming.

When the ambulance finally came, much quicker than I'd hoped because the neighbors had already called the cops, I stepped back from a comatose Farrah, collected an uncharacteristically subdued King and H.R. under my arm and watched the paramedics start to work on her.

"Where do we go now?" Harleigh Rose asked me quietly, her words harkening back to the song she'd chosen with eerie premonition in my truck.

I looked down into her face, in awe of her beauty given where she'd come from, what she'd experienced in this house of horrors, and I knew that no matter how strange it may seem, I'd do anything to protect her from further harm however immoral it may be.

I squeezed her shoulders as tears began to race down her cheeks and spoke before I'd even fully conceived of the idea, "You're both coming home with me."

CHAPTER TWELVE

Harleigh Rose

When I woke up, Danner was gone, but his iPod lay on the pillow beside me, a sticky note affixed to the screen that read:

MADE YOU A MORNING
PLAYLIST, LISTEN TO IT
WHILE YOU DRINK THE
COFFEE I MADE IN THE
KITCHEN. WHEN HERO
AND I GET HOME, WE'LL
MAKE YOU OUR SPECIALTY.

P.S. THE ALARM IS
ARMED, YOU'RE SAFE
OTHERWISE I WOULD'VE
LEFT THE DOG WITH YOU.

I smiled into the pillow, tracing my finger over his small, all-capital script, remembering the note he'd left me after my dad went to prison, remembering the many, many playlists we'd made each other over the years. I unlocked the iPod and opened the morning playlist, playing the first song there.

"Born to be Wild" blasted through the room.

I tipped my head back and laughed, loving that he could make me do so even after the horrible experience of the night before. Energized by my soundtrack, I slipped out of bed and danced into the bathroom, bobbing my head as I appropriated his toothbrush and washed my face.

By the time I hit the kitchen ZZ Top's "La Grange" was pumping out the surround system. I shimmied over to the coffee, kissed the Nespresso machine and slotted the mug Danner had left out for me under the spigot.

It read "feel safe at night, sleep with a cop."

I laughed knowing that he probably got it as a gag gift one Christmas and had never used it until he pulled it out for me that morning.

I was on my third cup of delicious, life-giving coffee reading the Globe & Mail newspaper and sitting at the island when the door opened, the alarm went off and my boys appeared.

Hero went right to me, jumping up to plant his paws on my thigh, but my eyes were fused to Danner.

There was a Canucks baseball cap on his head, shading the strong, sweat-slicked planes of his face and until that moment, I'd never known how sexy a cap could be. My eyes slid like one of the trickles of sweat down between his naked pectorals, keenly defined and dusted lightly in brown hair, to the neat boxes of muscles stacked like a ladder down his stomach leading to the hairier expanse of skin above his groin, framed by ridges of muscle that formed a deliriously sexy V. He was wearing grey sweatpants, hung low on his narrow hips to almost indecent levels, his boxers peeking just slightly above that, his feet sockless in black Nike sneakers.

I had a near-instantaneous orgasm at the sight of him.

Unaware of my lustful paralysis, Danner entered the code to stop the alarm, tossed his tee on the coffee table and headed my way with a small, sexy grin. He didn't stop until he literally hit my side, displacing Hero, his hands coming to either side of my face so he could run his thumbs over my cheeks and look deep into my eyes. Whatever he seemed to read there pleased me, because his smile widened a second before he slanted it over my mouth and kissed me.

I melted the second his mouth hit mine, his mouth cool and wet, his tongue silken against mine as he tilted my head to deepen the kiss and pressed his sweaty chest even tighter against my body. He ate my moan as I gave it to him then hummed his approval before breaking away from me.

"How's my thorny Rose this morning?" he asked, his eyes bright and carefree in a way I hadn't seen them since he was a teenager and I was just a girl.

I put my hand on the wrist of the hand he had on my face to orientate myself, dazed from our lip lock. "Huh?"

He chuckled, the feel of it against my nipples like a caress. "You look good. Like the sight of you in my stuff."

"Possessive," I noted, slightly surprised.

Danner didn't strike me as the caveman type of guy, one of those men who liked to lay claim to their women in every conceivable way, like my Dad had done with Lou.

He moved away, around the counter and pulled out two bowls then a couple of spoons in preparation for breakfast. "Got you tattooed over my heart, rebel girl. Don't know if it gets more possessive than that."

I realized that in my haze the night before, I hadn't really taken in his naked body, let alone the expanse of the tattoo that covered his entire left pectoral and up onto his shoulder. My eyes traced the intricate design as he leaned back against the counter and dropped his arms, giving me unobstructed access to it.

As Laken had described, it was a lion, exquisitely rendered mid-roar, fierce, proud and beautiful just like my human version. The animal burst forth from a thicket of wicked looking brambles and huge, gorgeously red roses, some furled and some spilled open into full bloom. It was the most beautiful tattoo I'd ever seen and all the brothers of The Fallen including my dad and brother had great ink.

"Yeah," I said, trying to downplay the way that tattoo made me feel, as if Danner had linked his heart to mine with ink and thought. "Guess not."

He reached into an open cupboard and grinned at me as he revealed a box of Cinnamon Toast Crunch. "My specialty."

I laughed, thrown back to the early mornings before school the ten months I spent living with the Danners in elementary school. On mornings that his mum, Susan, was busy with her charity work or shopping, Danner was in charge of making King and me breakfast. Cinnamon Toast Crunch was about the extent of his culinary prowess, so it was a good thing that both of us fucking love the stuff.

"My fav," I said as he slid a bowl drowned in milk over the counter to me and then took up a lean against the counter to eat his own portion.

"We should talk about a few things," he said, taking off his cap, tossing it to the counter and running a hand through the longer hair on the top of his head.

I tried to focus on what he was saying, but I gave myself a pass because any woman would drool over a man as ludicrously hot as Officer Danner.

"Talk?" I echoed lamely around a mouthful of cinnamon-y goodness.

He grinned. "If I'd known taking off my shirt was all it'd

take to make you docile, I'd've done it a long time ago, a helluva a lot more."

I glared at him and haughtily brought my mug of liquid heaven to my lips. "I just haven't had enough coffee yet this morning."

His eyes slid to the empty coffee pods strewn across the counter and then back to me, one eyebrow raised.

"Don't judge me," I warned him, which made his lips twitch. "Let's focus. What did you need to talk about?"

He sobered instantly, discarding his bowl of cereal and crossing his arms over his chest so that every muscle in his biceps bulged and glistened in the morning light.

I spoke into my mug before he could get started. "You want me to pay attention, I suggest putting a shirt on."

I smiled as I took a sip of coffee when he burst out laughing and stalked over to grab his discarded tee.

"Better?" he asked when the tight athletic shirt in a shade of green that exactly matched his eyes was glued to every inch of his beautiful body.

"No," I answered truthfully, but I waved the concern away with my hand. "Continue anyway."

"What happened last night, it's not going to happen again," he promised. "I called Sgt. Renner this morning and we're going to put a plainclothes officer on your apartment while you're at home. We've got the budget and thanks to that crap you pulled yesterday morning, you're worth it to the RCMP to keep alive so they're extending the funds to do it. You're also going to fucking obey me when I tell you to take Hero with you every-fuckin-where you go unless you're with me. He's a trained police and guard dog, Harleigh Rose, and he loves you. There aren't many situations he isn't an advantage in."

I chewed my lip, hating that I had to agree with him.

He continued despite my lack of agreement. "I'm really fucking unhappy with that stunt you pulled offering up your services as a fucking C.I. but now you've done it, there are some rules."

"They went over those with me," I interrupted, only to receive a glacial look from Danner.

"Yeah, they went over *their* rules, but you'll see Rosie, I got rules of my own. The most important of those being, you do not, under any circumstances, go off half-cocked without me. You understand? I know you're dead set on endin' this club for a variety of reasons I won't argue aren't valid, but you don't know shit about police work and that same passion that got you into this could end up ruining this investigation."

"I'm not a dumbass, Danner," I snapped.

"No one said you were. What I *did* say was that you got a tendency to go off half-cocked when you get your teeth into something big. Don't do that."

I glared at him. He stared impassively back.

"There goes my good morning," I muttered, staring into my empty coffee cup. "I need more coffee."

"You'll get an ulcer the way you drink that stuff," he told me as he walked to the other side of the counter, planted a forearm into it and leaned over to palm the back of my head. "And you'll still have a good morning, Rosie. We just haven't got to the good part, yet."

"Uh huh, sure."

He bit the corner of his grin. "You wanna get there, tell me you'll stick with me in this, okay? I need to know you're safe or I'll do stupid shit I don't need to do to make sure of it."

"Like what?" I asked, perking up with curiosity.

It didn't say good things about me that I loved when he was stupid for me, even more when he did bad for me.

"Like never leave your side."

"Oh."

"Yeah, now be good for me and say you get me."

I wanted to. God, I wanted to.

But the asshole had left me for three years without so

much as a fuckin' goodbye. How the hell was I supposed to trust him?

"Left me once, Danner. No reason, no fuckin' explanation. You think I'm goin' to trust a guy who could do that?"

"Trusted yourself with a guy that beat you," he snapped back, cruel with sudden anger. "You know I'd never do that. You fucking know if I left without sayin' goodbye it was for a good fucking reason."

"There is no reason on this goddamn planet to abandon your family," I shot back, standing up in my rage so I could snarl over the counter at him.

"What the hell do you call what you want to do now? Isolating yourself from The Fallen?"

"I'm doing it for *them*," I yelled, throwing my mug of coffee across the room because my anger had no eloquence and I needed him to understand. "I'd do anything to keep them safe."

"You think I don't feel the same fucking way about you?" he challenged, unfazed by the crash and clatter of the mug or the shards of it all around him. "I'd break my own heart a million times over if it meant keeping you alive."

He stormed over to where I stood panting, and wrapped a hand firmly around my throat, thumb over my pulse. It was such a dominant move, one that instantly made me weak in the knees and weak of resolve.

I was a badass biker chick, but I wanted to submit to him as he was now, transformed by anger and need into an alpha so dominant he demanded my obedience.

Only for him had I ever felt that desire, and only for him would I ever give in to it.

"I've been savin' you since you were six-years-old, Rosie," he said, eyes blazing. "I've done it again and again even when it meant going against what I stood for because in the end, what I stood for was you, safe and happy after all the shit you've been dealt. If I left you, you think it was for any other reason than that?"

"How am I supposed to know when you never explained it to me," I countered, leaning against his hand at my throat so it tightened like a collar against a rabid dog, so I felt leashed by him in a way that made me wet. "How am I supposed to ever know how you feel when you've never fucking told me?"

"Maybe you haven't been takin' notice, but I told you every time I played music for you, every time I hung out with you at Mega Music, and every time I stayed home as a young guy to look after you and King. I told you when I bought you that bike you wanted with fucking pink skulls on it and when I took you to pick out Hero and name him. That's not enough for you, I told you when I picked up your call, havin' kept that old phone for the sole reason that I wanted to have it in case you called, and dropped fucking everything to risk my under-cover cop and rush to your side."

He bent closer, his lips against mine. "You need more, I'll tell you now. You said you don't abandon family and that may be true, but you're doin' it now because your family needs that and I did it then to you because you needed it, even if you didn't know it. Wasn't right that our friendship was turning into something physical, not when you were a teenager, not when I am the way I am."

"And I didn't get a say in that?"

"No, Rosie, you didn't. Because whether you like it or not, I was the adult and you were the kid. We don't come from the same side of the law and more, our fathers would kill each other if they could. Anything romantic was, and is, impossible."

"So, you left," I whispered, hurt and so angry, lost again like I had been at eighteen when he'd left.

"I did, not saying now I know what that did to you, turning you to Cricket like it did, that I would do the same now. Maybe I could've found the strength to keep my hands off you and still protect you from all the ugly in the world. But I didn't, and Cricket's death is just as much on me as it is you."

"Yeah," I told him, because I was honest and it was true. "It is."

I'd been with Cricket to fill even a fraction of the void Danner left behind and after a year, when he still hadn't returned, I decided having any kind of love was better than having nothing at all.

"Not gonna leave you again," he told me sternly, in a voice low, smooth and dark as smoke curling around my body. "Swearing it right now."

"Don't know if I believe you," I countered.

"Don't fucking care, I'll prove it like I've proved it before. I'll show you."

"You get me?" he demanded.

"I get you," I breathed, then remembered myself, swallowed my instinctive willingness and rolled my eyes. "If you get on the same page as me, we shouldn't have any problems anyway."

The tendons in his neck were straining in a way I was trying not to find delicious. I wanted to focus on my anger, demand to know why he had left me. But now that I'd had those wide palmed, rough tipped hands on my body, I wanted more.

I wanted to gorge myself on his body until I had my fill so I could finally get Lion Danner out of my fucking system.

"You gonna keep your hands off me while you're protecting me?" I asked, licking my lips at the thought of that gorgeous body back on mine.

He ignored the last bit of my statement and shifted his grip so his hand cradled the side of my neck. "That brings us to the good stuff. We started something last night. Actually, we started something about three and a half years ago when you were still too young, but we picked up the thread last night and I don't mean to let it go again if I can help it. We've got to go slow, be careful, because our lives depend on it, Rosie. First sign of trouble, if I've got to leave you to keep you safe, I will. Do you understand that?"

The warmth of his declaration froze in my veins. "No. You just said you want to be with me. I've wanted you for fucking years. You can't say that shit one second and then take away from me the next. You're either with me or you aren't."

His jaw clenched, and his hand tightened hard in my hair. "I'm with you until being with you threatens to harm you, Harleigh Rose. You can fucking give me that."

I threw up my hands, wrenching my head out of his hold. "I can't believe you'd ruin the first time you've ever admitted you wanted me by being a fucking coward about it."

"Coward?" Danner said, his voice octaves lower, cold and heavy like the weight of steel shackles against me. "Wanting to keep you safe is cowardly?"

Hurt that he'd ever even consider leaving me after every-thing we'd been through, after I'd made it clear in actions if not in words how much I needed him, burned through my insides like lava wrecking ruin over Pompeii.

I got into his face and hissed, "Yeah, Danner. You care about someone you don't let them go in the face of a threat, you hold them tight, keep them safe and warm through the storm and hope to fucking God or whoever the fuck else that you *both* get out of it alive."

Danner stood there, implacable as a stone statue, his eyes darkly shuttered as I finished my tirade and breathed heavily into the silence.

"You obey me, Rosie," he repeated, this time in the dark tone that sent shivers down my spine. "You obey me in the field, and we do this, you obey me in bed, on the couch, in the back of my 'Stang, where I decide to fuck you. You want this, those are *my* rules."

"You want me to submit," I said, knowing that as I'd

known it when he'd taken me over his knee when I was seventeen.

"Fuck, *yeah*," he growled, his fingers fisting at the back of my hair and tugging so I was forced back, looking up into his cruelly handsome face. "This is the game we're gonna play, rebel. You can sass me, fight me and disagree with me all day long. It's you, and fuck knows, I like that. But now, when I've got my hands on your body, I'm your Dominant, and if you want my cock, you'll fucking well have to earn it by being my good girl instead of my rebel one."

Each of his filthy words piled like kindling in my gut, but there was a small part of me still that told me giving in was wrong, weak in the way of Berserker biker women who let themselves be used by their men.

"Why do I want this?" I whispered, clamping my hand over his on my neck. "It doesn't seem natural. I'm not that kinda woman."

"You meet me, you think I'm the kinda guy that wants to spank naughty teens and fuck them so hard they scream?" he asked bluntly. "No. Took me a long time to learn it, but I'm gonna teach you. There's only strength in submission, only care in Domination. We do what we do because we get off on it and we leave it mostly in the bedroom. You can still be badass little rebel Rose, and I can still be good guy Danner."

His free hand moved to cup me between my legs, over my shamefully wet panties. "But we'll both know the truth. It may be your body, Harleigh Rose, but *I* own it."

Then he kissed me.

I softened in his arms like melting butter until only his hands at my neck and over my pussy kept me upright.

He tasted good, like coffee and cinnamon and *man*.

I clung to him and opened my mouth farther so he could kiss me harder.

"Gonna take you, Rosie," he told me against the skin of my neck, his tongue licking over my throbbing pulse. "Gonna tame you, leave you just wild enough to fight back against every touch, buck back against every thrust of my big cock in your tight, wet cunt."

I groaned, my nails raking over his tee covered back. "Yes, fuck me."

His fingers rubbed over the cloaked placket of my panties then slipped underneath to run between my silky folds. "That's it, Rosie. So wet for me."

His thumb found my swollen clit, wrenching a gasp from me.

"I want to play," I panted. "I want you to play with me."

He grinned. "Did my naughty girl do some research after I played with her years ago?"

"Yes," I hissed as he sunk two fingers into my molten core.

"You ever played before?" There was a sharp edge of jealous that ran like a knife point through my leashed inhibitions.

I loved him jealous, I loved him mad with desire in a way I knew instinctively only I could make him be.

"No, but I thought about it every night when I lay in bed touching my cunt, thinking about you inside me, your fingers, your cock, your tongue."

"You want me to make you break for me," he said, his voice sinking into that low octave I remembered, that one that tied me with rough ropes to his will. "You want me to earn your submission."

My legs wobbled and the next instant I was on the counter, my legs spread wide by his palms so he could look down at my pussy. When he looked up at me again, his eyes were torches.

"I'll play with you, I'll even break you open with pleasure until you sob my name, but when you do Rosie, you call me by my name."

"Yes, Danner," I breathed, desperate for his touch on my cooling, exposed cunt.

He lashed out with one hand and spanked my pussy *hard*.

I cried out and tried to close my legs, but he held them open with his biting grip, leaned over and blew chilled air against my stinging clit before sucking it into his mouth for a full, wet kiss. When he straightened, his lips were wet with me and his eyes were ice cold against my heated skin.

"You say my name," he repeated.

I swallowed my instant resistance. It was a defense mechanism I'd honed well over the years, throwing sassy shields to hide my vulnerabilities.

I didn't want to hide them from him, not anymore.

So, I tipped my chin and looked him right in his blazing, beautiful green eyes as I said, "Yes, Lion."

He moaned raggedly, reached forward and twisted the tips of each breast with his hand before giving them both a sucking kiss that arrowed heat straight to my clit.

"I could keep you here like this all day. My good little whore presenting herself. I'd eat you for breakfast, torture you for lunch and then, when you were starved for it, I'd fuck you all through dinner and gift you my cum for dessert," he told me almost conversationally as his hand played with my pussy, his thumb rubbing hot, tight circles over my swollen clit, two of his fingers twisted and pumping inside.

I loved how he played with me, as if I was an object that existed only for his pleasure. It should have felt wrong, maybe even degrading, but it didn't because Danner was playing me the way he played his guitar, masterfully, removed only because he needed the focus to strum every string just right.

"Are you on birth control?"

I nodded, desperate for the feel of him bare inside me. "Yeah, and, sucks to say, but I got tested after Cricket and I'm clean," I told him.

His smile made the pain of the memory disappear like a phantom. "Never fuck without a condom, haven't touched anyone in weeks. You trust me?"

I didn't have to think. "Yes, always."

I moaned when he moved away, but he only smiled a cruel little smile that touched me like his mouth to my pussy and moved away. I watched with low lidded eyes as he pulled open a drawer filled with plastic bags, rubber bands, clothes pins and other catch-all materials.

"What are you doing?" I questioned.

He quelled me with a single, displeased glare.

I chewed on my lip as he moved back to me, his hands behind his back until he fell into a crouch and revealed a zip tie in one hand. He watched my eyes widen, my chest heave as he slowly bound my left ankle to the drawer of one cabinet and then the right to another. I could see the intent in his eyes, the gleam of wickedness and satisfaction that I was open and secured for him.

He watched his fingers trail up my ankle, tingling over the skin of my calf, a lazy circle around my knee cap and up over the thin skin on the inside of my thigh. When he reached the bare lips of my sex, his fingers danced over them up to the small rectangle of hair over my clit and then he tugged it sharply between his knuckles. My hips jerked forward, my head tipped back, and I panted at the perverse pleasure to be had in that pain.

"This is a game of Dominance and submission, Rosie," he told me, pinching my chin lightly with one hand as the other hand moved to cover my cunt. It was a possessive gesture, holding me there, his fingers gentle but firm as if it was his pussy to do what he wanted with. I tried to gyrate against him, get any kind of pressure on my aching clit but he stopped me by sinking two fingers into my sex and curling up, pinning my pussy from the inside out in a move that made me melt in his hand.

"And it's a game we've been playing with each other for a very long time. Only now, it's sexual and I need you to understand the difference. This isn't about pain," he told me even as he plucked at my nipples and made me hiss. "It isn't about you blindly obeying my every command because you feel you have to. It's about you giving me your trust, knowing that I arouse you and abuse you with my body, with my words and with my toys not to hurt you, but to *own* you so I can banish everything from your head—all the bad, all the worry and dread—and bring you peace."

Tears hurtled to my eyes and prickled in my nose. It was embarrassing to feel so emotional when he had his hand in me, when we were talking about something as simple as sex.

But it didn't feel simple. It felt like he was offering me dreams I'd never been able to voice, offering to take me to a place I'd never even be able to picture in my head.

It felt like he was going to guide me to a place where I could learn to love myself.

"Do you understand what I'm saying?" he asked, and I focused back on his face to find it hard with resolve, his mouth soft with desire and his eyes, his greener than freshly watered grass eyes were filled with love.

"Yes, Lion," I said.

His brows slammed down over his gaze, transforming his face with gorgeous intensity a second before he fisted the hand at my face in the back of my hair, tugged me back and crashed his demanding mouth to mine.

Instantly, my mind went blank.

There was nothing to me but my lips on his, the warm, wet slide of his tongue in my mouth and the way his stubble rasped over my cheek, his lean hips between my lewdly spread legs, his hand working between, in and out of my cunt, twisting, curling, turning until every inch of me sung with pleasure.

"So wet for me," he groaned into my ear then traced his tongue around the shell of it. I shuddered when he bit the lobe and scraped his teeth over it. "So willing to let me play with your gorgeous body."

"God," I groaned as he sunk his teeth into the strong cords

of my neck, working his way with soft nips and firm bites to the junction of my neck and shoulder where he bit so hard and sucked so long it was pure exquisite agony. I knew he was marking me, that I'd wear his love and ownership inked in the bruise for days afterwards. It was a dangerous badge of possession I would wear with pride, that I fucking *loved* because he did it out of madness, not logic, not as he usually did.

In that way, it said he was as much mine as I was his.

His lips trailed down to my chest, where he kissed around my left nipple in smaller and smaller circles without hitting the target. I tangled my hands in his hair and forced his mouth to me.

I cried out when he grabbed my hand in one of his, the grip firm, his eyes their own reprimand as he said, "No. You do as I say or nothing at all. Hands behind your back or I'll tie them there."

I thought for one brief, giddy second of disobeying him and then did as I was told. The flash of admiration in his eyes as he took in my lifted breasts, my willing movement, was better than any act of willful disobedience.

"I'm not going to stop. I'm not going to show you mercy. You can beg, but I won't be moved. I won't slow or give you pause so you can catch your breath. As soon as I put my hands on your body, you are my instrument to play. And I'm tellin' you right now, Harleigh Rose, I plan to play you all day long, until your strings are frayed and your tones are harsh as fuck coming outta that dirty mouth. Your pretty pink cunt is going to be swollen and weepin' when I finally pull my fingers and cock out and even then, I'm warnin' ya, I'll be makin' you sleep all night with one of my toys in your aching pussy so you feel me even in your dreams."

God, that sounded like a dream.

"Fuck me," I begged him.

He didn't answer, but he didn't have to. Instead, he slid his grey sweats down his thighs, revealing his long, curved cock.

"You want this?" he taunted, wrapping his fist around it so he could jerk himself off.

"Yes, give it to me."

"You think you can handle it?" he taunted, his eyes dark, feral.

"Try me," I challenged.

Then his cock was at my pussy driving forward in one brutal, delicious thrust.

"Fuck!" I cried out as he pulled out then slammed back in, setting a brutal pace that set my tits jiggling and my eyes rolling into the back of my head. "Fuck me."

One hand wrapped around my lower back to bring me close while the other arrowed up my chest to my throat where he squeezed.

"Take me," Danner growled as he pounded into me, as he clenched his hand around my neck in time with the brutal strokes of his cock. "And come for me."

Thirty seconds later, I did.

I exploded like shrapnel, pieces of myself flying in every direction, the explosion emanating from my wet pussy and travelling all the way through my body.

"Yeah," Danner groaned into my neck as he finally let go of my throat and planted a kiss there. "Now take my cum."

"Yes, Lion, give it to me." I panted when I felt the first kick of his cock and the resulting warmth in my pussy.

He sighed when we were through, collecting me gently against him the way I'd seen him do with his guitar, gently, deferentially.

"How was that, Rosie? You were such a gorgeous good girl for me."

I shivered at the praise, at the feeling of his cock still inside me, his hard-sweaty body against my own.

It was something I'd wanted for so long yet the reality was

so much more beautiful than the fantasy. I could smell his earthy scent, taste the salt of him in my mouth and feel the warmth of him between my legs. I could feel how *mine* he was.

"Loved it," I breathed then because it felt so fucking good to say, I added, "Love you."

Danner leaned back to smile in my face at the same time a pounding knock sounded on the front door.

We froze for one long suspended moment, insects caught in amber.

Then the knocking came again, louder this time and accompanied by Grease's voice calling, "Yo fuckhead, wake up and open the fuckin' door it's hot as a stripper's tits out here."

We jerked into action simultaneously. Danner reached for a knife lying on the counter and made quick work of cutting me from the zip ties before we dashed apart to pull on our clothes.

"Linen closet," he mouthed at me before calling out, "Yeah, yeah hold onto your panties, I'm comin'."

"You have a linen closet?" I asked before I could help myself.

But come on, my hot cop slash sexy undercover biker had a fucking linen closet? Fuck, I barely even knew what constituted *linens*.

"Just get the fuck in there," he ordered softly, harshly then tagged my hand as I moved away to press a hard kiss to my mouth. "Be quiet and stay there until I get you."

I nodded and dashed away to the closet midway between the bedroom and the living area, thankful when I opened it that there was a narrow space beside the shelves I could tuck my slim, straight form into with relative ease.

Two seconds after I closed the closet door, the front one opened and the heavy stomp of motorcycle boots sounded in the hall.

"Good, you're up," Grease grumbled.

"Yeah, brother, though you're knocking woulda done the job I was still asleep."

"Got shit to do today, need all hands-on-deck." A pause then an incredulous, "Eatin' kid cereal?"

"Got a sweet tooth and I like some spice," Danner admitted in a way that made me smile even through my fear.

"Well don't mind if I help myself while you put some fuckin' clothes on. Just 'cause you're some kinda pretty boy don't mean you can just go 'round not wearin' nothin'."

"Aye, aye, Serge," Danner said. "What's the gig?"

"We're goin' after a delivery of Fallen grass."

I felt the air compress out of my lungs.

"You shittin' me?" Danner asked, sounding mildly curious, but still down for it.

It was crazy how good he was at acting the part.

"Nah, got some intel a few boys are running some shit down the Sea to Sky tonight for a big party the Red Dragons are throwin'. We're gonna take it. If those Asian fucks really did do in Cricket, it'll be good to have The Fallen lookin' at them as shady fucks to distract 'em from the fact we're goin' strike them soon's the opportunity comes."

"And it's just a bonus that we'd get grade A marijuana in the process."

"You betcha. And you know the Prez, anythin' to poke at big bad Zeus Garro, ya know?"

"Sure. Give me a sec and I'll get dressed."

I heard Danner's step pass by as he went into the back bedroom and then listened closely to the sounds of Grease rustling through a few drawers, snooping because it was in his nature to be distrustful and because he relished any opportunity to find a brother wanting so he could enact revenge.

Once, he'd made a car bomb that took out a brother they suspected of snitching and his entire family, including their toddler and dog.

I tried to regulate my breathing as panic seized me then

tried to stop breathing altogether as the thud of Grease's boots moved closer and suddenly he was at the closet door.

I squeezed my eyes shut and held perfectly still, but for my madly pounding heart.

"Ready," Danner called out from the mouth of the hall and the feet shadowing the crack under the door shifted away from me.

I let out a slow, quiet stream of air and felt grateful I hadn't peed my panties.

"Let's head," Danner said as he walked by and clapped a hand over Grease's back.

I waited for what seemed like fifteen minutes after they left until I let myself out of the closet and scuttled back into Danner's bedroom. There was a burner phone on the basin in the bathroom and a note written in condensation on the mirror, the sink plugged and filled with steaming hot water.

Don't tell your father.

CHAPTER THIRTEEN

Harleigh Rose

I DOLLED MYSELF UP BIKER-STYLE, BIG HAIR, BLACK EYELINER, tight jeans with huge rips strategically placed right where my ass cheeks met my thigh, exposing the white fishnets I wore underneath, and my habitual black combat boots, before heading to the Berserkers compound.

I wasn't going off half-cocked like Danner had warned me not to do. I was just doing some gentle recon.

If Danner thought I could sit back while the club attacked my family, he didn't know me very well.

I parked my custom black Mercedes G65 in the gravel lane beside the clubhouse, taking a second to let the familiar sounds of AC/DC's "TNT" wash over me. It was my dad's favourite band, one of our favourite songs by the band, and sitting there in the car he'd built and customized for me, I felt closer than I had to him in weeks.

I was my father's daughter.

I'd been born that way then forged further into his image by the fire of trials I'd undergone in my formative years. It was a good likeness, one I was secretly proud to have more of than King, but for the first time in my life even after everything he'd done for us, I understood the incredible responsibility Dad must have felt knowing he had the power to keep us safe and happy.

Now, I yielded the same power, and I wanted to be strong enough, Zeus enough, to carry the weight of it through to the bitter end.

It was quiet when I made my way into the old Tudor house, not surprised given it was eleven o'clock on a Sunday and that was early as fuck by biker standards. I went directly to Reaper's office at the back of the house, hoping I could impose on him under the ruse of needing guidance after Cricket's death. Reaper was the kind of man that liked to hear his own voice and dole out wisdom like some kind of false prophet so I knew he'd be down.

Giggles emerged from behind the slightly open door, raspy feminine sounds that reminded me of the long-forgotten sound of my mother's own silly laugh.

Still, I knocked on the door because Reaper wouldn't have a problem sending away one of his many women if it meant some one on one time with me. I'd never been sure why, but the man not only coveted me, I think he truly loved me (as much as his black heart could) almost like a daughter.

"Yeah?" he called out, laughter in his gruff voice.

"'S me!" I hollered. "You got a second?"

There was conspicuous silence and then another husky giggle.

"Sure, babe, give me a second and I'll getcha."

I leaned against the wall across from the door and

unwrapped a square of Hubba Bubba before popping it into my mouth. There wasn't a huge likelihood of Reaper being loose-lipped about his plans to steal The Fallen's cache, but I figured I could at least find out what time they planned to meet and then maybe trail them from the clubhouse...

The door opened, Reaper's stocky frame taking up the entire width but not much of the length in the frame.

"Come in, girl," he said with a smile.

With a smile. Reaper Holt was not the kind of man who smiled easily and the sight of it stretching his pocked, bulbous features into some semblance of joy sent an echo of unease through the pit of my belly.

I followed him into the room, studying his face for some clue as to what had changed in his life to take him from ruthless curmudgeon to happy bastard when the scent hit me. The cloying sweetness of cheap, sugary perfume scored by the harsh char of cigarette smoke.

Then the laugh came again, sandpaper in the air, rough against my ears.

I knew before I turned to look at Reaper's desk who would be standing beside it.

My mum.

I hadn't seen Farrah more than twice in the ten years since the Danners took me in and then Dad got out of prison and made us a home again. Once had been when I was sixteen and she'd approached me at school, asking for money, the next and last had been when I ran into her on the street on a trip to Vancouver on my eighteenth birthday. She'd looked right through me.

The intervening years had taken their toll on her once considerable beauty. There were hard brackets around her thinned mouth, folds in her cheeks and beside her eyes that sagged slightly, her skin too loose and slightly waxen from the abuse she'd put her body through over the ages. Her hair was dyed the normal shade of bottle blond, her breasts were still big and fake but drooping in her slack skin, her chest marked with sun spots and moles. She was wearing tight jeans, biker chick boots and a low halter neck crop top that gave evidence to the fact that she may have looked about fifteen years older than her forty years, but her body was still good enough to pull off the trashy look at least relatively well.

It was her eyes though, that got me. They were the same bright tropical ocean blue as my own, the same wide, round shape and curly lashes. Only hers were filled with spite and bitterness that tarnished the edges like aged copper.

"Harleigh baby, Mummy's home," she cried dramatically, flinging her arms wide to invite me into her embrace.

I stayed where I was. "Mum, what are you doing here?"

Reaper chuckled with manly satisfaction and went over to wrap a meaty hand around her hip like a proud partner. "Farrah here's my new old lady."

"What the fuck happened to Jade?" I asked.

That old bitch wasn't the warmest woman in the world, but she was Madonna compared to Farrah. She'd also been through a lot sticking by Reaper's side, dozens of affairs and at least a dozen bastard children besides, I couldn't see her giving up her position without a fight.

Farrah waved her hand, her bedazzled bangles clinking. "Oh, that old bitch had to go. Don't worry about her."

I hadn't inherited my love of biker babes from my mother. She hated anyone with a vagina, specifically if that vagina was prettier than her or had something she didn't.

God, looking at her I was reminded that half of my DNA was formed from pure evil and I cut myself some slack for my not infrequent bad behaviour. It was only natural given my origins.

"Why aren't you greetin' your mama, girl?" Reaper asked, a frown crashing down over his features and setting me at ease again.

I did as I was told, moving forward to be enveloped in her

heavily perfumed arms. "Hey, Mum."

"Better," she whispered in my ear before smacking her lips in a loud ear kiss that almost made me deaf on the left side. "I knew you'd be happy to see me. The Maycomb women back together again."

I was no Maycomb. I never had been.

I was a Garro through to the marrow of my fucking bones.

But I'd play this game if she wanted to.

I perched on the edge of a chair, settling in. "So, how'd you two meet?"

"Met her 'fore your fuckin' dad did, babe," Reaper told me. It was obvious he hated that, that he had counted the minutes of difference between Zeus meeting her and him doing it, that he blamed the sixteen minutes as the reason they hadn't been together all these years.

Interesting.

Reaper had a lifelong hard-on for my mum.

Disgusting.

But useful.

I knew by the way Farrah's smile slithered across her red painted lips like a snake in the grass that she knew this to be useful as well.

"Ran into her at a bike show a few weeks ago. She gave me the runaround, but fuckin' got her in the end," he ended on a roar of laughter as he pinched her ass and she playfully slapped at him.

Gag me with a fucking gun.

"How nice," I said mildly instead.

"It's good to finally be with the man I should have had all along," Farrah preened, placing her hand on Reaper's bloated chest. "Now we can be a family again."

"And King?"

She made a face. "He chose your father, but then again, he never had your brains, did he?"

She was right, he didn't, he was *much* smarter than me.

"What about Honey?" I asked.

Farrah waved her hand again. "The little shit runs off sometimes, ungrateful girl, but she'll come back. She always does."

That "ungrateful girl" should've been in high school, not getting hooked on drugs and having sex on camera. Fury coursed through my blood so hot I felt like I glowed with it.

"Was tellin' your mum how proud she'd be to know you been with us for a solid three years, first with Cricket, RI-fuck-ing-P, now with my brother, Wrath."

He was proud of me for that, his chest puffed out, his cheeks ruddy with the force of his own compliment. In another life, a lesser one, without Dad and Danner and King, I wondered if I would have been weak enough to fall under his spell.

Pride was no equal alternate for love.

"He thinks you're loyal enough to know our plans for your daddy's club," Farrah sing-songed, her fingers walking a path over Reaper's chest and down. "I'm not so sure."

I shrugged as if I couldn't have cared less when really, bile was biting metallic teeth at the back of my tongue. "I don't need to prove anything to you, Farrah. At this point, Reaper is more my parent than you are."

I saw my volley score two points, one in the cruel twists of Farrah's lips, and the other in the shocked look of pleasure shown by the Prez.

Yeah, two could play at this game, bitch.

"We're going after The Fallen cargo tonight," she snapped, her patience gone. "What do you have to say about that?"

I shrugged again and looked at the chipped black nail polish on my fingers. "That's club business. You're new around here, but that kinda stuff stays between brothers. It's not my shit to disturb."

Reaper chuckled and when Farrah shot him a look he shrugged. "Told you she'd say that, sugar lips. Give the girl a break. Why don't you go get us some beers so we can celebrate this reunion fuckin' proper-like."

Farrah pursed her lips before her entire expression transformed into the perfect doting girlfriend. "Sure thing, Reaper honey."

As soon as she was out the door, I raised a brow and said, "Really?"

Reaper guffawed, moving around his desk to sit down in his big leather chair. "Sucks better 'an a Hoover and swallows too."

A full body shiver of violent disgust rocked me and I let out a little gag. "Fuck me for asking, eh?"

He laughed again then sobered. "You know not to screw us tonight, H.R.? You're the Berserker princess now, not part of them Fallen and I won't have you tippin' them off to the ambush off exit 78."

I stared at him for a long minute, watching as he stroked his mustache and kicked his dirty boots onto the top of his desk. There was absolutely no way, no matter how much he may have liked me, that he would give me the exact location of their heist unless he was testing me.

Which meant I couldn't save the club of my heart from the club of my present. Which meant, if Dad or King ever found out, they'd never forgive me for putting brother's lives in danger when I could have saved them.

My good intentions were quickly drowning in a riptide, waterlogged with impossible questions, choking on moral ambiguity as difficult to digest as ocean waves.

There was no clean way out of the situation. No matter what happened in the end, my family wouldn't trust me and my life might still be very much in danger.

I breathed deeply, filled my eyes to the brim with sincerity and told Reaper the truth, "I won't fuck up."

CHAPTER FOURTEEN

Danner

It was ironic that I'd only ever become involved in the biker life because it was my mission to dismantle it. There wasn't even a reason for my hatred of biker gangs, just something written in the code of my DNA, passed to me by my father and his father's father all the way back to the founding of the mother Fallen chapter in 1960. There had to be some twisted connection between one of my ancestors and the Garros, some illicit romance gone awry, a metal and chrome Romeo & Juliet killed in a hail of rival gunfire, the Mercutio equivalent downed by a blade and a man in the wrong leather cut. It was a romantic way to think about what I grew up believing to be my destiny, but I'd yet to see spilled blood for what it really was, just blood, just death smeared over pavement, guts trailing, brains splotched like ink blotches. There was nothing romantic in death, and nothing beautiful about my automatic hatred of an entire group of human beings.

But I didn't learn that until later.

175

Until Harleigh Rose showed up in a record store wearing a kid-sized AC/DC shirt and listening to Johnny Cash as if he spoke directly to her through the record player. It wasn't until I saw her plight, saw how *un*romantic the reality of their situation with their drug addict mother was, and how deeply wonderful she and her brother were as people that I began to reconsider how my system was programmed.

That I began to hack my Danner influenced mind and started to go from my traditional idea of good to one that was bad.

Therein lay the irony, because the more 'corrupt' I was in my father's own contemptible eyes, the stronger I felt, coated in titanium conviction and brassy with confidence in my own grey shaded principles.

Who would have ever guessed that a cop playing a biker to take down an MC would become seduced by the very lifestyle he was supposed to condemn?

I loved the freedom of the oceanside wind against my chest as I soared over the road straddling a metal beast that felt like one of my mustang horses, feeling the wildness of her in the vibration beneath my ass, in the weight of her power under my gloved hands.

Riding a bike never failed to make me hard as steel because it reminded me of the way Harleigh Rose would feel when I finally fucked her. All that power and untamed beauty required skilled hands and a firm touch to keep under control. I was Dominant, so both were exactly the kind of challenge I relished.

I focused on the road again when Wrath dropped his speed to slide into formation beside me where I rode gunner in our six man convoy up the Sea to Sky Highway. I looked over at him at the same time my phone rang in my leather cut.

"Yeah?" I answered over the Bluetooth in my helmet.

"You stick with me and keep your trap shut as in don't

repeat a fuckin' word of what's goin' to go down tonight. You get me?" Wrath's low rumble sounded over the speaker.

Curveball.

Interesting.

I'd been trying to evaluate whether or not Wrath Marsden could be turned into a confidential informant two out of the three years I'd been working undercover for the MC.

He'd never given me any indication he could be turned away from Reaper and Grease. Ever.

Until now.

I wondered how much that had to do with his new relationship with Harleigh Rose and rage burned in my gut like one too many shots of whiskey. It was hypocritical as shit, considering I was technically dating two women, one as a cop and one as a biker.

It was only Harleigh Rose I wanted with every multifaceted part of me. As a man elementally, powerfully could want a woman, to cherish her, guard her and plant his babies in her.

She hadn't mentioned Laken or Diana Casey with me though and I had the feeling that they didn't matter to her. She was just that sure of herself, of the effect she had on me, and she wasn't wrong.

I obsessed with dominating every inch of her life. I wanted to bend her with my hands, break her into beautiful pieces with my cock and then glue her back together with my mouth. Cut through the thicket of dangerous thorns surrounding her gorgeous, one-of-a-kind heart, so that I could hold the tender, fragile bud in my hand and watch it grow. Dominate her mind, body and soul until every molecule of her person was imprinted with my name.

I wasn't sure when it had happened, when I'd tipped over from a familial protector into the more dangerous role of forbidden lover, but it could have been the night she spied on me jacking off when she was sixteen. It was as if a flip switched in my bestial brain, and she was suddenly a *woman*, ripe with curves and sultry with sexual intent aimed at me.

I'd honed my moral code against the corruption of my father's greed-driven influence and against the thugs I'd taken down for petty crimes that led to despicable consequences yet it still wasn't strong enough to stand up to the allure of a teenage Harleigh Rose with all that streaky hair.

I thought of that hair now, as it had looked drying over my pillow, how it felt between my fingers as I combed through it while she slept, and I hoped like hell that she could find it in herself to forgive me for raiding her club's cargo tonight.

Grease lifted a fist at the front of our convoy and peeled off exit 78 to wait behind sparse shrubbery for The Fallen to ride by. It was a good place to ambush them, our bikes concealed, this stretch of highway 99 filled with steeply curving lines that meant the rival gang wouldn't have time to react and pull away when we descended upon them.

Still, my cop's intuition was scratching at the back of my neck, insistent and annoying. I scanned our surroundings as I swung off my bike and quietly pulled it into the vegetation off the side of the road with the others. It was a partly cloudy night, the light grainy and dark grey over the sheer cliffs at our back and the expanse of dully shining metallic ocean on the other side of the pavement. Perfect light to hide dark and dangerous things.

"Gonna fuckin' stick those mother fuckers," Mutt said to my left, his leg bouncing with restless energy, his eyes slick like an oil spill in the moonlight, filled with insanity. "Gonna taste their blood."

I had enough on Mutt to incarcerate him for life already. He was a sick fuck without much care for subtlety and I'd watched him beat a man to death in the back of a bar one-night last fall. No one in the club reported the incident or narc'd on the biker when the police finally showed up.

Berserkers were a well-known Vancouver menace, no one spoke out against them unless they wanted to die.

Of course, I'd witnessed the beating, how Mutt lost his shit at a man because he accidently bumped into him and spilled some of his beer. How Mutt then used the heavy stein to beat the man over the head until he dropped to the floor and then how he proceeded to kick him until his spleen ruptured and he died of internal bleeding. I told my senior officer in the joint task force even though I had also been wearing a recording device at my crotch and he told his superior in the RCMP.

We did nothing.

It was the hardest part of policing, the idea that one part was not a worthy substitute for the whole. If we started picking off individual bikers for their transgressions, it would tip off the MC to a greater police presence in their lives, and make it nearly impossible to get close enough to take out the entire club. The goal was the entire beast, not just cutting off one of its many heads.

So, we waited.

I was the first officer in British Columbian history to become a fully patched member of an outlaw MC despite multiple efforts throughout the years and the RCMP was not going to waste that opportunity.

Three years, dozens of transgressions on my soul for the sake of the greater good, and countless lonely nights, going home to a house that held my dog and nothing else. It was a life without real friends, with only occasional, risky nights spent in a hotel with Diana, and telephone conversations with a father I hated and a mother who was growing more and more absent because of her dementia.

All for the greater good.

It was a phrase I repeated to myself every day, sometimes multiple times a day.

I was doing the right thing.

But I was tired to my fucking soul and having Harleigh

Rose suddenly in my life blazing like a comet across my dark universe, the creeping doubt that I wasn't living the life I *wanted* to live came rushing back.

I wanted to be free.

The thunderous roll of motorcycles rolled over the warm night air.

"Secure the cargo," Grease reminded us. "Mutt, Roper, you take it back down the mountain, me and Hendrix will follow. Wrath and Lion will clean up the mess an' make sure as fuck they don't follow."

Meaning, Wrath and I should kill The Fallen brothers and dispose of their bodies.

This was the first time the Sergeant at Arms had seen fit to put me on clean up duty. Believe it or not, it was a promotion. It said he trusted me enough to do the dirty, do it well, and do it quiet.

I'd do it, hate it, and report it back to my handler.

It still wouldn't be enough to take them down. For that, we needed something bigger, accounts or cooked books, or, ideally, seizing a cargo of guns.

The bikes moved closer. I could taste the adrenaline leaking out of the men's bodies into the air and my heart pumped harder.

"With me," Wrath murmured out of the corner of his mouth from my right and then the bikes were rounding the corner and Grease called, "Go."

We went.

I was an auditory man, music a language I understood better than spoken words, so the fight happened for me with a series of cacophonic events.

The Fallen laid down their motorcycles, a euphemistic biker expression that meant the skid to a painful stop flattened to the asphalt. There the sparking hiss of metal on concrete, the rough cry of men as their exposed skin grated like cheese against the asphalt and then shouts of warning as they realized we were on them.

Wrath and I approached the man farthest away from us, sneaking up on him from either side so that when he sprung free of his bike, we were already on him.

It was King.

We stared at each other for a long second that seemed to stretch an eternity.

He'd grown in the three and a half years I'd been away from Entrance, filled out his tall frame so that it was thick but lean with power under his cut. My eyes caught on the patch over his left chest, "Prospect."

I wanted to close my eyes and observe a moment of silence for the good, smart kid I'd known and helped raise. King wasn't supposed to join the club, he was supposed to join Doctors Without Borders, head a coalition at the United Nations or start a billion-dollar hedge fund company. More than Harleigh Rose, I'd played a role in influencing King as a kid, cultivating the goodness, the morality in him until he was more white knight than black marauder, more me than Zeus.

That was obviously no longer true.

It was Wrath that broke the stalemate with a meaty fist connecting to King's jaw. The kid went reeling backwards, caught himself on his back foot and remembered he was in an ambush. He launched himself at Wrath.

I needed to join the fray, to wear the blood of The Fallen on my knuckles so that Grease and Reaper would see it later, how it anointed me irrevocably as one of them.

But fuck me, this was King.

He was the kid I'd fed Cinnamon Toast Crunch to nearly every morning for almost a year, who'd helped me turn my Mustang Fastback into a gleaming beauty I was proud to ride, who'd sat with me at the table in my mother's kitchen doing homework for hours on weeknights even after he'd moved back in with Zeus.

This was, in so many ways but blood, my brother.

I looked around for someone else to latch onto when I saw a flash of pale hair catch in the moonlight briefly peeking through the clouds.

A slight, black-clad body was moving through the calamity to the last biker laying half in the vegetation at the side of the highway, crouching beside it and fiddling through the saddle-bags filled with prime grade weed.

Harleigh fucking Rose.

"Fuck me," I cursed as I went ducking and weaving through the fistfights going on. The Berserkers were playing with the four Fallen bikers, if they were seriously in danger of losing the upper hand, I knew the knives and guns would come out.

I skidded to my knees beside her and hissed, "Get the fuck out of here right the fuck now."

She bared her teeth at me, deftly unbuckling the bags and tucking one then the other under her arms. "There are three bikes loaded with stuff. They probably didn't even see this one. They'll think they got the goods, but I'm saving my club thousands of fucking dollars by doin' this."

"You're also risking your life," I growled, looking over my shoulder to see Wrath land a punishing blow to King's temple that knocked him out cold before he even hit the ground.

The other members were similarly finishing off their fights and I could see Hendrix making quick work of grabbing the other bags a few yards away.

"You think I could sit by while I knew my family was going to be attacked then you're *whacked*," she seethed as she finally finished her task and began to slink on her belly deeper into the brush.

"Stay down, motherfucker," Grease yelled, and a gunshot rang out through the mountains.

Fuck.

I turned away from Harleigh Rose and slunk back to

Wrath. He turned to me with a raised eyebrow but otherwise didn't say anything. We walked together to Grease who stood over an enormous blond man that looked like an honest-to-Christ Viking. Blood spilled out over his gut, pooling under him.

I needed the Berserkers to get out of there so I could call a fucking ambulance.

"Get the shit and let's move," Grease ordered, delivering a kick to the fallen biker's wound then turning on his heel to hustle back to his bike.

Police sirens wailed in the distance, thankfully arriving from Entrance instead of Vancouver so the Berserkers could get back down the mountain unobserved.

"Clean this up!" Grease shouted over the shout of his revving engine as he and the others took off.

Wrath and I remained, arms crossed, shoulder to shoulder like sentries.

The second the group disappeared around the corner, we moved.

I crouched to the guy with the bullet wound and slapped his face to bring him to. "Hey, hey, need you to put pressure on this wound."

"Fuck," he said in a pain strained whisper. "Fuck you, you fuckin' 'serker."

"Shut the fuck up and put pressure here," I said, using his own hand to quell the blood flow. "The cops are comin' and they'll get you to the hospital."

He blinked up at me, sucked in a wet breath and then launched a wad of spit into my face. "Fuck you."

I rubbed the thick saliva off my cheek and left him to it to check on King.

Wrath was helping him up when I jogged over.

"Thanks, man," King grumbled, shaking his head to clear the cobwebs. "Did you have to hit me so fuckin' hard."

The goliath shrugged. "Had to look the part."

"Yeah, well don't think anyone's gonna be the wiser the way you clocked me. Jesus, have a headache for a week after this. Cress is not gonna be happy with my shiner."

"What the fuck is goin' on here?" I asked, the situation so far out of my realm of understanding that I couldn't make any sense of it.

King grinned at me and clapped me on the back. "Good to see you, man. Have to say, like the leather better than that Canadian cowboy look you usually got goin' on."

"What the fuck?" I repeated.

King threw his head back and laughed as if we were at my place in Entrance shooting the shit in my garage instead of on the side of a highway littered with bikes and bodies. "Yeah, betcha thinkin' what the fuck right 'bout now, but we don't got time to clue you in. I gotta see if Axe-Man's gonna make it and you two gotta get the fuck outta 'ere."

Wrath grunted his agreement and walked away to retrieve his bike.

King made to move away then stopped shoulder to shoulder with me before he moved past me and stared. His eyes were pale even in the darkness and they went straight to the center of the confusion and chaos in my soul.

"Good to see you, Danny," he muttered softly. "Stay safe."

"Lion, get movin'," Wrath called as King walked away and the sirens seemed to be right around the corner.

I got movin', my head spinning nonsensically in my head as I got my bike out of the brush and followed Wrath into the darkness back to Vancouver.

Only, Wrath didn't take us back to the clubhouse when he entered the city limits. First, he drove into the dirty bowels of East Hastings Street and turned off onto a filthy row of welfare housing. I pulled up beside him when he stopped before a peeling, white painted house and took off my helmet.

I didn't lay into him with questions or rage. I'd learned the hard way as a cop that silence was the best tool in garnering a confession, so I waited.

Wrath had his helmet off, his gaze tipped towards the house, face soft in a way I recognized by seeing King with Cress and Zeus with Lou.

He was in love with the person that lived in that house.

"Name's Kylie," he started, his voice gruffer than his usual deep rasp. "Met her when she was fifteen and her mum tried to convince Reaper to pay child support yet a-fuckin'-gain. He hit her mum, sent her sprawling right to the ground in the driveway at the clubhouse and then stalked off. Didn't know she was fucking fifteen, but the sight of her in this purple dress with her hair a riot of all these little curls, it knocked me on my ass just as surely as her mum. I helped her up and drove the both of them back home. Stayed while Kylie made me fuckin' tea, as if I'd drink it, but I did."

He looked down at his heavily scarred hands. "Doesn't care 'bout his baby mama's, hit or miss if he cares 'bout the kids. Coupla months, don't know how, he took notice'a Kylie and started pushing 'er to hang around the club. Mutt got to 'er."

I hissed, imagining the damage Mutt might have done to a young girl.

"She's a grown woman now, twenty-two, but she's a slight thing. Mutt sent 'er to the hospital. He cut open her mouth with a penknife so he could get his dick in there."

My gut rolled at the blasphemy of mutilating a woman like that. "Fuck."

"Yeah, took everything I had not to go into the clubhouse in a rage of gunfire, takin' out every damn brother I could. They were there that night, you get me? They saw Mutt take 'er into his room, heard her scream and cry out. Didn't do shit about it 'cause this crew doesn't stand for brotherhood and freedom, it stands for male supremacy, rapin' and beatin' women into submission, killin' those who oppose us even if it's over a fuckin' spilled beer."

He stopped, his breath fast in his chest. A light turned on, then off in the silent house, on then off again.

A signal.

"He'd kill me he knew she was mine," Wrath said, holding up a hand to the house even though I couldn't see anyone looking out. "Kill me and let his boys kill her 'cause his sense of loyalty is whacked and he likes us to prove we'd go to hell for him."

"What does this have to do with King, brother?" I asked quietly, using the endearment every brother in the club used for each other but using it in a way that showed I was with him, that I had his back and got his tragedy.

"Kylie went to university with him, they struck up a friendship. When shit went down, I went to King to buy protection for her, he didn't want money though, he just wanted the same for his sister. I fell down on that job, but Cricket was my cousin and it was complicated, but I'm rectifyin' it now by givin' her the protection of bein' my Old Lady."

I didn't even try to stem the tide of relief that flooded my chest at hearing Wrath and Rosie's relationship was a ruse. Guilt followed swiftly like red tide mucking up the clean when I thought about my commitments to Diana and Laken. I could get rid of Diana, we'd been dating for years, but we didn't have even a spark of what I had with Rosie. In fact, it was a dick move, but I decided to call her that night and end it over the phone. She deserved better, but then, so did Harleigh Rose.

The only problem was ending my relationship with Laken when she was crucial to the investigation. I was pretty damn certain that Reaper only trusted me because his favourite kid did, and getting rid of that security, especially now that

Harleigh Rose was involved in the MC, was a dangerous move I couldn't risk.

"Does he know his sister is involved with the cops?" I asked, because even though he loved his sister, I couldn't see the new prospect, King Garro, liking that idea.

Wrath's mouth thinned. "No, and actually, didn't know that 'til now. Just thought you two had a history."

"We do," I said, taking a chance on him just as he'd taken a gamble on me. "And she is."

"Right, well I'm guessin' you don't want me to tell King, that's fine, that's her business and it might fuck with my gig. King kept his part'a our bargain. Kylie's been stayn' up in Entrance until this week 'cause my girl loves her Mama and it's her birthday. She'll go back up after that. Can't risk it."

"She gonna stay up there with King forever?" I asked because I knew the answer was *no*.

His face hardened, and he turned to face me. "They call me Wrath 'cause I'm a big guy, strong enough to crush bones between my fingers, and when roused, I'm a vengeful beast, but they shoulda called me "Hound" 'cause I'm smart 'nough to see shit and know shit others don't." He paused. "Like the fact that Harleigh Rose or her daddy prob'ly killed my bastard ass cousin for beatin' her one too many times. Or that Reaper keeps an iron lock down on his source in the Port Authority, but he's got a new bitch in his bed he talks to so the opportunities ripe for the takin' to help you bring these sons of bitches down. Like the fact that you're a fuckin' cop and I knew it only 'cause I could fuckin' *smell* it on ya."

I rubbed a hand over my face, reeling from the sudden turn of events, trying to figure out how I could make this work to my advantage and feeling grateful I'd decided not to wear a wire that night, otherwise cops would be rolling up to turn Wrath C.I. even as we spoke.

"Why didn't you go to the cops? Why didn't you turn me in?"

"First, liked you," he shrugged. "Even 'fore shit happened with Kylie, thought 'bout leavin', defectin' to another club that stood for what I wanted, family and freedom to live without rules. The Fallen seemed to fit, made a deal with King that when the time came, I'd be welcomed there if I worked with them to take out the club."

"You're working with The Fallen," I echoed.

"They know they got an inside man, don't know who it is only that I'm feedin' them solid intel. Didn't want this shit spreadin' so only King knows."

I raised my brows and let out a low whistle. "Not even Zeus Garro?"

Wrath's smile flashed white through his beard. "Not yet."

"Fuck, well, why tell me this?"

Wrath looked back to the house. "We both got girls in this fight, I figure we need each other." He peered at me and for the first time in the three years I'd known him, I could see his soul shining in his eyes, wide and deep as a well, seemingly black but filled with something a fuckuva lot lighter than anyone gave him credit for. "You with me?"

I shouldn't have been.

It was my job to take him into the station, get him set up properly as a confidential informant, promise to get protection I knew wouldn't be given to his woman, and let the higher-ups make the bigger calls.

I was just a grunt.

But I looked into Wrath Marsden's eyes and saw a soul I could respect a lot fucking more than I respected the paper pushers I worked under, the father who'd taught me the police were elementally, eternally in the right, and I made another of a series of decisions in my life that were not morally good, that pushed me in the direction of another kind of brotherhood than the one with the men in blue.

I took Wrath's offered hand in mine and clapped him on the back.

CHAPTER FIFTEEN

Harleigh Rose

I LEFT THE WEED AT KING AND CRESS'S FRONT DOOR BEFORE I hauled back to Entrance going fifty kilometers over the speed limit so that I'd beat the brothers back to the clubhouse. I'd told Farrah and Reaper that I was going to take a nap in Wrath's room while I waited for him to get back from the job, then I'd climbed out the window, jumping to the garage roof and then the soft grass at its back. My car was still parked prominently in the front yard of the compound so it was a good thing I'd learned to hotwire cars when I was twelve and King was bored enough one day to teach me. Newer cars were a pain because of alarm systems and automatic start buttons, but I'd found a beautiful old model Aston Martin

DB5 just sittin' pretty in a driveway a few blocks away that did the trick.

I parked it in the same spot I'd found it and then couldn't resist using the pink lipstick I found in the passenger seat to press a kiss to the side window and write a little "xoxo, thanks for the ride" underneath.

I'd just climbed back through the window and changed into one of Wrath's tee shirts because mine were covered in dirt and it would better cement my napping story anyway when I felt the thunder of bikes rolling into the drive.

Still, I stayed upstairs.

It was only when the second, lesser growl sounded outside that I knew Danner and Wrath were back that I realized the danger of Danner coming inside.

Farrah was still there, and she knew him. Sure, she'd been high and obliterated as Ben Franklin's lightning struck kite each time he'd visited to have a chat with her about raising her kids right, but Danner was not the kind of man a woman could forget.

I jumped off the bed and raced down the stairs. Thankfully, Wrath and Danner were just climbing up the steps when I crashed through the door and launched myself at Wrath.

Instinctively, he caught me and my legs went around his waist even though he was too mammoth for me to wrap them fully around and I had long legs.

I dipped my face to his shoulder so that any of the onlookers would think I was giving my man a tender embrace. It was sketchy to warn him in front of Wrath, but I figured I knew enough about his secrets to blackmail him if he gave us grief about it.

"Farrah's inside," I whispered to Danner who had immediately locked furious eyes on me.

I guessed I wasn't forgiven for getting involved in the ambush.

"You cannot come in. Farrah's inside," I repeated.

The fury dimmed then flared to life again reminding me that he hated my mum even more than I did.

"Need ya to take my woman home," Wrath said loudly to Danner. "She's got school tomorrow and I'm gonna be 'ere awhile debriefin'. You got 'er?"

"Yeah, brother," Danner agreed easily then looked over my shoulder. "You cool with that, Prez?"

"Sure the girl's mum would like to spend more time with 'er. Why don't you leave her here while we finish up our business? Won't take long."

It was formed like a question, but we had no choice.

My heart was lurching in my chest, overtaxed by the amount of excitement I'd had that day.

"She's tired, Prez," Danner tried again.

It was the wrong move.

Reaper's anger lashed through the air. "Don't give a fuck, do I, boy? Now get your asses in here and Harleigh Rose go on up to your mother."

We trudged in dutifully, Wrath letting me go so that they could follow Reaper into the "chapel," a room in each biker clubhouse designated for just the patched-in members of the club, where they held their meetings.

I went up the stairs to find Farrah.

She was in Reaper's bedroom, a master suite at the back of the house that was covered in biker girl posters and strewn with dirty clothes.

My mother sat in the middle of the bed wearing black fishnets and lingerie.

"Jesus, do you seriously just hang out like that?" I asked, covering my eyes against the sight.

She laughed. "Word of advice, Harleigh, this is how you keep a man."

"Don't need your help with that. Can you please cover up?"

She sighed, but I heard the rustle as she got off the bed.

"Yes, I heard you kept a man for four years. Impressive, I guess, if you hadn't let him beat on you. You never did learn anything I tried to teach you."

When I was little, and my mother was being wicked or drunk and cruel, I came up with a game to distract myself. I tried to think of a positive memory and match it to a song.

I thought of that morning waking up in Danner's bed, of his fingers binding me to the cabinets and his mouth on my pussy, his cock in my cunt after so many years of wishing for exactly that.

I came up with a song by one of Cressida's favourite artists, "Can't Help Falling in Love" by Elvis.

The song started playing softly in my head as Farrah, finally covered by a silk black robe, continued her lecture.

"You never should have left me, prettiness, I would have taught you how to be a *woman*. Instead, you've become this rough, biker thing," she waved her hand, bangles jangling and I thought about how I wanted to rip those cheap bracelets off and choke her with them.

"Oh, I listened to the lessons you taught, Farrah," I said through gritted teeth. "I listened to the one about not doing drugs that you taught me when you'd overdosed three times by the time I was ten. I listened to the one about being careful not to drive away a good man, the best man by being unfaithful in all the ways that word means. And most of all, I learned that just because you think you're a good person, it doesn't mean you *are* because nothing you've ever done has been good or honest, and the fact that you don't even seem to understand that makes it so much worse."

Farrah stared at me for a long moment, her cruel face impassive, before she sighed. "You always were dramatic."

"I'm not dramatic, I'm *right*," I hissed.

I didn't want to be there after the night I'd had, seeing King fall to Wrath's punch, watching Axe-Man get shot in the gut by a man I despised while I just lay in the dirt doing nothing. I wanted to go home.

Not my apartment, Cricket had taken the home out of that place.

No, I wanted to get on the back of Lion's bike and ride with him to his little house, open the door to greet a happy Hero, take the punishment Danner was probably at the moment thinking up for me, and then fall exhausted into bed with him.

Instead, Elvis kept crooning in my head and my mother kept running her mouth.

"You don't get this because you were too young, but your daddy was a beast. He ordered me around like I was his fucking slave and then he took my kids from me!"

"He took us because you were a washed up, abusive, drug abuser," I told her flatly. "And I don't see you complaining about Jacob. He took Honey from you too."

"Yeah, well karma got the bastard. He died of a fucking car crash when Honey was five and I got 'er back."

"And look at her now! She's a high school dropout, drug-addicted porn star."

"It's just a phase," Farrah said, arranging herself back on the bed as if she was the queen of fucking Sheba. "You're clearly going through one now too. Don't worry, you stick with your Mama and I'll get you through the other side."

"Both Zeus and Jacob left you 'cause of your drug addiction, who says Reaper'll be any different?"

God, I hoped he was. I hoped he kept her and ensnared her in his filthy web so that when he went down, she did too.

"Oh baby, old Reaper and me go way back," she said with a childish giggle. "He's been in love with me since I was with your daddy. He'd do anything for me…" she shot me a sloe-eyed look. "Even kill for me."

Trepidation sliced through me. "Who would you want killed? You owe a dealer or something."

"Come sit with your mama," she ordered me softly, patting the bed beside her. "And I'll tell you."

Getting close to her was like willingly cuddling up next to a rattlesnake, but there was fear germinating in my gut and my intuition wouldn't let me dig it up without identifying the source.

I crawled onto the bed then ground my teeth when she patted her lap so I would lay my head there.

I did.

Her hideous perfumed, braceleted hand started to stroke through my hair. "It's really a shame you didn't get the same uniform blond from me as your brother did."

My entire body was clenched in an attempt to be boulder strong against her pike and chisel, but still, they wore away at me.

"Focus, Mum, who do you want dead?"

She hummed softly for a few long minutes, but I didn't push her again because I'd inherited my wild from her and I knew what happened when you pushed a feral animal too hard into a corner.

"You knew your daddy took a new wife?" she asked sweetly.

I grew tighter, even the blood in my veins calcified.

"What?"

"Your daddy, he got himself a sweet, young new wife. Reaper said you're not close with 'im. Did you know about her?"

Every instinct in my body screamed at me to lie and do it better than I'd ever done before. "No, mum. I haven't seen him since I moved back away from Entrance to start a better life."

"My girl," she murmured, her voice like sugar, her hand gentle in my hair. "Her mama's daughter."

No.

I was my father's daughter.

Only the spawn of Zeus would think to lie in the face of their mother, to be smart enough to see the poison in her sugar and the potential energy coiled in that gentle hand.

"You haven't been with Dad in years though," I ventured carefully.

"Did you know he went to prison for that little bitch? Your daddy's sick, he's loved her since she was a kid."

Wrong, my mind bellowed. Dad had saved Loulou from death that day in the parking lot. He'd chosen to save a little girl's life and go to jail to enact retribution instead of doing things like a coward. It wasn't until later, until dozens of letters had been written until dozens of obstacles had been hurdled and ten years had elapsed that they found each other as lovers.

There was absolutely nothing sick about that.

"What are you going to get Reaper to do about it?" I asked softly, as if I was sorry for my mum, as if I didn't care about dad's "little bitch."

"We made a deal, him and I. I'll be his and give him Jacob's brother's information at the dockyard so he can do more business through the Vancouver Port, and he'll keep me in comfort." She paused because I'd learned how to be dramatic from her. "And he'll have one of his brothers kill that slut and her babies. Maybe then Zeus will understand what it's like to have your children taken away from you."

CHAPTER SIXTEEN

Harleigh Rose

2011.

Harleigh Rose is eleven. Danner is twenty.

I WAS EATING CINNAMON TOAST CRUNCH BEFORE SCHOOL ON
a Tuesday, alone in the Danner's big, farm-style kitchen when
the music started. It was "Real Wild Child" by Iggy Pop, a
song I'd only recently discovered while exploring records with
Old Sam and Danner at Mega Music a few weeks ago. It was
a great song, but I wasn't sure why Danner was playing it as
he got ready for a Tuesday morning.

I turned back to my cereal, slurping up the spicy, sugary
milk at the bottom of the bowl, thinking that King better get
his butt out of bed or we were going to be late for school.

The music got closer and in it, I heard the familiar twang of a blue guitar and the throaty drawl of my favourite singing voice in the world.

A moment later, Danner came down the stairs into the kitchen, his blue guitar strapped over his chest, thrumming under his fingers, his mouth smiling around the words as he sang. Behind him was Susan Danner holding a tall cake covered in pink frosted roses, the top popping with sparklers and her sweet face alive with happiness. They filtered into the room and stood by either side of the door so that when King came down the stairs, he could do it with flare, jumping into the kitchen and sliding across the linoleum on his knees until he was right beside my chair, his fingers playing air guitar, his lanky back bent in back like some kind of rock star.

I sat there, my spoon frozen mid-air, milk dripping to the table, my mouth open and slack with shock.

The song ended and in unison, they cried out, "Happy eleventh birthday, Harleigh Rose!"

I blinked at them and the spoon dropped from my hand into the bowl with a clatter.

King got up off the ground, frowning and moving to my side as Susan walked forward to place the cake in front of me.

"Blow out the candles, love," she encouraged me with her wide, sincere smile.

I looked up at King, swallowing hard past the lump in my throat, trying to shove it back down into the dark pit of my belly where it'd lain dormant since my Dad went to jail so I could speak, but I couldn't seem to move it.

King put a comforting hand on my shoulder. He was thirteen, tall and so gangly that only his extreme handsomeness made him look anything other than silly. He had to bend to get close to my ear, but when he did, he whispered, "It's okay, H.R., I mentioned it was your birthday an' they wanted to celebrate. This isn't even the end'a it. You get to skip school and Danner's gonna spend the day with you. Then tonight we're gonna go to fuckin' Donovan's for a steak!"

"King," Susan reprimanded softly, trying to break him of his nearly lifelong swearing habit even though we all knew it was hopeless.

My brother grinned unabashedly at her. "If Donovan's famous steaks aren't worth cursin' over, I don't know what is."

Danner laughed with his mother, but his eyes were on me, gentle and assessing. He went to a crouch in front of me, forearms on his thighs, his face a little lower than my seated one but close enough to count the short, spiky lashes around his eyes.

His eyes were my favourite bit about his face, even though it made me blush to think about it.

"It's your birthday, rebel Rose," he said in his honey rich, molasses smooth voice. "We've got to celebrate."

I chewed on my lip. "It's just, well, we don't really celebrate anymore."

Anger flashed across his face like a lightning strike before he could clench his jaw and pretend he was unaffected. It warmed me to see that in his face, to know that he cared enough about me and King to be angry for us.

"Well, in the Danner house, we celebrate. Harold's already at work so he can get off early and take us to the steakhouse. Mum's going to work, King's going to school, but you, Rosie, get to spend the day doing whatever you want with me until dinner. How does that sound?"

It sounded like the best present anyone had ever given me, and when I was five, Dad gave me my first pair of real biker chick boots that were the *bomb* so that was saying something.

"Really?" I asked, staring at Danner, trying to make sure he wasn't joking even though he never joked. "Anything I want?"

"You got it," he said with a grin. "Now, first you've got to make a wish, blow out the candles and all of us are going to eat cake for breakfast."

I looked over my shoulder at King and grabbed his hand even though I knew it made me look like a baby. "Will you blow them out with me? I don't want to make a wish without you."

King's face, always so open and expressive, broke into my favourite of his smiles, lopsided and goofy with indulgent love. "Sure, H.R., let's do it."

Susan walked around the table to take a photo of us as we bent our heads close together to blow. I sucked in a deep breath, thought of my wish then panicked and blindly reached out with my spare hand to fumble for Danner's. He caught my questing fingers and held them tight.

A second later, King and I made our wish.

OLD SAM AND HIS WIFE MILLIE WERE WAITING FOR US WHEN we showed up after cake at Mega Music. As soon as we opened the door, Old Sam started playing the "happy birthday" song on his old, shiny saxophone and his wife started singing. Millie had been a backup vocalist for stars like Aretha Franklin and Whitney Houston so I told myself it was only natural that the beauty of her voice singing that song to me made my nose itch with tears.

We spent four hours there.

Old Sam closed the shop and put on record after record for us to dance to in a little section at the back of the shop by the record player I always used. Millie and Old Sam loved to swing dance and they taught Danner and me some of their coolest moves. I remembered swinging over Danner's fore-arms, my hair a stream of gold as I spun full circle then landed with his arms around me. When we were too breath-less to keep going, Old Sam put on some slow records, some Bob Dylan and Leonard Cohen, songs you could tip your head back, close your eyes at and really listen to. Finally, just before lunch, we left them, but not without a stack of gifted records under my arm.

"Having fun?" Danner asked with a bright smile as he held the door to his winter ride, a huge, new white Dodge RAM 1500 truck that I basically had to climb up to get into.

"Um, *yeah*," I said, with a happy roll of my eyes. "This is the best day *ever*."

I said it without thinking about it, but as Danner rounded the car to get into the driver's seat, the betrayal of my words hit me like a bullet through the heart.

It wasn't the best day ever. It couldn't be. Not with my dad in prison, not when I wouldn't be able to see him.

He'd write me a letter. I knew it would be at the Danner's when I got home from my adventures, a thick envelope filled with thin paper weighted with heavy, precious words. He wrote King and me a lot. A few times a week at least, and they never got old even though I knew there wasn't that much to do in prison. His letters were always filled with questions about our lives, with stories he shared of the family before he'd been locked up, of the wild things we would do when he got out.

They didn't help the missing of him, that phantom ache I felt in my heart as if it was missing a vital piece, but they made me smile.

I didn't smile then, looking out the window as Danner got

in the car, started it up so that "Snake Song" blew like smoke through the space between us and Main Street began to slide by outside my window. I touched my fingers to the cool glass and wondered when my Dad would see something new again.

"What's up, Rosie?" Danner asked, adjusting his navy Entrance PD toque over his head.

It was snowing out, just a light dusting, but it was nearly Christmas and the streets were covered in it, just as Danner was, snowflakes melting on the tips of his long lashes, on his broad shoulders under his heavy coat. I wanted to capture one of the icy flakes on his cheek and bring it to my mouth.

I was eleven, but little thoughts like that had begun to stud my thoughts, making the topography of my mind rough and dangerous, riddled with landmines of desire I didn't fully understand.

I pulled my own hat, a smaller one with skull and cross-bones all over, down over my cold ears and looked back out the window.

"Nothing."

He snorted. "Rosie, I hate to be the one to tell you this, but you got a personality that poisons or lightens an atmosphere dependin' on your mood. Right now, the air in here tastes like arsenic, so I'm thinking there's something wrong over on your side of the car."

I sighed, rolling my head against the back seat as if he was annoying me when really, I loved that he'd noticed.

"Fine, I'm missing my dad, okay? I know I'm eleven and too old to get all snot-nosed about something like that, but it's true so whatever, okay?"

"Okay," he agreed instantly.

"Yeah, like you don't need to make a big deal of it or anything," I told him.

"Right."

"I mean it, Danner," I said, because I only called him Lion when I was feeling uncharacteristically vulnerable.

"I hear ya, Harleigh Rose."

"Good," I said, looking out the front window as we turned off Main and the ocean opened up in front of us, gunmetal grey in the winter light.

"Good," he echoed.

I slanted him a look to see if he was making fun, but his lips were their normal firm, full and flat.

We were silent after that, our Lion & Rosie playlist the only sound in the truck as we drove. I leaned an elbow into the passenger side window sill and thought about birthdays with my dad before he went to prison. When I was four, he'd taken King and me to Whistler and taught me how to ski on the bunny slope. When I was five, the year he got me my first pair of combat boots, he'd invited the entire club over for a party in *my* honour with a banner that said "Happy Birthday, Princess" and everything.

I vaguely heard Danner making a call in the background of my memories, but I didn't want to listen or talk to him. It felt wrong to be with him and enjoy it when I couldn't share the day with Dad.

"Rosie," Danner called my name after a while and I adjusted so I could look over at him. "I've got two surprises for you today, and I'm not gonna lie, I'm a little angry with myself for not thinking of this one first, but it is what it is. We're here now, and then we'll go get your present after, okay?"

I frowned at him. "I don't need even *more* fun!"

One of his thick light brown eyebrows rose. "Excuse me?"

I huffed with frustration. "It makes me feel bad to be having fun on my birthday without my dad. *God*, I told you not to make a big deal about it and now we're talking about it again."

Danner bit the edge of his lip, trying to hide back a smile. "Well, I'm thinking you don't have to worry about that anymore."

When I just continued to glare at him, he tipped his chin out the front window and I followed the gesture to see Ford Mountain Correctional looming ahead of us.

Something that had been germinating in my chest for months, that had been planted there years ago by a teenage boy when he'd saved me from watching my dad go down in gunfire, that had been watered and tended to since then with act after generous act, erupted through the malnourished soil of my soul and sprung into bloom. I could feel it unfurl, red and ripe and full of plump petals bowed into feminine curves.

It was the exact moment that I fell in love with Lion Danner.

My eyes shone with held back tears as I deep breathed to get myself under control. Danner let me have a moment, parking the car and walking around to my side to open the door like the gentleman he was even to an eleven year old.

I hopped out of the car into the crunching snow and followed my new, tender instincts by taking his hand in my gloved one.

"Thank you, Lion," I said, staring at his big hands, warm even in the cold air, mapped with veins and topped with long, thick fingers.

His hand clenched mine, then twisted so our hands were intertwined. "Come on, I called ahead and he's waiting."

CHAPTER SEVENTEEN

Danner

HARLEIGH ROSE SAT IN THE LARGE, OPEN ROOM AT A ROUND table talking to her dad and smiling so big, I thought it would split her face in two. She wasn't supposed to touch him, it was forbidden, but she kept forgetting, putting her hand on his arm and then glaring at the correction officers who told her to quit it.

I was outside the room in a viewing area, because it was only one visitor at a time. The distance was nice, it let me see how much better Harleigh Rose looked after the three months she'd spent with my parents and me compared to her time with her mother. Her hair was a clean, shining rose, yellow and brown gold streaming down her back, her clothes new and pristine. She'd gained such much-needed weight even though she was naturally long and thin, and her skin had lost its pallor.

There was a warmth in my chest that felt like something more than pride at doing a good deed. I was invested in the Garro kids. One might even say, I loved them.

My cell rang in my pockets and I knew who it was before I even answered it.

"Dad."

"Lionel, why the fuck are you at the correctional facility meeting with that *felon*?" he demanded. "You insisted on taking those kids in, and I get you, that kind of life is not meant for the lowest of the low, let alone children, but you have to keep them away from their parents! Whatever positive influence we may have on them won't take otherwise."

I rubbed my hand over my face and leaned a shoulder into the glass as I watched Harleigh Rose tip her head back in tandem with her father and laugh her bold, brassy laugh.

"Not going to keep her away from her father, Dad."

"You know what those thugs are like, Lionel. You went to the academy, you worked with Sgt. Renner and I know you saw how brutal those biker gangs can be."

I did, and I had.

The club in Vancouver, where I'd done my police training, called Berserkers MC, was one of the most despicable organized crime syndicates I'd ever had the misfortune of studying.

"Zeus Garro jumped in front of a bullet to save Louise Lafayette," I pointed out. "It's not like the man doesn't have a heart *or* an obvious soft spot for kids."

"You goin' soft on me?" Harold Danner said quietly.

It was when he went quiet that you had to be careful.

"No," I stated firmly.

"Takin' down The Fallen has been our family mission since your grandfather was in office and if I don't get the job done, it'll be *your* duty," he reminded again of something I'd grown up hearing about.

My grandfather had made some inroads, put a few of the brothers away back in the 60s for drug possession with intent to distribute and a few bodily assault charges.

My father hadn't made any unless you called Zeus Garro

killing a man for shooting a child good police work and not just an obvious arrest seeing as he'd done it in First Light Church parking lot.

I'd been on my father's force for six months at that point and some things were becoming painfully obvious.

Harold was corrupt.

And not inconsequentially.

He was rotten straight to his core, putrid to his marrow and greed-driven with every beat of his selfish heart.

I was still a rookie and even though I was his son, he was still feeling me out, so thus far, I'd been able to keep myself out of his "goon squadron," a collection of officers that he trusted enough to task with his dirty work.

I didn't know the specifics of that dirty work and I didn't want to not really, but I had a feeling that I was inevitably going to come to a crossroads where I'd have to decide what kind of man I wanted to be. My father's or my own.

"Listen, I've got to go, Harleigh Rose's time with her dad is up and I've got to take her to get her present," I said, my eyes to the little girl who had just thrown herself into her father's arms.

A guard moved forward to pull them apart then hesitated at the ferocity of Garro's frown. A moment later, she unlatched herself, turned to face the guard and flipped him the bird.

"Jesus," I muttered under my breath as she flounced away, waving at her dad over her shoulder in a cool way I knew she had to have learned from her biker brethren that was just a flick of her fingers.

I hung up the phone without listening to what my dad was saying, and grinned at her as the guard let her into the waiting area with me.

"So?" I asked.

Her smile widened, lips bright pink and full over straight white teeth. "Best. Birthday. *Ever!*"

"You deserve it, so I'm glad," I told her and as her smile collapsed, her mouth tight and her eyes big with the effort not to blink and let the moisture there pool.

God, that fuckin' bitch Farrah fucked her up so well it was a wonder Harleigh Rose believed she deserved any goodness at all.

"Dad wants to talk to you," she told me after taking a deep breath through her nose.

"What?"

She rolled her eyes. "He's not *that* scary, you know. Sure, he's like twice your size, but honestly, he's twice anyone's size so you shouldn't feel bad about it."

"Not feeling bad about my size, Rosie," I said after a startled laugh. "Just wondering why he wants to talk to me."

"He said," she cleared her throat and affected Garro's voice, "'Man's takin' care'a my princess, better look 'im in the eye while I threaten 'im if somethin' happens to my girl. Wanna make sure it sticks in his brain.'"

I chuckled again despite myself. "Guess I better go talk to him then. You're going to wait here and not move an inch?"

She rolled her eyes. "I've got to move to breathe and like, walk over to that bench over there. Is that cool?"

"Brat," I told her fondly, ruffling her hair as I moved toward the door and waited for the guard to allow me entry.

Walking across the space to Zeus Garro who sat with his powerful thighs spread, huge hands resting on the table and chin tilted up like he was still holdin' biker court from prison, was one of the longest walks of my life.

When I made it to the table, I gestured to the chair in front of him and asked, "May I?"

"Clean cut, rookie cop with down-home manners," he muttered instead of answering. "Takin' care'a my kids."

I sat anyway. "Yeah, Garro, my parents and I are taking care of your kids because the province granted us temporary custody while you're in prison. Not that my decision had anything to do with you, but you should be grateful I didn't let the system get them or they'd be separated and placed anywhere between here and Newfoundland."

"That why you're doin' this, so I'll thank you? So, I'll think I owe you one?" he asked in a low growl.

"I'm doing this because I was there that day you got shot saving Louise Lafayette and despite what I've been raised to think, I don't think you're entirely bad. More than that, I met Harleigh Rose that day, saw her faint with the force of her scream as she watched you go down and people form bonds over something like that. We did. I kept in touch vaguely over the years then saw her three months ago stealing candy bars just to feed herself. Fed the kids dinner and took them home to have another chat with your cunt of an ex-wife and King and Harleigh Rose found her dying on the floor. What's a man to do when he's faced with a situation like that but take them in?"

Garro stared at me for a long minute with eyes the same colour and cut as a blade. There were tattoos that ran from his wrists up under the pushed-up sleeves of his orange jumpsuit and a huge, ragged scar at the junction of his throat and shoulder like someone had taken an axe to him.

They probably had.

I didn't know how the two of us were supposed to sit there and have a meeting of the minds. We had nothing in common, no shared history, similarities in past or plans for the future.

Yet, there was something about the way he'd been with his daughter, so obviously overjoyed to see her, so comfortably doting, more like a typical suburban dad than a biker outlaw. Something too in the way he sat there, relaxed, but coiled, casual but cunning that made me want to gift him my respect, even after years of being told bikers and Zeus Garro most of all, were filth.

"Great man, maybe he calls the cops, makes sure the kids

get placed in a good home or pushes for a distant relative to take 'em in. Good man, he drops 'em off at their mum's house and drives away, feelin' like he did his good Samaritan work for the day or the month or the fuckin' year. A bad man never even notices Harleigh Rose run outta a building at the sound of gunshots and chases after 'er so he wouldn't be sittin' 'ere like this with me now."

He paused, his eyes drilling into me until he seemed to find the gold he was looking for. "Nah, got the feelin' that despite you bein' that son of a bitch Harold Danner's son, you're something altogether different than any'a those kinds'a men. You got heart and morals the like I've never seen, doin' what you're doin' with my kids. You want my thanks or not, you got it."

"Don't need it," I agreed. "But I'm happy to accept it."

"Things'll change when I'm out," he said over the rattle of chains as he steepled his fingertips together.

I shrugged. "Of course, they'll go live with you, but I don't see why I can't be in their lives."

"It's the rookie in you sayin' that. You know somewhere deep that this isn't their life and it isn't yours. You don't go to prisons to visit cons, you put 'em there in the fuckin' first place. They want to see you after, hey, I'm not stoppin' 'em because God fuckin' knows those kids need some good and some lovin' in their life. I plan to give it to'em. I also plan to raise 'em like Garros, like bikers, and your people got a pretty big fuckin' problem with that."

He shifted forward to stare at me, his pale silver eyes intense. "Right now, you're the kind of guy who saves kids from the other side of the tracks just 'cause they're in need even though it's none'a your business. Doesn't mean few years down the line, doin' more work for your daddy, you don't turn different. Don't want that kind of bigot 'round my kids, you get me?"

"Got you," I gritted through my teeth, hating that he

would think that was even a possibility and hating even more that it probably was.

"Harold's had a big, fuckin' fat red target on my back for years, on the club for even longer. There's a chance you stayin' friends with 'em after will put them in an uncomfortable position, maybe even a criminal one. You want that?"

"Fuck no," I cursed. "Why do you think I took them away from Farrah in the first place?"

Garro raised his hands in a gesture of goodwill. "I'm not sayin' this as your future enemy, Danner. I'm sayin' this as a man who loves his kids more than life an' I still put 'em in danger by givin' 'em a shit mum. You get where I'm comin' from?"

Fuck me, but I did.

My moral compass couldn't find it's true north around the Garros, first Harleigh Rose and King and now even with Zeus. The guy was smart, clearly loved his kids, and was the sort of man to save an unknown child's life by risking his own.

In strange, uncomfortable ways, I noticed a kind of parallel between the two of us.

I ignored it.

"Listen, it's Rosie's birthday and we have to pick up her present before we grab King from school and pick up dinner so, we done?" I asked, already standing up to leave.

Garro tipped his head back to maintain eye contact with me and nodded. "Rosie? Can't believe my biker princess lets you call her that."

"Told you, the sort of things we've been through you form a bond that never withers."

"Yeah," Garro said, scratching his beard as he looked away into the far distance at a thought I could see. "Yeah, sure fuckin' does."

I rapped my knuckles on the table and turned on my heel, leaving the uncertainty Zeus had sown in my head behind with him.

"Oh my God, oh my fucking God," Harleigh Rose repeated, dropping to her knees as soon as the breeder opened the gate to the backyard where the puppies were playing in the snow. "Oh my god."

I should have told her to watch her mouth, but I didn't. She was having a moment and I didn't want to ruin it for her.

"Lion," she called out as the puppies noticed she was there and started their clumsy puppy runs over to her. "Get in here, quick!"

"Thought you could pick one," I told her from where I leaned against a tree outside of the enclosure.

"I want to do it together," she said in a tone that brokered no argument. "Now, get in here."

The breeder smiled at me as I shook my head and moved through the gate into the pen.

"On your knees," she ordered again, patting the snow beside herself as the first puppy reached her and jumped up into her arms.

With a huge sigh, I dropped to my knees in the cold, wet snow.

It was worth it when two seconds later a burnished gold puppy put his little paw in the air and batted at me.

"Whatcha want, little buddy?" I asked, bending forward to look in his huge brown eyes.

He jumped up with a little woof and planted a short, quick kiss on my cheek.

Harleigh Rose laughed beside me as the pup did it again.

"Okay, little guy." I picked up his ridiculously soft body and held him in front of my face so we were eye to eye. "What're you lookin' at?"

Again, Rosie giggled beside me, abandoning the four puppies frolicking all over her to shift closer to me and the one in my hands.

"He likes you," she noted as he tried to kiss my face, his tongue lapping a mile a minute even though he was too far to make contact.

"Yeah, I guess so."

"I think we should take him," she said suddenly leaping to her feet to say to the breeder. "Can we take this one?"

"He's going to be a police dog, Rosie, don't you think he's more of a lover than a fighter?" I asked as the dog growled then tried to launch himself forward in my hands so he could get to me.

"He loves you already, imagine what he'll do for you if you're in danger," she said easily, as if it wasn't heartbreaking that an eleven-year-old would know enough to say that.

I nodded at the breeder. "We'll take him."

It was after dinner at Donovan's Steak House, a dinner my father recused himself from because of my earlier decision to take Harleigh Rose to see Garro, after we had more cake at home and King gave his sister his gift of an iPod, one I'd helped him pick out but he'd bought with mysterious money I chose not to ask about.

I was tucking Rosie into bed even though she declared she was too old for it. It was her birthday though, so after my mother finished speaking quietly to her about whatever women talked about, I took the new puppy and went to say goodnight.

"He can sleep with me?" she asked immediately.

I laughed. "For now, but I think it's important in his training that he sleeps with me. We have two months until he's old enough for the ten-week program, so we have time."

"Fuck yeah!" she shouted with a little fist pump.

God, she was a cute kid.

I sat on the edge of the bed and let the puppy go. He instantly ran up the bed, tripped over one of her legs and did a head plant into her belly.

Harleigh Rose laughed brightly, happier than I'd ever seen her.

Words couldn't describe how warm that made me feel. King had looked just like that earlier at dinner too, his plate practically licked clean, his laugh a frequent addition to the ambiance as he charmed my mother and me with his mature-beyond-his-years sense of humor.

I did that for them.

It was, by far and away, the best thing I'd ever done in my nineteen years.

"So, what're you going to name him?" I asked as she lifted the puppy and placed it on her chest for a snuggle.

"I can name him?" she asked, bewildered by the responsibility.

"Uh huh, think you're not getting that he may technically be *my* police dog, but I got him because I thought you could also use a friend."

She blinked at me, the lamplight turning her eyes a deep turquoise. "I think you're the best man I'll ever know."

It was my turn to blink. "What?"

She shrugged, suddenly embarrassed by her confession. "It's true. It's not like a compliment or anything. It just is."

I didn't know what to say to that to make her feel less awkward for saying it or me less awkward for hearing it.

"Hero," she said suddenly, lifting the golden retriever so she could turn him to face me. "His name should be Hero."

"Yeah?"

"Yeah, 'cause he's going to be a police dog and he's going to be yours so the name suits him twice."

God, she was killing me.

"Three times over then. He'll be part yours and if anyone deserves a hero, it's you," I told her honestly, unable to keep the words in my mouth.

"I've got one already," she said, glancing up quickly before looking back at Hero. "But with the life I live? I could definitely use two."

CHAPTER EIGHTEEN

Harleigh Rose

I LEFT FARRAH AS SOON AS I COULD, BUT THE BROTHERS WERE still in church so I drove home to Danner's without him and let myself in using the code for the door and the other for the alarm that he'd texted to me on the burner phone.

Hero was waiting by the door when I walked in, his pink tongue lolling out of his mouth as he gave me a wide doggy smile then stood up on his back legs to give me kisses. I let him out briefly, too on edge to take him for a walk, and then, dressed in one of his RCMP tees, I settled in Danner's bed with Hero and my laptop to do some digging on Jacob Yves's brother.

I remembered very little about Jacob from the two years he lived in my father's house with my mother. He was a good man, taken in by Farrah's wiles until she was pregnant and it was too late to turn back. I recalled him making us pancakes some mornings when mum was passed out or hungover in bed, how he'd let King sit on his lap one time in his huge work truck so he could yank the horn. Farrah was only negligent instead of cruel when he was around, but unfortunately, that wasn't often because Jacob was a long-distance trucker, so our life wasn't all that different with him in it. It wasn't even all that different when Farrah got knocked up either, because she only cut back on injections and still hit the bottle hard every weekend at her parties.

It was a wonder, really, that Honey only arrived with her little heart on the wrong side of her chest instead of brain damaged or dead.

Even at six, I'd told my mum Honey was a stupid name to give a kid, but she'd insisted it was sweet. She hadn't had much of a choice in naming King or me, because Zeus decided our names soon as he knew our genders, and I think she believed giving "Honey" such a bubbly name would help her be a bubbly girl.

Born the daughter of that woman, there was no way Honey was going to turn out that way, and it was obvious given her current predicament, that she hadn't. I felt a brief flash of guilt grip my heart that I hadn't tried to find her after Jacob had taken her away, but until now, I'd always assumed she'd stayed with him and she was better off without us.

I searched Jacob Yves on the internet, found his obituary and then found mention of his brother "Grant." I typed in his full name, found his Linked-In account and discovered he was a transport operative for the Port of Vancouver.

Ding, ding, ding!

I'd successfully found Reaper's newest drug smuggling connection.

"Fuck yeah!" I said, shooting my hands in the air, laughing because it was appropriate that Johnny Cash's "God's Gonna Cut You Down" started playing through the stereo.

Hero let out a soft whoop of encouragement then panted into my face when I grabbed him by his soft ears and bent close to say, "We're gonna cut them the fuck down, Hero. You with me?"

He whined in response, which made me laugh again.

"Why the fuck isn't the alarm on?"

I gasped, spinning around to face Danner, Hero moving to straddle my lap and growl at his master for scaring me. "Jesus, Danner its three o'clock in the fuckin' morning and we've had a tense fucking day. You couldn't have warned a girl you were there a little more gently?"

"Good boy, Hero," he said to his dog, completely ignoring me. "Now, bed."

The golden retriever jumped off the bed and trotted over to his plush cushion in the corner then lay down with a happy groan.

The music changed and suddenly the band Glass Animals was playing, their smoky, beat-filled music filling the room.

I looked back at Danner to find him suddenly looming over the end of the bed, his brow knotted into a fierce tangle, his hands white-knuckled against the cushion as he leaned down into my face to clip, "You bought my displeasure today, Rosie. You ready to pay the consequences for it?"

My breath left my body in one fell whoosh, my nipples tightened into painful points hard enough to cut diamonds and my pussy clenched.

This was dirty Dom Danner and he wanted to punish me for my recklessness.

"Are you going to spank me?" I asked, trying to keep the excitement from my voice.

Danner's smile was a long, slow curl of his lips. "No."

"Why not?" I sassed back.

"You enjoy it too much," he drawled, yanking off his tee to reveal the mouthwatering length of his muscled torso. "It's not a punishment and after the stunt you pulled, you need to be reminded of who is in control here."

I tilted my chin and glared at him even as I licked drool off the corner of my mouth. "You don't control me, *no one* does."

He stilled completely, but his stillness wasn't empty. It was filled with harnessed energy, with the promise of explosive action.

I'd never known stillness to be sexy but fuck me, Lion Danner half naked and posed like a predator about to take me down was the sexiest thing I'd ever seen.

"You're mistaken," he murmured, deceptively soft.

"What're you gonna do to me?" I was squirming, but I couldn't help myself. It was like I had eaten an entire bag of fuzzy peaches and my skin was buzzing from the inside out.

His frown was immediate, brows slamming down over eyes that glittered like wet jade. "Who is in charge here, Harleigh Rose?"

"You," I gasped immediately.

He fisted a hand in the bed at my hip and leaned down into my face until his eyes were the only thing I could see. "You seem confused about that. Do you need a reminder?"

I trembled, *yes* on my lips because I wanted him to test me and *no* low in my throat ready to be shouted because I didn't want to disappoint him.

"If you want to remind me," I finally whispered.

His gorgeous eyes flashed, and good guy Lion was gone.

"Get on your knees, open your mouth and get ready for me to feed you my cock," Dom Danner ordered.

I was on my knees before my rational brain could kick in. Truthfully, I didn't want it to. I was tired of thinking, of planning and scheming to save my family, to take down their enemies and save myself in the process. I didn't want to think anymore, to worry or even complain.

I just wanted to feel.

Danner unbuttoned his jeans just enough to pull out his cock, so thick it seemed impossible, covered in tantalizing veins I wanted to trace with my tongue.

"You want a taste?" he practically purred, seducing me with the sound.

"Yes," *yes, yes, yes*, I thought in a manic loop.

My mouth was already open, my tongue resting on my bottom lip, my eyes looking up through my lashes at the man above me. The power of my submission pulsed between us and lit a flare in his eyes, settling something between us.

He fisted his big dick and pulled hard so a pearl of precum glistened at the tip. One of his hands found the back of my head, fisted in the hair to hold me still so he could paint himself across my lips.

My pussy spasmed and I wondered if it was possible to come without actually being stimulated.

"Touch your cunt while I use your mouth."

God, *yes*.

My hand arrowed down my belly and curved through my wet folds to find my clit. I played, but I did it distracted, my entire focus on my man before me.

I panted, my mouth open for Danner to sink his cock into and he did, straight to the back of my mouth and then with only a brief hesitation, enough for me to prepare, down my throat.

"That's it," he encouraged me, his voice guttural. "Take all of that thick cock down your throat."

He pulled out, let me circle his plump head with my tongue and lap up the delicious salty precum there before his hand clenched in my hair and he pulled me down again, this time without stopping until my lips hit his lightly furred groin.

I loved the ache of it, the fight to keep him down and hold him tight. My eyes watered, tears dripping down my cheeks and I loved that too because he'd see me struggle and know I was being a good girl.

Out again, tongue swirling like I was licking an ice cream cone only his cock was infinitely more delicious.

In. Down my throat smoother now, fucking my face with a steady rhythm, my hand on his thighs not pushing him away but clawing at him, desperate for him to move faster, use me harder.

The next thrust, one of his hands pressed tight to my throat so he could feel the swell of his cock there and we groaned simultaneously at the sensation.

"Look up at me."

He pulled out enough that I could suck on his tip while I tilted my head to look up into his stern, handsome face. He looked like a God standing above me, demanding my worship, wonderfully unimpressed with my prostration.

His thumb swiped away one of my tears and went to his mouth so he could suck it away. I trembled.

"Work harder and I may let you come tonight."

The thrill of the challenge scorched through me like a lightning strike. My body buzzed and burned with electricity, with the power he'd gifted me to work him over as I wanted. I brought the hand at my pussy to his steel shaft and twisted, tugging up towards my sucking mouth, my tongue flat against the sensitive underside of his head, my other hand at his balls, tugging gently down.

He hissed and the sound was oratory gold.

I fucked his cock with my mouth, laying waste to his reserve until his hands were in my hair, clenched and pulling me forward and back against his thrusting hips. My mouth made obscene wet sounds as I slurped and drooled over the thick, veined length of him.

"Open your mouth and keep it open wide for me," he ordered suddenly, his fist tight around his dark, angry red cock. "Hands behind your back."

I moved my hands and opened my mouth before I could even consciously rationalize his request.

"I'm going to use you to come, but you worked hard so you get a choice. Do you want my cum in your mouth or on your gorgeous face and breasts?" he asked as he slowly pulled that tight fist over the pulsing length of himself, twisting his grip over the head in a way that made his legs quake slightly.

My inner thighs were soaked to the knee with wet, a separate pulse in my clit that beat even faster than my overworked heart. I wanted his cock back in my mouth. I felt delirious with the loss of it, rabid with the desire to taste it again, but I was torn by his question.

I wanted his cum on my tongue, to know I'd pleased him in the most obvious way by having the evidence of it between my lips.

But I wanted it on me, searing hot and wet on my skin, because I was a wild thing and the animal in me wanted to wear his smell, reveal in his ownership.

So, I said the only thing I could. "I want you to come wherever you want to."

Danner's eyes dilatated until his eyes were black pools revealing the darkness he tried to keep hidden inside him.

Now, he wasn't hiding.

Now, he was made of iniquity and built for temptation, a sinner ready to debauch his ultimate craving.

Me.

He pushed me down so I sat on my ass and with his hand still gripping the base of his cock, he straddled my knees, put a hand in my hair and *thrust*.

Again and again into my open, hungry mouth.

My body hummed with power each time he groaned, every time he sunk his cock into my mouth and I knew I was bringing him pleasure.

"Good fucking girl," he groaned, his thrust erratic, his breath fast through his chest. "Now hold still and take my cum."

I didn't close my eyes as he stepped back slightly, jerked his cock hard and started coming into my mouth. His face was tortured, pink mouth open, eyes crushed closed, his hair sweaty and hanging golden in his face, so beautiful I couldn't breathe. His boxed abs clenched and unclenched, a bead of sweat rolling through his treasure trail down over the base of his straining cock as he worked it, pumping his seed over my lips and cheeks, bursting across my reaching tongue.

The taste of him was ambrosia, a gift from the god-like man I'd been in love with for forever.

I closed my eyes, licked the residue from my lips and hummed. When I looked up at Danner his face was soft with satisfaction, but when he spoke his voice was still mechanic with purpose. "Ready for more, Rosie?"

My entire body shuddered and I smiled up at him. "With you? Always."

I squealed when he rolled off the bed, tagged my ankle to drag me closer and then hefted me onto his shoulder as if I was a little thing and not four inches shorter than his six foot two.

"Lion!" I cried out through my laughter as he slapped my ass and took us towards the bathroom. He dumped me in the shower then cranked it on to cold.

"Fuck you!" I screeched at him as he laughed, safely out of the spray.

He grinned at me and it hit me harder than the cold spray that I'd never seen him happier. "You looked like you needed cooling off."

It took seeing it written in his face bold and bright as graffiti to make me realize that it was true for me too. I could feel the levity of my heart, warm and comfortable in my chest for the first time in my life, as if it was wrapped in felt.

"And you look dirty, Danner," I said with a beaming smile that made him blink. I jerked forward to grab his flaccid dick and force him to walk forward into the spray. "Why don't you let me clean you up?"

LATER, AFTER WE'D SHOWERED, AFTER DANNER MADE ME RIDE his face to three orgasms, his fingers in my pussy and my ass so that I fucked back against them every time I bucked my hips, after Hero had jumped up on the bed so he was pressed against me on one side and Danner the other, Danner took me in his arms and laid it out for me.

"Need you to understand something for me," he murmured, his voice gentle but his tone firm in a way that I knew his words were going to hurt me. "I get that you're a wild thing and fuck me, but I love that about you. Got no desire to tame you anywhere but in the bedroom and even there, I'm willing to fight for it. But I need you to recognize that every time you put yourself in danger is a time that I'm either going to join you there or be unable to get to you despite my best efforts. If something happens to you 'cause I wasn't there to protect you, you're condemning me to a life of disability. I don't mean physically, Rosie, what I mean is, if you die, I'll go on breathing, but I won't go on livin' 'cause the most beautiful part of my life would have ceased to exist."

He squeezed me gently as I burrowed into the crook of his neck, trying to hide from the beauty and pain of his words. But he wouldn't let me. He was everywhere, his body wrapped around me, a section of his lion's heart entwined with mine, his phantom touch in my pussy. I couldn't escape the terrifying fact that what he said was very, very true.

"If I do make it to you," he continued, his hand brushing through my hair, his voice devastatingly casual as if what he said was only obvious. "You also need to know, I'm happy to die for you. If that's what you need somewhere deep inside, to know that at least someone in your life loves you better than anyone else, that they would sacrifice themselves without fucking blinking if there was even a one percent greater chance of you surviving, then I can give that to you. Keep livin' reckless, keep throwin' yourself into situations not knowing and not totally carin' if you survive. But like I said, you need to know that I do care, very much. I care enough to die for it."

I was crying again, for what felt like the dozenth time in the past few weeks after years of dry eyes.

It wasn't that I was unloved, because I was. My family loved me so beautifully that sometimes I ached with affection for them, my heart too burdened by the weight of my regard for them that it didn't beat right.

It was that I knew how gorgeous love could be because I felt it and I saw the romantic glow of it between King and Cress, Dad and Loulou, even old Buck and Maja, but I'd never had that for myself. And it killed me to admit it, even to myself, but under all that thorny sassy and steely confidence, I sheltered the tender, greedy heart of a romantic.

And for years that heart had yearned for love, not just from anyone, but him, the man who held me wrapped tight in his strong arms. It had seemed like such an impossibility my entire life until he came blasting back into my life, ever the hero, saving me from myself with Cricket just as he had been saving me from myself all my life.

The reality of being his hit me between the eyes. I could feel the warmth in my chest as Lion's golden love slid over the cracks of strain and longing in my broken clay heart and healed it, made it so much more beautiful than any other heart could be because I was the only one in the world with a love so bright and kind and strong as his.

"You with me, Rosie?" he said after long minutes of allowing me to digest it.

I nodded then tipped my head so I could kiss his strong throat, my lips sealed to his pulse.

He squeezed me gently again and confirmed, "You going to be careful for me?"

I nodded again, sliding my legs between his so I could cuddle even closer. "I mean I'll look both ways before I cross the street and I won't get in the middle of an ambush again, but I can't promise I won't get into *some* trouble. I'm, ah, pretty sure it's just in my nature."

He laughed into my hand. "Yeah, rebel. My good girl in bed, and my bad girl outside, can't say I don't love it."

"Good," I whispered, because as much as I'd yearned to be good like him my whole life, I knew I was too biker, too Garro and too *me* to ever shy away from danger if it meant something important was on the line.

"Good. Now, we've got a lot of stuff to sort in the morning, so sleep, Rosie. I'm with you."

Yeah, he was with me, because he was mine.

And there was no way in hell I was ever letting him go.

But even as the thought drifted through my mind, my heart reminded me of another ache, the one that ached like the loss of a limb.

I was happy with Danner in a way I never thought I could be, but I wasn't whole.

How could I be when I haven't seen my family?

Every time they texted and I ignored them, every time they'd call and I sent it straight to voicemail only to desperately check it minutes later for a sound bite of their beloved voices, I felt myself grow hollower.

Carefully, I slipped out of Danner's sleeping arms just enough to grab my phone where it lay on the bedside table.

I had twenty-five missed calls and over thirty text messages unanswered.

Cressida: Okay, remind me why I love tequila again? I went out with the brothers to celebrate Bat's birthday and now it's the morning after and I couldn't tell you anything that happened last night. We missed you, by the way.

Loulou: Your dad's drivin' me fuckin' nuts, H.R.. Seriously, will you call him back so he stops walking a hole through our living room? I don't want the babies to fall through it when they come.

P.S. I miss you too.

P.P.S. Did I tell you we wanna give the baby girl the middle name Rose after her big sister?

King: Went to Mega Music today. Shot the shit with Old Sam. Said he hadn't seen you in a while and he's getting old, H.R., so I'd fix that fuckin' now. Come up and spend a Sunday with me like old times. We'll go to Mega Music and swing by Danner's old house to visit Susan. Ya know she left old man Danner, yeah? Don't blow me off, brat, or I'll drag you up the mountain my-fuckin'-self.

Lila: Miss you, bitch. Know you probably have good reason to stay away, whatever it is. But we all miss you so fuckin' much. How am I supposed to plan a weddin' without my biker bitch of honour?

Dad: left texts, voicemails, and fuckin' emails, Harleigh Rose. Don't make me send out a fuckin' carrier pigeon, 'cause I'll fuckin' do it. I don't hear from you in the next twenty-four fuckin' hours, I'm ridin' out, pickin' you up and never lettin' you leave home again.

My eyes were burning when I finished reading a few of the many texts and my heart felt fatally fragile, constructed of ash, barely held together by Danner's affection and constant attention.

I knew, without it, I'd break.

My hand found Danner's body in the dark, resting over the warm, pulsing skin over his tattoo, right over his heart.

I took comfort from it, then texted out the only thing I could in one mass text.

Harleigh Rose: Need more time. Miss you too xxxx.

CHAPTER NINETEEN

Harleigh Rose

2017.

Harleigh Rose is 17. Danner is 26.

THE STUPID GUY WOULDN'T GET THE FUCKING PICTURE AND back the fuck off.

"No, I'm good, man," I told Rick for the fourth time. "Just stickin' to the soft stuff, ya know?"

I did not, under any circumstances, do hard drugs, especially not the meth that Rick seemed moved by divine force to push on me. He was a cute guy, a little young being only my age, a teenage student at the fancy Entrance Bay Academy where my brother had gone to school. Too preppy for the biker chick in me, too hardcore for the little girl in me that remembered the exact shade of blue her mother's lips turned each of the three times she overdosed.

"Oh c'mon," he whined, moving closer so he had me caged up against the wall in the kitchen. "A little's not going to hurt you."

"No," I agreed with a glare. "But I'm going to hurt you if you don't back the fuck off."

He groaned, his brown irises thin frames around his blown pupils. "Fuck I love your spunk. Like me a taste of the wild side."

"Got a boyfriend, bucko," I warned him, wishing for the millionth time that Cricket had deigned to join me at this stupid high school party, or that I'd been smart enough to go with him to his biker one. But it was the start of my last year of high school, I wanted to at least try to enjoy it while I could.

"He's not here, is he?" he asked with a sloppy grin before swaying closer.

I turned my head so his wet lips hit my cheek and growled, "Warned you once, I'll warn you twice and not a-fucking-gain. Back. Off."

"I've got to see if there's some sweet under this act," he muttered to himself and then he pushed me flat against the wall with one hand and drove his other straight down my pants.

I was drunk. Intoxicated on half a dozen tequila shots, a coupla beers and some kid's shitty weed. But even drunk as a skunk and reeking like one from the booze, I was still Zeus Garro's daughter and I knew how to fell a man.

My knee jerked up hard, straight into his unprotected balls and when he doubled over with an exhale of pain, I drove the heel of my hand up into his nose. The bone crunched like gravel under the impact, but it wasn't enough for my alcohol strengthened sense of justice, so I unclenched my fingers, pinched the broken bridge and turned sharply so his blood gushed out of his nostril and covered my hand in warmth.

"Fuck!" he garbled through the blood in his mouth. "Fuck you!"

I kept hold of his nose, steadying his bent torso with a hand to his shoulder and bent close to whisper in his ear. "Next time you try to assault a girl after she says no, maybe you'll think again."

A strong hand clamped on my shoulder and I looked around just in time to see one of his buddy's shove a hand into my chest.

"Get the fuck off him, you psycho!" he yelled into my face before shoving me again back against the wall.

"He was the one who wouldn't get the fuck off of me," I snarled at him. "And you touch me again, I'll give you a matching broken nose."

The guy, taller than me but not by much because I was tall, snorted and cracked his knuckles. "Yeah right. Don't make me hit a girl."

"You already did," Lila pointed out, appearing beside me because my girl always had my back.

"This isn't any of your business, cunt," he spat at her.

Fuck *that*.

I leapt at him, locking my legs around his waist as I tore at his hair.

No one intimidated me, put a hand on me, but more, *no one* insulted Lila.

I could hear her drunken battle cry behind me and then a *thunk* as someone hit the ground.

Chaos descended, the party turning into a full-blown fight. It wasn't totally surprising given that we were teenagers trumped up on drugs, booze, and hormones, but I was still thrilled by the anarchy of friends turning on each other in infectious bloodlust.

I'd noticed cocaine going around, coke tended to do that to people.

It didn't last long, maybe ten minutes, before red and blue lights flashed through the front windows and the cops descended.

I was arrested for assault, Rick hollering out that he was going to press charges as a rookie officer cuffed me and escorted me into the back of his police vehicle. It wasn't my first time wearing cuffs or being in that cage in the backseat, and the fight was worth it to prove a point, so I didn't really care about spending the night in prison.

I'd have a phone call, I'd make it and my dad would get me out the next morning after making me pay penance by staying the night in an uncomfortable holding cell. It was his idea of parental justice and I had to admit, I kinda got it.

Only, I didn't get a chance to make the phone call because almost as soon as they'd locked me in a cell with what looked like a strung-out hooker and a low-level drug dealer, Danner appeared between the bars.

I hadn't seen him in three months. We both knew why but he hadn't spelled it out for me. I couldn't seem to stop myself from blatantly flirting with him, from goading him with sexual innuendos and wearing increasingly short shorts and deeper tops to catch his attention. I think we both knew that some-times, I got in trouble just so he would show up and spend time with me.

It was easy to blame our distance on the fact that he'd gotten involved in The Fallen business when my brother's babe Cressida got abducted under his watch and his fuck up resulted in Zeus's increased hatred for him and solidified King's growing disdain. But we both knew the truth. We'd find a way to spend time together even if it meant our family's wrath, even if that time was spent platonically because I was too young for him and he was too good for me.

He looked good standing there then, done up in a navy-blue suit that fit his long, lean body perfectly and made his jade green eyes pop like precious stones. His arms were crossed, his face creased into eloquent lines of censure that sent a strangely erotic tingle down the ladder of my spine straight to my pussy.

Fuck me, but I'd never seen a man so sexy with anger.

He didn't say a word as a uniformed officer unlocked the bars and opened them for me, and he didn't even look at me as I carried my personal effects and trailed him out to his waiting Mustang.

It was only in the car when I'd reached over to tinker with his iPod and "Short Change Hero" murmured quietly through the car that he looked at me from the corner of his eyes as he pulled out of the parking lot.

"Seventh time you've been in there in the last five years."

I shrugged because it was true and I didn't want to give him any more fuel to add to whatever fire he was working up to lay at my feet.

"The officers call you 'the wild one,' you know that?"

I shrugged again and brought my feet to the dash, licked my thumb to rub some dirt off my rose embroidered combat boots. "They aren't wrong."

"You proud of that? You're happy to know that those officers and their family, their friends, the people of this town you call home all know you by name and reputation as the princess of The Fallen, as "the wild one" that's predicted to wind up in juvie sooner rather than later?"

I stared at his hands as they clenched the wheel, the dusting of golden hair and the delicious map of veins running down to his strong wrists. I wanted to press a kiss to each calloused fingertip and trace those veins with my tongue in a physical plea for forgiveness.

Instead, I clenched my hands into fists and let anger overwhelm the hurt.

"You disappointed in me again, Danner?"

A muscle in his jaw jumped. "I'll be disappointed in you until the day you pull your head out of your ass and realize there's power in being good and kind as much as being wicked and fierce. It isn't the thorns that make a rose."

"It's what protects them, though," I argued.

"It's the contrast, the duality of hard *and* soft, dangerous *and* beautiful that make it covetable, Rosie. Don't know when you lost your soft, but the girl I just picked up from jail who was comfortable being there and liked what it said about her... that girl's lost sense of herself."

We were quiet after that, listening to the lyrics of the song, made even more poignant by Danner's lecture.

I wanted to spit at him, rally my forces to launch a counterattack that would leave him devastated. I wanted to see him burn with shame the way I did. And I could have, I could have dug up the grave of secrets I had on him, the fact that his dad was a corrupt asshole that was slowly forcing Danner into his gravitational pull, that he was too chicken shit to even think about what he wanted let alone go after it, that he loved me in a way that was more than white knight and damsel in distress and more Clyde with his Bonnie.

I didn't.

Because as much as his words hurt me, it would hurt me even worse to see him lacerated by the accusations. There was also the fact that I knew the day was coming when he'd have to choose, leave me behind for a life of austerity in righteousness or go bad in order to join me in sinful revelry. I didn't want to push him to that decision now, or really ever, because as much as I wanted him to pick me, I knew he never would.

We arrived at the wooden gates to his property, a sprawling acreage that had been in the Danner family for years that his father had gifted to him, because he hated the dirt and distance from town. It was a low ranch-style house that almost resembled a barn, the two garage doors and the front door like barn doors, the wood siding painted a buttery yellow and the deep wraparound porch white with scrolled detailing. There was a red barn a hundred yards behind the house to the left where Danner kept his two horses, Chief and Beauty, and an empty swimming pool that he hadn't gotten around to restoring.

It didn't suit him just as much as it did.

It was a family house and despite valiant efforts by the female community of Entrance, Danner was still a bachelor and only twenty-six, fresh from the RCMP training force and ready to make a name for himself in his hometown.

It was the house of a cowboy sheriff though, so I loved it for him.

I'd even helped him decide on a few items of furniture when he moved in right after King and I moved back home with our dad when he was twenty, and I'd been there numerous times since, especially after I'd misbehaved or got into trouble and he swooped in to save me.

He put me in the guest bedroom and closed the door before I could snark at him, or thank him. Both were bad ideas for different reasons, but his anger left me feeling hollow and wrong, as if the slightest breeze would have me caving in on myself.

I sighed loudly, rubbing at the dull pain of a coming hangover between my temples then decided that showering would probably help. I shucked my clothes, leaving them littered across the room as if it was my home because in a way, having spent so much time there and feeling about Danner the way I did, it *was*. I padded naked into the adjoining bathroom and ordered the music system to play "I Hate Myself For Loving You," so loud the walls reverberated around me as I stepped under the spray.

I soaped my body thinking of how strong Danner's hands were, how firm they would feel squeezing my smallish, pink-tipped breasts, the fingers abrasive with calluses from guitar playing. My nipples beaded as I slicked my sudsy hand down my belly over the soft tangle of hair I kept over my sex then down even further to the well of wet at my core. I slid my fingers through my silky folds, imagining Danner on his knees, his nose to my clit as he tongue-fucked my pussy, his fingers hard enough to bruise on my ass.

I was too naive to understand why I wanted that edge of pain, why it felt right that even on his knees before me, Danner was the one in control, dictating my pleasure like a ruthless, callous judge.

I just knew I wanted to please him. I knew that I wore his displeasure like a hair shirt beneath my clothes, itching and scratching until I was slowly driven insane enough to beg him for forgiveness however he saw fit to grant it.

Secretly, sometimes when I lay awake in the morning after doing something particularly bad with a hangover and somber regrets, I wondered if I didn't act out because some sick, twisted part of me actually craved his censure.

He wasn't an affectionate, open guy, but when he scowled at me, his whole face transformed by passion, and he reprimanded me with harsh words in that rough tone, I could feel the weight of his intensity for me like a fur mantle around my shoulders. It was a heathen way to feel acknowledged, but it made sense given the brutal savagery with which my teenage heart yearned for him.

I didn't bring myself to climax in the shower. It was tempting to orgasm when he was so close, just a few thin walls away, just as it was strangely depressing to get off in his house, thinking of him, without his actual hands on me.

I turned off the music as I rubbed myself down with the towel, then grabbed the Entrance PD tee Danner had taken to leaving for me on top of the dresser and slid it over my wet head.

A sound caught my attention, just something faint like the howl of a winter storm moaning through the house or the groan of a tree rubbing against the roof in the wind.

I moved closer to the wall of windows and heard it again.

This time stronger.

Another moan, another groan and now, a wail.

I inched along the wall running perpendicular to my bed and the noise grew more and more discernable until I hit the wall the headboard of the bed was pressed against.

The same one this room shared with Danner's.

My hand flew to my mouth as I realized what I was hearing.

I could hear him through the wall.

Not enough, not *nearly* enough to make out the specifics of what he was doing, but I had grown up with a brother and a father and a whole host of fake uncles, so I'd heard it before.

Lion was jerking off.

I ran to the glass Danner kept on the sink to hold my toothbrush, dumped that into the basin, and then climbed onto my bed, glass pressed to the wall, my ear pressed to the glass.

Better.

I could hear it now, the faint *thwap, thwap, thwap* of his hand sliding over his hard cock, the harsh gust of his breath as he exhaled and then, the even quieter sound of the porn he was watching.

"Spread them," a man's voice. "Spread them wide and show me that pink cunt."

I shivered at the order in that voice, at the way it sent a pulse from my brain down my spine and straight between my legs where it throbbed, wet and warm.

There was the sharp noise of flesh hitting flesh and then, "Do you like it when I spank your pussy?"

The woman moaned, long and low. I echoed her softly as I wrenched off my underwear and slid a finger through the molten wet at my core.

"Count them," the man ordered. "You'll take five slaps

239

and you'll thank me for them. If you please me, I'll let you suck my cock. Would you like that?"

"Yes, sir, *please* sir. I'll suck you off so well."

Danner groaned then and muttered, "Fuck *yeah*, open your mouth and suck me off."

My thighs quivered as I sunk two fingers in my pussy and curled them deeper. I couldn't believe this was Danner I was listening to, that the gentleman cop could get off on something so goddamn dirty.

I fucking loved it.

I listened with him to the man play with his woman, to the way he ordered her around in cool, commanding tones that brokered no argument and the way the woman got off on it, screaming as he ate her out and begging for his cock on her tongue and his cum in her mouth.

I was begging too, under my breath, begging for the same things from Danner.

When the climax happened on screen, it triggered my own. I came hard on my hand, soaking my palm and the inside of my thighs.

I groaned, "Thank you, Danner," as I came just as the woman in the video thanked her Dom.

Just as the man said, "You take my fucking cum."

And Danner did too, only he said, "Fuck *yeah*, take my fucking cum, Harleigh Rose."

I gasped loudly and the glass I'd been holding up against the wall slid from my listless fingers, falling to the floor with a discernable crash.

"Fuck," I said before I could help it, clasping my hands over my mouth, the fingers of one tacky with my juices.

"What the *fuck*?" Danner growled from the other room and then, before I could pull my panties back on over my swollen sex or pretend I'd been doing anything other than spying on him, the door to the bedroom swung open and he was there, growling low in his throat, his eyes tropical green with hot anger.

I watched his nostrils flare as he took in the sex sweet air in the room, as his anger grew darker and turned into something else, something I wasn't sure I should be terrified of.

"You fucking spying on me?" he demanded.

I swallowed thickly and dropped my hands, my own cum smearing slightly on my lips. Unconsciously, I licked them and watched Danner's jaw clench tight.

"Yeah," he drawled as he stalked towards me and I wasn't sure if he was going to strangle me or kiss me. "Fuck *yeah*, you were."

"I," I tried explaining, frantically digging into my reserves of sass and wit for anything to throw at him and stop his slow prowl across the room. "You shouldn't have been so obvious about it."

It didn't seem possible, but his expression burned with rage then blackened into something utterly wicked. He reached me, his arm snapping out to tug at one of my ankles so I went sprawling onto my back on the bed. Before I could recover, he sat on the bed and yanked my body belly down across his lap.

"You wanted me to catch you, didn't you?" he asked in a voice like fire and brimstone as he held my squirming form across his knees with an iron forearm banded across my back. "You wanted me to see what a dirty girl you've become."

"Oh God," I groaned, my thighs so wet with cum they slid together with an audible slosh.

I didn't know what was happening and at the same time, I did.

I was seventeen and even though I was a virgin for reasons that neither Cricket or I understood, I'd done oral and all that other stuff. I thought I knew enough about sex to take whatever was happening in stride.

I didn't.

Not even close.

"Fine, you want me to treat you like a responsible woman and not a little brat?" he asked as one hand, the one not holding me down, smoothed up one leg and over my ass, dragging my tee with it so my bare skin was exposed to his gaze.

Heat scorched through me, sexual enough to incinerate my inhibitions and shamed enough to find anger in the swirling vortex of fire in my belly.

"Fuck you, Danner. You wouldn't have the guts to hit me, you pussy!"

"Ah," he clucked his tone, his voice cold and mechanical as if from a machine even though his hand was hot and human against my butt cheek as it squeezed and soothed. "You don't seem to understand how much power is in a pussy. If you knew, you'd never use it as an insult. If you knew how fucking furious it makes me to want you when I can't have you because you're too young, too wrong and too wild for me to tame. But Rosie, if you knew how I wanted to tame you, stroke your pussy with my fingers, my tongue and my cock, watch you beg at first then break open for my touch, for my permission to come. If you had any fucking inkling of that, you wouldn't call me a pussy when you think I'm being weak."

I was panting, confused and aroused and so angry I felt made of fire, in danger of turning to smoke and blowing away the second his hands stopped kindling my flames.

"Are you going to hit me?" I asked, my tone betraying how much I wanted that.

"Hit? No. If you want to redeem yourself for your reckless, stupid behaviour tonight, if you want me to make you feel good by making you feel bad then I'll spank you."

A shudder snapped and popped through my spine. "Okay."

"Okay?"

"Um." I bit my lip, but I knew what to say, "Okay, Lion."

"It gets to be too much, you just tell me to stop, Rosie." His voice didn't soften, and I was grateful for it because it would have ruined the moment, but I could read his brief softening in the way he palmed my ass cheek and in the use of his nickname for me.

I nodded and an instant later, pain radiated across my bum. A second after that again, on the other cheek. He rubbed the burn of the impact deeper into my skin, taking out the sting but prolonging the heat that sluiced over the curve of my ass to nestle between my thighs.

"You like that, Rosie?" he asked, his voice in his throat.

"Is that all you've got for me?" I taunted instinctively, trying to ask for something I didn't even know the name of.

His low growl vibrated against my torso and I became acutely aware of the thick, long length of his cock pressed against my belly.

Slap.

The sound cracked through the air, adding drama to the strike that I felt like fingers thrusting into my clenching core.

Slap.

"Harder, Lion."

Slap. Slap.

"Give me more," I begged, my voice breaking as my mind fractured into charred pieces, dissolved into cinders.

"You'll take what I give you," he told me, both hands at my ass now, pressing the heat farther into the muscles with his strong thumbs and rough fingers. "You love it, don't you? You love being my good girl."

God, I did. For the first time in years, my spirit felt free from its cage of self-doubt and reprimands, liberated from social constraints and mores. I thought being an outlaw was as free as it got but I was *wrong*.

This was true freedom, giving myself over to the hands of a man who would let me run wild, but keep me safe as I did it.

I squirmed in his lap as his thumbs dug deeper, painfully

into my sore behind and then I gasped as he leaned down to take a plump section in his mouth, between his teeth. The bite was firm, sharp in a way that sat above the dull pulse of the hurt in my ass.

I was going to come.

I knew it even as it shocked me. He hadn't even touched me, not sexually at least, not really. And yet I was on the precipice of a tidal orgasm so strong, I knew I'd be passed out when it finally broke and carried me to shore.

"Lion," I groaned, turning my head into his calf so I could bite it sharply in silent demand for more.

"Hush, I'll give you more. Wait for it," he ordered.

The very octave of his voice, the weight in the air pressing against me, shackling me to his will brought the orgasmic tsunami closer.

"Please," I broke and begged. "Please give it to me."

"There she is," he praised as one hand slid down my ass into the sopping wet crease between my thighs. "There's my good Rosie."

Then he drove two fingers inside my cunt and cracked a vicious slap to the bottom of my ass cheek.

I screamed as I drowned in sensation, as it spun me in a breathless cycle of cold pain and hot pleasure, as I broke again and again like the tide against his curling fingers.

When I emerged from the depths, Danner was leaning over my burning ass to tenderly kiss each cheek. I smiled into his calf sleepily then allowed him to twist me in his arms and slide me into bed, under the covers.

I caught his wrist when it pushed the heavy weight of my hair away from my face and kissed his pulse there.

"Forgive me?" I asked, my eyes mostly closed because sleep was a hound biting at my heels.

I could feel his hesitation, then his hand turned in mine so he could run a thumb over my lips. "I'll always forgive you, Rosie. It's yourself you have to learn to forgive."

I frowned, dredging myself from the edges of slumber so I could argue his point, but when I opened my eyes, he was already across the room, closing the door behind him.

I didn't see him after that except for in passing for another six months and that was the last time I saw him for three and a half years.

CHAPTER TWENTY

Harleigh Rose

IT WAS EXAM TIME. HOW THREE WEEKS HAD PASSED ME BY IN such a blur of change, I wasn't exactly sure, but there I was sitting in the exam hall with hundreds of other students, taking the last test I'd need to take before I graduated to becoming a fully qualified nurse.

When I finished the exam, I swung by Tim Horton's for my much needed fourth coffee of the day and took out my phone, staring at Dad's name in my contact list. I wanted to call him, to tell him that I'd just officially finished my degree. He'd shout "fuck yeah" so loud it'd crackle through the phone, and then he'd tell whichever brother he was with, and Lou, that his princess was goin' to be a nurse. They'd pass the phone around, congratulations coming at me from Bat and Nova, Axe-Man and Lab-Rat, Boner and Curtains and more, all my uncles and best friends and brothers, then Lou, her voice rough with tears and sweet with pride as she told me how much she loved me.

I turned the screen off and pocketed the cell.

I hadn't returned anyone's calls in weeks, only perfunctory text messages that assured them I was doing fine, but needed time and space to get my head sorted.

They wouldn't leave me alone forever, but they trusted me enough to give that to me even though it went against their instincts to guard and cherish me.

I accepted the Double-Double coffee from the barista and took a necessary, steaming sip of coffee to center myself before making my way to the parking lot.

Danner was there, leaning against his black and gold Iron 883 Harley Davidson Sportster. He was in his Berserkers cut, his tawny hair in disarray around his handsome face, his booted feet crossed at the ankles as he sat sideways across the seat.

There was no crowd around him as there had been with Wrath, because even though Danner was less physically intimidating, there was something in his aura that told people to stay away or be damned.

His unapproachability in his biker persona made my nipples hard as rocks.

I sucked by my coffee in less than thirty seconds, scalding my throat, and then threw the empty cup in the garbage. Then, I sauntered up to him and leaned right in, plastering my body against his in a deep curve that had my little jean shorts riding up my ass cheeks. Danner's eyes flashed as his hand moved to my back, down and over so he could grab my slightly bared butt in a possessive cinch.

"Hey biker man," I said before pressing a kiss to his rough stubbled cheek, then his square chin and one more on his close-lipped smile. "What's up?"

"Club's meeting at Bernadette's, Reaper sent me to grab

ya. We'll do some time with them, see if we can't figure out what they're gonna do with that stolen Fallen weed, then I'm takin' my Rose out for a celebratory dinner."

"Yeah?" I asked, and I could physically feel my eyes sparkling at him.

He dipped down to press a firm, spine-tingling kiss to my mouth. "Yeah, rebel."

"You're the tits, I ever tell you that?" I asked, propping my elbows on his chest so I could take my chin in my hands as I stared up at him.

He bit the edge of his grin in that way that I loved. "Don't think you've ever said exactly those words, but I'll take it."

I nodded firmly. "Not a flowery, girl, so I'd take what you can get."

This time a low, short chuckle that rumbled through him to me. "Oh, I think you're plenty flowery. When I get you rooted to the bed with cuffs, you bloom for me, wet and open, so pink it's plush, and I've never seen a flower so pretty."

I shivered in his arms, a reaction I was beginning to equate to the submissive in me, that strange duality Danner had told me about for years. That I could be both hard and soft. And I was soft for him, tender, pliable and so eager to please.

"Did you get me a graduation present?" I asked, pressing my lips to his so he could feel the intent behind my words.

"Oh yeah," he growled, nipping my bottom lip with his teeth. "There's a new steel butt plug at home with your fuckin' name on it. Gonna use it to open up your sweet ass while I give my cock to your pussy, then I'm gonna give us both a treat by sinking my thick cock in your ass, four fingers in your cunt, my tongue in your mouth so you're taking all of me, everywhere you can. Only then, when you're takin' all I have to give you like the good girl you are, am I gonna fuck you until the only thing you remember is how to scream my name."

His fingers lifted to the waist of my shorts, his thumb dipping down to tease under the strap of my thong and raise it slightly, just enough so that the gusset of my panties pressed into the fresh wet of my pussy.

"You like the sound of that, Rosie?" he rasped into my panting mouth.

"Sounds alright," I tried to say casually, but I could feel the hot flush in my cheeks, the low lids of my eyes and the rush of my breath from my suddenly tight chest.

He laughed into my open mouth then kissed it firmly, before pushing me gently away. "Don't worry, I'll have you saying easy, pleading *yes, Lion*'s by the end of the night."

I waited to shudder when he turned to grab my helmet and by the time he handed it to me, I was mildly composed. He watched me throw my hair over my shoulder, clasp the dome to my head and climb onto the Harley behind him. I pressed a kiss then a bite to his shoulder and promised, "I look forward to seeing you try."

THE BAR WAS FILLED WITH BERSERKERS AND THEIR FRIENDS. IT was celebration time, a mini party to congratulate the brothers on a job well done stealing thousands of dollars' worth of weed from their rival MC. Every member of the chapter was there, their old ladies and one-night pieces, their kids if they had any, and trusted friends.

So, basically, I'd spent the last three hours separated from Danner and hating it.

I watched him from the pool table where I was playing a game with Reaper, Grease, and Wrath, as he held Laken loosely in his lap, nodding as she used her hands to illustrate some story, her huge breasts practically in his face.

It was easy to forget, when it was just the two of us, that Danner wasn't only mine.

He had two girlfriends, a biker chick and a straight-laced cop.

Both beautiful, both perfect in one way or another for his life.

It would have been easy to be jealous, but I wasn't.

Mostly, because when I'd left bed earlier that day telling him I was going to study in the library before my exam, I'd gone into the North Van PD and met with my handler, the one and only Diana Casey. I'd briefed her on the heist even though it was clear from her reaction, Danner had already told her most of the story, and I was annoyed to find out that she was not only beautiful, she was kind. She'd genuinely asked after my health after Cricket's assault, if I was having nightmares and if I'd met with the trauma counselor. I wasn't, and I hadn't, but only because I had Danner and Hero to keep the demons at bay.

I didn't tell her that.

But she did let slip, as we were walking out the door of her office, her C.I. notebook with my secret identifier #69 on the front, that she hoped Officer Danner was looking out for me in the field. I agreed he was then pushed a little more, asking if they worked closely together on the case.

Her lips had pursed, her eyes lost some luster and she gave a little blasé shrug that tried to mask how hurt she was.

He'd been her boyfriend, she said, for over two years, but he'd broken up with her over a week ago.

She looked horrified by her blunder. I was a criminal from

a criminal family and her confidential informant. There wasn't supposed to be an exchange of any personal information. But rules were meant to be broken, and Danner had told me that they usually were between handler and C.I. because it wasn't a relationship that could form without trust.

Diana Casey thought she could trust me, and I hated that that made me feel guilty and good at the same time.

I said nothing to Danner about it because he'd said nothing to me. It was obvious that she wasn't important enough to bring up, he hadn't even spoken about her once in the time we'd spent together, but Laken was another story.

"Stop starin' like a witch brewin' a curse and get playin'," Wrath murmured to me as he stepped up to the felt to take a shot beside me. "You're bein' fuckin' obvious."

I rolled my eyes, but I wasn't too concerned. Grease and Reaper were playing us, but they were distracted, muttering between themselves, Reaper checking his phone every few minutes.

"Something's goin' down," I muttered after Wrath sunk his shot and aimed for another.

"Yeah, they found a new way to smuggle guns in from the States. We're supposed to get a test shipment in tonight," he whispered into my ear, grabbing me as if to press a kiss to my hair.

He smelled good, classic and manly like Old Spice deodorant.

I hummed, my mind whirring. If a shipment was coming into the Port of Vancouver that night and I knew the man who'd be bringing it in, what other information did I need before I could act on it?

The shipping company and crate number.

I moved closer to Grease and Reaper's side of the table, pretending to study the table when really, I just wanted to eavesdrop. Wrath went with me, stopping me with an arm around my waist when he thought I was close enough.

"Who're we sendin'?" Grease was saying into his beer, his cruel face made uglier with excitement.

He wanted to go, he wanted to find trouble and dismantle it with his gun.

Reaper was smart enough, I knew, not to let him go for exactly that reason.

"It's small shit, thinkin' we can send Mutt and Roper. They won't even meet with my guy, just text 'em the number, they'll go straight to the container and get the guns."

"Black Knights gonna fuck us over on the number again?"

Black Knights, an American based 1%er MC that had links to the Irish IRA.

Laken's bright laugh rung out through the noisy bar like the peal of fucking bells, distracting me from what the men said next.

"Harleigh Rose," she called across the room, and when I looked over, she was waving at me from Danner's fucking lap. "Get your ass over here."

"Go," Wrath said when I hesitated, and I realized he could feel the fury in my tensed body against his.

I rolled my eyes but went.

"Long time no see, girl," Laken said, beckoning me to bend into her arms for a hug.

I could smell her sweet perfume mingling with Danner's manly, cowboy scent and it made me want to throttle her.

"Yeah."

"You avoidin' me or somethin'?" she asked, her eyes narrowed on me.

Laken wasn't the smartest girl in the world, but she was Reaper's favourite child, and she'd learned early on to be suspicious of people who might use her to get closer to her daddy. It was why we'd always got along, I understood the feeling.

"No, just finished my last exam today, I've just been way busy with school," I lied easily.

Her lips split into a wide, gorgeous grin. "Fuck, that's awesome, H.R.! Let's do some shots to celebrate. Li-Li baby, will you order some while I go fix my lipstick? I think you kissed it right off."

He had. There was more red on his lips than hers.

My heart burned.

"Sure thing," he agreed, carefully not looking at me until she had jumped up and strutted away.

"Li-Li?" I asked with raised brows, the bitter tang of jealousy on my tongue.

There wasn't reason to be jealous, I told myself. We'd spoken about Laken and it was *me* who'd insisted I was fine with his continued faux-dating. She was a font of information about Reaper, information that Danner had put to good use over the years laying the foundation to get him arrested, and he needed the security of being her boyfriend for his cover. Reaper was a suspicious, crazy motherfucker and he'd already taken notice of how aware of me Lion was.

So, logically, I should have been casual about it.

But my soul burned on.

"Harleigh Rose," he muttered, his booted foot finding mine under the table of the booth. "Only kissed her. Haven't done more than that since I found you covered in blood in your apartment."

"How'd you manage that?" I griped.

Bikers had a reputation for being horndogs, and it was rightly earned.

It would make Laken wary if her gorgeous man didn't want to fuck her gorgeous body.

Danner shrugged a shoulder. "Told her I got chlamydia."

I burst out laughing. "You did not. How'd she believe that? She let you sleep around on her?"

"She's of the belief that you can't hold a biker man down. Her daddy taught her that."

Right.

I knew that.

It was an argument I'd had with her once over tequila shots when I'd confessed to her that Cricket hit me sometimes. She'd sullenly wondered if that was worse or better than infidelity.

Clearly, she'd never been hit by the full force of a man's hand.

"Still don't like it," I admitted, because he was a magnet, forcing my confessions to the surface so they hummed on my skin, desperate to go to him.

"Me either. You think I want her lips on mine when yours are all I think about?" he asked seriously.

I pursed my mouth. "I'll remind you just how sweet they are tonight when we get home."

"Oh yeah," he groaned. "I have no doubt you will. Now, you promise to be good for the rest of the time we gotta be here? No glarin' or starin' or gettin' into fights."

I ran my finger over my head like an invisible halo. "Angel reporting for duty."

"Brat," he said fondly.

I winked at him then got up as I spotted Laken returning from the bathroom. "Tell her I went for a smoke."

I didn't wait for his reply.

The night was still warm, the July sun lingering in the pavements, emanating from the brick walls of the bar as I leaned beside the front entrance and lit up a Lucky Strike cigarette.

I didn't smoke often anymore because I was a nurse and I knew intimately what that shit did to your lungs. But it was a habit I'd picked up from my father then solidified over my years of teenage rebellion, so once in a while when I needed to clear my head, I indulged.

"Got a light?"

I slanted my eyes to the side where a lanky biker stood smiling at me. He wore a sleeveless leather vest without a patch. A nomad biker just popping into a biker friendly bar to have a good time.

Without speaking, I tossed him my Bic lighter.

He caught it, his grin widening before he lit his cig and joined me in a lean against the wall.

We smoked silently, watching the grey puffs of air curl through the air.

"Anyone ever tell ya, you're hot as fuckin' shit?" he asked me finally.

I could feel his eyes like hot hands grappling over my clothes.

"Yeah. My Old Man."

"Good thing them Berserkers aren't a jealous crowd," he laughed.

Then he moved closer, his hand going for my ass to either pinch or slap.

And I was done.

So done with men thinking they could touch a woman because she was pretty, she liked to dress well to suit her style and wasn't afraid of showing a little skin.

So done with them treating my sisterhood like disposable cum rags, like punching bags, like anything short of fuckin' gold.

So done with all they'd done to *me*.

One second his hand was reaching, the next it was caught in both of mine, his arm twisted behind his back so painfully, *this* close to breaking, he crumbled to his knees on the ground with a shocked cry of pain.

"You touch a woman without her permission, be prepared for the fuckin' consequences," I shouted at him as I planted my boot in his back and tugged harder on his arm.

The bones creaked, his shoulder popped, and he sobbed out a, "fuckin' bitch, let me go."

"I'm the bitch?" I asked him, my outrage enflamed by my history, his face transformed into high school Rick who tried to force me to do drugs, by Cricket who tried to rape me, and the Berserker brothers who tried to claim me against my will.

I shoved him to the ground with my hands and my foot, then quickly stepped over him, boot to his tender groin, pressing hard, and the gun from my purse brandished in my hand, pointed straight at his face.

"You're the bitch," I told him. "Only cowards don't ask a woman for permission 'fore they touch her."

"Rosie?" I heard from the door and looked up in time to see Danner close it behind him.

"Hey," I called around my cigarette still caught between my lips but droopy now. "What's up?"

"I thought I told you to be good?" he asked, eyeing me warily as I pressed the heel of my boot harder to the groin of the man lying moaning at my feet.

I shrugged. "I was bored. Maybe a little touchy."

"I didn't do a fuckin' thing," the piece of shit biker groaned out between his clenched teeth as he writhed on the pavement under my foot.

"Rosie?" Danner asked me, crossing his arms over his straight up kickass black leather jacket. He shook his head as he pushed his hand into his thick hair and pinned me with his hard gaze. "You wanna tell me why you got that man pinned to the ground by his balls?"

"'Cause she's a crazy fuckin' bitch!" the nomadic biker shouted.

I crushed my heel down on his sensitive balls as I leaned forward to bat my eyelashes at my Officer. "'Cause he grabbed my ass and no one grabs my ass but you."

Danner cut off his grin with his teeth. "Sweet sentiment, rebel. Appreciate it. But why don't you let that man up now. I'm thinkin' it's time to go home. Go back in, tell Wrath goodbye and meet me at mine in twenty minutes."

I looked down at the biker in contemplation then plucked the cigarette from my lips and leaned down to press the still burning tip into his thrashing neck. His skin sizzled faintly and he cried out.

I flicked the dead cig off the curb and took my foot off his balls so I could move to Danner with a big grin. "Cool, is it time for my present?"

He was hurting me.

Deliberately, calculatingly, excruciatingly.

My body was on fire with exquisite sensation, burning so hot I thrashed and moaned and begged for freedom.

But I wasn't free.

I was bound to the four corners of the coffee table by unforgiving leather cuffs and tethered to Danner's will by my own submission.

I would stay shackled because Danner wanted it and I allowed it.

No, I didn't allow it, I *needed* it.

Just as I needed the sharp bite of strong teethed clamps at my nipples, attached by a delicate chain to the wicked looking clamp Danner held open in his strong fingers just over my swollen sex. I had his thick cock in my cunt, stretching me and rubbing me ceaselessly in short thrusts right over my g-spot, and a deliciously heavy steel plug sunk deep in my greedy ass.

He thrust forward slowly, his own teeth gritted with concentration as he spread my pussy open, pinched my clit until it lurched with each beat of my pulse and then he clamped it with that innocuous, vicious little clamp.

I screamed, thrashing so hard he had to hold me down and work hard to pump his cock into my clenching cunt.

I wasn't body, I was electricity, humming against him, spasming like a current.

"Yeah," my dirty Danner rasped as he reached under his cock to twist the plug in my ass in a way that made me scream again. "Take it all, Rosie. Come apart for me, let me feel your cum on my cock."

The orgasm tore through me, devastating the infrastructure of my body like a cyclone, twisting up my thoughts until they winked into nothing, ripping sensation across every inch of my body until I was nothing but human debris.

I was still coming when he twisted and pulled the plug from my ass. When he grabbed my cheeks in one hand to tilt me up over his thighs, exposed to his gaze, to the warm coconut oil smeared across my closing hole. A mini orgasm exploded in the haze of the first when he worked his fingers in there, two then three, pumping and twisting against the hot walls of my ass until I was writhing, my pussy weeping all over his lap.

"You ready to take my cock like my good fucking whore?" he asked me, his voice like an extra finger in my ass, filling me up with his ownership.

"Yes," I panted. "Fuck *yes*."

"Good girl," he praised as he left me empty, clenching at nothing, so eager for it I moaned and moaned and moaned until I felt the searing press of his lubed cock at my entrance.

One of his hands found my throat and pressed firmly, cutting off just a fraction of my air in a way that heightened every inch of sensation.

And then he thrust, not stopping until his balls were pressed to my cheeks, his hair roughened groin pushed up against my drenched pussy, grinding slightly against my clit in a way I knew he was going to make me come again.

"Oh God, oh God, oh God," I chanted incoherently as my body possessed my brain, turning it base and heathen and so fucking greedy I couldn't take a breath without wanting more from him.

"It isn't God who owns this body," Danner ground out, his face a gorgeous mask of stark almost painful desire. "Say my name while I fuck your ass."

"Lion," I panted, the word so sweet in my dry mouth. "Lion."

"You want more don't you my greedy little slut?" he asked.

I loved the way he called me his slut, his whore. As if I was the personification of all his dirtiest fantasies, as if only I could grant him his ultimate carnal satisfaction.

As if he knew I'd do anything to bring him pleasure.

"Yes," I told him as his thick cock throbbed in my ass and my empty pussy pulsed. "More, please, Lion."

"Yeah," he drawled hot and low as he brought the hand not at my throat to my sopping cunt.

His fingers played in my cum there, smearing it from the front of my pussy to the back, just before where his hot cock filled me up. It was hot as fuck, his hand playing with the cum he'd forced from my pussy, lavishing me with my own arousal.

I shivered as an orgasm started to climb the ladder of my spine.

"Want you to take me everywhere, feel me in every inch of your body, in every facet of your goddamn beautiful soul," he growled before thrusting his fingers into my pussy and bending over to seal his plundering mouth to mine, his hand still hot pressure on my throat.

I was filled up and full up on pain, but I wanted more.

Danner was my Dom, my dealer, and he knew he had power over my ultimate craving.

And that wasn't the pain, it wasn't even the pleasure.

It was the slick, painful slide of his thick cock in my clenching ass. His hungry mouth eating at my cries as I moaned and thrashed against him. The rough tipped fingers twisting, pulling, plucking at my nipples until they throbbed red and angry as the lights on his cop car. How he took me to the brink of insanity, held me poised over the edge, suspended between pain and pleasure, fear and completion, who I pretended to be and who I was in my bones. And when he finally propelled me over into the abyss and after I was done wheeling, free falling without thought or identity, so alive I was just a spot of light, a sound bite of ecstatic noise, he caught me again. He wrapped me up in his big arms with his coarse hands, tucked my face into his neck so I could feel his strong pulse against my cheek, his marble slab torso protecting my fragile heart and trembling core like an impenetrable shield.

He held *me*.

Not an MC princess of a notorious motorcycle club.

Not a slightly trashy but rockin'-it university student with a juvie record.

Not a murderer.

Not even Harleigh Rose as anyone else knew her.

Just Rosie, stripped of her thorns and even of her petals, just a seed of self.

And he held her preciously, protectively and patiently as if he would do it forever and never fade or fail.

That, he knew, and I could just now admit, was what I craved and what my Dom Danner gave me.

"Have you always been a Dominant?" I asked after he'd unshackled me from the cuffs, carted me into his arms and laid me in his bed.

He was straddling my prone, heavy body, his hands covered in vanilla scented massage oil, strong fingers slick and powerful against my back as he worked me over.

I didn't need the massage. I was already boneless, the stress wrung out of my body like dirty water from a sponge, but I knew he needed to care for me after using me so roughly.

"I was fourteen when I had my first real crush on a girl named Brittany Goodman. I liked her neck of all things, the graceful, pale white column of it exposed by her short hair. I pictured it adorned with bruises from my hands and lips, by my teeth biting into her and holding her down as I fucked her. How pretty it would look marked as *mine*." I could feel him shrug into his hands as they smoothed over my triceps. "It freaked me the fuck out at first, but by the time I got around to fuckin her, I'd done enough research to know the urges I had were kink."

"Did you fuck her like you wanted?" I asked, deeply curious about his sexual history because he'd always kept it so goddamn quiet.

"No. I bit her nipples a little, gave her a hickey that didn't even begin to quell the need in me to conquer and dominate, but they say your first time is never that great."

I laughed at his dry comment and turned my head so he could see my smile. "So, how many submissives' have you had?"

"Eight."

"Including Laken and Diana Casey," I asked, giving into the jealous impulse.

He leaned down to press a kiss to the center of my spine, then pushed my hair off my neck to place another at the back of that. "Diana'd never done it before. She tried, but she didn't love it and it showed. Laken's got a submissive personality and she's a biker chick, she was willing to go there with me so yeah."

He felt my body stiffen beneath him.

"Hush, my thorny Rose, don't go sharp on me after what we just had." He dipped farther forward to run his nose from my ear down the slope of my jaw and then lifted my chin with one finger so he could kiss me softly. "You are perfect for me.

The only woman who could ever give me what I really need. Who could let me be the gentleman cop *and* the dirty Dom I need to be in order to be *me*."

"Yeah?" I whispered against his lips.

"Yeah. And I'm the only one who can give you what you need. Let you be my wild rose, bristling with thorns and red as blood, but also the soft flower, delicate under my touch and easily plucked between my fingers. I'm the only one who you give that kinda tender to."

"Yeah," I agreed, so happy he understood without me having to find the words to explain it to him.

He smiled against my lips then leaned back to grab the towel beside him and clean off my back. Then he rolled me under the covers, got up to turn off the lights and joined me in bed. Hero took his cue to join us and curled up over our tangled feet.

I smiled as I fell asleep, forgetting that even though I was safe in Danner's bed, there was more than one monster waiting outside the front door to devour our love.

CHAPTER TWENTY-ONE

Harleigh Rose

WHEN I OPENED THE DOOR TO MY APARTMENT TO GRAB MORE clothes the next evening after spending the day hanging out with Wrath at the clubhouse while Danner went to the station to work, I felt the heat of explosive anger trapped like a dormant volcano in my home.

Zeus was there.

Sitting on the same chair he'd occupied at our family breakfast two months ago, only this time he was sitting in the twilight, his head bowed, hands clasped loosely between his spread knees as he leaned into his thighs.

"Haven't been home in months, haven't been answerin' calls and when Cress came down to get some shit for 'er store last week, spent three hours waitin' outside for you to get home after class, but ya didn't. So, I got on my bike came down an' waited. Saturday, so figured you'd be home at some point. Got here at nine this mornin' and when you didn't show, I figured I'd do a drive-by of the Berserker compound, just to check on an impulse."

He looked up at me finally and his eyes were blank grey slates. "Saw ya on the back of their brother Wrath's bike, talkin' to Reaper as he stood in the doorway with your *fuckin'* mum, Harleigh Rose. One great big biker family."

A whimper was trying to work its way out of my throat like some small, disgusting bug, slithering, crawling toward the light.

Only, there was no light, not in this apartment, not in this situation.

There was only black tunnel.

"So, there I was thinkin' my girl was in some kinda trouble, the kind only she seems to find 'cause she's her father's daughter, likes to live wild an' free, flyin' through life like she doesn't have a fuckin' care. Thinkin' I needed to hightail my ass down the mountain even when my woman's nine months gone with twins, just to make sure my princess doesn't need some savin'."

God, his conversational tone played cruel contrast with the dead look in his beautiful eyes. He'd never been angry with me like this. We were fighters, the Garros, my dad and me especially. We burned bright and tall like whiskey on fire, then settled, mellow enough to talk through the trouble and work away the pain.

This was different.

This wasn't my affectionate, crazy cool father lecturing his wayward, beloved daughter.

This was Zeus Garro, outlaw biker, ex-con and righteous murderer sitting on his rebel throne accusing one of his soldiers for disloyalty.

Disloyalty.

The word burned a hole through my thoughts and fell like a hot coal into my gut, eating away at the lining there until my stomach cramped.

"Daddy," I tried to explain, my voice more helium than

sound, high and bright with terrified emotion. "Let me explain."

He stared at his ringed hands, at my name inked into the inside of his strong wrist. His other hand covered it up, as if it hurt him to bear witness to his love for me.

"Called home, tried to get Lou to help me understand where my little girl coulda been coming from. How she could be shunnin' her family for a mother that don't deserve the name, a man who's taken Fallen blood, a Prez who wants your family dead. Shocked the shit outta me when Axe-Man took the phone from 'er and told me he'd seen ya at the ambush coupla weeks ago, stealin' from your own goddamn family."

No, God, *no.*

My skin felt like it was coming apart at the seams, like my stuffing was falling out, instinct driving me to plug the holes, sew myself shut by confessing to my father all I was doing *for* him, not against him.

But I couldn't.

I'd been loved all my life by the greatest men I'd ever know.

A brother who beat up my bullies on the playground and stood up to our mother even when it meant going without food.

A father who treated me like a princess, placing me so high on a pedestal I was safe from harm, open to admiration and removed from the tragedies of reality.

And an entire battalion of brothers, uncles, and friends from The Fallen who enrobed me in a love so fine it felt like silk spun by fingers so rough from callous and stained by grease it only made the contrast more exceptional.

I don't know how I went wrong, how I chose a love so black it consumed me in its inky folds before I could think to break free. But I chose it over them even before I knew there was a decision to be made between the two.

And even though that lover was gone, I was still sunk deep

in that dark mire, battling to be free, to rejoin my family in light.

They said I was a thing of beauty, but all I'd ever caused was pain.

It wasn't intentional, but did that really matter in the grand scheme of things?

The same men who had loved me so well all my life would hate me now, reeling against the reality I'd forced them to face.

That I was no longer a member of The Fallen family.

That I'd turned my back on everything I'd ever known in order to take up with the very MC that wanted my father killed, my pregnant step-mum raped and my clubhouse burned.

In their eyes, I was fucking a man named Wrath who used his infamous fury to pound in the faces of Fallen brothers caught unawares on dark roads and crowded highway bars. I was no longer the princess of The Fallen, but an old lady of a Berserker.

To make matters worse, if they knew the truth, they'd be horrified to learn I was also fucking a cop, working undercover for the men in blue my culture was founded on hating.

I was involved in a war, but on the wrong side of the battlefield, a turncoat of the highest order. And I knew with a certainty I felt in the pit of my gut, in the marrow of my bones and the tick of my heart, that I would never be accepted back home.

Words clogged my throat, hard and sharp as stones, but I remained quiet. I remained resolved.

"Always been proud of my little badass. God knows you caused 'nough trouble over your life to earn that label but I was a proud dad 'cause you were smart as fuck and twice as noble at your core."

My lip curled under, wobbling precariously. This wasn't a

gift he was gearing up to give me, not after what I'd done, what he thought I'd chosen.

It was a condemnation.

An excommunication from the only religion I'd ever practiced.

Zeus Garro, President of The Fallen MC, stood before me, taller and broader and *fiercer* than any other man I'd ever known. I watched as that man transitioned like Jekyll into Hyde from my father to my Prez. The wet in his blade grey eyes froze over and his twisted, broken-hearted features smoothed out and hardened like battened down hatches. He stood to his tall, strong, dazzling height and walked a few heavy steps toward me in the open door. In those few seconds, he cut me out of his heart and closed himself off to me forever.

I choked on a monstrous sob but forced myself to look him in the eye as he delivered my fate.

"You've just proven to me, to everyone that ever thought there was good at the heart of all that bad, that they were fuckin' *wrong*. You turned your back on your friends, on your fuckin' family and you gotta know, Harleigh Rose, now we've turned our back on you. The home we kept open to ya even in your darkest, worst fuckin' hour. It's closed. If it'd'a been just me you fucked over, maybe I coulda let it pass 'cause fuck, you're my kid, but you put Lou in danger and your fuckin' unborn siblings and your goddamn brother. You think I can let that slide?"

He took a step away from me, just a small one but it felt like a million miles and he was already turning away from me when he landed the final punch. "You're done. In The Fallen and as a fuckin' Garro."

The words hit me worse than Cricket ever had, so hard my bones seemed to splinter beneath my skin, my organs bruised from the force, my body swaying visibly backwards so I had to catch myself on my back foot.

Impulsively I reached out for my dad as he moved passed then flinched when he evaded my touch and walked through the door without once looking back.

I collapsed to my knees, my fist in my mouth to try to stem the awful force of my sobs as my body shuddered with agony. Giving up on containment, I sunk farther to the floor, so my wet cheek was plastered to the cool floor, the same floor that had seen Cricket's blood, the same floor I'd nearly been raped on, the same floor that I laid against transformed again by tragedy, now orphaned and nameless.

I don't know how long I lay there for, but it was long enough that my tears dried, my bleeding soul shriveled up like a drying husk, and I was numb to everything but the feel of that floor against my cheek.

He came for me.

I should have known he would, but thinking was too painful, so I hadn't allowed myself to do it.

I heard the jingle of Hero's tags and the simple sound brought tears to my eyes again because it reminded me that I *did* have some family left at least.

My man and his dog.

Hero appeared in front of my face, whining sharply, bumping my face with his wet nose then licking gently at my salt streaked face. I wanted to hug him, to wrap my aching body around his warm, soft one and bury my face in his fresh air scented fur, but I was too weak and wasted to move an inch.

"Rosie."

There was so much pain in that one word, each syllable shaped like a gaping wound. His empathy soothed me. It reminded me that if anyone could understand my anguish, it was Lion.

He crouched beside me, only his worn Timberland boots visible to my eyes from where I lay. His hand found the damp hair in my face and pushed it back behind my ear, his fingers tracing the shell.

I didn't move.

"No one could do this to you, but your father," he noted softly, and when I hummed weakly in agreement, he punctuated his displeasure with a growl. "Fuckin' bastard."

"No," I whispered through my swollen throat. "I wronged him."

Danner sighed angrily then shifted, going to his belly on the ground beside me, displacing Hero so that he was lying face to face with me. His eyes were deep green pools, safe and still as lake water. His hand found my hair again and gently detangled the threads.

"You're doing this *for* him, for your family. He doesn't know that so maybe one day I can forgive him for gutting you like this. But you *have got to* remember it. You aren't a victim here, Rosie, you aren't letting life catch you up in this fierce fucking storm. You *are* the storm, this is your set up, these are your choices, and you're strong so you'll blow furious and true until you see this thing through. You're no victim, rebel Rose, but you are a martyr. So, I'll lie here with you as long as you need to absorb this blow, then we're gonna get up and I'm gonna take you home. Tomorrow, we're going to wake up together and face the day that way, side by side, every day from now until we break this case and then I'm going to be at your back again when you go up the mountain and let your family take you back."

His hand squeezed the back of my neck. "You with me?"

My withered heart shifted in my chest, the blood pumping slowly, painfully through the distressed chambers. But I could feel it moving, feel it beating again in my chest. It wasn't as strong as it should have been, but then again, I'd just lost most of my reason for living.

Now all I had left was Lion and Hero.

I reached across the floor to grab Danner's hand tightly in

my own and brought it to my mouth so I could bite his knuckle and kiss his palm.

"Yeah, Lion, I'm with you," I told him.

And I was, just as I had been since I fell in love with him on my eleventh birthday and just as I would be at my ninetieth.

It seemed life wouldn't allow me to be loved beautifully and platonically at the same time as brutally and romantically, and I couldn't say I would have knowingly made the same choice if I'd been given a calculated time to make it, but as I laid there on the ground, Lion on his belly beside me, Hero on his behind me, I knew I'd sacrifice everything I had left just to keep them with me forever.

CHAPTER TWENTY-TWO

Harleigh Rose

THE NEXT NIGHT, I WAS DONE WAITING.

My family hated me, it was done.

But I wasn't.

I needed to get the goods on the fuckin' Berserkers and I needed it done *now*.

So, I was already in my car, clothed from tip to toe in tight, black clothing including a pair of leather gloves with a toque on my head to contain my hair so I wouldn't leave behind any DNA when I called Danner.

"Rosie, thought you'd be home by now," he answered.

I loved that he called his house our home. We hadn't talked about it, but I hadn't spent a night without him since the hooded man held me at knifepoint in my car.

"Yeah, about that," I explained while I chewed anxiously on a wad of Hubba Bubba. "I'm not coming home for a while."

There was a long pause then a vicious curse, "What the fuck are you up to now?"

"I'm sitting in my car a block away from the Port of Vancouver," I told him. "I'm going to show up in Grant Yves office pretending to look for Jacob and Honey, and I'm going to get him to tell me which company and cargo containers the Berserkers are using to transport their illegal arms."

Another long pause. This one artic, frozen solid in a way that kept me from discerning what he could possibly be thinking.

"You remember that conversation we had about you bein' reckless?" he asked quietly.

I swallowed hard. "Yeah, Lion, I do. It's why I'm callin' you."

"You didn't think to tell me say, last night when we got home or this mornin' over fucking Cinnamon Toast Crunch?"

I chewed my gum, popped a bubble and tried not to let his anger touch the submissive place in me that wanted to stop, drop and roll at his commands.

"No, because then you'd have stopped me from being involved, and I know I can get Grant to talk about his brother, maybe even turn on the club and become a police asset."

"Good thinkin', Harleigh Rose. Only, are there any police there with you right now?" he bit out, already knowing the answer.

"Uh, no."

"No... so how are the police goin' to turn an asset if they aren't involved in this rebel operation you got goin'?"

"Well, that's where you come in. I thought you could bring your cuffs."

Danner let out a harsh laugh and I knew he'd be rubbing a frustrated hand over his face. "Listen to me carefully, Rosie. This is what we're going to do. I'm going to call this in. A truck is going to show up within fifteen minutes with two guys I trust for surveillance. They're gonna outfit you with a wire, then you're gonna go have a chat with Grant. If one *single* thing goes wrong with that chat, you're outta there, and I mean he even looks at you fuckin' funny, you're gone. You with me?"

"With you," I agreed, trying not to let my giddiness show.

He was going to let me do this.

"Know you're done with waiting and watching, Harleigh Rose, but we still gotta do this in a way we can bring them down *for good*. I don't want you in danger after it's revealed you were in on this, you get me?"

"Get you," I agreed.

"Fuck me, but you're fuckin' trouble," he muttered.

"You love it," I sassed, because sassing the patriarchy was my bread and fuckin' butter.

He grunted his agreement. "Gonna hang up and get this shit sorted. You wait there for me to call you back, and Rosie, if you move one fuckin' inch out of that car, I'm going to punish you so hard, you won't sit easy for a fucking month. You with me?"

"With you," I whispered through my sudden loss of breath.

He hung up.

I tried to get my breathing under control and flipped on "Gun in My Hand" by Dorothy to get my head in the game.

Fifteen minutes later, a black van pulled up across the street from me.

Two minutes after that, Danner's Mustang Fastback screeched to a halt behind that and he climbed out of his car wearing tip to toe black that made him look like a fuckin' biker god.

He knocked on my passenger side window then tagged my hand the second I opened the door to pull me back over the street to the van.

"You do everything I say," he told me as we power walked. "There'll be a piece in your ear so you can hear me and a microphone in the camera they're goin' to attach to your jacket. If I say move, you move. If I say get the fuck out of there, you get the fuck out of there before you take your next breath."

"Aye, aye, Officer," I said, turned on by his no-nonsense cop persona.

I wanted him to use the cuffs dangling from the back of his black jeans on my wrists, push me against the car for a full body search and then fuck me silly.

He turned to me with a glare as we reached the back of the van and he knocked on the door. "I want to hear you agree with me, seriously, Rosie."

"Yes, Officer," I said sweetly, hand to my heart. "I solemnly pledge to obey your orders."

He scowled, but before he could reprimand me again, the doors were opened and I was being pulled into the back of a van the likes of which I'd only ever seen in cop movies. There was equipment everywhere, three computers, speakers and two TVs, a rack bolted to the floor that carried weapons and police armour.

"Cool," I whispered, touching a vest that read "RCMP." "Can I wear a bulletproof vest?"

"No," said the huge black man I recognized as Sterling, one of the cops from the scene of Cricket's death. "But you can get over here so Johnson can get you set up and I can brief you."

"Aye, aye Officer," I repeated with a flick of my fingers in a mock salute.

Sterling cut his gaze to Danner who only sighed wearily.

They attached a camera to the necklace I wore with "Rosie" written in gold, affixing it to the skull and crossbones pendant that hung beside it. They explained to me the rules and regulations of doing a 'sting,' and what exactly I was trying to get Grant to say.

If I successfully got a confession from him, Danner, who

would be waiting outside the office, would cuff him and bring him into the station in order to offer him immunity in return for becoming a confidential informant.

When they were finished with me, I was restless with eagerness, so confident in my own abilities, I felt invincible.

I'd never been on the right side of the law before, but apparently, it could offer the same thrilling high flagrantly disregarding it could garner.

I practically skipped out of the van and across the street, pulling the gun I'd hidden down the back of my pants out and into my hand, Danner trailing behind me. He grabbed my arm as we reached the chain link fence dividing the port from the street and turned me to face him.

"Do we need to go over the plan again?"

"Show up. Kick some serious ass. Get the hell outta there," I said as I checked the safety on my gun and adjusted the cool, familiar, heavy weight of it between my hands.

"Are you taking this seriously?" Danner asked in that voice that shot wet straight to the core of me. It was his no-nonsense authority voice. The one he used to bend me over his knee and break criminals into pieces on the floor of interrogation rooms.

Still, it wouldn't do for him to know how it affected me, especially when we were about to put our lives on the line and he was doubting my badassery.

So, I did what any self-respecting woman would do in that situation.

I threw him sass.

"As serious as a bullet to the brain," I said, crossing my heart.

"Rosie..." he growled, all hot cop and restrained dirty Dom.

"Don't do it," I warned him.

"What?"

"Don't tell me I can't do it, because I'll do it anyway and

277

I'll do it well. Don't want you to have to swallow your words when I'm through because I proved you wrong." I slid the two feet it took to press up against him in the dark, empty street, pressed my lips to his stubbled cheek and one hand, the hand holding my gun, to the inside of his thigh so I could press my fingers to the bulge tenting his denim. Yeah, my man got off on the danger just as much as I did.

"I'm not an idiot, Danner," I reminded him on a rough squeeze of his hardening cock. "I read the rules before I break 'em."

He growled, but I broke free before he could kiss me the way his eyes told me he wanted to. We'd never get anything done if that happened.

"Now, give me a boost over this fence," I ordered, brazenly ignoring the massive sign affixed to the metal that said, "PROPERTY OF VANCOUVER HARBOR AUTHOR-ITY: KEEP OUT!"

I tucked my gun into my waistband as Danner sighed roughly and held out his hand for my boot so he could launch me up the fence. I scrambled up and flipped over to the other side, working my way down the ten-foot fence nimbly. Danner came after me, scaling the height as if he climbed fences every day of his life for years.

"You made that look easy," I told him with an impressed eyebrow raise.

"Been a cop a long time. Undercover three years. What's your excuse?" he asked, mirroring my expression.

I grinned. "Been a rebel a long time."

He snorted. "Fuck me, come on let's get this done so I can get you home and turn you over my fucking knee."

I shivered but ran after him as he jogged into the stacks of multicoloured cargo containers piled up in the massive lot.

Grant Yves office was a trailer at the top of a ladder beside a crane that was used to move the containers off freighters and onto land. The light was still on in his office.

"Good luck. Stay safe," Danner whispered when we reached the top of the platform and I moved forward to the door.

He kissed me roughly, relaying his anxiety in the only way he could.

I placed a soothing hand on his cheek, kissed him quickly then went to the door.

When Grant Yves answered, I was shocked.

He looked exactly like Jacob, his red hair so bright it shone like the orange outer ring of a flame in the light spilling out from his office.

"Can I help you?" he asked gruffly, looking passed me suspiciously.

"Yeah, um, I'm sorry to disturb you at work, but this was the only address I could find for you. I'm Harleigh Rose Maycomb, Farrah Maycomb's daughter."

Grant's eyebrows shot into his hair. "No fuckin' shit."

There was a chance that he was still friends with my mother, after all, she'd practically bragged to me that she'd gotten Reaper his contact in the Port Authority.

But I was willing to bet my life that that wasn't the case.

Farrah wasn't real good at keeping friends.

"Yeah, unfortunately for me," I said with a thin smile and a shrug. "I'm actually here to talk to you about Jacob and Honey, I'm hoping to find them. I'd really like to get to know my sister and thank Jacob for the small solace he gave me and my brother when he was in our lives."

His face transformed, the suspicion falling away to give way for sympathy. "Yeah, yer Ma was a real piece of fuckin' work. Sorry you had to deal with it growin' up."

I shrugged. "Shit happens to everyone."

"Yeah," he said, his voice suddenly heavy. "Why don't you come inside, darlin'?"

I smiled gratefully at him, hiding my inner triumph and slipped past him into the office. He took a seat at his L-shaped desk and gestured to me to do the same in the chair across from him.

"Listen, I'm sorry to have to be the one to tell you this, but Jacob died in a car crash years ago now. I tried to get custody of Honey, sweet kid, but the province wouldn't grant me shit with her mum alive and kickin' so I lost. Has to be goin' on two years now that I haven't seen the kid, though she's runaway to me before."

God, my heart clenched with sympathy for my half-sister.

I'd only lived with Farrah for nine years. I couldn't imagine what sixteen of those would do to a girl.

"Damn," I muttered, frantically trying to think of an angle to sway him to the blue side. "I really need to find her."

"Yeah? What's goin' on?" he asked, leaning forward, his weathered face further creased with concern.

He may have been a corrupt man, but he was a loving uncle.

Perfect.

My voice was shaky as I said, "I got a friend who's dating a brother of Berserkers MC. She told me they're on the lookout for Honey, that she owes 'em somethin' like five grand worth of drug money."

"*Fuck,*" he swore savagely, shock punched in block letters across his face. "Knew she was usin', didn't know she was doin' it outta Berserker pockets."

I nodded, carefully working a tear into my eye that wasn't entirely false. I was lying about Honey's involvement in the MC, obviously, but her real predicament with Irina Ventura's pornography company, was enough to spill tears over too.

"Not sure you know much about the club, but they're fuckin' ruthless. If she doesn't pay up and soon, they find her, they'll kill her."

"Holy fuck," he said, tugging on his orange mustache so hard it had to hurt. "Fuck me. I didn't know."

"You know the club?" I asked carefully.

He looked at me for a long moment, pulling his mustache compulsively. "Yeah, I do. Got a business deal with 'em, maybe I can talk to the Prez, work somethin' out."

"You got pull?"

"Fuck," he said again, planting his face in his hands. "Fuck."

"I'll take that as a no?" I said, sorrowfully.

"No," he agreed through gritted teeth, his eyes filled with turmoil as he looked up at me. "Let's just say I didn't want this deal I got goin' with them, but they can be fuckin' persuasive."

I tipped my head and frowned questioningly at him, as if I didn't understand just how persuasive an outlaw MC could be.

He sighed gustily and admitted. "They got me off the street walkin' home one day, beat me so good I was coughin' up blood and ended up in the hospital. Said it wouldn't be the last time unless I cooperated with 'em."

"What would they want with you?" I asked, digging carefully, an archeologist searching for confessions instead of ruins. "You poor man."

"Arms smugglin'," he admitted. "They got a few operations goin', but I get they want to expand and I was their way to do it."

Ding, ding, ding.

I grinned at him. "Thanks for that, Grant."

He frowned at me, his face murky with confusion for one glorious moment before it cleared like clouds, revealing the full force of his realized fury.

I pointed at the camera on my necklace and grinned. "Say cheese!"

"You fuckin' *bitch*!" He growled, launching himself across the desk at me.

I punched him hard in the esophagus just as Danner busted through the door, gun raised, yelling "RCMP, hands in the air."

Grant tried to lunge for me again, still choking on my punch.

"Careful," Danner warned, moving closer until he was at my side, his gun unwaveringly on target. "She'll punch you in the face if you get too close."

"Now that was fun," I said, beaming at him as he moved around the desk and began to read Grant Yves his rights.

Only, I spoke too soon.

We hadn't been thinking thoroughly. If the Berserkers MC had a stake in keepin' this guy on their side, of course they'd send protection.

"Everythin' okay in there, Yves?" a voice called up to us.

It was Runner, one of the prospects, a young kid who'd earned his name because he was flighty as fuck. Reaper had recruited him only because he was desperate for numbers.

It wasn't ideal, having to make our way past a Berserker to get to safety, but it was good that if something had to happen to Runner, the MC wouldn't question it. Runner was always disappearin' for a spell.

Danner stared at me as I thought this through, his face transforming into stern, disciplinarian planes.

"Harleigh Rose," he started to warn.

But I was off.

I ducked through the door and out onto the landing, seeing Runner peering up from the left side of the ladder.

I brought my gun up and shot. Not at him, I didn't need any more blood on my hands, but close.

"Fuck!" he cried out, immediately running to duck behind a container close by.

"Cover me and get him to the van," I told a wide-eyed Danner as he appeared behind me, a cuffed Grant behind him. "I'll meet you there."

"He'll fucking *see* you," Danner hissed as I tucked my gun in my waistband and started down the ladder. "He'll see you and tell Reaper."

"Not if I get him first," I said as I disappeared over the edge and scrambled down.

A shot rang out, pinging so close to my hand on the ladder that I could feel the arm move.

Another shot, this one from Danner, and then the sound of him speaking into his mike, "Sterling, need back up at the office. Shots fired."

I jumped to the ground and sprinted behind the container opposite Runner.

And like I knew he would, he ran after me.

I could hear his heavy boots striking the ground behind me, but I wasn't terrified. It felt like I was flying as my long limbs carried me between the towering stacks of containers, as I led him on a merry chase I hoped I'd be able to end back at the van.

Unfortunately, I miscalculated.

Runner had been providing protection for Grant Yves long enough to figure out the configuration of containers.

Suddenly, I couldn't hear his feet behind me.

I stopped running, my breath rasping through my lungs, hot over my tongue as it turned white in the air.

Nothing.

No sounds, but my thumping heart and wasted breath.

"Stop, police!" a voice cried from somewhere in the maze.

Then nothing, again.

Bang!

I jumped at the sound of the shot so close by and whirled around to see Runner fall to the ground at the mouth of the alley between containers, fifteen yards behind me. Then Danner, stalking over to his prone body, voice harsh but indiscernible as he read him his rights and cuffed him.

I jogged over, seeing the bullet graze bleeding lightly at Runner's shoulder as Danner hauled him to his feet.

"You got him," I noted, the adrenaline making me dumb, flooding my brain with too many endorphins.

Danner scowled at me then turned to Sterling who was coming up behind him with Yves. He shoved Runner at Sterling and said, "You got 'im."

The other cop's eyes shot from him to me, read the fury in the air and nodded curtly. "Yeah, got them. Meet you at the station. I'll tell Renner, you were doin' a scan of the area to make sure it was clean."

Danner nodded curtly at him then crossed his arms and watched the huge black man cart the two men toward the van.

Only when he was out of sight and hearing did I try. "Danner, listen—"

"Not listenin'," he growled, lunging for me so violently, I squealed.

He pushed me hard against the side of the container, his hand on the back of my head so it wouldn't hit, conscientious even in his rage. I gasped when his other hand moved up from my hip over my belly to my neck where he gently—eyes such an intense contrast to the movement that it took my breath away—plucked the camera from my necklace and dropped it to the ground. I heard the crunch of it under his boot as he broke it.

Still, he didn't speak. He stared at me for a long minute before his radio squawked and the other cop in the van, Henson, confirmed that Yves and Runner were contained.

Still, he waited, staring at me with a fury so palpable I felt it slide down my throat and scorch my insides. I wanted to explain myself, but I knew there would be no words to make Danner understand why I went off half-cocked.

Then, his radio sounded again.

"Yard is all clear," Sterling confirmed. "Got fifteen minutes then need you at the station."

"Copy," Danner growled into the radio.

Then his hand fisted tightly in my hair, tugging it back so viciously it brought tears to my eyes and his mouth crashed onto mine.

Immediately, I ignited. The stress and adrenaline the perfect kindling, his fury the gasoline and his lust the match.

I went up in smoke the second his hand found my tit and squeezed.

I was trembling, gunpowder residue on my hand that Danner wrapped around his thick cock.

"Jack me," he ordered through his teeth.

I fumbled with his belt and zip then sighed when the hot width of him hit my hand. I weighted his cock in my hand then slowly, firmly began to stroke it.

"That's it," he rasped as he clenched my t-shirt dress in his big, wide hands and tore it with a snarling rip down the middle. My braless nipples instantly beaded in the cool air, perfect targets for his cruel, pinching fingers. His face was screwed up into a glare of dissatisfaction as he stared at my reddening tits. I should have known my silence wasn't enough for him, that he wanted to taste my pants and moans like a Dominant's ambrosia on his tongue.

Still, I was surprised when he lashed out and slapped across both my taut nipples with perfect precision, sending an electric current of painful pleasure straight to my dripping cunt. I threw my head back against the metal container and let out a hoarse shout.

"That's my slut," he praised as he ripped a massive hole in my leggings.

He dipped down to take both my legs into his arms, and then hefted me high into the air so they landed not around his hips, but perched against his shoulders, only my back against the metal container keeping me upright, my cunt completely exposed for his use.

"You think you deserve this cock?" he demanded, the crown of said cock poised at my entrance, rubbing back and forth across my clit, lighting it on fire with the friction.

When I didn't answer, he slammed his thick dick straight

to the root in my grasping pussy, the wet sounds of our sex drowned by my scream.

"Look at me."

It took a long minute, but I was finally able to peel my eyes open to stare at his face, overcome with an intensity so stark it was unbearably beautiful. I wanted to cup his face, touch my tongue to his hard mouth to soften it with my kiss, and hold him to me softly, as if I trusted him to stay there with or without my hold.

But I didn't dare.

That wasn't how this game was played.

He fucked me like he hated me, and it was the best lie he ever told.

I took it like I didn't care either way, and it was a lie I didn't even believe myself.

He bit down on my neck and planted himself deep in my pussy as I came all around him, and then he did too, his cock thumping inside me as he came.

Carefully, he slid my legs off his shoulders, shrugged off his jacket and tugged off his shirt, before handing the latter to me so I could pull it on over my naked torso and ruined tights. Then he took my face in his hands and stared deep into my eyes, as if reassuring himself that I was there.

"Tell me a lie," I told him, to remind him of the duality of our game.

"I hate you," he replied like he'd been waiting for me to ask. "I hate you with my whole body and all of my soul."

I kissed him, my apology for being reckless more eloquent on my lips than it ever could be with my words.

And he accepted it, eating at my mouth until I was clean and absolved. Forgiving me as he always did, as I knew he always would.

CHAPTER TWENTY-THREE

Harleigh Rose

2017

Harleigh Rose is 17. Danner is 26.

THE PARTY WAS WILD.

The first time I'd ever enjoyed a high school party.

EBA and Entrance Public had joined forces to host a massive spring blow out in one of the fields on the outskirts of town.

Just minutes away from Danner's house.

I tried not to think of that as I sipped my warm beer and chatted with Lila.

"Seriously, it's like I'm sexless to him," she complained for the millionth time. "I mean, do I look sexless to you?"

I checked her out even though I knew what she looked like better than nearly anyone. Long dark hair that fell in straight, glossy sheets to her belly button, lots of exposed golden skin over muscle carved thighs, a toned tummy and round, full breasts currently pushed up in a sleeveless, torn tee that read "reckless."

She was definitely *not* sexless.

Any of the boys at the bonfire would have been happy to dissuade her of that ridiculous notion.

But she didn't want any of those high school boys.

Much like me, she was into older men.

One in particular, 'Nova' Booth, one of the brothers in my father's Fallen MC. He was like an older brother to me, but he'd always been more than that to Lila.

Hell, he was the reason she was a de facto part of the club in the first place. He'd been the reason I'd met her in elementary school, and he was the reason the club kept her close despite her not being his old lady.

She was like his kid sister.

Twelve years younger than him.

Not that age usually stopped Nova from tapping a hot piece of ass, but Lila was different. They'd grown up next-door neighbors and been through a lot of shit together. There was absolutely no way he would go there.

I knew it and Lila did too.

She just didn't like it.

"You could be Marilyn fuckin' Monroe and he wouldn't touch you, babe," I told her. "We know this."

"Whatever," she mumbled into her beer, then brightened again. "I've decided to get a tat."

I groaned. "Jesus, Lila, are you that desperate to have Nova's hands on you?"

"Don't be a bitch," she groused. "I'm not a bitch to you about the fact that you have a thing for a fucking *cop*."

"You know he's more than that," I shot back.

"And you know me wanting a tattoo is more than what you implied it was," she countered.

We glared each other for a minute before I hit her softly with my hip in a physical version of an apology.

"What do you want and where?" I asked, waving the white flag.

She smiled dreamily. "Flowers."

I snorted. Nova called her his "flower child" because she was always dressing like a slutty hippie. Acting like one too, minus the slutty, because she was saving her v-card for Nova.

She'd be a virgin for life.

"I'm gonna go grab some more beer, want any?" I asked.

"Nah, I'm good, I'm gonna go shoot the shit with Taylor and Kelly."

I tipped my chin at her and weaved through the crowd towards the kegs situated on the far side of the bonfire to keep them sorta cool.

A couple of guys were manning the kegs, but I pumped my own beer before turning to make my way back to Lila.

Only Rick was in my way.

I stared into his sneering face and scowled. "Get out of my way or I'll beat you down like I did at the last party."

"Bitch," he spat just as someone walked into my shoulder and made me stumble back.

Rick reached forward to steady me and my drink.

"Thanks," I muttered before quickly ducking around him.

I could feel his eyes like darts aimed at the back of my targeted head as I hurried away, but I put him out of my mind, determined to continue enjoying myself.

It was only twenty minutes later when my head started to feel like a boulder on my shoulders, the inside just as dead and heavy, that I saw him again lurking at the edge of the group I was in. His eyes were black in the low light, his grin a dark curl on his face as he started toward me.

"Here, sweetheart, why don't you let me help you sit down," he said when he stopped in front of me, his hands gently but firmly pulling me away from my group of friends.

Through the muck in my brain, alarm bells started ringing.

"Come on, why don't you and I go over here and I can show you how to be a little sweeter to a man, huh?" he asked in a low, wet whisper he pressed to my ear.

Then his head dipped lower and he kissed me, his breath sour in my mouth, arsenic on my tongue. I tried to pull away and stumbled slightly.

"Lila," I whisper-yelled because my lips were going numb.

She stopped mid laughter talking to one of the EBA boys a few feet away and turned to me with a frown. "You okay, H.R.? You don't look okay. And what the fuck are you doin' talkin' to that shit head?"

"She's fine, I think she's just had too much to drink," Rick told her with a small, hateful smile.

Only Lila didn't smile.

She knew I was a biker chick.

I could hold my liquor.

She stepped closer as I tried to lift my hand to prop my aching head up.

"Call Lion," I said weakly, but then my head seemed to tumble off my shoulders and I succumbed to the weight and the blackness.

CHAPTER TWENTY-FOUR

Danner

I WAS ON A DATE WITH A CUTE WOMAN WHO RAN THE LOCAL library when I got the call from Rosie's phone. It was rude to take it, but I did anyway because it was Rosie. Only, it wasn't. It was her best friend Lila, her voice frantic as she told me what had happened, that Harleigh Rose had passed out in the arms of the boy she'd been arrested for assaulting six months ago.

I hadn't seen her since that night, since I'd turned her over my knee and laid into that sweet ass, taken my fingers to her sopping wet cunt and made her come on my hand.

But there was no way my guilt or morals were going to keep me away from my girl when she was in distress.

That fucking fucker had tried to roofie her.

I said my abrupt goodbyes to my date, knowing that she liked me enough to reschedule at the same time knowing that I wouldn't, and then I drove to the field with my police lights on, tearing through town well over the speed limit.

When I arrived, Lila had done what she was told, and the

cops were there. I'd walked up to the paramedics leaning over a totally out of it Harleigh Rose and gotten debriefed.

She was going to be fine, she just needed to sleep it off and she hadn't been assaulted, thank fucking Christ.

I turned to my partner Gibson, who was on call that night and demanded to know what was being done about the fucker who drugged her.

He'd hesitated before explaining that nothing tied Rick Evans to the drug and she hadn't been assaulted so there was nothing to be done.

Nothing to be done.

Without another word, I'd collected Rosie from the paramedics, swallowing my fury as she curled into my arms and carried her to my car.

I told the officers on duty that I'd get her home safe and debrief Garro on what had happened.

And I would, but not that night.

She was staying with me so I could watch her through the night and make certain she was going to be okay.

I put her in the bedroom I'd come to think of as hers, the same one she kept a toothbrush in, the same one I'd spanked her in months ago.

Tenderly, I took off her tight jeans so she would be more comfortable and slid her into bed, brushing her heavy hair back from her face and giving in to the impulse to kiss her soft cheek. Hero jumped onto her bed, licking her face with a low whine before he settled against her.

She turned her head to me, eyes heavy but clearing before I could move away.

"He kissed me," she whispered, mouth twisted with disgust. "He put his lips on me."

"Hush, I'm with you," I told her, stroking back her hair again.

"Lion," she said in the voice soft and silky as rose petals. "Make it go away."

"What, Rosie?"

"His kiss. I can't sleep with it on my mouth," she told me, her eyes blue as melted gemstones.

I shouldn't.

I'd been careful to draw distance between us again after the spanking incident and I didn't want to confuse her. But looking to her eyes, seeing the fragility of her soul shining out from them, I knew I couldn't deny her.

"Okay, rebel," I said softly. "Close your eyes."

She immediately obeyed.

Gently, I leaned over to press whisper light kisses against each of her fluttering lids, then when she opened her eyes, her mouth parted to protest where I'd kissed her, I pressed my open lips to hers.

She sighed into my mouth and melted into the bed.

It was a short kiss, as sweet a one as I knew how to give.

And it rocked my simple world temporarily on its axis.

In the span of that minute with her plush lips on mine, her silky tongue in my mouth, and the scent of her floral skin and bonfire imprinted hair in my nose, there was no future for me but her.

An MC princess from the same biker gang my family was determined to see ruined.

A girl ten years younger than me that pretended to be seasoned, but who was as fresh and beautifully untouched as morning dew. I wanted to smear that innocence with my rough hands and taint it with my cock at the same time I wanted to preserve it, fight to defend it.

It was an impossible contrast, but in those seconds we kissed, it seemed wildly possible.

Natural, even destined.

I pulled away abruptly, my heart thumping hard, my deviant cock pulsing.

Her eyes remained closed, but she smiled and mumbled, "Love you, Lion."

And then she was out. I could see it in the way her head drooped, and her breath deepened.

My rebel Rose looked so peaceful in her sleep, so at odds with her waking hours when she seemed provoked to take on the world. That was the beauty of Harleigh Rose, she was a walking contradiction, the rebel and the saint, the good girl and the sinner.

I sat in a chair beside her bed and watched her for hours.

I thought sitting sentry and seeing with my own eyes that she was going to be okay would be enough to quell the nuclear rage that blasted through me on repeat, but it wasn't.

It only grew stronger.

There wouldn't be justice for Harleigh Rose because sometimes, too many times, there was nothing the police could do.

I was faced for the millionth time with my own impotency in the face of unjustness and the feeling burned cleaned through my rational brain until all that was left in me was pure, bestial instinct.

I left her.

The alarm armed, my dog at her feet.

But I left her.

I got in my 'Stang, Hozier's "It Will Come Back" pumping through the speakers because the singer reminded me of Rosie, and I drove to Evergreen Gas where teenagers from Entrance Public like to hang after parties.

The stupid fuck was there, laughing with his buddies as if he hadn't just tried to rape an innocent girl.

I parked my car in a darkened lot across the street and waited.

I didn't have to do it long, it was late, and they were still children even though they pretended not to be.

Rick Evans said goodbye to his friends and went into the gas station to buy a snack before heading home himself.

Fate was smiling on me.

I was waiting in the shadow by his car when he finally ventured to it and I had him pressed to the metal with his arm wrenched behind his back, one hand over his mouth before he could even call out.

His open packet of Skittles fell to the ground and tumbled out like a broken rainbow.

I leaned into him, my voice hard in his ear. "Next time you think to mess with any woman, let alone Harleigh Rose Garro, you'll fuckin' think again."

"Fuck off man," he said when I released his mouth slightly. "That bitch deserves everything she gets."

"*Wrong*," I growled, "That *bitch* deserves all the good she can get, not shit the likes of which you tried to give her tonight. You don't get that, boy, I'm happy to teach you."

"Fuck you," he tried to shout behind my hand.

So, I taught him a lesson.

One I wrote on his body in bruise blue ink, with punches I wove like calligraphy around his torso and face, the flourish of my signature in his matching black eyes.

He was contrite when I left him there, crying on the ground like the pathetic boy-man he was.

The beast in me, that savage I'd tried for years to curb with platitudes and substitutes raged glorious inside me, beat its chest like a heathen warrior claiming victory, like an alpha who had successfully protected his mate.

The guilt would come, I knew. It always did when I gave into the darkness at the pit of my person. But for now, I reveled in the wickedness, the rightness of vengeance.

My phone rang just as I pulled back into my driveway and I knew who it would be, as I always did when he called, before I answered.

"Dad."

"Lionel."

There was a heavy pause that relayed much. My lack of

regret about my moral collapse, my obstinacy against his censure, and strangely, his willingness to cede to that.

"Listen, son, I'm prepared to cover this up for you," he said the voice of the devil asking me to sign my soul over in blood ink. "Easy enough to do, the Rick Evans kid is scared brainless and barely admitted to Percy that you were even the one to beat him up. But kids get bold with time, as I'm sure you know," he paused to let his thinly veiled point sink in, "So, it's best we sweep this under the rug now, while we still can."

My silence was my answer.

"Just need to know that I can count you as my right-hand man. There're things goin' down in the town and I could use a good man, the *right* man and my son as a player in it."

"No."

I could live with my crime. I'd lose my badge if it came to it, which would fucking suck, but I was willing to take the hit. I'd done a bad deed for the right reasons and I was okay paying the price for it.

"Not gonna let anything bad happen to you, son. It's already dealt with, just wanted to loop you in. Join me for dinner at mayor Lafayette's house this weekend. I'll be introducing you to a good friend of mine, Javier Ventura. And, Lionel, next time I call, be ready to serve your brothers in blue."

I stared into the silence after he hung up, furious with myself for not understanding the depth of depravity my father had succumbed to. He'd been waiting for this, some slip-up so that he could blackmail me into working with his crooked cops.

And I'd played right into his fucking hand.

I sat in the car staring at my grandparent's old house, now mine, imagining as I often did the family I was going to plant inside, the wife and kids and dog that would brighten the empty farmhouse until it rang with laughter and noise.

I'd always pictured the white picket fence kind of life for

myself, but I realized as I sat there, my father's voice in my ear, Rick Evan's blood on my aching knuckles, that the kind of woman I craved wasn't that kind of woman.

She was the kind of woman that would climb a white picket fence just to graffiti the pristine house. The kind of woman who would punch a bully in the throat and toss her hair as she did it, magnificent and wild.

The kind of woman, seventeen years old and sleeping in my bed.

As bad as she played herself to be, as good as I acted, the truth was, of the two of us, she was the one who was too good to settle for me.

I needed to get out of town, away from her. She was too young and innocent for my deviancy and secret darkness, for the tangled web my father had just thrown me into with force.

I sat in my car and made two resolutions that changed the course of my life.

One, I was going to take down my father, or at least, part of the organization he worked for.

And two, I was going to stay away from Harleigh Rose Garro.

CHAPTER TWENTY-FIVE

Danner

OLD SCHOOL ROCK MUSIC PULSED THROUGH THE HOUSE LIKE A heartbeat, too loud for a weeknight in a quiet, residential area, but no one would call the police.

Berserkers were partying.

It was their annual summer blow out so even though the night was still young, the empty bottles of booze were racking up and the acrid taste of cocaine was in the air, white clouds of it floating through the halls like chalk dust.

The highlight of the night was starting soon.

The Fight.

A tradition the Berserkers had of throwing each brother into the proverbial ring to see who came out the winner in the end.

There were thirty-nine brothers and all of them were expected to fight but Reaper, who proceeded over the fight like the Emperor of Rome over in his colosseum. I'd helped the brothers set the stage, a small circle of earth in the backyard that was marked with stakes and strong white rope and highlighted by huge industrial lights that would blind the competitor's eyes. We'd had a summer rainstorm through the night so the grass was slick, the ground beneath it soft and sucking.

It would make for one hell of a spectacle when the time came, and I knew if Reaper could have filmed that shit and sold it as entertainment, he would have.

Maybe he did.

But the fucked-up part of the fight wasn't the fact that it pitted men who were supposed to be brothers against each other.

No.

It was the fact that each man had to put up collateral and that collateral was only accepted in the form of a woman. If you lost, the winner could claim a fuck from your woman. If you won the entire fight, you could have your pick of as many of the girls as you pleased for one night only.

It was disgusting. Barbaric in the extreme. But the MC was famous for it through North America. Men prospected the club just for a chance to participate and brothers from other clubs petitioned Reaper for an invite like most politicians campaigned for President.

It was a biker's Olympics.

Only the gold medal was pussy in any form you wanted it.

Most brothers picked up trailer trash or hookers as collateral, but Reaper liked it best if you had an Old Lady that you used her. He thought it bred unity throughout the club, a warped rendition of the philosophy 'what's mine is yours.'

It was my first time participating in the fight because only patched-in members were granted the honour and I'd only made that rank nine months before.

But I'd watched two of those fights to their very bloody end.

Brothers had died and so many women had been offered up as bounty it made me physically ill to think about it.

"Not puttin' you up," I told Laken for the twelfth time, pressing my lips to her silky black hair in order to do so.

I hadn't spent much time with her in the last six weeks, something she was officially done putting up with. She'd showed at my house that morning, thankfully while Harleigh Rose was out with Wrath, and demanded to spend the day with me.

I'd narrowly avoided fucking her by dragging her around Vancouver for hours, taking her for Earnest Ice Cream, walking along the sea wall and making out with her in Stanley Park. I'd never taken her on a date like that and she was fucking thrilled.

Obviously, I didn't tell her that I'd taken Harleigh Rose on the same one the day before, that my rebel girl loved Earnest's whiskey hazelnut flavor, and that when we'd sat beside the ocean she'd kept one hand in mine and the other twisted in Hero's silky fur, her face contented because she was with two of her men even though the other had excommunicated her.

It had been reckless to take her on a date like that, but after all she'd been through, I'd wanted to spoil her.

My eyes searched for her in the backyard, the air filled with the haze of weed smoke and the burn of the huge fire on the other side of the lawn.

She was under Wrath's enormous arm, tucked into his side like she was made for him, tall enough that he didn't have to bend in half to touch his lips to hers the way he was doing then.

My heart burned with rage even though I knew it was just a ruse, even though I currently had a woman under my arm myself.

Laken pressed into me, grabbed my face with one hand and glared up at me. "You think I don't see you always lookin' at my girl Harleigh, think again, Lion. I'm not educated, but I'm not dumb neither. I'm your Old Lady and it's thanks to me you got your cut at all, so how about a little gratitude?"

I snarled at her, half-biker persona, half because I hated

that I needed her. Reaper still didn't trust me much and whatever trust I'd earned, Laken was right, it'd come through her.

"Why the fuck you think I don't want you bein' fucked by some other guy or fuckin' *multiple* guys tonight? Don't want that for my girl."

I didn't, but I meant the girl across the yard, the one Wrath was putting up for collateral because she was his and Reaper had ordered it.

The burn in my heart spread through my chest and down into my gut where it started to blaze.

There was no fuckin' way I could stand by and let Harleigh Rose get fucked by one of these psychotic fuckers.

She'd only avoided it in the past because Cricket, somehow, had kept her away.

His one redeeming quality.

Now, I had to count on Wrath winning The Fight to keep Harleigh Rose safe.

"It's my duty," Laken told me, pulling my focus back to her. "It's my honour as your Old Lady."

"That shit is just straight up fucked, Laken," I told her.

"It's tradition," she seethed.

I wondered how many deplorable things were done for the sake of tradition. The Chinese had used it as justification for foot-binding, the horrible act of tying a woman's feet to stunt their growth, the Aztecs had used it as a motive for sacrificing humans to their antiquated Gods. My own family had turned wiping out biker gangs into a kind of legacy even though The Fallen did more good than harm within the community, and many outlaw biker cultures used it as a reason to indiscriminately share their women regardless of getting their permission.

Tradition as I'd come to know it was a false God I refused to worship at.

"Fucked up," I repeated.

"Don't care, I'm doin' it. You care so much, don't lose," Laken said with a wide smile.

I grunted my affirmation and turned back to our conversation with Mutt, Roper, and Twiz.

Seconds later, Reaper joined us with his new old lady under his arm.

Farrah.

Fuck.

Harleigh Rose had been playing interference all night with her mum, trying to keep her out of my sight so she wouldn't recognize me, but I'd known that it was inevitable, especially with The Fight.

My only hope was that the bitch didn't recognize me.

I was older for one and I wore that in my face, craggier than ten years ago, lined and brown from spending too many hours out of doors. Dressed in a cut with my hair in my face and a different kind of attitude in my air, I hoped to hell it was enough. It should have been given that the times I'd seen her back in the day, she'd been high out of her fucking skull.

But Harleigh Rose had warned me.

Farrah was an addict, but she was too cunning to be taken for granted.

So, when she approached under Reaper's arm, I knew I'd have to use every tool in my arsenal to get her to believe I was someone else.

"Brothers," Reaper said with a chin tilt and then addressed Laken with a smile. "Girl. You ready for The Fight?"

"Fuckin' born ready, Prez," Twiz said, jumping from side to side lightly on his toes like a boxer, throwing a few air punches for good measure.

Reaper jerked his chin up at him then looked to me. "You ready for your first time, brother? There isn't a thrill like it in this whole goddamn world."

"Ready to win, Prez."

He threw his head back and laughed. "Wrath's won last two years runnin', you beat 'im, I'll give you permission to fuck any'a the Old Ladies for a week, not just one measly night. You'd fuckin' deserve it."

"Dad," Laken said with a loving eye roll as if her dad was just being silly and indulgent, not immoral and psychotic.

"Shame to get such a pretty face knocked about," Farrah input, her eyes thin, red slits. It was clear she was high as fuck.

I shrugged. "Don't got much care for my face, pretty or not. It's my woman I wanna keep at my side and it's why I'm gonna win this."

Farrah stared at me for a long moment then turned to bat her lashes at her Old Man. "Why don't you let this handsome Lion go first, Reaper? He wants to prove himself to his woman, why not make him go all thirty-nine rounds to prove it."

There had been no flicker of recognition in her eyes, but the way she threw that at me had me convinced she knew who I was.

Then I remembered she was a despicable bitch who liked to play dangerous games for sport.

She probably just wanted to see me beaten and bloody, probably got off on it like the hell demon she was.

Reaper kissed her long, wet, and sloppy before pulling back and declaring, "Done. Twenty minutes, you're up first, shirt off and in the ring."

"This is going to be so hot," Laken breathed into my ear as Mutt and Twiz gave me pounding slaps on the back for good luck.

It was going to be a lot of things, but I very much doubted it was going to be hot.

My eyes searched the yard for Harleigh Rose again and I frowned when I saw Wrath lead her into the house by the hand, his usually stoic face broken apart by a wide smile.

Harleigh Rose was smiling too.

304

That rage came back, primal and too strong to stem.

"Better use the john 'fore the fight," I muttered, unwrapping myself from Laken and heading inside after the fake lovers.

Fake.

I told myself.

But the beast in me that I'd gentled over the years into the Dom in me, seethed at the idea of her touched by a man.

Be damned that he was with her like that to protect her.

I was her protector.

I had been since she was six and I would be until she was fuckin' dead in another hundred or so years if I had anything to say about it.

My feet took me up the stairs to Wrath's room before any hope of my rational mind could kick in.

I paused outside the door, struggling to lasso the wild thing in my chest and bring it to heel.

A laugh.

The sultry, full-bodied laugh that I'd recognized anywhere as Harleigh Rose's.

A grunt.

Deep, manly.

Not hers.

Wrath's.

I could feel the tear between personalities come down, the moment where my Dr. Jekyll, my good guy cop, gave way to the heathen that was Hyde.

My foot pounded through the door so hard the side splintered and then I was storming through, body so tight with contained fury it was a wonder I could move.

"What the fuck, Danner!" Harleigh Rose yelled at me from where she sat cross-legged on the floor beside the bed. "The door was fuckin' open."

I tracked every inch of her body with my eyes, tested the scent in the air for sex like some kind of fucking hound, and then I went to her, not satisfied she was clothed and untouched, and *mine* until I had my arms around her and my mouth on hers.

I ate her growl of protest until it was a moan and she melted the way she always did in my arms.

Yeah. Mine.

"Brother, ever heard of fuckin' knockin'?" Wrath asked from behind me.

I whirled, shoving him in the shoulder hard. "What the fuck were doin' in here gigglin' and moanin' anyway?"

Wrath stared at me implacably for a moment and then burst out into a rusty laugh. "Fuck me, that's good. Oh, fuck."

Harleigh Rose laughed lightly from behind me. "Not complainin', but that was an awesome alpha rage."

"I asked you a question," I told Wrath, fists clenched to hold back the urge to punch him.

He was big, too big, and I knew I'd need my energy for The Fight.

"Dude, I grunt. Not got much to say, most of it can be said in a grunt," Wrath explained, actual tears of mirth in his eyes. "And your woman laughs, from what I can tell it's a Garro trait."

Harleigh Rose came up beside me and wrapped a hand around my waist. "You know me and Wrath are just friends. It's…it's cool to have someone else to talk to about my brother." Her eyes were wide and shining with sorrow as she looked up at me. "Miss him."

My arm slid around her and pressed her to my front. I closed my eyes, took a deep breath of her floral scent, so perfect for my Rosie and so at odds with the world's Harleigh Rose.

"A little on edge," I muttered finally, looking at her then at Wrath in silent apology. "Gearin' up for the fight."

Wrath snorted. "Little jealous, more like, but whatever you gotta tell yourself, brother."

I glared at him. "If you'd stop fuckin' kissin' her, might help with that."

Wrath grinned, unrepentant. "Kiss again it means you fight with that much fury tonight. Fuck, you could take down me with that rage you had in your face when ya first busted in."

"Was a close call," I admitted, unashamed of my jealousy, because I was unashamed of the way I loved her. "Didn't want to fuck you up for the fight. Countin' on you to keep Harleigh Rose out of anyone else's hands."

Wrath's mirth fell off his face and dropped to the floor like a stone. "Fuckin' count on it, brother."

I offered him my hand and we clapped each other on the back.

"Now get lost for a second, but mind the door," I told him, pulling away and turning to Harleigh Rose.

"You got it," he muttered with a grin as he walked out of the room and closed the door behind him.

"Danner, what are you doing?" she hissed as I walked her to the edge of the bed then pushed her on to it.

I ignored her, flipping her over and yanking her hips up so her ass was tipped like a ripe fucking peach.

It was dangerous to fuck her in the Berserker's house. Wildly inappropriate to risk us both by giving into my basic needs.

But nothing could have stopped me in that moment from claiming what was mine.

"Danner," she snapped.

"Think you need reminding of who you belong to, Rosie," I clipped, knowing by the way she shivered that she knew the tone of my voice. "A reminder of who owns your wet cunt and your wild soul. Who's bed you've been sleeping in and who's cock you've been worshipping."

I reached around, undid her jeans and then yanked them down her thighs so the denim would keep them trapped closed. She gasped when I grasped the T of her thong and jerked it so the fabric snapped in half and then again when I dropped to my knees and spread her ass cheeks open with my thumbs so I could see her wet, pink center. So fucking pretty my mouth watered.

"Be quiet while I eat you," I ordered before licking from her clit to her ass, her sweet taste exploding on my tongue, honeyed and heady as mead. "You make one noise and I'll take you over my knee later and crop this fine ass with a paddle."

She moaned softly, her body relaxing into her position as she ceded defeat to my domination. Fuck, but I lived for that moment of victory, for the second she turned pliable as warm wax in my molding hands.

I slapped her ass sharply. "What do you say to me?"

"Yes, Lion," she moaned, rocking forward on her toes as I swatted her other cheek.

Then I dipped my head and feasted.

I bit the inside of her thighs until they glowed red and trembled, sucked her sweet lips and licked her straining, aching clit until her legs quaked all around me. My cock ached, the tip so wet with precum I could feel it dampen my boxers, but I didn't touch it because having my mouth on her was revelation enough.

She was half-heaven, half-hell, each meeting at the apex of her thighs. And when I worshipped there, it was both a prayer and a sin.

I added three fingers to her pussy even though I knew it would be too much, eager to see her struggle to follow my orders.

A whimper cut off in her throat as she bucked back against my pumping fingers, against the thumb I swirled around her ass.

"Every single inch of you is mine to do with as I please," I told her before leaning over to bite her gorgeous ass. "Your ass, your pussy, and your pretty mouth."

"Yes, Lion," she agreed on a short breath. "Use me. Fuck me anywhere where you want, just please give me your cock."

"No," I said, pressing a wicked smile against her thigh as I swatted her cheek again.

"Please," she repeated.

Another slap.

"God," she gasped, her legs shaking, her wetness sliding down her legs for me to lap up like melting cream. "Please, you fucking bastard, fuck me."

There it was, the sass that came through the submission, the desperation that made her untamable, wild even as she succumbed to my will.

I stood up, shoved my athletic shorts down and slammed into her drenched cunt.

Immediately, she groaned, "Need to come."

"No."

I curved over her body taking her beaded nipples into my hands to tug, twist and play. My mouth at her neck, I bit and sucked, desperate to mark her and doing so until she cried out because I knew she could blame it on Wrath. I kissed the bite mark on her neck and thrust harder into her tight pussy.

"Gonna come," she repeated.

"Not until I tell you."

"Fuck," she groaned roughly.

I reared up and pushed her down so her spine dipped and her ass raised higher.

"Take my cock like my good slut and I'll let you come," I grunted as sweat beaded on my forehead and fell to her pink ass.

I slapped it again for good measure, loving the feel of the bounce. Both my hands grasped her ass, opening it up so I could spit on our connection and thrust into her even harder, loving the sight of my ruddy cock sinking into her hot, pink folds.

"Lion!" she shrieked into the pillow, her legs shaking wildly. "Please, God, Lion, I'm yours, yours, *yours.*"

"Good girl," I praised, feeling her words in my balls. "Come for me."

She broke.

Shattering between my hands and over my pounding cock like waves crashing into a rocky shore. Her cunt pulled at me, a sucking tide that made my cock swell and finally erupt inside her.

"God, I can feel you," she breathed in awe as my cum pumped inside her.

I ran my finger around our connection feeling her swollen folds tight around me and jerked my hips forward again with a groan.

"Suck," I ordered, lifting my wet fingers to her mouth so she could taste our juices. "Suck our cum from my fingers and know you are mine, Harleigh Rose."

Her lush mouth wrapped around my fingers and sucked before they formed the words against my skin. "Yours," she agreed as if I didn't even need to ask.

As if she always had been.

Mine.

THE SICK THUD OF A FIST CONNECTING TO FLESH WAS LOUD even amid the roar of male voices yelling their advice and praise into the ring. I reeled back from the impact, taking that punch on the corner of my chin, the pain like a shockwave through my jaw and into my brain.

I shook it off and wiped the mud from my eyes as best I could with my blood-soaked, dirt-crusted hands so I'd be ready for the next attack.

It was hours later.

Three or four, at least.

I'd beaten twenty-one brothers into the ground and I was on my twenty-second, but I wasn't sure it was going to end as the others had in victory.

My body was one live bruise, each limb so heavy from fatigue it was a wonder I hadn't already fallen to the ground in defeat.

I'd already set a record for The Fight, beating Wrath's of sixteen rounds undefeated by a landslide.

I wanted to be done. I wanted to lay down in the face of Mutt's rabid punches and let him take the victory.

But I couldn't do that to Laken, even if she thought sleeping with another man for me was some kind of twisted version of romantic.

I didn't love her, had never even come close, but I liked her. She was sweet and sassy, a woman who loved her family and loved to laugh. She didn't deserve to be passed around like beer from a championship cup.

So, when Mutt ducked to the left to fake me out, I mustered up the dregs of my energy, fortified it with my steely sense of justice and swung my fist in a brutal uppercut that connected with Mutt's chin just as his momentum came forward.

His eyes widened before the pain set in and then they rolled to the back of his head as he swayed then fell in a heap to the churned-up mud at my feet.

The crowd fucking roared.

Twenty-two men down, seventeen to go.

Sweat rolled down my bare heaving chest, taking blood and dirt with it, staining the waistband of my grey sweat shorts so that nearly the entire fabric was heavy and saturated. I wanted to shuck them off, lie in the cool dirt and die the way my body seemed to want to.

But I focused my mind by chanting, *just one more, just one more.*

Then Grease was stepping over the rope and into the ring, middle-aged but packed with dense muscle he'd accrued over a lifetime of work in the gym. His smile was mean, sharp like a blade, his fists curled into meaty hammers.

"This is it, brother," he taunted me. "Time's up for you."

Reaper signaled the start of the fight by hollering, "Blood up and body down. First to hit the ground, loses."

Before he was even finished talking, Grease sprung forward, his fist going at my temple.

I wanted to move, I could hear Harleigh Rose's voice begging me to be careful in the cacophonous jumble of yells from the crowd, but I couldn't find the speed to escape that fatal punch even though I tried.

It connected with a sound I felt more than heard, the knuckles crunching against that soft spot over my ear, the fist meeting bone with a dull boom that exploded in my brain and tossed it bodily against the other side of my skull.

I struggled to find my way through the disorientating darkness, to stay conscious so I could keep Laken safe, make sure Wrath won The Fight so Harleigh Rose was never touched.

But I couldn't.

And a second later, I fell to my knees in the stinking mud and passed out.

CHAPTER TWENTY-SIX

Harleigh Rose

I WANTED TO GO TO HIM, BUT I COULDN'T.

Instead, I had to watch as Hendrix and Pope dragged him from the ring and into the house, Laken fluttering around them in distress. I wanted to knock her buzzing body away with a fly swatter and take my rightful place at Lion's side.

Instead, I stood beside my mother as she frequently made out heavily with Reaper and continued to watch the muddy bloodbath that was Berserker tradition. It was only when Wrath bent down to whisper in my ear, that I stopped thinking about Danner and started worrying about myself.

"Gonna win this thing, no worries, Harls," he said quietly with an oddly comforting squeeze to my arm.

He'd started calling me that recently when we realized that we actually liked each other enough to turn our fake relationship into a real friendship.

"That'd be good," I told him.

His grin was a white ray of hope in his dark beard. "Gotcha."

I stood back so he could pull his black tee off by the back of his neck and reveal the huge, muscled and tattooed length of his torso. The women around me sighed at the sight, but I only rolled my eyes.

"Show off," I muttered.

Wrath surprised me by winking.

Then he swung his leg over the rope and entered the ring to fight Grease, who was still standing after another fifteen rounds.

This would be the last fight.

Winner takes all.

As in, winner takes *me*.

Reaper didn't announce the beginning words to the fight as he normally did the second the fighters entered the circle. Instead, he whispered softly so that Grease would approach us where we stood in a VIP section of the crowd.

He spoke to his Sergeant at Arms too quietly for me to hear, even standing so close to him, but I watched as he slipped something to Grease that glittered metallic in the bright stadium lights.

I blinked, and Grease was back on his side of the ring, Reaper was saying the words and the fight was on.

Wrath started off fierce, his fists so powerful that one punch seemed to rock the older fighter to his very core. It was an amazing thing to see, like David versus Goliath only this time, I hoped like hell my Goliath won.

I could hear some of the women yelling at him lasciviously, tossing panties into the mud at his feet.

It wasn't nearly as many as already littered the ground from Danner's fights.

Wrath may have been a powerhouse, but it was Danner who was lethal as the sharp edge of a blade.

I could still feel the wet in my panties from watching him,

his cut muscles emphasized by the strain of the fights, glittering in the white light like a marble warrior but covered like some savage warrior in blood and mud.

I'd never seen anything hotter than him, weaving around punches and ducking into bodies with a vicious array of punches, landed perfectly on kidneys, cheekbones and the narrow ledge of the jaw.

I'd been looking forward to fucking him when he got home, to worshipping him like a soldier returned from war, only now he was comatose somewhere with that slut, Laken, and I was watching another man defend me.

A man, I realized as I clued back into the fight, that was suddenly losing.

"Fuck," Wrath roared as Grease landed a malicious punch right to the left side of his gut, his skin opening up under it as if he'd been cut through with a hot blade.

Blood spilled down his side and into the sloshing mud at their feet.

Wrath retaliated by lunging at Grease, locking him in one arm and delivering two quick blows to his head.

But Grease was close enough to hit short, sharp punches to Wrath's stomach that bloomed again and again into gaping wounds.

What the fuck was happening?

Wrath released him with a pained grunt, his hand going to a particularly gruesome cut.

Something caught and winked at me in the lights, something affixed to Grease's hand.

Wicked looking brass knuckles, curved at the ends into short blades.

I gasped and looked immediately to Reaper who wasn't looking into the ring at the fight, but at me, my mother tucked under his arm and a massive grin on his face.

"Weapons aren't allowed in The Fight," I accused.

Reaper's eyes glimmered with wet satisfaction. "Think you

forget this is my club and I'm the one makes the rules here. I want weapons, I'll put guns in my motherfuckin' soldiers' hands and no one will say fuckin' shit 'bout it."

"I'm saying shit about it," I spat.

"Yeah, you are," my mother added with a sly smile. "Why do you think this is happening, sweet pea?"

I gaped at them.

"You wanna be Berserker now, girl, you gotta be christened with Berserker style, anointed with the cum of my brothers," Reaper declared.

A shiver caught my spine and wrenched it backwards. "No."

"Loyalty is everythin', princess," he told me as Wrath let out another low growl of pain in the ring. "The brothers prove it with blood in that ring and the women prove it by takin' care'a 'em when they're done."

"That's so fucked up," I shouted over the roar of celebratory shouts as Wrath staggered and nearly fell to his knees. "Mum, you can't seriously be okay with this?"

"Okay with it?" she asked, her face so similar to mine creased in shock. "Harleigh baby, it was *my* idea."

The crowd screamed again, pulling my gaze to the mud where Wrath had fallen to his knees, swaying but still, somehow upright. His eyes, one already swelling shut, red with blood from a cut in his forehead, found mine and they were filled with agony. Not only for him but for me.

"It's over motherfucker," Grease crowed, then landed one last brutal blow to Wrath's left cheek.

And Goliath crumbled.

"No," I screamed, so long and loud I was thrown back to the day my dad had been shot in the chest, only this time I didn't have Danner to shield me from the truth.

Grease had won The Fight. And I was his prize if he wanted me.

Immediately, I turned away on my heel and sprinted from the circle.

I made it ten feet before Grease caught me, his arms slippery with mud and blood but unyielding around my torso as he lugged me up the stairs into the house yelling, "Got me my prize!"

I was still screaming, kicking and wailing and scratching deep welts into his arms as he carted me to the living room and dropped me on the couch.

Twiz appeared above me and locked down my wrists, Pink Eye at the foot of the couch holding my kicking boots. Grease sneered down at me as he straddled me then bent farther to whisper in my ear.

"This is how you smoke out a rat."

I hesitated for one brief second.

What the fuck?

And then pandemonium broke loose.

Danner was suddenly there, still filthy from the fight, his face a black mask of rage as he let out a roar, one so mighty it shook the walls and launched forward to attack Grease.

This time, quickly, he gained the upper hand, dragging the older man to the ground so he could land punch after punch to his manically laughing face.

Then Wrath was there, pulling Twiz and Pink Eye off me even as he bled all across the floor from his wounds.

"Mine," he grunted to them, then smacked his chest. "Fuckin' mine."

I took the opportunity to jump up and deliver a kick to Pink Eye's inner thigh, just above the knee that had him howling and dropping to the floor.

I'd just torn his ACL.

"ENOUGH," Reaper bellowed from the mouth of the hall, his gun raised at us all.

Everyone stopped, but Danner who landed one more blow to Grease's pulpy face.

"You're done here," Reaper said in a voice like a gavel strike. "Turn in your cut and get the fuck out of this clubhouse."

Danner glared at him over Grease's gurgling body. "This shit is fucked, Prez. Doesn't mean I can't do my part for the club."

"That's exactly what it fuckin' means, you fuckin' pussy," Reaper spat. "You deny your brothers 'cause 'a woman? One who ain't even yours? Fuckin' disgusts me. Brothers before all else, that's the fuckin' motto 'ere and you've proved again you can't swallow it. So, get the motherfuckin' fuck out 'fore I get Hendrix to drag you outta 'ere."

I made to step forward, to say something to rectify the situation before the last three years of Danner's work went down the drain, but Wrath stilled me with a careful hand and subtly shook his head.

Danner got up slowly, his eyes locked with Reaper's even when he hocked a wad of spit onto Grease's body and then still when he said, "Came here for a fuckin' brotherhood and freedom. Not for more fucked up rules forced on me."

Reaper sneered at him. "Out."

He didn't look at me, but I knew he wanted to as he stalked out the front doors and into the night.

Reaper turned his gun on Wrath, squinting one eye in focus. "You do somethin' like that again, Wrath brother, I'll not only excommunicate your ass, I'll put a fuckin' bullet in it, ya hear?"

Wrath grunted.

"And you," he told me, cocking his gun between me and the hall behind him. "I got another way to prove you're loyal, you're too prude to take a fuckin' cock. Get to my office."

He turned on his heel without waiting for me to follow.

I didn't want to, I wanted to go to Danner's and make sure he was alright, ask him what the fuck we were going to do next, because at this point, there was nothing I wouldn't do to take these fuckers down.

"Go," Wrath ordered me quietly. "You want'a bullet to the brain? Fuckin' *go*."

So, I did.

But first, I kicked Grease in his prone belly and added my spit to his face.

Reaper was waiting in his office, door open, stroking his gun where it lay on his desktop.

"Close the door, girl."

I did, then moved into the room to sit at one of the chairs on the other side of the desk from him. Anger coursed so swiftly through my veins, I was worried I wouldn't be able to dam the flow of it from my mouth if he asked me to speak.

"We got a mole up in here," he opened, clearly hoping for a telling reaction from me.

I was too tired, too angry to give him anything but a straight shot of sass. "No shit."

His eyebrows jumped. "You know it?"

I shrugged. "Grease just sneered it into my face before he tried to get in there with me."

"It's Lion."

I shrugged again. "Not close with him, don't know enough to give you my opinion."

"Yeah," he said nodding, clicking the safety on his gun on and off with an audible *click, click, click.* "Thing is your mum told me she recognized him a while back, but couldn't put her finger on how. Was only when she met him 'fore the fight she realized she knew him as a fuckin' pig back in Entrance. So, I'm thinking, Harleigh Rose Garro, there's no way you coulda forgot that either, is there?"

My heart was hammering, my palms so slick that they slid off the arms of the chair and into my lap. "Like I said, not close to him, can't say I gave him much notice."

"Fuckin' bullshit," he roared, standing so abruptly his

chair flew back and then he was leaning over the desk, his Glock aimed at my forehead. "You knew. Why the fuck would you know and not tell me, huh? 'Less you're here for your fuckin' father."

"I'm not," I rushed to say. "I thought I recognized him, but I didn't remember from where. I must have been a kid when he was a cop there, and I was a biker's kid, what did I know about cops?"

He hesitated, breathing heavy, his dark eyes sinister. "Hard to believe you girl, 'specially when you wouldn't let yourself have Grease. How am I gonna trust ya?"

"You can," I said with a small smile as if being held at gunpoint was no big deal because I wasn't guilty. "What do you want me to do to prove it?"

His grin was wicked sharp like the edge of a blade. "Wanna make it clear 'fore you say no to this. Got a man watchin' your family, 'specially that sweet piece Garro's got pregnant with his seed. You don't prove to me that you've renounced The Fallen by doin' what I'm now gonna ask you to do, I'm gonna have my man gut her, pull those babies outta her while she's still livin' then put a bullet in all three'a their heads. You feel me?"

I'd never been so frightened in my life.

Fuck the gun pointed at my forehead.

I'd rather have him blast that bullet in my brain than even *think* about doing something so grotesque to someone so goddamn beautiful.

"I'll do it, Reaper," I said, my voice surprisingly steady. "I'll do it, just tell me what the fuck it is."

Reaper studied me, scouring me for sincerity, then finding what he needed in my desperate eyes, he clicked the safety back on his gun and settled into his chair with a placid smile.

"You're gonna kill Lion for me, princess. And you're gonna do it tonight."

CHAPTER TWENTY-SEVEN

Harleigh Rose

THE HOUSE WAS SURPRISINGLY CALM WHEN I WALKED THROUGH the door, "Die For You" by The Weeknd playing through the speakers as Danner chopped vegetables at the counter, Hero curled up by his feet until he heard me and came running to my side.

I dropped to my knees to give him an ear scratch but kept my eyes on my man. He didn't say anything and even his eyes were indecipherable as I gave the dog a kiss on the head and made my way over to him.

He'd had a shower, clean from gunk and gore, and he smelled so good that I almost burst into tears.

God, I'd miss the smell of him.

"You okay?" I asked, proud that my voice didn't wobble.

"Better question, are you?" he said, lunging forward to grab my hand when I hesitated to go to him so that he could tug me into his arms.

"Yeah," I mumbled against his chest. "Thanks for saving me. Again."

"Anytime, Rosie," he said, and there was a hidden wealth of meaning in it.

I leaned back in his embrace to study the strong angles of his face, finding a deepening bruise at his jaw and a swollen cut above his eyebrow that he'd already pulled closed with medical tape.

"I would have cleaned you up, I'm a nurse now, you know?"

It was a lame tease, but he smiled at me. "Didn't want you to worry about it when you got back. The shower and tending also gave me time to get my shit under control. You were gone a while, what happened after I left?"

I chewed my lip then forced myself to stop before I gave anything away. "Wrath got in trouble, Reaper reamed me out for not being a team player a.k.a team slut. Nothin' too serious."

"Good," he said before kissing me firmly, turning me around and slapping my ass. "Take a seat, I'm makin' you my one and only dinner specialty."

"You mean you can make more than cereal?" I said with a faux gasp so he would smile.

He did.

I wanted to collect all his smiles and put them in a jar to take out and look at later when this was all over, and I never saw him again.

"Yes, brat, I happen to make the best fuckin' sausage mac n' cheese this side of the border," he told me proudly.

"You're in a good mood, which I totally wasn't expecting given that you just got excommunicated from the club you've been trying to take down for three years."

He resumed chopping, the huge butcher's knife gleaming in the overhead lights. "Yeah, that'd be because I have a badass woman at my table who's gonna keep me on my toes all night until I decide to bend her over and turn her into my good girl while she takes my cock. I'm makin' my kickass dinner and my dog is at my feet. Things are good."

"Again, I'll mention that three years of your life's work just went down the drain... do I need to check you for a concussion?"

He smirked, playfully like only I could make him do.

I saved that one in my jar too.

"Wanted them gone, *still* want them gone. Don't care that they're bikers, I care that they're horrible people doin' horrible things to civilians who haven't bought that. I hope the RCMP finds a way to do that and I think in my three years of service, I got them way fucking closer than they were before. Already called it in and got a meeting with the Sergeant tomorrow. I'll probably be reassigned. Sucks I couldn't finish that job, but that meant letting someone rape you, so got to admit, Rosie, most of me is fucking thrilled we're out of there."

"We?" I asked softly.

He froze, that stillness he could affect that was artic, the room gone solid with him. "You're not with me?"

"I'm with you, I just need to see this through," I whispered, my heart failing like a sick thing in my chest.

"Even if I could get back in with Reaper, it's too fucking risky," he said, his arms crossed and feet parted, ready to do battle with me over this.

"I know I can do it."

He didn't notice that I wasn't using a universal 'we.' He stalked around the counter to stare down into my eyes. I tried to memorize the way he looked gazing down on me like that, gorgeous and righteous like the angel Gabriel come down from heaven to slay all my demons.

"This isn't Romeo and Juliet, Rosie. You think only one person's gonna die if we get found out? No. We both know, if you'll just let yourself think about it logically for one second, that we keep doin' this and we get found out, it isn't only you and me in jeopardy. It's your friends and family, your dad, Loulou and her fucking unborn children, your brother and his girlfriend, one of your best friends, Lila, Nova, and Bat, and Maja and Buck. You want to see all those lives go up in flames because we were too selfish to let go of this thing we got between us?"

He shook me gently by the shoulders, his eyes so green they burned through me like acid.

Something in me broke at the poignancy of his words and anger went flooding through me. I wanted to rally at the moon, curse the gods and sacrifice anyone but him. Instead, I shoved him away hard with a two-handed push and snarled at him even as I felt my heart beat and throb for him, the kick beat to every word I yelled.

"Loving you was never a decision I made. There was nothing conscious about it so how can I be logical about it now? I know it doesn't make sense, the two of us, the good guy and the bad girl, with your family and my family. I know I make you crazy and I make you mad. You think I don't know all that? Well, I do. So, stop telling me to think logically about this shit. There's no logic to our love, only a feeling I've got so deep in the heart of me if I rip it out, I just know I'll stop living."

"You telling me you love me?" he asked, so low I almost didn't hear the words, but I felt them. Each one hit a note deep inside me, plucking at an instrument only he knew how to play.

I blinked at him, chewed my lips and cursed myself for letting my hot head get me into such a fucked up, vulnerable situation, especially in the face of what I had to do.

But then it occurred to me that Reaper, Mutt and Twiz were outside waiting, guns at their belts and wicked knives in their boots. There was no getting out of what I had to do to guarantee my family's safety.

It was Danner or them. And there were so many more of

them, countless names that he had just reeled off like a grocery list.

One or a dozen.

The love of my life or the people who had given me life and raised me.

I knew what the answer would be.

So, I sucked in a deep breath and decided to be selfish like only I could be.

I decided to enjoy the only moment I would ever have with him where I could love him freely.

"Yeah, so what?" I said, sassy because he liked it and I knew it. "It's not like you don't love me too."

"Yeah, that's true," he agreed instantly, in that long, honeyed drawl he used when I said something that affected him. "I love you and know the way most people know the sun rises in the east and sets in the west, that bikers know the sound of Harley pipes, and cops know the difference between fucking right and fucking wrong that you and I are made for each other."

"Fuck," I breathed through the rush of tears attacking the backs of my eyes. "You're going to make me cry again. Jesus Christ, what is *wrong* with me lately?"

Danner bit the side of his grin but then gave up and blasted me with the beauty of his full smile, creases cut into his cheeks and pressed beside his glittering eyes. I even loved his strong, square teeth so white against his skin.

"Fuck," I repeated again, feeling overwhelmed nearly to the point of hysteria. "I feel like I might faint or something equally wussy."

His head tipped back as he laughed, exposing the long column of his throat. Before that moment, I'd never known an Adam's apple could be so goddamn sexy. Before I could shake myself out of my stupor, he was on me, lifting me into the air so that I instinctively wrapped myself around him.

"You love me, Rosie?" he asked, looking up at me with carefree joy, his face boyishly open.

I wanted to rip him apart limb by limb with my teeth and fingers turned into claws. I wanted to hold his lion's heart in my hands too tightly and feel it beat and throb for me, against me. I wanted to disassemble him, piece by bloody piece, to satisfy my burning passion, my crushing rage at the changes he'd wrought on my life and me.

But then...I wanted to sit crossed-legged in the middle of the mess, smooth my claws turned fingers over the jagged edges of him and put him back together again. I wanted to trace the outline of each of his limbs, knot together his muscles and slot his bones into their joints. I wanted to sew myself into every atom of his DNA and live there forever, intrinsically tied to him so that if any force tried to tear me away like I knew they would, they'd have to kill him to separate us.

It was a gruesome way to love someone, but it was the way I felt about Lionel Danner and I knew that would never change.

"Yeah, Lion," I said, placing a hand on his strong-boned face. "I fucking love you, okay?"

I gasped as he slid me down his body, each hard plane gliding against my slight curves like a rough caress, and he took advantage of my parted lips by sealing them with his own.

He kissed me like he owned me, one hand going to the skin over my heart and pressed there, warm and heavy, and the other diving into my hair so he could hold me how he wanted. I felt his claim almost painfully as he tattooed himself into every inch of my skin, synchronized himself to every beat of my reborn heart.

"Fucking love you too," he rasped against my damp lips before pushing me back against the counter. "Brutally, savagely, fucking endlessly."

I felt my broken heart in my chest, the poisoned blood beating through each chamber until it pumped out through my veins suffused with light so my plasma felt like champagne. Giddiness swelled in my belly and I let it out with a diaphanous giggle that didn't suit me at all.

He was a good man.

The kind to help old ladies across the street, save kittens from lofty tree branches and open car doors for his dates.

But he was a bad man too.

The kind that liked to mark my skin with ruddy bruises and stripe my ass like a fucking candy cane with the harsh lash of his belt.

He was good gone bad and it was all because of me.

The truth of it shouldn't have razed through me like a forest fire until I was just cinders and ash in his hand, but it did.

He wasn't all good and I wasn't bad.

Not separately, and definitely not together.

Together we were a lot of things, and none of them made any sense, but all of them worked.

I focused on his lips on mine, the feel of his warmth around me, the way his hands cradled my face as if I was precious. And I realized that rotten seed in the center of my soul was gone, that implant from Farrah that had always told me I wasn't worthy eradicated by his love.

Danner was the best man I knew, and he loved me.

Actually, loved me.

Tears pooled in the backs of my eyes and slid down my cheeks.

I held him close, kissing him with the entirety of my ferocious passion for him and carefully moved one hand across the counter to the cutting board. My fingers clenched around the cool handle, the weight of the knife so similar to the cleaver, but the situation in such contrast to the one with Cricket that for a brief moment, I hesitated.

I pulled away from him so he could see my eyes, filled with tears and the wreckage of a self-broken heart and I whispered, "I'm so sorry."

Then I plunged the heavy blade into his soft flesh.

His breath froze in his throat, his lips parted over mine in stunned confusion.

I slipped off the counter and gently pushed him away so I could step back.

He swayed, his hand moving to the weapon protruding from the top left of his chest.

"Rosie," he whispered and there was so much bewilderment in the word, my heart collapsed under the weight of it and I started to sob. "Why are you doing this?"

I wasn't doing this. It was done.

But I said, "Never gave a fuck about you, Danner," because I didn't want him to get up and follow me if he could, if he was stupid enough to do so after I stuck him like a pig.

I watched as he tried to take a step forward and fell sideways, slamming to the ground on his opposite shoulder and rolling with an anguished groan to his back.

Hero barked at me, growling and yipping beside his master, unsure if I was the threat or under attack as well.

I don't know what I expected except that I'd always thought of Lion as immortal, a deity of old, made of flesh and bone but animated by something stronger, surer of spirit than mere mortals ever possessed. I guess that's why I was so stunned when red blood flowed out of the wound gouged in his muscle-plated chest and spilled in silky torrents down his front.

I blinked at the sight of Danner caught like a fly in the web of his own sticky blood. Then I blinked again at the sight of the thick handle of the butcher's knife sticking out of his flesh.

The butcher's knife I'd put there myself.

I wanted to go to him, prove to him that we weren't the

modern re-telling of Romeo and Juliet yet, that I wouldn't let him die and that I wouldn't be moved to kill myself if he did.

But that would've been a lie.

So, instead, I dug my phone from my back pocket, took a picture as Danner lay there in shock, bleeding out on the floor, then walked straight out of the house and onto the back of Reaper's bike.

"Good girl," he praised as I showed him the photo.

But the words were daggers in my ears.

Because I knew that no matter what happened, I'd never be a good girl again.

CHAPTER TWENTY-EIGHT

Danner

I KNEW BEFORE I OPENED MY EYES WHAT HAD HAPPENED, BUT I didn't know if I was alive or dead. Part of me hoped I was dead. If I could fall head over ass in love with a woman who was capable of literally plunging a knife into my heart, death was the most peace I could hope for. Otherwise, I'd spend the rest of my life like a mad archeologist going over every square inch of my past with Harleigh Rose to see where I went wrong.

I didn't want to believe she would do something like that to me, of course I didn't, but there wasn't exactly a *reasonable* excuse for her to stab me with a fucking butcher's knife, was there?

"You open your eyes, we can have our chat quicker than not and I can get the doc in here to do a check on ya."

Fuck.

It was official.

I wasn't dead.

There was no way I could be, because I'd lived a good life, I didn't deserve to go to hell and that was the only place cruel enough to tie me in eternal damnation to a man who had been my career-long enemy.

Zeus Garro.

I peeled my sandy eyelids apart and sure enough, there he sat in an almost comically small orange chair beside my hospital bed. He looked rough, bags under his stale eyes, his normally wind-swept tangle of brown and gold hair more than its usual mess.

"Look like shit," I croaked.

He threw back his head and laughed the same way Harleigh Rose did.

Pain lit up my body like a light board, concentrated in my heart and the throbbing wound under my left clavicle.

"Always said cops don't have a sense'a humor, but you been provin' me wrong for years." He shook his head, pushed back a lock of errant hair and leaned forward on his forearms. "She left ya a note."

"What?"

"H.R., she and King used to do this thing when they were kids. Leave each other notes in weird places, inside shoes, books, shit like that. King came home last night, found a note in the keyhole'a the front door, that one led him to one she left in her apartment, hidden in the ceilin' fan."

He jerked his head to the tray attached to my bed and angled to the right of me.

I'm sorry I stabbed you.
I'm sorry I said I never gave a fuck
about you.
The opposite is true.
I give all the fucks, I'm a glutton, a
slut, an addict of fucks when it comes to
you.
But "I'd break my own heart a million
times over if it meant keeping you alive,"
so I hurt both of us to save you.
I only hope you can forgive me.
xx.
Your Rosie.

I looked up from the note with blind eyes, seeing Rosie standing over my body with tears streaming down her face and a look of painful resolve in her eyes. I remembered the weird vibration she was giving off when she walked in the door, how she kissed me desperately, aggressively as if she would never get enough of me.

"Girl knew what she was doing," Garro interrupted, jerking his chin at my bandaged shoulder and upper left chest. "Stuck you close to the heart so they'd know she meant business, but through nothin' important. You'll be sore, need some therapy for the shoulder, but they had you in surgery for an hour and said you'd be fine."

"Who found me?"

"She sent a message from some private number to Cressida sayin' to meet at your address if she wanted to chat. Cress's a soft touch so even though we'd shunned 'er, Cress went. Got there as the bikes were pullin' away, called King from 'er car and the ambulance from inside when she saw ya bleedin' out."

Jesus Christ.

"Now, that's all squared the fuck away, why don't you tell me what *the fuck* you an' my daughter been up to the past two months?" he growled, leaning forward on powerful arms to get near my face. "Might be laid up, but I'm the kinda guy don't mind addin' to your misery."

"Jesus, Garro, I was just fucking stabbed by the love of my fuckin' life, why don't you give a guy a fucking minute here?" I snapped at him, then winced when I pulled at my shoulder.

He stared at me, the stillness of a predator about to strike. "Love of your fuckin' life?"

Fuck, at least I was in the hospital already so they could give me the paddles of life after Garro tried to kill me.

I sighed heavily. "Yeah, Garro, you think the man I am I can't love the woman she is? 'Cause I know she's your daughter, but I've taken care of her as a girl, watched out for her as a teen and now loved her as a woman. She's mine in a way, honestly, I don't give a fuck if you approve or not. She's gonna stay mine."

"You sayin' this lyin' in a hospital bed with a stab wound she gave ya," he pointed out, but there was a smirk in his voice and I watched him rub a thumb over his thick wedding band, knowing that he got me.

"She had an impossible choice and she made it the only way someone as brave and loyal as Harleigh Rose could make it. She hurt me to save me and save her family. She's broken her own heart over and over to make sure of it."

"Thinkin' you better fill me in now, Danner" he growled. "And tell me just what kinda shit she put herself through for me and mine, and fuckin' *why* she did it?"

I tipped my head to the ceiling and for the first time in my life, I told Zeus Garro everything.

OVER THE NEXT FEW DAYS, I RECOVERED PAINFULLY THOUGH not solitarily in the hospital.

I had many visitors.

My mother was there frequently, so upset about the wound that I didn't have the heart to tell her it was Harleigh Rose who'd done it.

My mother loved Harleigh Rose. She loved King.

She'd never fully understood the dynamic between the Danners and the Garros even though she was one of us, and she complained over the years of separation between our two factions, that she missed the kids.

She'd wanted a big family, kids and animals running around the way she'd had on her parent's ranch outside of Entrance, the same one she'd given me as a graduation present.

Dad hadn't.

He wanted one perfect son and got it.

Well, he got the gender anyway, and the perfect son up until the day I blindsided him by taking down the Nightstalkers MC, the same club his shady business partner Javier Ventura had financially backed.

I hadn't talked to him in three and a half years.

He was not one of my visitors, and my mother, in the process of divorcing him because he'd driven away her beloved son and never given her much love himself, didn't speak of him.

The Garros, though, were there every day.

It started with Garro, sitting sentry by my bed as if he was concerned the Berserkers wouldn't buy the police and Harleigh Rose circulated version of my death.

At first, we didn't speak much. I lay there, he sat there, two very different kinds of Alphas with very different types of lives.

Only, maybe, not so different after all.

We talked about Farrah and Garro let me read the shameful anger in his tone when he spoke about how she'd turned like Lilith after the fall, how it started the year before he went to jail, but with shit going down in the club, he hadn't gotten around to divorcing her and then it was too late.

Divorce proceedings in jail took time.

He didn't thank me for taking care of his kids, but I told him some stories about the time we spent together because he seemed to need it, pressure on a knotted muscle. I told him about teaching King to shoot his first gun, how he'd fallen on his face from the recoil on the shotgun, how Harleigh Rose had once convinced Old Sam to let her put on a concert for her friends and then only invited brothers from The Fallen.

He laughed.

It was weird, making the Prez of an outlaw MC laugh.

But it was oddly, deeply gratifying too.

The end of the second week, Loulou, Cress, and King showed up.

Loulou waddled right up to the side of my bed, her hugely pregnant belly partially exposed by a cropped top that read "Biker Mama," and pressed a kiss to my temple.

"Nice to visit you in here for a change," Cressida joked as she sat on the edge of my bed and placed a book on my thigh. "Midnight In The Garden Of Good And Evil. It's about moral ambiguity and faith."

I blinked at her. "Right."

"You don't have to read it," she said happily, leaning

forward into the bed with happy eyes. "I'm opening my own bookstore, you know?"

"Ah here she goes, Danny," King laughed, tugging on a lock of his woman's hair as he passed her to lean against the window. "Once she gets started on books, it's hard to stop her."

"This is true," she said with a shrug.

I looked bewilderedly at Loulou as she settled herself in Garro's lap, but she only laughed huskily and said, "You took care of Harleigh Rose when we didn't, Danner. Welcome to the fold."

CHAPTER TWENTY-NINE

Harleigh Rose

I'D NEVER BEEN ALONE IN MY LIFE.

Not like this.

Not by myself and hating it but knowing that there was no one to call.

My family thought I'd betrayed them.

My lover was hospitalized because of me.

Even my fake family wouldn't come when called. They weren't that kind of MC, and wasn't that the reason I was doing this?

I tried to fill the void yawning open all around me with that reason and others. I was doing this for a purpose. The Berserkers MC were a threat that needed to be eliminated. My dad had taught me from a young age that evil couldn't be excused or ignored. It had to be decimated, torn out from the roots and incinerated. I'd never been so directly faced with evil as I was now, embroiled in the Berserkers, but now that I was, I had a duty to end them and it was my dad who'd taught me that. So even if he couldn't understand, wouldn't even love me after I'd done it, I'd stay until the bitter, blackened end of them. Because it was simple, I'd do anything for my family. Even if it meant going to war against them.

It was two weeks after I'd stabbed Danner in the chest, but the moment still haunted me at all hours of the day. I'd called a nurse I trusted, Betsy, at the hospital to make sure he was okay, and she assured me that with rehab, he'd be right as rain in a few months.

Thank *fuck*.

I'd had a pretty good idea that stabbing him high in the left chest would cause the least amount of damage, but if my hand had slipped or I'd miscalculated at all, if Cressida wasn't a softie and she hadn't gotten to the house when she did, Danner would have been killed.

And I would have been his murderer.

My only solace was the fact that Sergeant Renner and my handler Diana Casey were thrilled with the progress I'd helped them make on the case. Grant Yves was organizing a massive shipment of guns in from California that would be arriving that very night and they were ready to make a bust. It might not be enough to take all of them down, but it should be enough to dismantle the organization.

Thank *fuck*.

I was tired to the marrow of my bones, my spirit a dead thing I carried dragging behind me like road kill. I needed this to be done so I could figure out what to do with my life, a life that would no longer involve Danner.

I thought my family might forgive me. There was hope like burning coal inside my chest that convinced me of it, and it fueled me through every pain-soaked day without them.

But how could Danner ever forgive me for what I'd done?

I parked in front of the Berserkers clubhouse with Hero in the passenger seat.

He'd showed up at my apartment two days after the stabbing, sitting on my doorstep with his leash in his mouth, his bag of doggy stuff beside him.

I didn't question how he got there.

He was the only creature I had left to love.

So, I fell to my knees in the door and burrowed my face in his fur as I sobbed and sobbed and sobbed until there was no moisture left in my body to give.

I'd taken him everywhere with me since.

I was at the clubhouse looking for Wrath.

In the last two weeks, we'd spent a lot of time together, so much that he'd even trusted me enough to meet Kylie.

It shocked the hell out of me, but they were adorable together. She was a short, curvy black woman about my age with a gorgeous array of honey tipped brown curls and a sweet smile. Wrath was Wrath, huge and imposing. But somehow, like Danner and I had, against all odds, they worked.

She made him laugh.

He made her feel safe.

Hanging out with them had been like punching a tender bruise, but I'd enjoyed it.

If I couldn't be happy, at least I could watch others be happy.

Wrath hadn't been around in three days.

For another biker, that may have been normal, but Wrath liked to keep his pulse on the action both because he was VP and because he needed that to make sure Kylie was safe.

So, I was concerned.

I opened the door, swung out of the car and waited for Hero to follow.

No one had commented on my sudden addition of a dog, and I realized Danner had never brought him around before, so they assumed he was mine.

He kept close as we walked the stairs then entered the eerily quiet house.

"Yo," I called out. "Anyone here?"

No one responded, so I dropped Hero in Wrath's room just in case something bad was going down before I went exploring.

I turned the corner into the kitchen, finding Twiz, Hendrix, Pink Eye, Roper, and Pope all sitting quietly drinking from opened bottles of whiskey.

"What the fuck is going on?" I asked, and I knew they'd tell me.

Since I'd 'killed' Lion, the club trusted me with everything.

"Was wrong," Hendrix admitted, looking stricken. "Wasn't Danner was the mole."

My heart seized. "What? Who the fuck was it then?"

The front door crashed open with an explosive bang that heralded a coarse, agonized roar, "*Where the fuck is she, you fucking bastards!?*"

Wrath.

My heart dropped to the beer stained carpet.

The boys looked around the table at each other, but only Twiz and Pope got up.

"Tell me *where the fuck* my girl is!" Wrath bellowed again, and we could hear him throwing shit in the living room before his heavy boots made their way down the hall.

Pope had his gun out and trained on the door by the time Wrath filled it with his body and his rage.

He was utterly terrifying, his face brutal with anger, his fists clenched into hard stones that would crush bones as easily as a metal scrapper.

Pope flinched then held the gun steady. "Stay there, Wrath. We know you're the fuckin' snitch."

Wrath's glare condensed further until his eyes were only thin, glittering slits. He stalked forward slowly toward Pope who took a step back then held his ground.

"Stop right fuckin' there," he yelled out as Wrath got closer.

Wrath ignored me and walked straight into the barrel of

the gun, the mouth at his right shoulder. His hand went up to grab Pope by the throat just as the gun fired.

He hissed loudly, jerked slightly as the bullet tore through his shoulder, but otherwise, he was unstoppable. He lifted Pope into the air with one hand and snarled into his face, "Where the fuck is my girl? You tell me in the next three seconds or I'll snap your neck."

Pope dropped the gun to clench at Wrath's hand pressed around his throat, but he didn't say anything.

Three seconds later, his neck snapped loudly, the sound like a foot stepping over broken plastic.

Pope fell to the ground dead and Wrath turned to face the others in the room.

"WHERE THE FUCK IS SHE!?" he roared so loudly, spittle went flying and the hanging light rattled.

"Dead."

The one word punctured the furious air in the room like a popped balloon.

Reaper stood in the doorway, a placid smile on his face.

"Killed that boy you had protectin' her, killed her mother and then dragged her outta that house by her fuckin' hair," he informed us. "Didn't even wait to take her to the container. Just shot her dead by the side of the road and shoved her in the ocean."

I threw my hand over my mouth to stop the sob from erupting as Wrath's face went grey and ashen.

"That's what happens to snitches in this fuckin' club, in my fuckin' family," Reaper sneered. "We kill them like the animals they are."

The air went suddenly electric and then it happened.

Wrath went berserk.

His roar filled the room, louder even than the shot Hendrix fired into his belly as he lurched forward towards the table. He ground an empty chair and brought it down over Roper's head before he had a chance to move, grabbed a butter knife from the table and sunk it into Twiz's eye as he shoved forward to take him down and then punched Pink Eye so hard in the throat something audibly broke.

Another shot fired, this one from the gun in Reaper's hand from where he stood in the door, his smile visible through the gun smoke.

The bullet hit Wrath in the stomach but didn't stop him.

He pushed Pink Eye's choking body aside and prowled towards Reaper.

Another shot, this one getting him in the arm.

He continued forward until he had Reaper by the throat and he lifted him into the air.

"Where is my *fucking girl*," he cried out in confused fury.

"Dead," Reaper smiled even though Wrath was choking him out. "Like you."

Then another shot fired, this one from Grease who'd snuck into the room from the other doorway. The bullet sunk deep into his right shoulder, the one holding Reaper up.

Wrath collapsed to the ground.

I sobbed and tried to go to him, but Grease was suddenly there holding me back. I struggled against his arm as more brothers filed in, grabbed Wrath by his feet and started to drag his big, bleeding body out of the room.

"Kylie's photo," he called out, his voice filled with pain.

"Shut the fuck up," Reaper said before kicking him in the head so hard, he passed out.

But it was too late.

Wrath had given me his message and it had been received.

I raced up the stairs after Grease let me go, after the boys had taken Wrath out the back and loaded him into a truck I heard start up and tear out of there.

Grease let me go, probably thinking I was just emotional.

I was.

But I was also on a mission.

My fingers shook as I lifted the framed photo of Kylie Wrath kept in his closet and worked the back flap open.

The picture fluttered out onto the ground.

But so did thin pages and pages of accountancy papers.

I hugged them to my chest for a minute, Hero whining at me and nudging my back, confused by the ruckus and my quick sliding tears. I wrapped a hand in the fur at his back and whispered in his ear. "We got 'em."

CHAPTER THIRTY

Harleigh Rose

It was two days later that it happened.

Too late really.

Wrath was gone, presumed dead.

Danner was presumed dead but gone to me forever.

And I'd undergone so many trials to get to that point that it almost didn't feel worth it.

But it did because it meant the threat they'd posed against my family was done.

The Berserkers had fallen.

I watched from the front seat of a massive GMC SUV as dozens of RCMP officers and local PD swarmed the Port of Vancouver. Red, blue and white lights flashed across the night scene, highlighting the last of the brothers who'd been there to unload the ship getting hauled into cop cars and driven off to be processed then, hopefully, convicted for life for arms dealing, smuggling, and a litany of other offenses.

It was too surreal.

I unbuckled my seatbelt and got out of the car even though they'd told me not to.

I didn't have a reason to listen to anyone anymore, so I didn't.

Instead, I walked under the yellow police tape, hugging the borrowed RCMP jacket around my shoulders, and watched up close as officers taped and categorized the guns in a massive open shipping container, how Mutt cursed at two officers who pushed him up against a car roughly before shoving him inside.

I looked down at the police lights flashing on my skin, smelled the brine from the ocean at my back and closed my eyes to hear the police chatter over the radio, the not too distant call of reporters showing up to get the scoop.

It sunk in.

I'd done it.

Somehow, against so many odds, I'd helped protect not only my family but the city of Vancouver and the entire province.

Berserkers MC was responsible for a third of the illegal guns in the city, for over twelve confirmed homicides and dozens of unsolved ones in the last year alone.

They were an evil I'd dug down into the dirt to dig up by the roots and weed out.

I closed my eyes, tipped my face up and tried not to cry.

"Harleigh Rose Garro."

I opened my eyes and smiled slightly at Sergeant Renner.

He had his hand extended to me, a smile bigger than mine on his face.

I stared at his hand blankly then back at him.

The grin widened. "Like to thank you, Ms. Garro, for your invaluable help with the case. It's the biggest seizure of illegal arms we've had to date, not to mention the fact that we have Berserkers MC tied up in that so tight, they'll be going away for years."

"It was Danner," I told him truthfully, his name hot in my throat. "He did everything, really."

"And he'll be commended for that. For obvious reasons that I'm sure you understand, you will not. So, if you will, I'd like to shake your hand."

A cop wanted to shake my hand.

I swallowed the strangeness, unsure if I was proud or horrified, and took his dry palm in my own.

"Thank you," he repeated seriously, his dark eyes pinning me with the intent of his words so I couldn't hide from it.

"Don't sweat it," I muttered.

And in the middle of a crime scene I wasn't a felonious part of, I made a cop laugh.

I WAS HOME, READY FOR BED BUT SNUGGLING IN FRONT OF THE TV with Hero watching Game of Thrones because it reminded me of Loulou, when there was a knock at my door.

Hero and I both perked up, looking at each other.

"Are you gonna get it, or me?" I asked him.

He woofed softly, and I laughed, giving him a gentle ear rub before I got up and walked to the peephole.

Farrah stood at my door, mascara darkened tears streaked down her face.

I chewed my lip.

She was a hideous person whose worst transgressions included plotting to see me raped by a biker.

She was also my mother.

And she'd done some terrible things, but I knew there was good in her because my father had loved her once, and on odd days at odd times in my childhood, she could be kind.

I dug my phone out of my pocket just in case and sent off a quick message to Renner.

Then I opened the door.

"What're you doing here, Farrah?"

She sniffed loudly. "Are you really going to be so rude to your mother when I'm clearly distressed?"

I sighed heavily. "I'm only talking to you if you can explain why you were okay with letting Grease rape me."

It was her time to sigh, as if I was a stupid kid again and she could never make me understand. She took my face in her hands even though I flinched, and her wet blue eyes the same as mine scoured over my face.

"You were such a beauty," she whispered, suddenly morose. "I loved you so much. You were this precious little thing and I had no idea what to do with you, but I tried my best."

"I never felt even a breath of that love," I told her bluntly.

She bristled. "My mum died when I was four. Be grateful you even have a mother."

"Be grateful I'm even talking to you now," I snapped.

"Let's start again," she begged softly, grabbing at my hands to swing them softly between us. "I just want to be in your life. I have it right now. I can be better, and I don't want to be alone."

"You did that to yourself," I told her, yanking my hands away. "You can't just pick and choose when you want to have a family, Mum. You've had one all along and did nothing for them. Don't expect me to want to be there for you now," I said, starting to close the door as my phone rang.

"At least let me in so I can call a cab," she asked prettily, crocodile tears in her eyes.

Renner calling.

I swiped open my phone and lifted it to my ear, tucking the device between it and my shoulder so I could tug her into the room as I answered the call.

"Hey."

"Ms. Garro, I need to inform you that Reaper Holt was not picked up by the separate RCMP team that swept the Berserker compound tonight. There was no sign of him there or at any of the usual club haunts. We have reason to believe he has a mole in the department. I'm sending a squad car to you now. An officer will come to your door and the other will stay outside for your protection while we get this sorted."

I listened mutely, careful to keep my face blank because my mother was pretending not to watch me as she fixed her makeup in the front entrance mirror even as she was.

Casually, I reached for my purse on the table beside the door, my other hand going to the lock to flip it.

A second later a gunshot fired and a bullet tore through the doorknob.

I leapt back, my hand blazing with pain, bleeding all over the ground from the bullet graze in the flesh of my thumb, as the door pushed open and Reaper appeared.

"Hey baby," Farrah called out as if he'd knocked on the door and was visiting for tea. "The door was open. I think you caught Harleigh with that shot."

Hero growled long and fierce from behind me.

Reaper lunged toward me, the butt of his gun to my temple. "Come the fuck on 'fore the pigs get here."

Farrah checked her hair in the mirror quickly then slipped by us out the door. "Careful with Harleigh, baby."

He grunted, but I knew he had no intention of being careful with me.

There was only murder in his eyes.

He knew.

He knew I was the rat. He probably even doubted that Wrath or Lion had been snitches now that he knew it was me.

And he was going to kill me for it.

My dumb, pathetic mother thought we were going to be a family again.

Maybe we would be, if he killed her too.

"Yeah, bitch," he sneered against my ear, feeling the fear turn my body rigid as a corpse. "You're gonna die tonight."

There was another growl from the couch and then a smear of gold flying through the air as Hero leapt into action.

He lunged at Reaper's groin, sharp teeth digging into his thigh in a way that had him bellowing and trying to shake him off.

I wrenched out of his hold and went for his eyes with my thumbs.

He swiped the gun madly in front of his face, trying to dislodge Hero and evade my sharp fingers. One of my nails connected with his tear duct and I pushed, feeling the wet squish as I cut through the corner of his eye.

"Fuck!" he screamed, lashing out so wildly that the back of his hand caught me in the side of the face and sent me flying.

I fell back to the ground with a sharp yell, cracking my head against the wood.

When I looked back up, Hero was wrenching his head away from Reaper's blood-soaked thigh with a rough growl and a sharp jerk.

Reaper howled in pain and madly, sightlessly fired his gun.

I closed my eyes as the pain burned through me, bright as if I'd been run through with a broadsword.

There was a short whine then a dull thud as a body hit the ground.

"No," I sobbed, crawling backward with my eyes shut, refusing to open them to acknowledge what had happened. "No, no, no."

A hand tagged my ankle and roughly pulled me towards the door. My fingers raked so hard against the wooden floor, splinters erupted under my nails.

"No," I screamed loudly. "No."

I felt the blood as he pulled me past the door onto the carpet of the hallway.

"What's going—" one of my unfortunate neighbors asked.

Reaper shot him.

Another thud.

But I was too preoccupied with the first.

I'd opened my eyes when Reaper dropped me in the door.

I was laying a foot away from him, his sweet brown eyes empty, his tongue hanging out of his mouth, but not in his usual happy way.

Reaper had shot him in the back of his neck.

But facing me like he was, if his eyes hadn't been open, he almost looked asleep.

"Hero," I groaned through the sobs spilling endlessly through my mouth. "Hero, no."

I clutched at his fur, rubbing my fingers through the still warm, utterly familiar strands and tried to memorize everything about him.

"No!" I screamed at the top of my aching lungs when Reaper pushed the neighbor and then leaned over to yank me up, gun at the center of my spine just under the base of my neck.

If he shot me there, I'd die of paralysis.

For one, horrible minute, I didn't think that would be so bad.

The last piece of my heart had just died on the floor of my cursed apartment.

Was there a reason to fight?

Reaper dug that gun into my back then pulled the door shut so it dislodged Hero's body, sliding it across the blood-soaked floor carelessly.

Fury ignited in my blood and fight surged back through my body.

Reaper wanted to kill me.

But if I was going to die tonight, I'd do it trying to kill him.

CHAPTER THIRTY-ONE

Danner

I WAS ALREADY ON THE WAY WHEN I GOT THE CALL FROM Renner.

Reaper'd evaded arrest and gotten to her.

Using her fucking mother to do it.

Renner had heard the entire exchange on Harleigh Rose's cell phone after it dropped from her hand when he busted in.

It had been two weeks since I'd seen my rebel Rose. Two weeks of painful recovery, too many crazy conversations with the crazy-ass, absurdly charming Garro family, and two weeks of living with the knowledge that my Rosie was suffering for what she'd done.

But Garro and I had talked about it just as I'd discussed it with Renner and we'd decided. Harleigh Rose's safety hinged on that fact that Berserkers MC thought I was dead and she had cut all ties with her father. We couldn't just go barging in, alpha male-style ready to save the day.

So, we'd waited until Harleigh Rose did in two months

what I'd been trying to do for three years. We waited until she took out the club and Renner gave us the all clear.

Only now, it was Harleigh Rose who wasn't in the clear.

I revved the engine, flipped on the lights and called the man who was trailing behind me on his bike.

"Garro, Reaper's got her," I snarled into the phone. "Keep close behind me, I'm breaking the limits."

"Where the fuck would the fuckin' fuck take her?" Garro growled.

I drummed my fingers on the wheel, mind turning over the sheaves and sheaves of information I'd amassed on Berserkers MC and their Prez over the last three years.

"He's got women. Last one used to own a storage facility, name's Jade Yeller. I'll call my unit and get them to pull up anything useful."

"Fuck that, callin' Curtains. He'll find the shit 'fore your cops and what you told me 'bout what went down, from what I know of this fuckin' motherfucker, we don't got time to mess around here."

Then he hung up.

I checked in my rearview that he was close then pressed my foot harder on the gas.

If Reaper had her, he'd kill her.

There was no doubt in my mind.

He'd 'killed' me, and most recently according to my friends in the force, he'd killed Wrath.

Another biker with a soul I would have liked to have a beer with.

He'd kill her, but the question that haunted me was if he'd rape her.

He was nearly cultish about his obsession with sharing women, and I'd felt his rage when Harleigh Rose had refused to let herself be degraded by multiple Berserker men.

There was no doubt he'd be furious enough to do it himself now.

It should have been another half an hour into the city center, but the glow of blue Vancouver city lights swallowed us up fourteen minutes after I hung up the first call.

"Hold On Storage," Garro said when I picked up his call. "W Third Avenue and Fir."

I gunned the engine.

Minutes later, we were there.

I grabbed my gun even though I knew I'd be a lousy shot with my arm, and got out to meet Garro. We checked the perimeter of the building, no lights, no noise, and decided on a game plan.

The warehouse was fuckin' empty.

Curtains gave us another location a few blocks away.

Nothing.

Ten minutes later.

No Reaper, no Farrah. No Harleigh Rose.

We were arguing about what to do next—I wanted to call the cops and he wanted to wait for The Fallen to descend from the mountain—when Garro's phone rang again.

"Yo," he said, then froze.

My gut clenched. If it was news that they'd found Harleigh Rose in any other condition than perfectly fucking healthy, I was going to lose my shit.

Garro flipped his phone into his palm to put it on speaker. "Speak while you can, motherfucker. Soon's I find you, you're a fuckin' dead man."

"You for the girl," Reaper's voice came through the phone, sending rage through me so violently, it felt like I'd touched a live wire. "That's the deal."

Garro looked up at me, eyes dark in the dim street lights. "Done."

Reaper laughed. "Always such a fuckin' pussy."

"You got daughters?"

"I got daughters and sons a-fuckin'-plenty. Wouldn't lay down my life for any goddamn one 'a 'em."

"Difference 'tween you an' me," Garro said quietly, quiet because he was trying to control the revulsion in his tone.

"Difference 'tween you an' me is, I got your fuckin' kid. You get here in ten minutes, she's alive, after that, make no promises."

"Where the fuck are you?" he growled.

Reaper laughed again. "The scene of her fuckin' crime."

Zeus hung up, an animal noise of frustration in his throat, but I was already moving back to the 'Stang.

"Take it you know where that cryptic asshole meant," he called out, stalking to his bike.

"Yeah," I said. "Port of Vancouver."

CHAPTER THIRTY-TWO

Harleigh Rose

I WAS TIED UP AND GAGGED.

Farrah had been displeased about it, but then changed her tune when Reaper agreed to use two of her pretty silky scarves to bind my hands and feet, one pressed over a sock stuffed in my mouth. She had me sitting up at the desk, chattering at me as she painted her nails a pink she called "Crushed Hearts."

Wrath lay in the corner of the room, and I didn't know if he was breathing. Only that it looked like he'd been there for a while and the carpet all around him was stained with blood.

"Reaper's gonna kill your daddy," she went on, pausing in her manicure duties to snort another line of coke off the table beside her nail kit. "And I know you'll get all *righteous* about it, but you'll realize he deserved it. He abandoned you to go to prison for his little slut, and now he's left you again. Reaper'll do what he needs to do and then we'll go somewhere new."

She paused, saw the drool dripping out of my mouth because the gag was stretching my lips too wide, and leaned forward to dab at it with the ends of the scarf.

When she sat back, she beamed a wide, happy, high off her fucking face smile at me. "I'm thinkin' Colombia. You know it's the coke capital of the world?"

She laughed that giggling, raspy laugh that I'd hated since I could remember and then, over that, a hoarse shout.

My heart kicked up dust in my chest, stirring old hopes.

Renner had been on the phone while I was taken.

Maybe the police were there.

Instead, there was a creaking groan as someone joined Reaper on the metal platform outside and then the door was opening, and he was stepping through with a wild grin.

Not the police then.

But I still gasped, nearly choking on my gag, when I saw Dad bend slightly to step through the door, his huge presence making the trailer seem unbearably small.

"Hey baby girl," he muttered softly, his heathen face creased into a slight smile.

God, *Daddy*.

I regressed to a little girl so instantaneously, I didn't even try to hold back the tears.

It had been weeks since I'd seen his handsome face smiling at me. And now it was happening in a trailer in a cargo yard with fucking psychos present.

If I hadn't been so tired, so sick to my gut with fright and grief, I might have laughed because our reunion was so Garro.

But I didn't.

Reaper lifted a gun, his arm high above his head to aim it properly at Dad's temple.

"You piece of shit. Thought you always deserved all the good, never thinkin' anyone else was better 'an you. But now look, I got your woman," Farrah laughed as she popped up from doing another line, rubbing her fingers across her gums to get the dregs of powder. "And your fuckin' rat of a kid."

Dad's fists clenched slowly opened then closed to control the rage emanating from him like radioactive waves.

"You don't deserve *shit*," Reaper yelled at him. "Get on your fuckin' knees."

I yelled behind my gag as my dad locked eyes with me and dropped slowly to his knees.

No, Daddy, no, no.

Reaper pressed the gun to his temple and smiled at me. "This is for you, Farrah baby. For you and me."

"He's gonna kill 'er," Dad rumbled. "Farrah, he's gonna kill H.R. for rattin' on 'im."

"No," Farrah laughed uproariously. "We're gonna move to Colombia."

Her eyes searched Reaper's and slowly, her smile slipped, "Reaper baby?"

"We'll talk about it," Reaper hesitated then pressed the gun harder to Dad's temple. "After I kill 'im."

For the first time in my life, I was happy my mother was such an idiot. The scarves against my wrists were silky enough to work myself out of and I'd been twisting my wrists for the last forty minutes.

I broke free just as a gun fired and Dad dropped to his side.

I screamed behind the gag, tore off the scarf, ripped at the one around my ankles and was pulling off my gag when I noticed Dad roll and come up into a crouch against the wall, gun in his hands aimed at Reaper who was staring like he'd seen a ghost at the suddenly open door.

Dad shot him in the head.

I watched as Reaper's head snapped back on his neck and then his entire body crumpled forward. Done.

I moved forward only to feel cool hands grabbing me from behind and the press of something small and sharp at my jugular.

Farrah was holding nail scissors to my neck.

"Drop it," Dad barked at her, gun raised and trained unwaveringly on her.

She turned to face him and sneered, "No, you won't do a fuckin' thing to me while I'm holding your precious kid. You're gonna let us go."

Dad stared at me, his eyes filled with something I'd seen thousands of times and never once disobeyed even in my deepest days of rebellion. Trust.

Slowly, he lowered the gun.

Farrah laughed and did a little dance that punctured my skin with the scissors. Blood beaded and rolled into my hair as she leaned forward to whisper, "Come on, baby, let's blow this place. You and me'll go to Colombia. All I need is my girl."

I let her walk me to the partially opened door, leaned forward to open it for us and immediately obeyed Dad when he barked, "Drop."

I fell to the ground as the door crashed open.

Bang!

So loud, right over top of me.

"Huh?" my mother gasped then gurgled behind me.

I rolled to my back to see her clutching her throat, a hole right through the center of it, as she fell to the ground.

"Rosie."

My eyes closed automatically against the burn of tears there.

"No," I whispered, afraid I was stress hallucinating, or I'd inhaled too many nail polish fumes.

But no.

Rough tipped hands gently reached under my armpits to pull me up then planted on my shoulders to spin me around.

And he was there.

The green-eyed teenager playing guitar in a record store.

The rookie cop letting me get away with shoplifting.

The undercover biker who gave up his cover to save me.

My fierce, loyal, handsome Lion standing before me, holding me, looking at me like I was the lost treasure of Atlantis and he'd never need for anything again.

"Lion," I whispered, the word all hope. "I did something bad."

"Nothing to forgive, nothing to forget. I love you, rebel Rose. You hurt me to save me. You broke your own heart a million fucking times to keep me alive and I love you so fucking much for that." He grasped my face in his hand and spoke against my lips. "My lion-hearted girl."

And then he kissed me.

CHAPTER THIRTY-THREE

Harleigh Rose

THE SHEET SHIFTED SLOWLY OVER THE SLEEP-WARMED SKIN OF my back, bearing my ass to the cool air. Fingers followed, skirted the slopes of my muscles and the hollow of my spine, the two depressions at the base of my torso like a sculptor molding precious clay. Another hand moved the thick curtain of hair obscuring my face off to the side of my head on the pillow and warm lips teased my ear.

"Good morning my thorny Rose," Danner whispered there, planting the words like a secret.

My heart surged with gratitude so warm, it sent a flush through my whole body.

Lion was back.

Back in my life, in my bed, in my arms.

My protector, my best friend, and my lover.

I finally had everything from him I'd ever needed.

I could still feel the echo of Hero in my heart, the loss of his head beside me in our bed, but I knew this is what he'd died for. To keep not just me alive, but this dream, his family together in bed again.

My mother was gone, dead by Danner's unwavering hand. He didn't seem to feel remorse and neither did I. But, we didn't call the cops until Dad had taken Farrah's body away to be laid to not-so-peaceful rest with the pigs at Angelwood farm. I didn't want to get Danner in trouble for saving me.

And Dad didn't want to be there when the men in blue showed up.

There was an ache in my thumb from the bullet graze and I knew Danner's scar was still bright pink on his chest, fresh but healing.

We had scars.

We'd had battles.

But that was finally done, and I had to believe the horrors we'd been through only made us stronger, as individuals and a pair.

I started to flip over so I could see his face but the hand on my back flattened and pressed me into the mattress.

"Got a craving to suck your sweet pussy from behind until you melt all over my tongue," he said, then sucked my earlobe into his mouth, releasing it with a sharp nip of his teeth. "Be a good girl and stay still for your Dom."

God, I'd missed that.

Almost a month without that strong voice in my ear, those firm words summoning the submissive from the depths of my soul. I was wet from his first word.

"Yes, Lion," I breathed more than spoke as he shifted over top of me, one of his strong arms visible and clenched deliciously as he slowly lowered his weight and then slid down my body to lay himself between my parted legs.

He swatted my ass sharply and ordered, "Hands and knees. Tilt those hips and show me that gorgeous cunt."

I slid my knees under me and practically purred as I

arched my back deeply, my ass a high steep, my legs parted for him to worship at the altar of my pussy.

He bent his head and prayed.

I groaned as his hot mouth met my pussy, as he tongued my clit and fingered my cunt until I was thrusting wantonly back on his lips.

"Please," I begged, so close to coming that I was scratching and clenching at the sheets with desperate fists. "Let me come."

He pulled away, ignoring my groan, and sat on the edge of the bed. I glared at him as he patted his thigh and ordered, "Climb on, but don't touch me."

"You bastard," I hissed, my pussy throbbing so violently I knew it would take only one touch to my clit to set me off.

"You make one wrong move, I'll cuff you, Rosie," Danner drawled lazily.

"Fuck you," I ground out between my clenched teeth.

His chuckle was a soft, dark rope he bound around my neck. "You'll do as I say, or I *won't* fuck you."

My thighs quivered as I straddled him, balanced precariously just above his thick shaft but careful not to touch the hot crown with my slick center.

That was the game.

Do not move.

Not one inch.

Not even when his rough fingers lashed out to twist my nipples and pull at them like taffy.

Not even when one hand cracked loudly, painfully against my ass and I had to brace my aching legs to keep from falling out of position and into his perfectly carved torso.

Not even when my wetness slid from between my thighs and began to drip down his shaft in an obscene display of want that made me whimper and moan and fucking ache to feel that wide shaft split my swollen folds in two and power straight to the end of my cunt.

He spanked me sharply once again but kept his hand on the hot flesh, kneading strongly so that the ache deepened and spread straight into my pussy.

"Don't. You. Fucking. Move," he ordered me again and even though his face was composed, I could see the hot storm thrashing behind his jungle green eyes.

His thumb slid over my cheek into the sweat-dampened crease of my ass and as he leaned forward to take one of my nipples between his teeth, he reminded me, "Not one fucking inch."

And then he drove his thumb into my ass and two fingers into my pulsing center and I detonated all around him, coming all over his teasing cock like I was a tropical rainstorm burst forth from the clouds.

Through it all, I barely moved. I held my muscles so taut they burned and sweat rolled down my body in waves. The only concession I allowed myself was closing my eyes. It was impossible to absorb the impact of Danner's fingers in my body *and* stare into his glowing green eyes. It was too easy to read into the possession there, to know it meant so much more beyond sex and kink.

My fragile heart, new born from the ashes of the one before, spasmed painfully at the sight.

So, I closed my eyes and kept them closed until the tempest passed and I was a weak, straining mass straddled over him.

"Look at me."

I shivered lightly at the heaviness of his order, as the words rasped over my oversensitive skin. He was staring at me under lowered brows, his eyes so intense that I nearly flinched.

"Spectacular," he offered me, but he didn't look satisfied.

"I didn't move," I defended.

One golden brow rose. "Didn't you?"

"I've got the shaking thighs to prove it! I was still as a fucking statue," I said, anger and shame swirling in my gut.

I wanted to please him, and I was pissed that I hadn't and even more pissed that I cared so much.

Strong, independent woman, I tried to remind myself.

"You closed your eyes. I could have forgiven you for falling out of position but closing your eyes... ah, Harleigh Rose, you took away the one thing I won't do without."

He watched my mouth fall into a trembling pout. His thumb swept the full lower lip and his eyes flashed as I curled my tongue, sucking it into my mouth. I was so eager to please him, to rectify my mistake that tears stung the backs of my eyes. I wanted to beg him to forgive me, to let me make it right.

"Shh," he hushed me because he was my Dom, he knew how shaky my emotional state was after a scene, after I had let him down. "You can make it up to me."

"Yeah?" I pressed myself against his iron-plated chest, my hand to his freshly healed stab wound, and licked the curve of his left ear. "Tell me."

"Ride me hard like the wild thing you are and make me come."

Instantly I reached down for his obscenely long cock, placed it at my entrance and slammed down, taking him to the root.

He tipped his head back and groaned long and low then swatted my ass. "Show me how much you love my cock."

So, I did.

I used my teeth and lips at his mouth and throat, my hands clasped for leverage over his good shoulder so I could buck, gyrate and roll over his straining shaft until his thighs were shaking his fingers were hard around my hips, urging me forward.

"Faster," he demanded, slapping my ass with series of quick, stinging hits that spurred me on and broke me open.

I came all over his cock, my cunt clenching so hard it triggered his own orgasm as he groaned it into my mouth, kissing me until we both needed breath.

"That's my good girl," he muttered into my damp chest, soothing a hand over my red ass.

I hummed my agreement, lazy with satisfaction, completely content to know that I was safe with my man, my dad was sleeping in the other room and I'd see my family later that day. It felt worth it, every single thing I'd had to go through to get to that moment, and the feeling was so beautiful it bloomed like a prize rose in my chest.

"I'm quittin' the force," Danner said into the silence.

I jerked in shock then leaned back to look into his face. "Excuse me?"

His eyes were serious, but he bit the edge of a teasing grin. "Realized recently I'm not as good as I thought I was, and I'm okay with that. Besides, I want to move back to Entrance with you and there's no way in hell I'm gonna be on my father's police force."

"What're you gonna do?" I asked, unable to conceive of any reality where Danner was not a cop.

He grinned and pushed my hair back behind one ear. "Gonna open a private investigations firm."

Except for that. *That* suited him just fine.

"Oh my god, you're going to be a *killer* P.I.," I told him. "Will you fuck me over your desk?"

He laughed. "Let's not get ahead of ourselves, Rosie. First, I need an office and a desk."

"Right."

We beamed at each other.

"I never really thought we'd get it," I whispered, almost too afraid to say the word out loud.

"What, rebel?"

I looked into his jungle green eyes and let myself be vulnerable the way he'd taught me to do. "That we'd ever get our happy."

His hand convulsed on my hips and his face softened. "Rosie."

I shrugged as if it wasn't a big deal, but we both knew I was a liar.

"We're gonna have our happy, I promise," he swore. "Do you believe me?"

I closed my eyes and pressed my lips to his, my hand to his heart so my fingers rested lightly over the scar I'd given him in order to get us to this moment.

"Yeah, Lion, I believe you," I whispered into his mouth.

And I did.

We were eating cereal in the kitchen when Dad came barreling in, his eyes huge, his hair a mess around his smiling face.

"My babies are fuckin' comin'!" he roared triumphantly. "Fuckin' *fuck* yeah!"

Danner and I laughed at him, his joy infectious.

"Congratulations, Garro," my man called to my father.

Dad's face warmed slightly as he stared at me standing between my man's legs at the bar where we were eating.

"Call me Zeus," he said.

My heart warmed with the beauty of that gift and I felt Danner stiffen then soften around me as he realized it.

"Now get your asses in gear, we gotta get to the fuckin' hospital," he yelled before disappearing down the hall again.

Danner gave me a bemused look. "Guess we better get dressed."

I laughed, feeling more carefree than it felt I ever had before.

Dad took his bike to the hospital and we followed in Danner's Mustang. We didn't talk as he drove. Instead, I made a playlist of songs for our love story and played it for him all the way to Entrance. When we parked, Danner turned to me to take my head in his hands and kissed me, long, slow and savory.

"Wouldn't change a fucking moment with you, it brought us here," he told me as his thumbs rubbed over my cheeks.

"Even the part where I stabbed you?" I asked without even trying to hold back my smile.

"Nothing," he said so fiercely that my humor fell away. "Not one fucking second."

I kissed him this time, quick, hard and sweet.

A knock at the window had us jerking apart, but I scowled at the sight of Dad leaning down to scowl at us.

"Make out on your own fuckin' time, my babies are 'ere," he ordered before turning and prowling through the front doors of the hospital.

We followed him in and up the elevators to the maternity ward. I'd never seen Dad so hyped up, his eyes electric and his body restless, rolling and moving like a fighter going into the ring.

"You okay, Dad?" I asked, reaching out to take his massive, beautifully scarred hand in mine.

He gave it a squeeze and admitted, "Never been more fuckin' nervous in my life."

"You're kidding," Danner chuckled.

Dad leveled him with a glare, but my man didn't even blink.

God, he was sexy.

"My girl's 'bout'a give birth to two babies. Got Curtains to do the research an' that shit gets dangerous for the mother real quick."

"Dad, nothing's going to happen to Loulou," I told him gently.

But I knew it was a nightmare he'd lived before and his edgy energy wouldn't dissipate until he saw her for himself.

The elevator doors opened, and we all stepped out, my men connected by me in the middle. My heart lurched then settled more comfortably in my chest than it ever had before.

"Gonna go on ahead," Dad muttered, already letting go of my hand so his long, powerful thighs could take him down the hall quicker than eyes.

"Garro nervous, never thought I'd see the day," Danner muttered.

"You and my dad in the same room *not* fighting, can't say I ever thought I'd see that day either," I pointed out.

He laughed, and he stayed laughing as we rounded a corner and saw the entire Fallen crew sprawled across a waiting room.

I froze.

Dozens of eyes came to me, the weight of their collective gaze like sinking sand sucking me down.

I didn't know what to do.

I wanted to say sorry, but I was shit at apologies.

I wanted to hug them, but I didn't know if they'd let me.

So, I stood there like an idiot and gawked.

King was the first one to move.

He unraveled from his seat and started walking toward me, his gait quickening, lengthening until it was a run and then I was wrenched from Danner's hold and swung up in his arms.

The smell of him, fresh air and warm laundry, hit my nose and it immediately started to sting with tears. I burrowed my face in his lush, gold hair and held on as my heart exploded inside my chest, a tidal flood of elated relief sweeping through my ravaged system like rain through the desert.

"H.R.," he croaked as he swayed me gently back and forth in his arms, my feet dangling and swaying like a pendulum. "Fuckin' welcome home."

I burst into loud, uncontrollable sobs that shook my whole body.

A soothing hand ran down my hair and a sweet voice spoke close to my ear. "My sweet Harleigh Rose."

I cried louder, my hand blindly reaching out to grab Cress and bring her into our hug. She folded into us and held on as tightly as we were.

"Babe," Lila said as she pressed against my other side and wrapped her arm around my waist. "Fucking missed you."

"Can I get in on this action?" Nova's voice called from beside us. "You know I love a good group hug."

"God, don't be gross," Lila griped and I felt her jolt as he joined the huddle, his weight against her and long arms wrapped around me.

"Ah fuck, if there's one reason I became a fuckin' biker it was to avoid this shit," Buck groused from somewhere nearby, but then I tasted his cigarette scent in the air and felt burly arms crush us all together from the left. "But fuck it, not every day we get our princess back."

I kept crying, softer now as the entire MC, as my entire family, crowded around me and accepted me back into the fold.

When we broke apart, I kept hold of my brother, Lila, and Cress and turned us all to look at Danner who leaned against the wall, Timberland booted feet crossed, dark denim shirt unbuttoned just enough to see the sexy hollow at the base of his throat and a dusting of chest hair, his aviator sunglasses pushed back in his hair.

He was back to his cowboy look, still rockin' it, but doing it now with a tat peeking out of his shirt, a scar through his eyebrow and a biker chick's heart in his hands.

I liked the look on him.

"Danny." King grinned, stepping forward to take his hand in a firm shake that ended with a back slap. "Fuck man, it's good to have you back."

Danner raised an eyebrow. "Yeah, I recall you not likin' me much when Cress and Lou went through your shit."

King grinned at him, unrepentant. "Water under the bridge, you were conflicted back then. You're on the right side'a things now."

"You tell him I was leaving the force?" he asked me.

I shook my head where it lay on Cress's shoulder.

"Fuck yeah, ya did," King whooped, clapping him on the shoulder again. "Wasn't talkin' 'bout the right or wrong side'a the law though. Was talkin' 'bout bein' on our side again, mine and H.R.'s. We missed ya there."

God, but I loved my brother.

Danner's face softened as he tipped his chin up at King. "Yeah, King, I missed you too."

"Here to stay, I'm thinkin'," King added with a cheeky wink.

"Here to stay," Danner confirmed.

I pulled away from my girls and went to my man, slipping under his arm the way I'd seen Lou do with my dad so many times.

It warmed my recently thawed heart like firelight.

"*Fuck, yeah!*" Dad cried out from the mouth of another hallway, clad in blue scrubs that looked almost comical on his big, biker body. "We got two healthy kids and a healthy Lou. Walker and Angel Garro."

Maja jumped on a chair, spun her fist in the air and started cheering.

We joined her so the entire maternity word rung with cele-bration.

"Zeus Garro," a voice cut through the joyful clamor.

We looked to the two officers coming down the hall toward him.

Danner stepped forward, "Robson, Hatley, what's going on?"

They hesitated, gazes swinging from Dad to Danner.

The shorter cop cleared his throat. "Good to see you, Danner, but this is official business."

"The fuck?" King asked, already moving forward.

They made it to Dad before he did.

"Zeus Garro, you're under arrest for the murder of Officer Gibson. You have the right to remain silent. An attorney will be provided to you by the province..."

EPILOGUE

Harleigh Rose

ONE YEAR LATER.

I WOKE UP FROM SWEET DREAMS, A SMILE ON MY FACE AND MY hand already reaching across the bed for Danner.

He wasn't there.

That wasn't unusual. Even though my man mostly kept his own hours working as a P.I., he was still an early riser and he often got his morning run out of the way so he could be home in time to shower with me before I headed into the hospital. So, I kept my eyes closed and let myself drift a little longer, feeling my body loose and slightly aching from the working over Danner gave me the night before. I could still feel the sting of the new paddle on my ass and the press of the nipple clamps like a phantom hold on my breasts. I loved it. The aches and marks he gave me made me feel loved and desired even when we were apart. After a year of solid bliss together, with time to explore, he'd only discovered more and more ways to unravel me like a spool of dropped thread.

I smiled into the pillow and shoved my hair out of my face even though I kept my eyes closed as I heard the tell-tale signs of the front door opening and closing, the alarm going off.

"Lion," I called softly, sleepily as I felt his presence hit the room.

He padded over the wooden floors to my side and I could tell he crouched beside me in order to run his thumb over my parted lips before he pressed a kiss to them.

"Morning my Rose," he murmured against me before moving back slightly.

I hummed in my throat and squished my face into the pillow. "Come back to bed and have a lazy Sunday morning being energetic with me."

He answered me with a rough lick to my cheek that made me giggle at the same time as I frowned. "Ew, since when do we lick each other's faces?"

Another lick, then another, from a tongue I realized was too abrasive, too small to be Danner's.

The second before I opened my eyes there was a tiny animal whine and my heart seized as I realized what he'd done.

My lids snapped open to reveal a tiny German Shepherd puppy about an inch from my face, currently chewing on an errant piece of my hair.

"Holy fuck," I breathed as tears instantly sprung to my eyes and I jolted into a seated position so I could cart the tiny bundle of black and gold fur into my lap up against my steepled legs. He was such a little thing, fuzzy with downy, baby hair and overlarge, upright but slightly lopsided ears topped with gold tufts. I lifted his squirming puppy body so I could look into his sweet, intelligent brown eyes and I felt my heart turn over in my chest as it added the weight of my new love to its collection.

I turned shining eyes to my man as I brought the puppy to my chest and cuddled him like a baby. "You bought me a puppy?"

"I bought you a puppy," he agreed, still crouching by the bed, looking impossibly hot doing it in a tight white tee with his aviators tucked into the collar.

"I didn't think I could handle one after." I swallowed the lump of sorrow that rose in my throat. "After Hero."

"I know, rebel," he said softly, reaching out to trail a hand down the wriggling puppy and then down my leg to squeeze my foot. "That's why I made the decision to get one for us when I knew it would be a good hurt instead of a bad one. We're dog people, it would have been wrong not to get another one."

"You're right," I said, reaching out to touch his harshly stubbled cheek.

He shrugged a shoulder. "Honestly, I'm surprised my smart girl isn't used to that by now."

I hit him in the shoulder, but couldn't stop smiling as I looked back down at the beautiful creature in my lap.

"Hello handsome," I cooed. "He's a him, right?"

Danner chuckled, "Yeah."

"Good, you know I love my men."

"Yeah," he said in a way that drew my gaze to his, the green of his eyes glowing with love so bright they shone neon. "I know my girl loves her men."

"What should we name him?" I asked, rubbing my hands over his crazy soft ears.

"Why don't you check the collar?" he suggested.

I lifted the dog close again, this time higher so I could look at the collar under his fur. Something shining caught my eyes and I frowned as I parted the black coat to investigate.

A small gold plate said "Saint," the perfect name, but that wasn't what made me gasp, fresh tears rolling out to join the dried ones on my cheeks.

It was the sight of a huge gold ring molded into a perfect rose that hung from the dog tag.

When I looked over at Danner again, he'd shifted onto one knee, his forearms in the bed so he could lean over and work at taking the ring off the collar. He called out to Alexa to play "Like Real People Do" by Hozier as he worked and then he said, "Love you, Harleigh Rose, love you in a way that I know I'll never stop doin' it, just like I haven't stopped doin' it in one way or another since I met you. Some men want women that are all sugar and sweetness, dependable and staid, but I've always preferred the kind of woman that's roses and thorns, strength and sass, that's so wild at heart I never know what I'm going to get. You make me feel alive, Harleigh Rose, filled with a love and purpose so strong it eclipses any other reason I may have to love living."

"Yes," I shouted through the ugly tears that had seized control of my body, curling the puppy in one arm so I could throw myself at my man with the other. "Yes, fucking yes, of course."

"Haven't even asked the question yet, rebel Rose," Danner griped playfully against my hair.

I pulled away from him only to readjust so I could say the words against his lips. "You ask me today, tomorrow, yesterday, any of the days since I met you when I was six years old and didn't even know the meaning of love, I'd've said yes to you Lion Danner."

"Yeah," he said, sweet and long and slow, the way he did when I told him something worth savoring.

Then he kissed me.

He kissed me in a way that said safety and security, sexy

and sensual, love and loved. He kissed me like he played music for me, more eloquently than words could accurately express.

"Yeah," I repeated in his tone when he pulled away to place the fucking awesome gold rose on my ring finger and I officially became engaged to the love of my life. "Yeah."

Danner

EIGHT YEARS LATER

BANG, BANG BANG.

Gunfire rang out across the four acres of land behind our house, the leaves rattling on the trees as birds took flight and a few of the horses we kept let out high whinnies of protest. Saint only stared at me, laying under my feet where I sat on the back porch, ass to the swinging chair Cressida bought for our last wedding anniversary. My dog was unfazed by the sound of the shots, he knew his people were home safe and sound, that the only thing to fear was the very real possibility that my wife was turning our kids into gun nuts.

I patted my dog on the head, took a pull of my cold Vancouver Island lager and looked to my family congregated to the far back left of the porch. Harleigh Rose was bent nearly double so she could speak to a six-year-old Cash about gun safety, our little girl, too young to handle the gun herself, stood with them, a pout on her tear-streaked face, still holding onto her tantrum like only the daughter of Harleigh Rose could do.

"You're askin' for it, showin' 'em how to use a gun," Lysander said as he emerged from the house, two newly cracked open beers between his fingers. "Not sure I know any other kid sleeps with a plastic gun like it was a stuffed animal the way Taz does."

"Yeah," I agreed, endlessly amused by the fact that Tasmin insisted on sleeping with a bright pink water gun we'd bought her for her fourth birthday. "She's a little badass-in-training."

"Not sure I envy ya, man," he said, leaning against the railing, one foot crossed over the other, thick arms folded over his chest.

He'd been out of prison for over a decade at that point, but the look of it had never left him. There were still horrors at the backs of his eyes, a careful threat to every one of his coiled movements and sloe-eyed looks, as if he didn't know how to be intimidating, as if he didn't even trust the world enough to try.

I hated that for him. We'd formed an unlikely partnership the last few years and now that he was going through his own personal shit storm, I was determined to take his back.

"You give yourself the chance to fall in love with a woman who'll steal your breath away and gift it back to you the next beat, you'll know enough to be envious," I told him.

He laughed. "The cowboy sage sittin' on his fuckin' porch swing, drinkin' a beer with his loyal companion at his feet, his woman happily playin' with the children she gave him... yeah, man, maybe I'll get there one day."

He didn't believe it, I could hear it in his voice, but I let it slide.

There came a time for all of us: Zeus, King, Bat, hell, even Nova was this side of his happily ever after and if that didn't prove any man could fall hard in love, nothing did.

"Daddy," Taz screamed as she sprinted over to me on her little legs, streaky blond hair flying out around her. "Daddy!"

I didn't respond. My girl had a way of yelling for me even when I was right beside her. At first, it had concerned me, like maybe she was afraid I'd leave her or something.

It was Harleigh Rose who'd decided it was something much different, that my little girl was proud of her daddy and wanted to shout it to the world. She knew the feeling, she'd said, staring into my eyes with those huge aquamarine blues, because she'd felt the same kind of pride since I made her mine.

"When're the others coming?" Lysander asked as Taz bounded up the wooden steps and threw herself into my arms.

I pressed a kiss into her floral scented hair. "Any time now."

"Was a time you'd tell me the both of us would be at a birthday party with The fucking Fallen, I woulda told ya you were off your fuckin' rocker."

"Yep," I agreed as Taz shifted in my arms, giggling as I tickled the soft slope of her little belly.

Peals of high, girlish laughter rang out and I thought it was without a doubt the second most beautiful sound in the world.

The first was hearing her mother say her soft and sweet "Lion."

As if I'd conjured them up myself, the roar of Harley pipes broke free on the air, a trail of dust on the horizon the tell-tale sign of the club coming up the dirt drive.

"Daddy Papa's coming!" Taz screeched from my lap,

diving off the bench and then screaming into Saint's face. "Puppy, Daddy Papa's almost here!"

Needless to say, my kids loved their grandfather.

"Cool," Cash called like the burgeoning cool guy he was, his chin tipping up in acknowledgment of his sister's freak out.

Taz ran to them, arms wheeling and crashed into her brother's side so hard she almost fell over. Cash caught her under his arm and held her tight.

Harleigh Rose's laugh drifted to me and I watched her long legs encased in itty bitty jean shorts as she strolled across the yard with one arm around our son and the other holding an empty, open shotgun.

Jesus, even as a mum she was hot as fuck and badass as livin' hell.

She separated from the kids at the base of the porch so she could climb up while they jogged farther along the driveway, eager to meet the bikers rolling in over the dirt.

My woman climbed the steps, a biker chick in her combat boots at home on a farm.

I'd never seen anything so pretty.

She handed the gun off to Lysander with a wink. "Deal with that for me, will ya?"

He snorted, but there was a smile in his eyes as he watched her hips sway over to me, at her sweet ass as she bent to kiss me.

"Ready for your birthday, Lion?" she asked.

I tipped my head back against the swing to smile lazily at her. "More excited for later, when the guests are gone, and the kids are asleep, when I can fuck you bound in rope, your ass red from leather."

"Mmm," she hummed under the sound of the bikes as they pulled up. "Should I tell the family to turn around and go back to where they came from?"

"Nah, think your father would cry," I joked.

I touched my thumb to the corner of her wide smile and swallowed her laughter with a kiss.

"Get your lips off my girl," the man in question yelled as he rounded the porch with Taz in one arm and his baby girl, Angel in the other.

They were both mini versions of their mothers.

I teased Zeus ruthlessly and often about the men he'd have to beat away from his daughter. She was only eight years old, but her beauty was already so bright, she seemed to shine.

"Not gonna stop, old man," I said, standing up so Harleigh Rose and I could meet him at the top of the porch.

He dropped his babies to wrap his arms around his adult girl. She ducked her face into his chest and held on tight.

She never took her loved ones for granted, not for one minute since she put her own life on the line all those years ago.

Sometimes I'd wake up and catch her staring at me, hand to the tattoo I'd gotten for her, fingertips on the scar she'd given me, her face full of sorrow. I'd kiss it from her face, seduce a smile or tickle away the frown, but there was always a fraction of her soul that would remain haunted by the day and the decision she'd had to make.

I'd only recently learned to live with it.

It was Cressida who had told me, "She has you to hold that feeling at bay, you don't need to worry about the times it moves her, Danner. It'll pass. And it's a good reminder that the happy she had now, she *earned*."

This was true, but I needed a wise woman I'd once condemned for fucking her teenage student make it clear for me.

Zeus released my wife and slapped a big palm on my shoulder, shaking it slightly. "Happy fuckin' birthday, Lion."

I grinned at him. "You make me a cake?"

"Fuck off."

We moved out of the way to greet the others coming up

the stairs, Lou with her son Walker who everyone had started to call "Monster," King and Cress with their kids, Bat with his family, Nova with his wife, Buck and Maja, Old Sam, Smoke and Riley, Curtains, Boner and Axe-Man, Cy with his Tay. They filtered up the steps in their leather and their black, their smiles wide with pure joy at hangin' out, at celebrating my birthday.

An ex-cop who'd spent years trying to put them away.

I tagged my wife's arm and pulled her into my side so I could lay a wet kiss to her mouth. "Love you, rebel Rose. Love the family you've given me."

She melted into my side, her aquamarine eyes I loved so much full of love, my rose in full bloom. "Love that you loved me enough to save them so I could give them to you."

Thank you so much for reading GOOD GONE BAD!

After the Fall (The Fallen Men, #4) is LIVE now!
Inked in Lies (The Fallen Men, #5) is coming next!

If you want to stay up to date on news about new releases and bonus content join my reader's group Giana's Darlings or subscribe to my newsletter on my website gianadarling.com!

If you loved Harleigh Rose and his dirty Dom cop, Lion Danner, you will love her father Zeus's forbidden love, age gap romance! Discover what happens when an outlaw motorcycle

Prez saves the life of the mayor's daughter and they become entangled for good…

"Taboo, breathtaking, and scorching hot! I freaking loved WELCOME TO THE DARK SIDE."
—**Skye Warren**, *New York Times* bestselling author

One-Click WELCOME TO THE DARK SIDE now!

Or you can see where The Fallen Men series started by reading about Harleigh Rose's brother, King Kyle Garro, and his torrid affair with Cressida Irons, who also happens to be his high school English teacher!

Sexy, forbidden, and a touch of sweet! Lessons in Corruption by Giana Darling hits all the marks when it comes to a taboo relationship, a badass biker, and a yummy love story! This book draws you in and tethers you to the Fallen Men MC world. Once you're in, you're never getting out! Five KING & QUEENIE stars!
—**K Webster**, *USA Today* Bestselling Author

One-Click LESSONS IN CORRUPTION now!
Turn the page for an excerpt…

(The Fallen Men Series, Book 1)
Excerpt

He was eighteen.
The heir to a notorious, criminal MC.
And my student.

There was no way I could get involved.
No way I could stay involved.
Then, no way I could get out alive.

Book One in The Fallen Men Series. A standalone.

One.

Preview of Lessons in Corruption

I saw him in a parking lot when I was picking up groceries. Not the most romantic place to fall in love at first sight but I guess you can't choose these things.

He had grease on his face. My eyes zoomed in on the smear of motor oil, the aggressive slash of his cheekbones protruding almost brutally under his tanned skin so that they created a hollow in his cheeks. His features were so striking they were almost gaunt, nearly too severe as to be unattractive, mean even. Instead, the softness of his full, surprisingly pink mouth and the honeyed-coloured hair that fell in a touchable mess of curls and waves to his broad shoulders and the way his head was currently tipped back, corded throat exposed and deliciously brown, to laugh at the sky as if he was actually born to laugh and only laugh...none of that was mean.

I stood in the parking lot looking at him through the heat waves in the unusual late summer heat. My plastic grocery bags were probably melted to the asphalt, the ice cream long gone to soup.

I'd been there a while already, watching him.

He was across the lot beside a row of intimidating and gorgeous motorcycles, talking to another biker. His narrow hips leaned sideways across the seat of one, one booted foot propped up. He wore old jeans, also with grease on them, and a white t-shirt, somehow clean, that fit his wide shoulders and small waist indecently well. He looked young, maybe even a few years younger than me, but I only guessed that because while his structure was large, his muscles hung on him slightly like he hadn't quite grown into his bones.

Idly, I wondered if he was *too* young.

Not so idly, I decided that I didn't care.

His attention was drawn to the group of college-aged kids who pulled up in a shiny convertible, their brightly coloured polo shirts and wrinkled khakis dead giveaways even if their gelled hair and studied swagger hadn't given them away already. They were chuckling as they reached the two motor-cycle men I'd been watching and it struck me that compared to the newcomers, there was no way the sexy blond I'd been lusting after was young. He carried himself well, regally even, like a king. A king at home in a grocery store parking lot, his throne the worn seat of an enormous Harley.

I watched without blinking as he greeted the crew, his expression neutral and his body relaxed and casual in a way that tried to veil the strength of his build and failed.

There was something about his pose that was predatory, a hunter inviting his prey closer. A couple of the college kids fidgeted, suddenly uneasy, but their leader strode forward after a brief hesitation and extended his hand.

The blond king stared at the hand but didn't take it. Instead, he said something that made the fidgeting increase.

I wished I were close enough to hear what he said. Not just the words but also the tone of his voice. I wondered if it was deep and smooth, an outpouring of honey, or the gravel of a man who spoke from his diaphragm, from the bottomless well of confidence and testosterone at the base of him.

The kids were more than nervous now. The leader, one step ahead of the others, visibly shrank as his explanation, accompanied by increasingly more agitated hand gestures, seemed to fall on deaf ears.

After a long minute of his babbling, he stopped and was met with silence.

The quiet weighed so heavily, I felt it from across the lot where I lurked by my car.

The blond king's sidekick, or rather henchman seemed like a more fitting word for the frankly colossal, dark-haired friend beside him, stepped forward.

Just one step.

Not even a large one. But I could see how that one movement hit the college crew like a nuclear blast wave. They reeled back as a unit; even their leader took a huge step backwards, his mouth fluid with rushed words of apology.

They had obviously fucked up.

I didn't know how.

And for the first time in my life, watching a potentially dangerous situation unfold, I wanted to know.

I wanted to be a part of it.

To stand beside the blond king and be his rough and tumble queen.

I shivered as I watched the men before him cower, his loyal friend at his back. Slowly, because he was clearly a man who knew the impact of his physique and how to wield the sharp edge of power like a literal dagger, the blond king rolled out of his slouched position on his bike and into his full height.

The sight of him unraveling like that made my mouth go dry and other, private, places go wet.

It had a different effect on the college kids. They listened to what he had to say like men being read their last rites, clinging to any hope he could give them, desperate for salvation.

He gave it to them. Not much, but a shred of something to hold on to because as one they practically genuflected before sprint-walking back to their fancy silver car parked on the street.

Blond king and henchman remained frozen in position until the car was out of sight before they clicked back into movement. Simultaneously they turned, staring at each other for a few long seconds before the laughter started.

He laughed and the sound carried perfectly to my ear. It was a clear, bright noise. Not a chuckle, a guffaw or a mumbled *hahah*. Each vibration erupted from his throat like a pure note, round and loud and defined by unblemished joy.

It was the best thing I had ever heard.

I gasped lightly as his joy burned through me and, as if he heard it, his head turned my way. We were too far away to truly lock eyes but it felt like we did. His friend said something to him but the blond object of my instant obsession ignored him. For the first time since I noticed him, his face fell into somberness and his jaw tightened.

I may have loved him from the moment I saw him but he clearly did not feel the same.

In fact, if the way he abruptly cut away from me was any indication, throwing one long leg over the seat of a huge chrome bike and revving the engine before I could even think to tear my eyes away, he may have even hated me on first sight.

Paralyzed, I watched him peel out of the lot with his buddy. It hurt. Which was insane because I didn't even know the man and more importantly, I refused to be taken in by a pretty face.

The last time that had happened, someone had died.

I pulled myself together, collecting the grocery detritus that spilled out of some of the melted bags and moved to my car. It was hot as hell in the compact sedan, the leather seats nearly burned the skin off my bottom when I sat down. I got back out of the car and manually cranked open all of the windows before I started the drive home.

Home was a sweet white-shingled house in the quiet residential area of Dunbar in Vancouver where real estate prices were crazy and desperate housewives were a real thing. My husband had grown up in the ritzy grove about eighteen years before I'd been born and grown up in the house next to his. Everyone *oh*ed and *ah*ed over our little love story, the older neighbor falling for the quiet girl next door.

Once, I'd done the same.

Now, as I rolled up the asphalt drive and saw William's car parked in the garage, I felt only dread.

"I'm home," I called when I opened the door.

I didn't want to say the words, but William liked the ritual. He liked it more when he came home to me already in the house, dinner on the stove and a smile on my face, but I'd gone back to work this year after three years of staying at home waiting for kids to come when none ever did. I loved working at Entrance Bay Academy, one of the most prestigious schools in the province, but William thought it was unnecessary. We had enough money, he said, and things around the house grew neglected in my absence, especially when you added on my hour-long commute there and back to the small town north of Vancouver that harbored the school. We had no children and no pets, a housekeeper with a more than mild form of OCD who came to the house once a week. I didn't notice much of a difference but I didn't say anything. This was because William wasn't a fighter in the traditional sense. He didn't yell or accuse, bruise with his actions or words. Instead, he disappeared.

His office became a black hole, a great devourer of not only my husband but our potential conflict and our possible resolution. Every fight we could have had lingered in the spaces between his leather-bound law books, under the edges of the Persian carpet. Sometimes, when he was late returning home, I would sit in his big wingback leather chair deep in the heart of his office and I would close my eyes. Only then could

I find relief in my imaginations, yell at him the way I wanted to so many days and so many nights across so many years.

We'd married when I was eighteen and he was thirty-six. I was head over heels in love with the curl in his mostly black, slightly graying hair, his incredible *manliness* next to the boys that hung around me in school. I was infatuated with him, with how I looked beside him in pictures, so young and pretty under his distinguished arm. I'd known him my whole life so he was safe but also, I thought, *not safe*, older and worldlier and, I hoped, dirtier than me. There were so many things an older man could teach a naive girl. I used to touch myself at night imagining the things he would do to me, the ways he could make me pleasure him.

Sadly, I still did.

"Beautiful," William said, smiling at me warmly from where he read in a deep armchair in the sitting area off the kitchen.

He presented me with a cheek to kiss, which I did diligently.

Every time I did, I wished he would grab me, haul me over his lap and lay into my ass with the flat off his palm.

I had these aggressive sexual fantasies often. Wishing that his sweet gesture smoothing back my hair was his fingers digging deep into the strands to puppeteer my head back and forth over his erection. Switching out our separate showers before bed with a shared one, where I bent double with my hands around my ankles as he pounded into me and the water pounded against us both.

I'd tried at first, a long time ago, to make these fantasies realities, but William wasn't interested.

I knew this, I did, but I was more than a little hot from the blond guy in the parking lot, the way he had commanded those men without even lifting a finger. It was only too easy to imagine the way he might command me if given the chance.

It was him that I had to blame for my actions.

I dumped my messenger bag beside William's chair and dropped to my knees between his legs.

"Cressida..." he warned softly.

He couldn't even scold me properly.

I ignored him.

My hands slid up his stiffly held legs until they found his belt and made quick work of undoing it. His cock was soft in its nest of hair but I pulled it into the light as if it was a revelation. It was silky in my mouth and easy to swallow.

William's hand hit the top of my head but didn't grab me, didn't even push me away.

"Cressida, really..." he protested again.

He didn't like oral sex. He liked vaginal sex: missionary, me on top or sometimes, if I forced him, doggy style.

I sucked him hard until basic biology took over and he grew in my mouth. I slammed my head down his shaft, taking him into my throat and loving the way it made me want to gag.

"Damn it," William said, not because it felt good, though it did, or because he liked it but because he didn't *want* to like it.

I didn't care. I squeezed my eyes shut tightly as I jacked the base of him and imagined the way the blond king may have held my head down until I groaned and gagged around him. How he might have praised me for taking him so deep and pleasuring him so well.

Instead, I got, "I'm going to come and I don't want to do it in your mouth."

"Please?" I panted against his dick, my tongue trailing out to lick over his crown.

It was his turn to squeeze his eyes shut. His legs shook as he orgasmed, his semen landing in my open mouth and over my cheeks. It took him harshly, wrung him up dry and useless afterwards like a used napkin in his chair.

I leaned back on my haunches and wiped my mouth clean

with my tongue and then the back of my hand. My pussy throbbed but I knew he wouldn't touch it so I didn't try to make him. Sex was for the dark hours and I was already in violation of his unspoken code of sexual conduct.

I knew what his reaction would be but, since I was a glutton for punishment, I waited patiently on my knees for him to recuperate. To open his eyes and pierce me with their disappointed, confused condemnation. He reached forward to touch my cheek softly as he asked me, "Why do you degrade yourself like that, Cressie? I don't need *that*."

I closed my eyes against the hot prickle of tears that threatened to elucidate my shame and leaned into his hand so that he would think I was sorry. In a way, I was, because I knew he didn't need *that* to love me. William loved me in a beautiful way, the way one might love a perfectly formed rose, a sentimental trinket. But he didn't love me in the way I needed, the way I'd wanted secretly since I was old enough to feel a heartbeat in my groin, the way one animal loved another.

"I'll make dinner," I said quietly, unfolding from my knees and going into the kitchen.

"That sounds nice," William agreed, easily forgiving me for my exploitation.

He efficiently did up his pants and went back to the book he was reading while I uncovered the Shepherd's Pie I'd already prepped the morning.

Our night continued from there in a normal way—happy, trivial conversation about our days over mashed potato-topped meat and veg, an hour or so of reading side by side in front of the fire because we didn't own a TV and then our nightly, separate showers before going to bed. We didn't have sex. We rarely did anymore because the doctors had said that the odds of William having children were slim and my husband was of the mind that sex was for a purpose, not recreation.

So, I lay next to him in our beautiful house long into the night until it was the darkest of the evening hours. Only then did I quietly turn onto my back, lift my nightgown and sink my fingers into my burning hot pussy. I came in under two minutes with my clit pinched between my fingers and another two shoved deep inside, thinking of the sexy young blond king and how he would rule me if I were his queen. It was the hardest I had come in years, maybe ever, and right on its heels came the tears. I cried silently and long into my pillow until it was steeped in salty wet and I was steeped deeply in shame. It was in all two hundred and six of my bones, so entangled with my molecules it was an essential strand of my DNA. I'd been living with it since I was pubescent teenage girl and I was so tired of it.

I was tired of boredom. The monotony of my loving husband and our life together, the hamster wheel of our social life with shallow suburban moneyed folk and the irrefutable fact that I was not attracted to my husband.

I lay in the dark for what seemed like an eternity, dissecting my thoughts like an academic at a conference. Slowly, with no discernable evolution, I was furious.

I was a twenty-six-year-old woman acting like a depressed middle-aged housewife. I had decades ahead of me still to live, to live a life where excitement, spontaneity and change could be a constant. Why was I lying in the dark like a victim? Because I was ashamed that my perfect life and husband didn't make me happy?

Pathetic.

Then, I wondered if I really was. William loved me because I was beautiful and obedient, because he had trained me to be this way since I was an impressionable girl. He did not love the side of me that was scratching and wailing to break free of the social constraints he'd bound me in so beautifully for years. It was the part of me that wanted to lie, steal and cheat; to sin a little every day and gorge myself on a steady diet of thrills. That side would bring the Irons name shame and the most important thing to William was his wealth and reputation.

It was his wealth that gave me pause. I had no real money of my own unless I counted the few thousand dollars my grandpa put into a small trust for me. I didn't know if it would be enough to start a new life. I didn't even know if I was savvy enough or strong enough to strike out on my own, not after an entire life of obedience to my father, and then my husband.

I didn't know, but as I lay there cradled in the dark night, I decided that I didn't care about the certainty. That, in fact, it was part of the thrill.

I rolled over to look at William lying beside me, his face slack and peaceful in slumber. Reverently, I traced his thick eyebrows, the slightly jagged edge of his hairline down to the winged ear that I liked to kiss. I peeled the covers away from his body carefully so that I could run my eyes over the entirety of my husband for the last time.

The finality settled in me like a bright thing, something light that made the heaviness in my bones fizzle and pop into nothingness.

"William," I whispered, pressing a thumb to the corner of his lips. "Wake up. I have to tell you something."

Now FREE on Kindle Unlimited!

THANKS ETC.

Good Gone Bad was one of the hardest books I've ever written because Danner and Harleigh Rose had minds of their own. They wanted to be together more than their next breath, but they didn't feel they deserved each other, or even a happily ever after. Sometimes too much of a good thing, like loyalty in their case, can lead to bad. I think they may have the best souls of all the characters I have ever written (with the exception of Mute) and I love that their love story was just as much of a struggle for me to write as it was for them to endure.

A note on their sexuality. There are very many forms of Domination and submission, and very many forms of Doms and submissives just as there are very many varieties of people under multiple labels and subheadings. Danner is a good man, a moral man, and a gentleman. His sexuality and kink may seem like a complete deviation from his character, just as the stubborn, sassy, independent Harleigh Rose may seem like a bizarre submissive. The truth is, most of the time, it is very difficult to peg someone correctly as one or the other. A powerful career woman sometimes needs to forget the stress of control and responsibilities by ceding that to her partner, who may in turn be an affable, beta-type male in social situations, but a man who craves the weight of a whip in his palm in the bedroom to assert his dominance and strength in another way. It's important for me to note this because a lot of BDSM books portray Dom's as big, bad, control freaks who act the same way inside and outside the bedroom. That happens, and that can be super-hot. But if you're curious about BDSM, do your research. You'll find an amazing array of lifestyles, from 24/7 Dom/sub or Master/slave situations to people who Dominant in a way that is completely non-sexual. Harleigh Rose and Danner are only one example of a community that is deep, varying and incredibly tantalizing, probably why there are so many books written about it!

Also, music is a huge part of this book, so I encourage you to listen while you read <3

I have so many people to thank for loving and supporting my own rose with thorns and this book.

Serena McDonald is my lifeline, one of the ultimate loves of my life, and a book Queen I feel very blessed every day to have in my corner. I can't believe I only met her this year when it feels like we've known each other our entire lives. I know I drive you crazy sometimes with my creative process, so thank you for being endlessly patient with me. I can't wait for many more books and many more adventures together, my S. #McDarling

To my second mum, my best girlfriend and my confidante, Michelle Clay. I don't know how you do it, but you know my soul and how to soothe it better than almost anyone. Thank you for your secrets, your praise and your endless love.

Becca, you are one of my best friends and I haven't even met you yet. Here's to a lifetime of love, future travels and possible projects.

K Webster was one of my ultimate favorite authors and she still is to this day. She's also, straight up, one of my favourite humans and not just because we share a love of hot daddies, surprise pregnancies and all things taboo.

The day Sarah from Musings of a Modern Book Belle reached out to me before the release of Welcome to the Dark Side is a day my life changed for the better. So grateful to have your insight and artistry in my life, Sarah.

Ellie McLove from My Brother's Editor, you saved my ass with your edits and you've seriously rocked my world with your new friendship. I'm so thrilled to finally have found my dream editor and I can't wait to give you all the projects.

Najla Qamber is my cover designer and all-around graphics guru. She brings my world to life in beautifully rendered ways that make me teary-eyed. Love you Najla, thank you for being on my team since the beginning.

To Stacey from Champagne Formatting, thank you for making this book gorgeous, and all the books in The Fallen Men series as beautiful as the men between the pages.

To Marjorie Lord for her proofreading expertise, I'd be a mess of errors without you.

Giana's Darlings, you ladies are my favourite. I never dreamed I could have such a beautiful, dedicated group of loyal readers and I am humbled every day by your love and support.

The biggest shout out has to go to the readers and book bloggers in Dirty Danner's ARC Team! I love you for your enthusiasm and willingness to share my work with others. Your support is essential to me and you've helped get this book into countless hands so thank you!

I believe that you create your own family and I am so blessed to have so many friendships with beautiful women and authors in this community. I can't possibly name them all, but I need to shout out a few special people.

Sunny, I cannot wait to hug your face and dance our asses off to Shawn Mendes this summer. Your love for me and my

Fallen Men makes me want to cry, but I'm being a biker babe and holding back the tears to save my street cred. Seriously though, you rock.

Leigh, I love you, I love your work, and I love that you always answer my sometimes dumb or inane questions. I feel like you know who I am and love me even though we haven't met yet and I can't wait to rectify that!

Kristie Lewis, my darling girl, I love you so much. We've been on this mad, wonderful journey together for a while now and it never gets less interesting, but I'm always glad to have you to talk to.

Ella Fields, I wish I could make a CD of our FB messenger voicemails to listen to whenever I'm down because your beautiful Aussie voice, easy wit and insight always make me laugh and smile.

Cassie, babe, I just straight up love you. You've been my friend from what feels like the start and you always around to support me and give me endless doses of love. Every time I write about Daddy Z, I think of you.

To all the other author friends who participated in my release parties and make me feel like this community is my home, thank you and I love you all. You know who you are <3

I can't list all of the book bloggers who make my day with their reviews and teasers but special thanks goes out to Sarah at Musings of a Book Belle, Allaa at Honeyed Pages, Keri at Keri Loves Books, and the girls at Kinky Girls Book Obsessions. My Instagrammers @booknerdingout, @bookmarkbelles, and @peacelovebooksxo.

My best girl, Armie, is my constant cheerleader and sounding board. She listens to me read out loud for hours, to ever-changing plot points and future project ideas. She okays cover photos and gives me love when I feel unsure. She's the best friend I always read about in books growing up, a friend I never thought I'd be lucky enough to have for myself.

And as always, last but never least, this book is dedicated

to you, my love, because if anyone can understand how over-coming obstacles can strengthen your love, it's us. Thank you for loving me the way you do, endlessly, beautifully and, occa-sionally, roughly ;) I am grateful for nothing in this life so much as I am your love.

OTHER BOOKS BY GIANA DARLING

The Evolution of Sin Trilogy

Giselle Moore is running away from her past in France for a new life in America, but before she moves to New York City, she takes a holiday on the beaches of Mexico and meets a sinful, enigmatic French businessman, Sinclair, who awakens submissive desires and changes her life forever.

The Affair

The Secret

The Consequence

The Evolution Of Sin Trilogy Boxset

The Fallen Men Series

The Fallen Men are a series of interconnected standalone erotic MC romances that each feature age gaps love stories between dirty-talking, Alpha Males and the strong, sassy women that win their hearts.

Lessons in Corruption

Welcome to the Dark Side

Good Gone Bad

ABOUT GIANA DARLING

Giana Darling is a USA Today, Wall Street Journal, Top 40 Best Selling Canadian romance writer who specializes in the taboo and angsty side of love and romance. She currently lives in beautiful British Columbia where she spends time riding on the back of her man's bike, baking pies, and reading snuggled up with her cat, Persephone.

Join my Reader's Group
Subscribe to my Newsletter
Follow me on IG
Like me on Facebook
Follow me on Goodreads
Follow me on BookBub
Follow me on Pinterest

Printed in Great Britain
by Amazon

22110073R00235